American Mythology

American Mythology

A NOVEL

GIANO CROMLEY

DOUBLEDAY   NEW YORK

FIRST DOUBLEDAY HARDCOVER EDITION 2025

Published by Doubleday, a division of Penguin Random House LLC, 1745 Broadway, New York, NY 10019.

DOUBLEDAY and the portrayal of an anchor with a dolphin are registered trademarks of Penguin Random House LLC.

Title-page illustration by Mercy / stock.adobe.com
Book design by Betty Lew

Library of Congress Cataloging-in-Publication Data
Names: Cromley, Giano author
Title: American mythology : a novel / Giano Cromley.
Description: First edition. | New York : Doubleday, 2025.
Identifiers: LCCN 2024038609 (print) | LCCN 2024038610 (ebook) |
ISBN 9780593688182 hardcover | ISBN 9780593688199 ebook
Subjects: LCGFT: Novels
Classification: LCC PS3603.R6535 A44 2025 (print) | LCC PS3603.R6535 (ebook) |
DDC 813/.6—dc23/eng/20250324
LC record available at https://lccn.loc.gov/2024038609
LC ebook record available at https://lccn.loc.gov/2024038610

penguinrandomhouse.com | doubleday.com

PRINTED IN THE UNITED STATES OF AMERICA
10 9 8 7 6 5 4 3 2 1

The authorized representative in the EU for product safety and compliance is Penguin Random House Ireland, Morrison Chambers, 32 Nassau Street, Dublin D02 YH68, Ireland, https://eu-contact.penguin.ie.

For Brento the Great,

a practitioner of magic

What would an ocean be without a monster
lurking in the dark? Like sleep without dreams.

—WERNER HERZOG

American Mythology

29 August 1853—Our crew has made its autumn camp. Neither Mr. W—, Mr. B—, Mr. J—, nor I have spent much time in these so-called "Elk-Horn" mountains. Immediate impressions are thus: game bounteous, topo-graphy well-suited to our endeavours, food for men abundant, weather appealing, &c.

1 September 1853—Crew has spent 3 days in autumn camp. Pelts harvested thus far: 8 beaver, 4 rabbit, 3 muskrat, 2 otter, 1 red fox, 1 marten, 1 fisher. Traps fill as soon as snares are set. If luck holds, we shall be wealthy men upon our return to Fort Henry come winter.

3 September 1853—Pelt harvest continues apace: 9 beaver, 6 rabbit, 4 muskrat, 5 otter, 3 minks. A cow elk was killed and her meat is being smoked. The land continues to look favourably upon our labours.

5 September 1853—6 beaver, 8 rabbit, 3 muskrat, 4 marten, 2 minks. Mr. J— spotted a sow grizzly catching trout with her cubs in a nearby creek. He managed to wound the devil, but she fled upon taking fire and we were unable to locate her body. Cubs were destroyed and skinned, though juvenile pelts are of little value.

7 September 1853—1 beaver, 3 rabbit, 1 muskrat, 1 marten, 1 mink. Weather has turned inclement, with early snows and frigid

temperatures. Crew reports finding large prints of unknown origin around camp.

11 September 1853—2 rabbit, 1 muskrat. Several snare lines cut overnight. Strongly suspect sabotage to be the work of local Indians. Nevertheless we remain undaunted. Crew spent halve-day making repairs. Tonight we shall keep watch in the hope of foiling the vandals.

12 September 1853—Mr. W— claims on his watch he saw unidentified creature. Gunfire missed or was otherwise ineffective. He describes it as large, hair-covered, walking upright like a man. I believe it was the sow grizzly shot earlier by Mr. J—, though Mr. W— disputes this hypothesis. Mr. B— now claims to have seen a similar creature 3 Sept., but did not mention it due to fear of ridicule. Myself and Mr. J— do not know what to make of these outlandish claims.

13 September 1853—No sighting of Indians. No sighting of grizzly. No sighting of creature. Traps empty.

14 September 1853—A queer sound was heard by all in the night— reminiscent of several people whispering at once. An investigation of surrounding woods turned up no obvious perpetrators. Mr. J— never returned to camp, despite numerous attempts to summon him. Mr. B— and Mr. W— believe he has lit out on his own. I suspect otherwise, as he did not take his firearm, ammunition, clothing, pelts, &c. Crew spent entire day searching for him. Returned at dusk. Traps empty.

15 September 1853—No sign of Mr. J—. Traps empty.

16 September 1853—More whispering noises coming from the forest in the night. Mr. B—, an unassimilated Irishman, claims the sound is that of a Banshee, that most feared witch of Celtic magic. Mr. W— and I scoff at such balderdash, yet we cannot deny some thing is making that infernal noise. And, too, Mr. J— remains missing. Traps empty.

17 September 1853—Weather continues to sour. Search for Mr. J— called off. Traps empty.

<u>18 September 1853</u>—Traps destroyed in the night. Snares appear to be chewed apart and are beyond repair with materials on hand. We have awakened something ancient in this forest that does not want us here. Remaining crew has decided to depart at once. If Mr. J— is yet alive, he must needs save himself.

Chapter 1

All his life, Jute Ramsey had been hearing tales of a mystical lake nestled at the top of an unnamed peak deep in the Elkhorn Mountains. Its location was a tightly held secret, known only to select members of the Ramsey family. When Jute turned eleven, his father finally took him there.

Those few days they spent in the woods together would shape the next thirty-five years of his life.

Luther Ramsey III kept a loose grip on the steering wheel as their Jeep thudded over deadfall on a long-abandoned logging trail.

"Tell me about Ramsey Lake again, Dad." Jute had the map spread out across his lap, finger pinned to the spot where his father had said their destination lay.

"My gramps, your great-gramps, Luther Ramsey the First, was a cartographer for the U.S. Forest Service back in the day. Mapmaker by trade. Had some mountain man in his blood. Some Crow too—or so he claimed." Luther took a swig of coffee from his green VFW mug as the Cherokee crested a steep rise. "My gramps was a mean cuss. So was his little man, my pops. It's why you're Julius Ramsey, instead of Luther Ramsey the Fourth. That's one family tradition that dies with me."

In Jute's memory, his father was a colossus of a man. He worked as a mechanic at the garage down by the interstate, but he also had a keen intellect and a voracious curiosity about the world. When he wasn't working, his nose was buried in library books on philosophy, physics, botany, religion. And he was a natural-born raconteur. Wherever he went, people would soon gather around to hear what he had to say.

"Credit where credit's due," his dad went on, "Luther the First was a hell of a woodsman. Ended up mapping most of the Elkhorns. Did such a good job, when he was done his bosses at the Forest Service said, 'Luther, pick any lake you want and name it.' So that's why we're heading to Ramsey Lake."

Thick brush scraped along the undercarriage of the Jeep. Twice his father hit dead ends and had to back up until he found another path.

"If they said he could name a lake, then why isn't it on this map?" Jute asked.

Luther glanced at his son. "The old man could've picked any lake he wanted. But he knew there was this extraspecial one out there, so he said, 'How about this, Boss: I'll pick one tiny old lake way up them hills, but what I want in exchange is this one doesn't go on any of your maps. Leave it off.' So that's what they did."

This part of the story had always sounded far-fetched to Jute, though he never knew how to dispute it. "What's so special about this lake?"

"First of all," Luther said, "it's the only body of water in the world known to contain wizard trout."

"What's a wizard trout look like?"

"I never landed one." Luther turned the wheel sharply to avoid a rock. "My old man told me they got purple spots on their flanks and they taste like heaven on earth."

Jute tucked his hands under his thighs to keep from fidgeting. "You haven't seen one though," he said.

Luther took another sip of coffee and frowned. "Who knows, they might be extinct by now. But I sure do hope there's a few left. It'd make the world a more interesting place. Don't you think?"

"So Ramsey Lake is special because it's got wizard trout in it?"

Luther tucked his chin into his Adam's apple for a moment. "Don't be surprised if you see some mighty strange stuff up there," he said. "Ramsey Lake is what some folks call a thin place."

"What's a thin place?" Jute asked.

"Every culture's got spots like this," he said. "Where the veil between our world and the spirit world is so thin they practically overlap."

"Do you really believe that?"

"There's no doubt certain places in the world are holier than others." Luther scratched at a mosquito bite on his arm. "You know there's this hill out there in the Middle East called the Temple Mount. Three separate religions all believe something important happened there. Now tell me, what are the odds of three separate religious events all happening in the exact same spot?"

"Probably not great?" Jute ventured.

"Exactly! But this place is so special, so sacred, it gives people a powerful feeling, a sense that their version of God is talking to them. So they figure something big *must've* happened there. Next thing you know, they make up a story to explain that feeling and build a church, or a synagogue, or a mosque to help bottle it up."

Jute nodded, even though he didn't know what a synagogue or a mosque was.

"I guess what I'm saying is where did that feeling come from in the first place? It must be something about that site, some property it has." Luther paused to look over at Jute. "Whether you believe it or not," he said, "places like this deserve to be treated with respect."

The logging trail was practically nonexistent by this point. The Jeep inched along, raked by heavy pine boughs on all sides. A short while later, they crested a small hill that overlooked a gently sloped clearing. Luther cut the engine.

"This is as close as we get by car," he said. "Couple days' hiking and we'll be there."

They unloaded the Jeep and hoisted their backpacks, taking time to adjust the straps. Luther's was an aluminum-frame pack. Jute's was a canvas army bag. Once they'd gotten them properly shouldered, Luther strode to the western edge of the clearing.

"Now this isn't like the kind of hiking you're used to," he said, turning to Jute. "We're gonna be off-trail, so you need to stick close." Luther scanned what little of the horizon was visible over the tree line. "See that mountain over there, buddy?" He pointed to a peak with a shallow crater at the top. "Up there's Ramsey Lake."

"Then why are we heading west?" Jute asked. "Shouldn't we go straight toward the mountain we want to reach?"

Luther turned a fretful gaze into the forest north of the clearing. "We don't want to go through there today, buddy."

"Why's that?"

"My dad called those the Whispering Woods," he said. "Told me they were strictly off-limits unless you really knew what you were doing."

Whispering Woods. The phrase gave Jute goose bumps. Did wind make the trees move in a way that seemed like whispers? Or was there something else out there that did the whispering? Jute sensed his father didn't want to talk about it anymore, so he kept his questions to himself.

It was late morning by the time they set out west, pushing their way through the forest. Jute had never hiked off-trail before and was surprised by how slow the going was. They constantly wrestled with tree branches and underbrush. Every so often, they had to disentangle themselves from vines that had gotten wrapped around their ankles.

Jute found himself getting disoriented; he lost track of time, distance, and direction. At one point, they paused to wolf down granola bars and chase them with canteen water. Jute had spent a great deal of his life in the forests of Montana, but this felt different. The colors here were grayer, the air heavier; sounds felt strangely muted.

Sometime after noon, Jute sensed they were veering north, and the trail started to rise. Then suddenly it opened up onto a wide field of scree. A bare, featureless hilltop covered in rock shards that were sharp as broken glass.

Without trees to block the sight lines, Jute realized it was significantly later than he'd thought.

"If memory serves," Luther said, "there should be a good spot to camp up ahead."

They reentered the forest on the far side of the scree field. An hour later, they came upon an egg-shaped meadow, where they peeled off their packs and took out their gear. While Luther pitched their tent in the tall yellow grass, Jute set off into the forest with instructions to gather firewood. The trees surrounding the meadow grew tight together, and the creeping juniper was so thick it was hard to see more than a few feet in any direction. But Jute found a half dozen game trails that mazed through the woods in all directions. He chose one and followed it.

The trail narrowed the farther it got from the meadow. It reminded him of a story he'd read in school, of Theseus finding his way through the labyrinth to slay the Minotaur. Behind him, his father was singing, *"What shall we do with a drunken sailor, what should we do with a drunken sailor, ear-lye in the morning."*

Eventually, the trail widened and Jute saw ahead of him a perfectly shaped Douglas fir, eight feet tall, trunk as thick as Jute's thigh. Without thinking, he set upon the tree with the camp hatchet. Chips flew as the blade dug past the bark and sank into the soft white sapwood.

He worked up a good sweat and his hands began to blister. When the tree teetered and finally fell, Jute felt powerful, like he'd accomplished a great task. He couldn't wait for his father to see what he'd done. Jute lifted the tree by its trunk, his hand warm and sticky with sap, and dragged it back down the game trail.

Luther looked up from the camp stove when Jute emerged from the forest with his freshly cut tree. "What's this now?" he asked.

"You told me to get firewood," Jute said.

"Did you chop that tree down just now?" His father stood and approached him.

Jute sensed he was in trouble. "I thought you'd be proud of me."

Luther shook his head. "Never cut down a tree for a campfire, Son. First off, that wood's too wet to burn good. Secondly, look at all the fallen trees around here. That's the stuff we need to use. That's how you keep the living trees healthy."

Jute looked around the forest to show he was listening. He hoped it might lessen the trouble he was in.

"Trees are the wisest thing in the forest, Son. They talk to each other. And they'll talk to you, if you know how to listen to them. So you ought not to cut one down without a damn good reason." Luther squeezed Jute's shoulder. "Now apologize to this tree here," he said.

Jute put his hand on the trunk and whispered, "I'm sorry."

"Lesson learned," Luther said, nodding his approval. "Now find us some wood we can use. And be quick about it. Dinner's almost ready."

The next morning, it took Luther a few minutes to figure out which direction to go. Once he did, they pressed on through dew-covered trees and brush, until they reached the base of the hollow-peaked mountain. From there they started climbing a seam of black basalt that zigzagged up the face.

Jute's lungs burned. His skin prickled. He wanted to stop, or at least catch his breath, but Luther didn't look back. And Jute wasn't about to disappoint him again.

They began passing pockets of snow, melting in the shadowed nooks and crannies between boulders. Ahead on the trail, Jute could see the peak of the mountain they were on, like a chipped tooth against the blue sky. The other peaks nearby seemed so close he could practically touch them. The world felt both small and impossibly big.

A half hour after they'd climbed above the tree line, they reached a narrow saddle where the ground was smooth, covered with springy moss. Then it dropped down into the crater.

Luther reached back to grab Jute by the shoulder.

"There it is," he said.

Ramsey Lake was figure eight shaped, with the smaller circle close to them and relatively exposed. The larger circle, on the far side, was obscured by a stand of trees growing along the shoreline. Jute was struck by the color of the water, which started as a pale turquoise at the edges and became nearly black toward the center.

"According to your great-grandfather, they never did figure out how deep this puppy is," Luther said. "Their equipment couldn't reach the bottom. I think that's how the wizard trout survive. They need that real deep water, where it gets so cold it's practically ice."

As they made their way to the edge of the lake, Jute imagined himself sinking through the watery depths, from blue to black, with no bottom in sight.

Luther propped his foot on a small boulder and scanned the pebbly shoreline. "Yes, sir," he said, "this here is your ancestral homeland."

Years later, Jute would remember this moment as a nearly religious experience, like the feeling pilgrims got when they traveled thousands of miles to bathe in a mystical river.

"Come on," Luther said, "let's see what's what."

They worked their way clockwise around the lake, stepping carefully along the shore. At one point, Jute glanced down and saw at his feet the perfect skipping stone. The temptation was too great. He picked it up and slung it sidearm. But when the stone touched the surface of the lake, instead of it skipping, a dark hole formed in the water and swallowed the stone with a quiet slurp.

"Did you see that, Dad?"

"What did I tell you?" Luther glanced down at his son. "This here is a special place."

The air was cold this high up. Jute started to shiver.

"Let's keep moving," Luther said.

They reached the far edge of the lake, where the woods grew right up to the shore, making it dark and shadowed. Tree branches seemed to sway and move, even though there was no breeze. Luther stood very still, staring at something deeper inside the forest, a dense knot of branches and limbs braced against each other. Mud was chinked into crevices between logs. Grasses and moss thatched a roof. Jute realized it was a primitive shack, like something out of a fairy tale.

Without saying a word, they slowly approached. Once they were upon it, Luther reached out and tugged a gnarled branch, which turned out to be a door. They stepped inside.

In the center of the shack was a flat rock, on which rested a rabbit-skin pouch. Next to the pouch was a green leather book. Luther picked up the book and flipped through a few pages.

"What's that, Dad?"

His father snapped the book closed. He took off his backpack and stuffed the book inside.

Jute nudged the rabbit-skin pouch. Its mouth fell open and a half dozen small white bones spilled out onto the rock. Luther's eyes went wide with fear. He grabbed Jute hard by the wrist and pulled him outside.

"Do you think Luther the First knew about this place?" Jute asked once they were back in the forest.

"Could be he built it." Luther kicked lightly at one of the logs. "It's hard to know how old something like this is."

"What was that book?"

Luther looked up at the sky. Gray clouds, big as battleships, were moving in. "Listen, we don't want to get caught up here when that weather hits." He cinched the belt on his pack. "Let's try making it back to last night's campsite."

"You mean we're not staying here tonight?"

Luther shook his head. "Best not."

Jute was disappointed he wouldn't get a chance to catch a wizard trout, but he wasn't about to argue. They made their way along the shoreline. When Luther found the trail leading up out of the crater, he set off with long, forceful strides. Jute had to scramble, using his hands for balance. He wanted to show his father how well he could keep up, how big he was becoming.

Once they crested the crater, the route seemed steeper going down the mountain. Jute couldn't believe how far they'd hiked in such a short time. They got back to the egg-shaped meadow as night fell. Jute used a flashlight to scavenge firewood while Luther prepared hobo pies for dinner.

Jute didn't want to enter the trees, so he gathered wood from the edge of the meadow. He felt unsettled by all the things they'd seen at Ramsey Lake that day. But most of all, he was frightened by the look on his dad's face in that hut. Up until that moment, Jute didn't think his father was afraid of anything.

After dinner, Jute sipped hot chocolate while Luther drank cowboy coffee. Firelight reflected off the trees, making the forest look impenetrable. Around them, the first stirrings of the night creatures commenced. Bats, field mice, raccoons, owls. In the distance, the flat yips of a coyote pack on the hunt.

"What was that hut we found in the woods?" Jute asked.

"Might belong to a mountain hermit." His father's voice was ponderous. "Some crank who lives back there."

A log shifted in the fire. The flames died down. The coyote yips were closer now, more enthusiastic. They'd picked up a scent.

Just then, one of the coyotes let out a piercing screech, primal in its distress. Jute's head shrank into his shoulders. Luther leaned forward and scanned the forest.

"Some animal's going to eat good tonight," he said.

"What animal around here eats coyotes, Dad?"

That was when they heard it. A long howl, but human—like a person wailing. It lasted a good ten seconds, rising in pitch until the air vibrated and the sound rang in their ears.

Luther shot up. "I'm not liking how close those coyotes sound," he said, tossing the contents of his mug. "Let's go ahead and hit the rack."

"Should we at least douse the fire?"

"I think it's okay to let this one burn out on its own."

This was a direct contradiction of the first rule of camping his father had taught him: *Never leave a fire unattended.* Something was terribly wrong.

Once they'd climbed inside the tent and zipped the flap closed, Luther pulled a worn-looking Colt .45 from his pack. The gun had been given to Luther III by Luther II, who'd gotten it from Luther I. The story went that he'd been issued the firearm during the First World War and kept it afterward because they'd never asked for it back. Luther III had always said it would one day be Jute's, though Jute wasn't sure he wanted it.

"What do you think made that howl?" Jute asked, worming his way deep into his sleeping bag.

His dad thought for a few seconds. "Can't say as I know," he said. "But just because you don't know something doesn't mean you have to be afraid of it."

"So you're saying, don't worry?"

"I'm saying worrying won't help anyways, buddy."

It wasn't the most reassuring point his father had ever made, but the sleeping bag was warm. Jute's eyes grew heavy. There was no way he could have known this would be the last time he'd feel safe around his father. If he had, he would have tried to stay awake longer.

When first light broke, Jute awoke to find his father's sleeping bag empty. Next to it he saw the green journal. Jute flipped it open to a random page near the beginning. It appeared to be filled with diary entries dated from a long time ago. When he fanned to another page, this section was dated several years later. Jute skimmed to the most recent page and froze when he recognized his dad's handwriting: *We're being watched. I don't know by what. I hear the voice. It's beginning. Can't fight it anymore.*

A loud noise caused Jute to slam the journal shut and claw at the tent zipper.

Outside, he was relieved to see his father standing nearby. But his relief evaporated when he took in the condition of the campsite. The fire ring had been kicked apart, ashes strewn in black streaks. Much of their gear was missing, but most of what remained hung in tree branches ten feet off the ground.

Luther bent down and picked something up, puzzling over it. Jute took a step closer to his father, who was holding a mass of sticks and twigs, snapped and bundled and twisted into the shape of a human stick figure.

"What is that, Dad?"

Luther shook his head. His hair was a mess. His shirtsleeve was torn at the elbow. His eyes were tiny and lost.

"Dad, what happened?"

Finally, his father's face cleared. He dropped the stick figure.

"We're getting the hell out of here," he said. "Now."

Jute was surprised by the decision, but didn't know what to say. He knelt down and dragged his sleeping bag out of the tent. He began rolling it from bottom to top, using his knee to pack it tight.

"Forget about that," Luther said. "We've leaving it."

"What about our gear?" Jute looked around the site. "Shouldn't we take the tent at least?"

His father paused for a second. His shoulders sagged as if a great burden had been placed on them. Then he spun and slapped Jute hard across the face.

"Always with the questions," Luther growled. "If I tell you once to goddamn do something, you do it."

Hot tears formed in the corners of Jute's eyes. He had no idea what was happening, no idea that the man who had been his father was now gone.

The hike out was the hardest Jute had ever done in his life. His father maintained a blistering pace and didn't bother to see if his son was keeping up. When they finally got back to the Jeep, Jute's head throbbed. His feet were sore, and his legs were so stiff he could hardly walk.

As he grabbed the door handle, Jute noticed a smudge on the window. When the light angled just right, he saw a handprint the size of a dinner plate. Jute wiped his index finger across the smudge and it came up sticky. When he smelled it, his neck hairs hackled.

Jute knew instinctively what had made the print, and that it was a message left specifically for him. He looked around the woods, hoping to glimpse a shadowy figure keeping watch, but all Jute saw was forest.

Luther climbed into the car and fired up the engine. Jute had no choice but to follow suit if he didn't want to be left behind.

The trip to Ramsey Lake was the last time the two of them went camping together. Afterward, Luther became meaner, angrier. He lost his job at the garage and could never hold another one. He'd sometimes disappear for days, even weeks, on end without explanation, until one day when Jute was sixteen years old, he never came back at all.

But Jute lost his father that day in the forest. And he would spend the rest of his life trying to find out why.

Chapter 2

A raucous delirium had already settled over the capacity crowd seated in the Helena Civic Center Auditorium as they awaited the emergence of Dr. Marcus Bernard, professor of evolutionary biology and legendary expert on the existence of an uncataloged, possibly mythical North American wood ape. The atmosphere was part Metallica concert, part tent revival.

Vicky Xu was *not* among the crowd, though she was arguably more invested in tonight's main event than the audience was. She was wandering around backstage in the dark, right hand holding a camera, left hand empty and outstretched, feeling for obstacles in her path.

"Dr. Bernard?" Vicky shout-whispered. "Where are you?"

She received no response and continued to grope.

Her favorite teacher, Professor Moss, had a line in the opening lecture of his Intro to Doc Filmmaking class that seemed to speak to this moment. "Never doubt your authority when the camera is on." His lecture did not, however, discuss what to do when the subject of your documentary was treating it like a game of hide-and-seek.

"Dr. Bernard, are you there?" Vicky bumped into a wall, turned, and started moving in a new direction, like a Roomba.

She wasn't sure how she'd gotten him to agree to this project in the first place. More than persuasion, persistence had been key. For all her preparation, her careful research and planning, in the end she seemed to have simply caught him at an opportune moment.

She'd first gotten the idea to focus her thesis on him two months ago, when she saw him walking across campus trailed by a coterie of adoring students. Here was a man who'd voluntarily chosen to become a pariah in the scientific community, yet whose classes were routinely filled months in advance. Vicky wondered if he really believed the things he said on TV, or if it was all part of an act. And it struck her that there had to be a story in there somewhere.

She'd started with a carefully composed email, introducing herself and asking him to sit for a series of interviews. When he failed to respond, she began showing up outside the lecture hall where he taught, ambushing him in the hallway after class.

"Doctor, I'm interested in talking with you about a documentary I'm making."

"You'll have to speak with my agent," he said, putting his head down and waving a hand over his shoulder.

"It's for my graduate thesis here at Idaho State."

"Not interested." He picked up his pace. "No thank you."

"But I really think it would—"

He bolted through a side door into the faculty parking lot and climbed into the soundproof safety of his Ford Explorer. Vicky knocked on his window, but he ignored her and peeled out of the lot, leaving her standing alone in a cloud of exhaust.

She'd already researched his career—from promising grad student studying gorillas in the Democratic Republic of Congo, to his eventual metamorphosis into schlocky TV personality, serving as a sort of scientific referee on a seemingly endless number of Bigfoot shows.

Then, two days ago, she wandered down into the bowels of the life sciences building, where Bernard's colleagues—embarrassed by his Bigfoot shtick, yet powerless to do anything about it on account of tenure—had relegated his office. She navigated the twisty corridors, past an open janitor's closet and stacks of cardboard file boxes. She had her camera out, filming as she went.

"This is where they've sequestered the most popular professor in the Biology department," Vicky said out loud as a voice-over. "The academic equivalent of solitary confinement." She panned the camera to a slop bucket filled with dirty brown water, a stale mop propped against the wall.

"I've come here to stalk him in his natural habitat," she went on. "Will he once again prove as elusive as the creature he purports to be looking for? Only time will tell."

She rounded a corner and noticed a dim light coming through a half-open doorway. Vicky couldn't believe her luck. She finally had her prey cornered, defenseless.

When she peered inside, she saw Bernard—late fifties, light brown ponytail, neatly trimmed beard—staring at the computer screen on his desk. She zoomed in and noticed that he appeared to be crying.

Vicky must have made a noise because he looked up, startled. "You again?" he said, dabbing at his eyes with a shirtsleeve.

"I didn't mean to interrupt," she said.

"I'm pretty sure that's exactly what you meant to do." He closed his browser and turned to face her. "What is it you want again?" His eyes were so alarmingly blue she nearly lost the nerve to speak.

"My name is Vicky Xu, and I'd like to interview you for my thesis project. I'm an MFA student here in the film program."

Bernard glanced at her camera. "Do you have any idea how much I get paid for appearances?"

"I don't have any money." Vicky stepped into his office and sat down in a chair facing the desk. "But I'd love to let the world know how you became . . . *you.*"

His gaze shifted down to his hands, resting on the desktop. "I don't think people are interested in getting to know the real me."

It seemed like an odd thing for such a public person to say. "I disagree, Doctor."

Golden light spilled through a basement window well, highlighting the dust motes that hung in the air. His gaze got far away and dreamy. "Have you ever felt like you had something important to say?" he asked. "But you weren't sure the world wanted to hear it?"

"I feel like that literally all the time," Vicky said.

Bernard sighed. He aimlessly nudged the mouse with his finger and stared for a moment at his screen saver, which was an image of an electric-green junglescape.

Vicky noticed his hair was mussed, his shirt wrinkled. "What were you looking at?" she asked. "On your computer just now?"

Bernard didn't answer at first. When his gaze finally snapped back to Vicky, she detected a different look in his eyes, something off-kilter, manic. "You want to show the world who I *really* am?"

"That's why I'm here."

Bernard leaned back in his chair, and the backrest creaked grievously. "Fine," he said, a smile creeping across his face. "Follow me around for the next forty-eight hours, and I'll give you a story the world won't forget."

After they shook on it, Vicky left his office, giddy. Once she was outside, however, she realized she didn't know what exactly they'd agreed to. For the next day and a half, all she'd gotten from Bernard was radio silence. Then eight hours ago, she received an email directing her to meet him here in Helena (a four-and-a-half-hour drive away from Pocatello), where he was scheduled to deliver a keynote address to the Montana Bigfoot Researchers Consortium. The speech was supposed to have started twenty-three minutes ago, and Vicky was beginning to wonder if this whole thing had been some kind of prank.

"Dr. Bernard," Vicky tried again. "I know you're here."

She heard the crack of a broom handle hitting the floor, back near a stage set for the local rep theater's production of *Moby-Dick*. Most likely that's where he was hiding out. She was about to investigate when a round of applause swelled in the auditorium as William Jennings, president of the consortium, took the stage.

"Ladies and gentlemen, it is with great delight that I get to introduce one of the true luminaries in our field."

Vicky assumed a spot in the wing, knowing her quarry would eventually have to surface if he wanted to claim his honorarium. She panned across the audience, taking in a sea of camouflage baseball caps and Carhartt overalls. Most of the hats and a good deal of the other merchandise worn by the crowd were emblazoned with the slogan WHAT WOULD BIGFOOT DO, Dr. Bernard's signature catchphrase, which he managed to shoehorn into every appearance.

Vicky had heard about these Bigfoot conventions before. And she'd viewed more than her fair share of clips on YouTube to prep for tonight. But witnessing one in real life felt surreal.

At the podium, Jennings ticked through Bernard's professional and academic highlights as if they were the least interesting things about him. Then he hitched his head to the side and gave a slight smirk.

"Oh yeah, there's one more thing you need to know about our guest tonight . . ." he said. "This guy's a straight shooter, folks. He calls 'em like he sees 'em, and he ain't afraid to tell it like it is."

Hoots from the audience. Hollers.

"Not that it's winning him any popularity contests in the so-called mainstream media. But that's exactly why we love him!"

Red meat for this crowd.

"He's the only living person to be named Bigfooter of the Year two years in a row by the *Bigfoot Times*. No one—and I mean no one—has been a bigger advocate for all of us here in the Bigfoot research community. So let's give a good old Montana welcome to one of our own, the legend, the GOAT, Dr. Marcus Bernard!"

Jennings pumped his fist over his head, and the crowd started chanting, "W-W-B-D! W-W-B-D! W-W-B-D!"

Vicky spun in time to catch Bernard emerging from behind the plywood bow of the *Pequod*. He wore a tweed jacket and a denim button-down shirt with a red bandanna tied around his neck—an ensemble that made him look like a cross between Indiana Jones and Ernest Hemingway.

Bernard blew past Vicky without so much as a nod to her or the camera. When he walked out onstage he was greeted with a roar from the audience.

"Thank you, everyone, for being here this evening," he said, stepping on the last of the applause. He untucked his ponytail from his jacket collar. His eyes darted around the auditorium.

"Umm . . ." He looked up at the ceiling, at the ropes and catwalks and stage lights suspended overhead. He exhaled, sending a raspy hiss through the speakers.

As America's best-known and most beloved Bigfoot talking head, he'd spent the majority of his professional career thriving in spotlights such as this. But tonight, something was off.

Bernard mopped his brow with his jacket sleeve. He tapped his hands on the lectern and looked down at them, blinking his eyes wildly as if he were trying to wake himself up. Finally, he stepped up to the microphone.

"It's wonderful to see so many familiar faces in the crowd tonight," he said, then paused and nodded for a moment. "So many people I've spent long hours with in the field."

Vicky detected an elegiac lilt in his voice.

"But I have an important message for you this evening," he went on.

Someone in the crowd shouted, "What would Bigfoot do!"

Another W-W-B-D chant started to pick up steam, but he held his hands out to quash it. "No, no, no, I won't be saying that tonight." He gave a weak smile. "In fact, I won't be saying it ever again."

The crowd took in a sharp breath all together.

"What I *will* be saying is this . . ."

He adjusted the microphone closer to his mouth.

"Bigfoot isn't real."

The words echoed around the plaster walls of the auditorium.

"As a myth, as a legend, sure. But not as a living, breathing creature."

The audience chuckled.

"I'm not joking," he said. "I've read all the eyewitness statements. I've examined all the track casts, pored over all the many, many blurry photos and videos. Trust me when I tell you they amount to nothing more than false identifications and hoaxes. The by-products of magical thinking."

Half the crowd still thought this was a joke and continued giggling nervously. The other half saw this speech for the affront it was and started to clamor in their seats.

But Bernard pressed on. "More than that, I've tromped through countless acres of forests, often right alongside many of you in this room tonight. Yet somehow not one of us has managed to turn up a single scrap of credible forensic evidence. No body. No fur. No bones. Not even a single pile of scat. Nothing that would allow us to scientifically catalog this thing. And why do you think that is?"

Several people stood and huffed out of the auditorium, hands balled into fists.

"I'll tell you why," Bernard continued. "It's because the only bipedal primates walking around the forests of North America are humans."

"What happened to you, man?" someone in the audience shouted. "You used to be one of us!"

"I know this is painful to hear. Believe me, I get it." He surveyed the rapidly dwindling audience. "Some of you are probably asking, Why now, Dr. Bernard? What brought on this sudden change of heart?"

He wiped the flop sweat off his brow again.

"Friends, we stand on the precipice of our planet's sixth mass extinction event. The world's biodiversity is dying off at somewhere between one thousand and ten thousand times the natural extinction rates. The impact of these losses will be felt by every man, woman, and child on earth. And unlike all the other mass extinctions, this one won't be caused by natural phenomena. It will be caused by us."

A woman near the front lobbed a cup of beer at the stage. Bernard gripped the podium and ducked, but a spray of lager managed to catch him across the face.

"You can laugh this off and say who really cares about spotted owls or the western ground squirrel," he said, wiping himself dry with his jacket sleeve. "But ecosystems rely on every single creature in them. Take one out and the system transforms. Take out too many and the whole system collapses."

The booing had become so loud Bernard could hardly hear his own voice.

"Listen, this is real science, friends. These are undeniable facts. I did my fieldwork—hell, I got into academia—because I care about the natural world."

Someone had pushed their way into the control room and was arguing with the soundboard operator.

"I know this is a lot to take in. And it's not my intention to pull the rug out from underneath you," Bernard said, picking up the pace because he could see he didn't have much time left. "I don't want to leave you bereft, with no hope for the future. So let's imagine for a moment the impact we could make together if all of us in this room tonight channeled our collective energy for good. I want you to join me on a new crusade. And it starts by letting go of *pseudo*science, so we can embrace *actual* science."

A loud pop rang out as the sound to the microphone finally got cut off. Bernard turned to his left, eager to see if Vicky had caught it all, hoping this might become the video that would propel him into the next phase of his career—whatever that turned out to be. But even his young documentarian had abandoned him.

Bernard staggered offstage to a sustained chorus of boos. He stumbled around in the dark, looking for the emergency exit, but instead ran into a hand truck leaning against the wall. He felt a searing bite of pain at his ankle, while his forward momentum sent him hurtling headlong through the air. He hit the floor chest-first, jaw snapping shut, wind sailing from his lungs with a groan.

While Bernard waited for his breath to return, he rolled onto his back and stared up at the ceiling. He'd finally delivered the speech he'd been aching for years to give. He'd uncoupled himself from Bigfoot World in the most spectacular, most irreversible way imaginable. And yet, in this moment of release, he didn't feel the satisfaction he'd been expecting. Instead, he had the nagging sensation that he wasn't quite done. The job, he feared, was incomplete.

When his lungs finally stopped spasming, Bernard lifted himself from the floor, dusted himself off. He tested his weight on the ankle. It held but didn't feel good. When he finally caught sight of the red-glowing exit sign, he pushed open the door, limped outside, and climbed into his rental car. At the far end of the alley a group of his former audience members was milling about, looking for a suitable outlet for their rage. Bernard locked the doors.

His foot felt moist, pooling blood. Definitely needed stitches. Probably a tetanus shot. He dimly recalled that the hospital in Helena was called St. Peter's, so he typed it into the car's GPS and let it pull up the route.

As he eased the car down the alleyway, he tilted his seat back and ducked behind the steering wheel, which allowed him to pull away from the mob almost entirely unnoticed.

When the crowd started filing out of the auditorium, Vicky had to make a decision. She recalled a lecture Professor Moss had given on narrative craft where he advised his students to *anticipate* the story, not follow it. Vicky's instincts told her the real action tonight would unfold outside, after the speech. In any case, the crowds' booing had gotten so loud she could hardly make out what Bernard was saying anymore, which didn't make for very good footage. So she made her way out of the auditorium, around to the front of the building.

Hordes of convention goers wandered aimlessly, seething. Some of them spoke surreptitiously in small groups. Others railed at the Civic Center façade, as if the building itself were responsible for what had happened inside. Vicky made herself inconspicuous as she circulated among them, picking up snippets of anger and betrayal. Any minute now, they'd start burning their "WHAT WOULD BIGFOOT DO" merchandise.

As she filmed the mob, she glanced down a dead-end alley that ran along the west side of the Civic Center. A rusty metal fire door opened, and a tweed-jacketed figure hobbled forth. Dr. Bernard had nowhere to go but straight this way, into the jaws of the mob. Vicky congratulated herself for anticipating this imminent conflict. Now all she had to do was sit back and let the camera roll.

But then, a car door opened in the alley. Headlights snapped on. Vicky realized with horror: The subject of her film wasn't about to face the music; he was about to flee the scene.

. . .

The GPS voice was telling Bernard to turn left down an unmarked, unlit road that certainly didn't look like it led to any kind of hospital you'd voluntarily admit yourself into.

As he started to make the turn, he realized too late he was pulling onto the interstate. And with another car riding his rear bumper, he had no choice but to get on it.

Several miles later, a green exit sign glowed against Bernard's headlights. He let his foot off the gas, eased the car off the interstate. When he reached the end of the ramp, the GPS voice was telling him to take a right, to go deeper into this strange, dark land. He had no idea where it was trying to take him. It seemed increasingly likely he wasn't headed to St. Peter's Hospital.

He hit the gas and flipped the wheel to the right.

The road through here was two lanes. Rock walls loomed close on either side. Bernard kept his speed below thirty miles an hour, craning his neck forward, alert. Then . . . lights ahead. A sign.

Welcome to Basic, Montana. Pop. 484.

Bernard followed the purple line on the GPS straight into town, toward the checkered flag.

There it was. Neon lettering: *St. Pete's Tavern.*

No chance of getting his ankle stitched up here. But it also wasn't the worst place in the world to hunker down and figure out what came next.

Chapter 3

The last operating bar in Basic, Montana, was a run-down watering hole called St. Pete's Tavern. One of its most notable attributes—aside from still being in business—was a sprawling stained-glass window that hung behind the bar, a biblically themed triptych presiding over all who'd ever hoisted a beverage inside its cinder-block walls. The window hadn't been cleaned in years, but if you happened to be day-drinking and squinted just right, you could make out Noah building his ark in the first panel. The second had him loading the animal pairs. And the third showed the ark bobbing on waters sent by an angry God to wash the wicked from the world.

Local lore held that the window had been salvaged from the Presbyterian church a few miles up the road in Richardton, a silver boomtown that never saw the benefits of a second boom, and had long since disappeared off the maps. No one alive in Basic today could verify the window's origin though. Like all myths, this one became history the moment enough people chose to believe it.

On nights like this, Vergil Barnes would lean back in his chair and stare up at the triptych as he contemplated life's perplexing questions. Tonight, his questions were more perplexing than usual. His eyes settled on the image of Noah hurriedly hammering two boards together while storm clouds mounted in the background. The man in the window was engaged in a race against time. That faint, omnipresent whisper of mortality had, in an instant, turned into a roar. And he only had a little time left to get his shit together.

Vergil could relate.

The man sitting across from him—his oldest, best, and only friend in the world—had no idea what was on Vergil's mind tonight. Nor would he. At least not for a little while longer.

Jute Ramsey was wedged between the armrests of his chair, knees grazing the underside of the table, causing the empties to clink and wobble. A small man trapped inside a big man's body.

As was often the case, Jute's eyes were red and misty. He'd just finished hijacking the Basic Bigfoot Society's monthly meeting agenda to recount the same traumatic childhood camping story, which invariably left him blinking back tears and blowing his nose into a cocktail napkin. As usual, Vergil had listened dutifully, offering bromides here and there when appropriate. Given enough time, Jute would sputter and run out of steam on his own.

The tableau at St. Pete's this evening appeared much the same as it did every Friday night. Near the front, a table of sheep ranchers who called themselves the Chamber of Commerce, headed up by Brodie and Dustin Dodge. At the far end of the bar, the Swintons and Loabs, two married couples, arguing over their nightly game of Yahtzee. Mixed among them were a dozen or so serious drunks, the true economic engines of any small-town bar. An aproned Tammy Reynolds was wiping down the taps, getting ready for close, though it was still an hour away.

The only thing different tonight from every other Friday night was the presence of a slightly rotund man with a light brown ponytail and an out-of-place tweed jacket, who sat alone at the bar chasing shots of Canadian Club with an Old Milwaukee tallboy. The stranger seemed oddly familiar, his identity hanging at the edge of Vergil's recognition.

"It feels like it was yesterday." Jute was peeling the label on his beer bottle with giant, trembling fingers. "My old man got screwed up on that camping trip." He shook his head slowly. "Threw my whole life off track."

Vergil took a swallow of beer. "It's hard to make sense of the past," he said, "and the things we choose to remember from it." This was one of three or four stock responses he kept on hand for these situations, meant to acknowledge his friend's pain while leaving open the possibility that it wasn't quite as bad as he recalled.

Jute looked up from his bottle. His eyebrows were two fuzzy caterpillars squared off on his forehead. "I didn't *choose* to remember anything, Verge."

This was a more combative response than usual. Vergil would have to modulate his tone if he wanted to nudge this meeting back onto the rails. "I just meant it's not always helpful to look for meaning in things that happened so long ago."

Jute frowned and took a long swallow of beer.

While Vergil privately questioned some of the more fantastical elements of what Jute claimed to have witnessed all those years ago, there was no doubt the experience haunted him to this day. And proving the existence of what he'd encountered on that trip was the entire raison d'être of the Basic Bigfoot Society. Even still, it was clear that Jute was looking for something more than an elusive cryptid; he was searching for a way to heal the parts of himself that were broken.

"I can't help wondering what things'd be like if we'd never gone on that trip." Jute ran his fingers through his graying crew cut. "I mean, what if? Right?" He shook his head slowly, side to side.

As children, Vergil and Jute had both been labeled oddballs under the rubric of small-town social norms, even though they'd only been close for a six-month window before high school. One night, during that time, they'd watched the special two-part episode of *The Six Million Dollar Man* where Steve Austin fights a Sasquatch. Jute then told Vergil his own Bigfoot story, and it dawned on them that they shared a passion for the unknown. Gassed up on Mountain Dew and Milk Duds, they formed and swore allegiance to the Basic Bigfoot Society that very night, though they never held a single meeting, or went on any hunts. The club was a statement of identity—to each other at least—of who they were, like saying you belonged to a particular religion, even if you never went to church. Neither boy could have known in that moment, as the caffeine and corn syrup coursed through their veins, that less than a year later, when Vergil entered high school, the centrifugal forces of adolescence would pull them apart. Their brief window of friendship would close, and the Basic Bigfoot Society would soon be all but forgotten.

It wasn't until Vergil moved back to Basic a dozen years later, with a wife and infant daughter, that the two misfit boys, now misfit men, resumed their friendship and reinaugurated their childhood club. The Basic Bigfoot Society—it turned out—filled a fundamental need for both of them.

That man in the tweed jacket was looking in their direction again. Probably overheard Jute blubbering about Ramsey Lake. Vergil felt embarrassed for his friend, even if Jute didn't have enough sense to be embarrassed for himself.

"Should I move to adjourn?" Vergil suggested.

"Move to adjourn?" Jute said as if he'd been slapped. "We've got one more agenda item."

He put on his half-moon reading glasses and peered down at the sheet of notebook paper next to his beer. "Item number seven: Location Scouting."

"About that," Vergil said. "I can't go tomorrow."

"But the expedition's right around the corner! And we don't have a location yet." Jute rested his meaty palm on the table. "I had to beg Pluto to take an extra shift at the car wash."

"Rye's coming home tomorrow."

"She is?" Jute perked up. "What's the occasion?"

Vergil didn't know how to answer this without first revealing to Jute the news he'd been trying like hell to keep from him. "I thought I mentioned it already."

"Location scouting's been on the calendar for a month," Jute said. "I'd remember if you told me you weren't going to make it."

"What do you want me to say?" Vergil held his hands out.

"I want you to say you'll help me scout expedition locations like we do every year," Jute said. "Last I checked you're still a member of the Basic Bigfoot Society."

The tweed jacket guy turned on his barstool and openly stared at

Jute and Vergil. Everyone else around here knew enough to ignore them when they started squabbling like this. A sweaty wave of embarrassment washed over Vergil.

"You can handle scouting on your own," he said, through clenched teeth. "I don't think that's asking too much."

They locked eyes across the table. The jukebox was playing an old Garth Brooks song, which Vergil could remember being a new Garth Brooks song not that long ago.

"Fine, I'll scout for both of us," Jute finally said. "On my own."

Vergil hoisted his bottle and took a swig. A wave of nausea climbed the back of his throat. He almost spit out the beer, but he managed to keep everything down.

"You okay over there?" Jute asked.

"Yes, yes, fine," Vergil assured him. He could tell Jute now. The same thing he'd be telling Rye tomorrow. This could be a chance to do a dry run. Vergil opened his mouth, waited for the words to come tumbling out. But when he looked into his friend's watery eyes, magnified by the lenses of his reading glasses, he didn't have the heart to do it.

Soon. But not tonight.

"I move we adjourn the June meeting of the Basic Bigfoot Society," he said, closing the notebook where he'd been recording the minutes.

"Second," Vergil said.

"All in favor?"

Both men raised their hands and said aye.

"Opposed?"

Respectful silence.

"Meeting adjourned," they said at once, in what might have been the first time they'd agreed on anything all night.

As they made their way to the door, past the big round table at the front, Brodie Dodge watched them with a wolfish grin.

"Hey, look!" he said, pointing at Jute. "It's Bigfoot!"

The rest of the Chamber of Commerce cackled, even though it hadn't been a particularly funny or inventive quip. Still, Jute's head dropped, his shoulders hunched, and his brow beetled darkly. This was his default response to ridicule, honed over a lifetime spent as the butt of every joke.

Vergil put a hand on his friend's waist and steered him past the table.

Dustin Dodge, not to be outdone by his older brother, pointed at Vergil. "Look at that," he said. "He's got Bigfoot's girlfriend with him!"

Even the drowsy drunks at the bar joined in now. And laughter followed them out of the bar.

It was quiet on the sidewalk, aside from the faint sounds of Whitesnake seeping under the door. The sky above was Prussian blue, carelessly daubed with a scrim of pale stars. Vergil used to look at the sky and think about ways to paint what he saw up there. But that was long ago, practically a different lifetime.

The entirety of Basic, Montana, stretched out before them. Seven or eight blocks of ramshackle buildings huddled against each other, the hulking husk of the old mill at the edge of town, and the towering smelter stack behind it. Then miles of wilderness, and the jagged teeth of the Elkhorn Mountains in the distance. Seen from above, Basic would have appeared as nothing more than a tiny speck of light in the middle of a black canvas, as isolated as every single one of those stars above.

Both men stood outside the door for a moment, hands buried in their pockets, breath visible in the cold spring air.

"Something's bothering me," Jute said.

"What's that?" Maybe his friend had sniffed out the news on his own. Vergil braced himself.

"I get how I'm supposed to be Bigfoot on account of my size," he said. "But why would they call you Bigfoot's girlfriend? Shouldn't you be Bigfoot's boyfriend?"

Vergil laughed. As he did so, an arpeggio of pain climbed up through his spine, sounding a different note with each vertebra.

"What's with that limp?" Jute asked, suddenly serious.

"Threw my back out changing a tire last week." Vergil kept his eyes on the stars.

Jute nodded suspiciously. "Seems like it's getting worse."

"It's nothing." Vergil pushed back. "Why don't you leave the worrying to me?"

Just then the music from inside the bar got louder as the door swung open. Vergil instinctively stepped forward to shield Jute, in case the Dodge brothers had decided to continue heckling him outside. But Vergil was surprised to see the man in the tweed jacket emerge.

"Excuse me, gentlemen, I couldn't help overhearing you inside the bar." An accent, East Coast maybe. Definitely not from around here. "I have a proposition which I believe you may find to be of interest."

He seemed to be waiting for them to respond, but they both stared mutely at the stranger.

"My name is—"

"You're Dr. Marcus Bernard," Jute said, stepping out from behind Vergil. "I'm a huge fan of your work."

Bernard performed an at-your-service arm sweep.

Hearing the name out loud finally jogged the pieces into place for Vergil. The red bandanna, the preponderance of denim and khaki, even the jacket, which lent him an air of professorial gravitas.

"What are you doing here?" Vergil asked. No one famous ever willingly came to Basic, at least not since the silver mine shut down a second time.

"Had a bit of a snafu with my GPS," he said. "But it seems that fate has dealt us all a winning hand."

The bar door swung open again and "Livin' on a Prayer" suddenly got louder until the door whooshed closed. The person emerging this time was a mid-twenties Asian woman with shoulder-length hair and a look of general annoyance. She'd been holding a video camera low at her hip, and now she swung it up to her shoulder.

"Gentlemen," Bernard said, gesturing to the new arrival, "this is my videographer, Vicky Xu."

The woman gave Bernard a cockeyed look. "I'm an independent documentarian," she said. "I'm working *with* Dr. Bernard. Not *for* him."

"Yes. Well. Now that we've gotten our job titles cleared up," Bernard said, "I couldn't help but overhear you've got a Bigfoot expedition in the works."

"Were we that loud?" Vergil wasn't sure why he was even more embarrassed now that he knew who the stranger was.

"What I'm wondering is"—Bernard looked around the empty street to make sure no one else was listening—"would you gentlemen have any interest in partnering up on this expedition of yours?"

Chapter 4

Jute's mind was already busy cataloging the opportunities this new partnership would open up, but he forced himself to play it cool, keep a steady pace as he strolled down Central Avenue, through Basic's darkened commercial district. Past First Federal Bank, which had been closed since 4:30. Past the Kit Kat Café, closed since 7:00. Then the Silver Museum, which wasn't open at all on Fridays anymore.

The world's foremost Bigfoot expert had shown up at St. Pete's—out of the blue—and offered to join the Basic Bigfoot Society's summer expedition. It was like winning the lottery when you didn't even know you'd bought a ticket. Jute put his hand in his pocket and felt Dr. Bernard's business card to make sure it wasn't a dream. He ran his finger along the edge until it nearly gave him a paper cut. Felt real enough.

The sidewalk began to slope upward as Jute trudged past the public library, which Vergil had closed up at 5:01 as usual, past Hoo Yin's Chinese Restaurant, closed since 7:30, and Ten Pin Lanes, closed since 1982.

Pretty much everyone in town viewed the Basic Bigfoot Society as a laughingstock, their endless quest for Bigfoot nothing more than a childish fantasy. What the doubters didn't understand—what they *couldn't* understand—was that Jute knew where to find Bigfoot. All they had to do was get back to Ramsey Lake, and the mystery would solve itself. He was sure of it.

Problem was, Jute had been too young at the time of that first visit to remember how they'd gotten there. Despite years of searching, he'd never been able to find his way back. You would've thought with the advent of satellites and GPS navigation, it'd be a snap. After all, they could now see hundreds of mountain lakes that weren't listed on any of the old topographic maps. Yet he and Vergil would hike in to a lake that seemed on Google Earth to have all the characteristics of Ramsey Lake, only to wind up disappointed. This one was a shallow, swampy depression. That one was dried up and likely only held water in the springtime. Sometimes it felt like Ramsey Lake didn't *want* to be found.

At the crest of the hill ahead stood the Swanser Hotel, once the finest lodging in a three-county radius. The Swanser closed its doors for the last time in 1979, when it became clear the second silver boom was well and truly kicked.

But anything seemed possible, now that the BBS was teaming up with Dr. Bernard. If Jute and Vergil found evidence to prove Bigfoot was real, they'd instantly become household names, probably get their own TV show, maybe a book deal, and they'd take their place alongside the brightest stars in the Bigfoot firmament. More than that, though, people would flock to Basic from all over the world. They'd open a Bigfoot museum, an interpretive center. Jute and Vergil could run guided expeditions. A discovery like that could lift the fortunes of the entire town, and places like the Swanser would open their doors again. This was Jute's personal version of the American Dream. And now, it was starting to feel entirely within reach.

As he turned left onto Second Avenue, a stiff breeze pushed down from the foothills. Jute picked up a strange odor, an old scent that reminded him of something from long ago.

The front yard was more overgrown with weeds than usual. His mower had been acting up again, and no matter how many times Jute took the motor apart and put it back together, he couldn't figure out what was wrong with it. He climbed the rickety porch steps to find his mailbox choked with envelopes and catalogs. It had been like this ever since the post office cut back Basic's mail service to once a week.

Jute grabbed a chunky Cabela's catalog and tugged. The aluminum mailbox groaned until the jam gave way, and a flurry of loose mail flew into the air. The heavier stuff hit the porch first and skittered under the railing down into the weeds. The letters fluttered longer, dropping gently like snowflakes.

Jute gathered the items off the porch floor first. Down in the yard, he beat around in the weeds, scooping up the catalogs. It was hard to tell in the dark, but he was pretty sure he'd found them all. Once inside, he tossed the mail on the coffee table and flung himself onto the couch.

One of the living room walls was entirely papered over with photographs taken on BBS expeditions through the years. Each one contained blurry anomalies that had at first seemed mildly curious, but which, upon closer inspection, had proven to be nothing more than tree trunks, rocks, oddly shaped branches, out-of-focus bugs sitting on the camera lens. *Blobsquatches* was the term for what they'd caught. Years' and years' worth. Most people would think this was a waste of time, but Jute saw it as playing the odds. If you took enough photos, shot enough videos, eventually one of them *had* to pay off.

He sat up and began sorting through the mail. Catalogs in one pile, Bigfoot magazines and journals in another, bills in a third. Then his eye caught on something that didn't belong. A sheet of paper. No envelope, no stamp, no postmark, accordioned into the back of the mailbox by the rest of the mail.

Jute cleared a space on the coffee table and flattened the paper, which felt moist and heavy with mildew. All it contained were a few hand-drawn lines. He put on his half-moon readers, tried rotating the paper different ways to see if it was a picture. From one angle, it looked like it could be a pair of disconnected legs. From another, maybe half a face. But what did it mean? And what was it doing in his mailbox?

Jute leaned back on the couch and took off his readers. His entire field of vision was filled with blobsquatches. He liked to think of it as an accent wall, which he learned about from watching that home-decorating show on Discovery Channel. Jute let his eyes go unfocused for a moment, then looked down at the yellowed paper again. He rotated it ninety degrees and squinted.

Without knowing why, he stood and went out the back door, across the yard to the former toolshed, now better known as the Bigfoot War Room. Inside, Jute took a seat at a rickety card table and pressed the power button on an ancient desktop. He opened a browser and pulled up a map of Basic. He zoomed out several clicks, then held the paper next to the monitor.

There—on the sheet and on the screen—was the distinctive hitch Coyote Canyon Road made when it doubled back over the south fork of Hell Creek.

Jute's throat went dry.

He was holding a map. And he had a pretty good idea what it showed.

Back inside the house, he picked up the wall phone in the kitchen. For a moment, he thought about retrieving Dr. Bernard's card from the coffee table. Instead Jute dialed the only number he knew by heart.

Vergil was probably asleep by now, but Jute didn't care. This was too important to wait.

Chapter 5

As usual, Vergil watched until Jute had turned the corner out of sight before beginning his own walk home, juggling even more questions than before. What was Dr. Marcus Bernard doing in Basic, Montana? More important, why would someone of his stature want to partner with a couple nobodies like Vergil and Jute? What did he hope to gain?

Regardless of what the answers might be, there was no way they could pass up the opportunity. Vergil saw how Jute's eyes lit up when Dr. Bernard made his proposal. Working with him could change their lives—or at least Jute's life.

Vergil turned down Silver Street and took a right onto Batten Avenue. When he got to his house two blocks later, he slunk around the side, through the backyard, to the western edge of his property, which ended at the bank of Hell Creek. On a chilly spring night like this twenty-three years ago, he and Melody made an emergency trip back to Basic after Vergil got a phone call informing him that his mother had passed away. When he pressed the caller for more details, he was told she'd had a heart attack, that she'd been on life support for three days before finally succumbing. Vergil couldn't understand why no one had called to tell him sooner, why they'd let him fritter away his mother's final hours in Seattle, while she suffered and died alone.

The night of her funeral, as the town mourned one of its last true matriarchs inside the house, Vergil stood right here on the bank of Hell Creek wondering what he should do with his life. Melody crept up behind him. She rested one hand on his shoulder, the other on her growing belly.

"Let's move here," she'd said.

"To Basic?" he said. "Are you joking?"

"Believe it or not, I like this place." A gust of wind blew her hair into wild black tendrils. "My residency's almost over. I'm sure I can get on rotation at one of the hospitals in Helena or Bozeman. It'll be a bitch of a commute, but look at this view." She spread her arms wide, did a slow turn to encompass Hell Creek and the Elkhorn Mountains in the distance.

"What about my work?" he asked. Vergil's art career back in Seattle was starting to achieve liftoff. He'd had three paintings selected for a thirty-under-thirty exhibition at a gallery in SoDo. His work had been deemed to "hold promise." Which in Seattle art-speak meant he'd be getting a solo show soon. He was close—so close—to becoming who he was supposed to be.

"That shed over there." Melody pointed with her chin. "We'll convert it into a studio. Who needs fancy galleries when we can make our own?"

Vergil stood very still as her words washed over him. Melody didn't know it at the time, but he hadn't painted anything new in months. Every morning, he'd stand in front of a blank canvas, waiting for inspiration to strike, but it never did. The longer the paralysis went on, the worse it became. It had gotten so bad he was afraid to even pick up a brush anymore. But this place, at this most unexpected time, might be the solution to his artistic dry spell. Moving back to Basic, back to where it all began, could be exactly what he needed to kick-start his creative motor.

That was the idea anyway.

Tonight Vergil went back around to the front of the house and shouldered open the door, lifting the knob so the hinges wouldn't squeak, even though no one was around to hear them. A week's worth of mail was scattered across the floor. When he bent down to sweep it up, the low ache in his back rose to a high trill that pealed out through his whole body. Vergil wasn't even sure where the pancreas was located, or what it was supposed to do, but his was now apparently killing him.

As it turned out, a change of scenery hadn't helped. For months, Vergil stood in that shed out back, paints mixed on the palette, blank canvas leaning on the easel, only to find his mind utterly devoid of ideas or inspiration.

"I think they need help down at the library," he announced one night early on when Melody got home from a shift at St. Peter's.

"You want to volunteer at the library?" she asked over a glass of chardonnay. "What about your painting?"

"It would only be for a little while," he told her. "With Mom not around anymore they could really use an extra set of hands."

Melody frowned and nodded as a way to give her blessing.

As the months wore on, Vergil's hours at the library grew while his time in the studio shrank, until it became, essentially, an unpaid full-time job. Whenever Melody brought up painting, he would deflect by talking about a set of reference books he wanted to order, or a new periodical he thought they should subscribe to. Eventually, he moved his art supplies out of the studio and converted it back into a toolshed. They didn't talk about it anymore.

The people in Basic did though. They'd immediately sniffed out the real reason Vergil came back. He was a failure, a washout, the same nerdy little kid who'd left town nine years earlier. Couldn't hack it out there in the real world, so he finally scurried back to the only place that would have him. No better than anyone else around here. It was then that Vergil realized: Towns like Basic didn't let people change, and they never forgave the ones who tried. The only person who didn't seem to share this sentiment was his childhood friend, Jute Ramsey.

Vergil stepped into the kitchen, sifting through the mail. Most of it was from St. Peter's Hospital in Helena. No need to open it. The doctor's phrase still rang in his mind: *worst-case scenario of a worst-case scenario.*

On the counter, the answering machine light was blinking. One message. He filled a glass from the tap and watched the clouds settle before taking a sip. He pressed play.

"Okay—yeah—Dad? I think I heard a beep. God, that machine is old. You know, people use voicemail now." There was a pause as if she were expecting an argument. "Actually, no one even uses voicemail anymore. Nowadays, humans *text* other humans. That's the evolution we need you to undergo." Another pause. "Umm . . . so, anyways, I can't hang out long tomorrow. Whatever this announcement is, I'm not sure why you couldn't tell me over the phone." Vergil detected a tremor of fear in his daughter's voice as she said this. He gripped the water glass tight in his fist.

"Okay—so—I'll text when I'm on my way. Please keep Flippy on. It'll make things a lot easier. Okay? Okay. So. Then. I guess that's it. But I just want to say—"

The machine let out a slurred beep. The tired motor started to rewind.

Vergil pulled open the junk drawer next to the fridge. He dug through a nest of receipts and orphaned keys until he found his old cell phone, which Rye had either affectionately or disparagingly nicknamed Flippy. He set it on the counter next to his perfectly good house phone. When he turned Flippy on, he cringed at the twinkly power-up jingle. What a worthless, redundant device.

The plan was to tell Rye tomorrow. Her first instinct would be to interrogate the doctors. Demand second opinions. Explore treatment options. Investigate experimental therapies. The whole nine. Vergil would have to explain how he didn't want to go through all that suffering if it only bought him a few more extremely unpleasant months.

This decision would not sit well with Rye—or Jute. But it was his choice, and he'd already made it.

Vergil remembered coming across a proverb in his mother's diary, written shortly before she died. "The world ends at the foot of one's sickbed." At the time he didn't understand what it meant, but now he saw it so clearly. Soon enough his world would shrink precipitously, and he wanted to put that moment off as long as possible.

He refilled his water glass. In the living room, he reached for the remote but thought better of it. Watching the news right now would only make him feel more anxious. Instead he went to the stereo cabinet, finger-stepped through the old vinyl until he found *Callas Portrays Puccini Heroines,* the one where the singer stares out from the cover, fingertips touching her cheeks. Melody always put it on after she got back from her shifts at the ER. A few crackles and pops and then strains of ecstasy and joy, sadness and sorrow would swell until the whole house felt full of life.

He slid the record from its sleeve and set it on the turntable. The speaker hissed as the needle settled into the track, before the orchestra struck up the first notes of *Manon Lescaut.* A moment later Maria Callas's voice came through, fragile as frozen glass.

Melody never sat down while the record played. She would put her hand flat against the wall to brace herself—still dressed in her hospital scrubs, eyes closed, face tilted toward the ceiling. She'd sway her head in slow motion, the corners of her mouth turned up into a beatific smile. Something ineffable was happening to her in those moments, some kind of transcendence. More than almost anything in the world, Vergil used to love watching Melody listen to this record.

Tonight, as the music came through the speakers, a ringing ache sounded in his chest. It was the same feeling he had the day he got the call from the sheriff's deputy to tell him about the accident. Vergil thought it had been a mistake at first, a wrong number. He kept saying no, no, no, no, no, because as long as he kept saying no, it wouldn't be real, and Melody would still be alive. But he eventually ran out of nos.

"I'm sorry, Melody," he said out loud now. "I'm sorry I won't be around to take care of our daughter. To help her find her way in the world."

The phone started ringing in the kitchen.

Vergil didn't want to answer it. But it could be Rye. So he pulled himself together, and picked up the receiver before the machine had a chance to click on.

June 11, 1911—As Supervisor of this fifty-two-person mining operation, I am compelled to notate our endeavors in this ledger I chanced upon at the site of an abandoned camp nearby. I cannot discern if previous writings in it are factual or fabrications. However, my notes here are intended to serve as a true account of our labors and achievements in these mountains.

June 15, 1911—Decision to begin mining operations so early in season is bearing fruit. Progress on primary tunnel into mountainside has been steady. Depth approx. 25'. Fresh water supply is conveniently located. Wildlife is abundant. Air is clean. Scenery is beyond compare. This is well and truly God's country. Engineer and geologist believe mine will be ready to begin extraction by end of month. A rather large crow has made itself a fixture in camp. The men have taken to feeding it and even named it Old Thom.

June 20, 1911—Tunnel depth approx. 30'. Weather has been disruptive, but our work proceeds apace. Workers have found several abnormally large footprints which are most intriguing. I suspect one of the laborers is playing pranks on his fellow companions, though all plead innocent in the matter. The men claim they have taught Old Thom to dance and count to three. He is the source of much merriment and delight. Despite our recent setbacks, morale is strong.

June 26, 1911—Tunnel depth approx. 35'. Preparations are under way to start first exploratory tunnel traveling in southerly direction. Anticipation of striking gold is high among the entire company. One team of diggers, in their off time, has discovered a lovely lake atop a nearby mountain with signs of recent human habitation. Alas, footprint pranks have continued unabated, though I have ceased to find humor in them. I am determined to identify the culprit and dismiss him, with no claim on our eventual yield.

July 1, 1911—The exploratory tunnel has reached a length of 15'. We have not struck gold vein that geologist predicted. Debate is under way whether to start another exploratory tunnel, or dig deeper into the mountain. Old Thom has not been seen around camp in some time. Morale of workers is low.

July 6, 1911—We have abandoned first exploratory tunnel and resumed deeper excavation. This afternoon, traces of gold were detected in extracted ore. Failing light forced us to cease operations for the day, but we will begin again tomorrow with renewed vigor. Also, someone has begun leaving trinkets around camp. Small figures woven from tree branches and reeds. It is an unnerving enterprise. Suspicion is high on all sides. But I believe striking gold will cure us of the lassitude that has beset us.

July 8, 1911—Assayer has determined that gold mentioned in previous entry is nothing more than pyrite. Spirits are low. Decided to penetrate deeper into the mountain until it yields its gold to us.

July 13, 1911—Company is in tumult. A stranger wandered into camp last night. His gaunt and bedraggled appearance gave entire company a terrible fright. Thus far, he is unable to speak, due to an exhausted and nervous state, though many suspect this fellow is responsible for the footprint pranks and the odd trinkets. Some among us wanted to turn him away, but mercy prevailed and we will give him succor until such time as he may provide an accounting of his deeds. He has not awoken in twelve hours' slumber. I hope to ask him, when he awakes, if he knows where the gold may be.

<u>July 15, 1911</u>—The stranger has risen. He declines to provide his name, and only states that he goes by the title the watcher. Whereas he was nearly mute not three days ago, he now speaks nonstop. He talks of a beast lurking in the forest, of curses on the land, and the certain doom to befall those who encroach upon it. His bizarre prophesies bedevil the company. Old Thom has reappeared. He is a constant companion of the watcher, often alighting on his shoulder like a familiar. Mining operations have nearly ceased. He knows nothing about the location of gold. I regret the weakness that prompted us to take the watcher into the bosom of our generosity.

<u>July 19, 1911</u>—The company is beset by sloth, listening all day long to the ravings of the watcher. The man fancies himself a prophet, speaking in wild psalms of pestilence and flood. He states that our mine is a blight upon the land, that we are sickening and fouling the soil. I have tried explaining that Earth is God's bounty given to man for his use and pleasure, but he will not listen to reason. At night, he and Old Thom cackle in a strange animal tongue. There are times, I admit, when it feels like they are mocking me.

Those of us who are yet clear-headed have begun digging another exploratory tunnel. I still believe we are close to striking the vein of gold, and that doing so will resolve the troubles we face.

<u>July 23, 1911</u>—All day, every day, the watcher talks and talks and talks and talks and talks. Even in the tunnel, filling bucket after bucket of rubble, I hear his voice echo in my ears.

Food stores are depleted. We are delirious with hunger. There is no gold. One wonders if it was ever ours to find. I must try to sleep, to clear my mind and find a way to go on.

<u>July 25, 1911</u>—I could not take one more night of infernal ranting. I waited until all were asleep. I trod softly toward the watcher, who was caught in a delirium, frothing like a rabid cur. Old Thom sounded an alert to my presence, but I hazed him off. Then I seized the nearest rock and struck a fatal blow upon the watcher. I slept deeply for the first time in many a night. We are free now to resume our true purpose on this

mountain. And I am convinced my account toward heaven remains spotless.

July 28, 1911—Our troubles deepen. In an effort to assign blame for the watcher's death, men have begun attacking each other. The situation is made more dire by the fact that a significant number of the company departed on a hunting expedition two days ago and has not returned.

August 1, 1911—The followers of the watcher have regressed to a primitive state. They wear no clothes and sleep on bare ground. Some, I fear, have begun to consume their fallen comrades out of hunger. I have resisted this temptation, though I have grown quite weak as a result. The others watch me, their mouths slavering in anticipation. I am reminded of the old admonition: "Blood follows gold." While we have not found the latter, we have spilled our fair share of the former.

August 4, 1911—I hear them plotting. They know what I did to the watcher. I have been sentenced to death. It is to occur tomorrow at dawn. If I cannot escape tonight, I intend to take my own life, and thus deny them the satisfaction of their diabolical ritual. I shall not write another entry in this ledger. May the Good Lord bless and keep my soul forever.

Chapter 6

A boxy Subaru Forester labored north on I-15 as it wound through the western foothills of the Elkhorn Mountain Range. The driver was cautious around the curves, even though she knew these roads well.

A sudden ping caused Rye Barnes to glance over at the passenger seat. Her phone was facedown, but she knew who the text was from and what it said. She cut her eyes back to the road and the approaching mountains, which felt like they were about to swallow her up.

Most Montanans considered the Elkhorns to be a second-tier mountain range, lacking the sheer size of the Bitterroots, or the jagged scale of the Beartooths, or the enigmatic cache of the Crazies. The Elkhorns were best known for being riddled with abandoned mining tunnels, pocked with piles of toxic tailings left over from the silver boom days. Sure, growing up she'd heard whispers, rumors of people seeing things in the forest that shouldn't exist, people losing their minds or even disappearing without a trace. But those were nothing more than legends, tall tales meant to give people a sense of shared history, a kind of social glue that held towns like Basic together.

Being guilted into driving home from school simply because her father had an announcement to make was not where Rye envisioned herself at age twenty-two. She should have been wrapping up her BS in kinesiology at San Francisco State University, a healthy eighteen-hour car ride from Basic. If she'd done well enough, she would right now be getting ready to transfer into the doctoral program in physical therapy at UCSF. It was a plan she'd been honing for years, busting her butt to make it a reality.

What she hadn't planned on was a late spring snowstorm her senior year of high school. What she hadn't accounted for was a snowplow crossing the median on I-15 without properly defogging its windows. Rye's mother had been rushing to St. Peter's Hospital in Helena to conduct an emergency appendectomy when that snowplow T-boned her car. And Dr. Melody Barnes wound up as a patient in the ER alongside the guy with the ruptured appendix.

He lived. She died.

Rye deferred at SFSU so she could stay at home with her father. It made sense. They needed to mourn together in that moment. But as that year wore on, Rye began to feel like life was passing her by. The next fall, he suggested Rye stay in-state for school: Bozeman, a couple hours away.

"Sure would be nice to have you close by," he'd said.

"What about San Francisco State?" she said.

"They've got a kinesiology program in Bozeman too," he said.

Rye didn't have the heart to tell him the whole point of San Francisco had been its lack of proximity to Basic. "MSU won't help me get into the UCSF doctoral program," she said. "You know that's my dream school."

"In-state tuition would be a lot easier for us to swing right now," he'd said, and looked down at his shoes.

That had been the end of the discussion.

Rye lifted her foot off the gas and held her breath as she approached her mother's crash site. The only evidence something out of the ordinary ever took place here was a shallow furrow gouged into the asphalt where the snowplow's blade had dug in. A permanent reminder of life's random, fundamental cruelty. Rye had loved her mother, yes, but it was complicated. They'd never been close the way it seemed like moms and daughters were supposed to be. Melody had always been prickly, judgmental. The kind of person with a lot of opinions she was keeping to herself, while making it widely known she was keeping them to herself. As Rye emerged from her teens, she believed they would grow close again—once she became an adult, once her mother got the chance to see who her daughter really was.

But neither of them got that chance.

Rye eased the Forester onto the exit ramp. Her phone chimed again. The fifth text she'd gotten on this drive. Almost certainly all from Jenny. Almost certainly saying something to the effect of *I'm confused.*

And who could blame her?

Rye's intention had been to break up with her before she left campus this morning, but as soon as she started to do the deed, Jenny's eyes welled up behind her glasses and her upper lip trembled, and, well, it was hard to know how things shook out in the end. "I've got to go now," Rye said once she'd loaded her things into the car. "We'll talk when I get back. Okay?"

Rye nosed her way up Coyote Canyon Road toward Basic, bracing herself for this announcement her father was planning to make. She hated open-ended surprises. More than likely, it had something to do with money. God knows he didn't make anything volunteering at the library. But Rye was ready for this possibility. She'd been working extra shifts at the coffee shop for a year, saving every threadbare dollar from the tip jar. And she could always take out loans if she had to. San Francisco may be out of reach for now, but at least she'd finish up in Bozeman and plot her next move after that.

Up ahead she saw the sign that let her know she was officially home: *Welcome to Basic, Montana. Pop. 484.* The day she left for college, her dad had joked that they'd have to change the sign to 483. A second later, they both realized that no one had ever revised the sign after Melody's death, and they choked on their laughter.

Rye hung a left onto Front Street and slowed down as she cruised past Basic Car Wash. Didn't look like Uncle Jute was working this morning. Instead, his sole employee, Pluto MacIntyre, sat in the glassed-in booth surrounded by windshield wipers and air fresheners, staring at his phone. Rye had gone to high school (and middle school, and grade school) with Pluto and liked him well enough. He was smart, creative, and had a quirky sense of humor. Now here he was, working for Uncle Jute at the car wash. Not that there was anything wrong with that. Hell, Rye worked there the year after her mother had died. But this was what small towns did. They caught you in their nets, kept you from going out into the world and growing into the person you were supposed to be. Pluto was just one more casualty of this godforsaken place.

Rye had no desire to catch up with Pluto today, so she took a quick right onto Batten Avenue. Straight ahead three blocks until she coasted to a stop in front of her dad's house.

She switched off the car and checked her phone. Six texts from Jenny. Rye started to type something back, but found she had nothing to say, so instead she let the screen go dark. She popped the hatchback and pulled out her laundry bag, which she balanced on her head as she started up the walkway to the porch. The front door, as always, was unlocked.

"Dad, I'm home."

Her voice rang hollow in the house.

"Dad?"

Nothing.

All at once, a dark thought took root. Rye dropped the laundry bag and raced into her father's bedroom, certain she was about to find him sprawled out on the floor.

"Daddy!"

He wasn't there.

Bathroom was clear too.

She forced herself to breathe again.

She tried his cell phone.

Flippy started vibrating on the kitchen counter. Because of course her father wouldn't take it with him.

She walked back out to the living room. On the wall over the recliner was a series of photos of Rye playing soccer—ball at her feet, galloping down the left sideline, ponytail flying behind her. Another photo of her regional club team posing with the trophy they won at the tournament in Denver. Rye made her parents take down every single one of these pictures after she blew out her knee. But once she'd gone away to college, her dad immediately rehung them.

Rye drifted into the living room. She noticed a record on the turntable. The one with Maria Callas on the cover—with those killer cheekbones and the eyeliner that curled up at the edges. Her mother used to listen to that record practically every night when she got home from work. Hearing it from bed always let Rye know she'd gotten home safe. Now, the thought of that ethereal voice gave Rye an empty feeling in her chest.

Was it possible Vergil had forgotten about this enigmatic announcement and gone Bigfooting with Uncle Jute instead? If that were the case, maybe it wasn't such a big announcement after all.

Rye should have felt reassured by this thought, but instead the empty spot in her chest grew bigger, pressing against her lungs. She pushed her way out the back door and took a deep breath.

Looking out over the porch railing, she saw her father standing alone on the bank of Hell Creek. He looked thinner than usual, smaller. In the background, the Elkhorn Mountains were marbled with snow. Rye didn't want to disrupt him, so she sat on the porch steps, elbows resting on knees, watching her father down by the water's edge. And the empty space in her chest knit itself nearly closed.

After some time passed, she lifted her chin and clicked her tongue three times against the roof of her mouth. It was a sharp sound that cut through the noise of the raging creek. Her father turned slowly, a heavyhearted smile on his face. He looked at her for a moment, then clicked four times back in response.

Chapter 7

Shrouded mummy-like under the covers of her motel bed, Vicky Xu traced the cracks in the ceiling tiles above her. A vent somewhere near the bathroom blew stale air into the room, though she wasn't sure whether it was pumping heat or AC. When her eyes got to a tea-colored water spot (possibly a burn mark?) over the TV set, she sensed the onset of a weighty existential crisis and had to avert her gaze before the feeling overwhelmed her.

Three years ago, she was embarking on her senior year of college, gearing up for the law school application grind. It was a plan her parents had devised long ago, and thoroughly instilled in her over the years. Though Vicky never saw it as a plan so much as the path of least resistance. That all changed early in the fall semester when she tagged along with a roommate to a screening of Werner Herzog's seminal classic, *Aguirre, the Wrath of God.* Witnessing that film on the big screen was a raw and nervy experience, less like watching a movie and more like driving a car with no brakes down a poorly maintained mountain pass.

That night shook something awake inside Vicky. She began consuming all the Herzog movies she could find, and realized she was especially drawn to his documentaries. Stories about weird outsiders, told by a weird outsider.

For the first time, possibly ever in her life, she found joy in what she was doing. And as she worked her way through his filmography, an earnest question began to surface in her mind: *Why can't I do that?*

Soon enough, law school applications were replaced by film school applications. Nineteen rejections and one acceptance later, Vicky announced to her family that she'd be attending film school at Idaho State University in the fall. Her parents' first reaction had been to ask where Idaho was. Their second reaction had been to cut off all communication with her for the next six months.

The irony was that it had been on the weekly trips with her father to Jingletown Video that she'd first felt cinema's tug. More than the movies themselves, she remembered wandering up and down those chaotic aisles, marveling at the constantly changing genre placards taped to the shelves. Vicky was fascinated by the elaborate categories the employees at the store dreamed up: Gross-Out Horror, Pee-Your-Pants Funny, Zero-Calorie Tearjerkers, Willfully Abstruse Foreign Stuff. Every time she'd visit, there were new subgenres to discover, representing ever narrower bands of taste. Her dad always ended up renting something from the Retrograde Westerns section, but Vicky dreamed about all the other genres out there, and wondered if someone would ever have to invent one for her.

The heat (or AC) cut off, and the room grew frighteningly quiet. Vicky knew she ought to get out of bed and check on Dr. Bernard, who was sleeping in the room adjoining hers. She reached for her camera on the nightstand, hit record, and swept the room, narrating her thoughts out loud.

"Last night, Dr. Bernard suddenly distanced himself from the Bigfoot community," she said. "A shocking heel turn for someone with his reputation. The question is why?"

Vicky found her jeans, folded on the chair next to the TV. She stopped recording and pulled them on quickly. Then she picked up the camera again and resumed filming.

"But instead of clarifying the speech's meaning, instead of doubling down on his heresy, he flees to this tiny hamlet and offers to go on yet another Bigfoot expedition with two strangers he encountered at a local bar. It's all quite curious."

Vicky panned the camera at the window to make sure her car was still parked in the gravel lot out front. Her vision for this thesis had been a simple talking-head documentary. She hadn't planned to drive to Helena, let alone wind up . . . wherever this place was.

"Checking the fallout on social media this morning," she went on, "it appears his attempt at earth scorching wasn't entirely successful. In fact, a surprising theory has taken root on the Bigfoot message boards, claiming last night's speech was part of a false flag operation meant to weed out nonbelievers in their midst."

Vicky turned away from the window, letting the camera linger on little details in the room: a dented lampshade, the parrot-green curtains, the rust-orange carpet, which felt slightly damp under her feet.

"Bigfoot World, it seems, isn't ready to cut Dr. Marcus Bernard loose. Even if that's what he really wants. Is it possible he's legitimately come to the conclusion Bigfoot isn't real?" Vicky thought about that for a moment. "Or perhaps he's experiencing a psychotic break of some kind." She approached the door to the adjoining room. "I guess there's only one way to find out."

She knocked twice softly. "Dr. Bernard?"

No response.

"Are you awake?"

She jiggled the handle, and the door creaked open. His room was stale, gloomy, and Bernard was nowhere to be seen. At the foot of his bed, next to a mound of rumpled bedsheets, Vicky noticed a dark stain. She moved in closer.

Blood.

She froze, unsure what this could mean. Had she unwittingly walked into a crime scene? What would she say to the authorities? She didn't have an alibi. She couldn't even explain why she was here.

Just then the bathroom door swung open. Dr. Bernard emerged and sat down on the edge of the bed. Vicky breathed a sigh of relief and brought the camera to her shoulder.

"You know there's a pool of blood in your bed." She tried to make her voice sound cold, dispassionate.

"Workplace injury." Bernard pulled up his pant leg to display a gash on his ankle two inches wide, the skin puckered and purple. "I was trying to take myself to the hospital last night after the speech, but ended up . . . Where are we again?"

"Let's talk about that speech, shall we?"

Bernard smiled at the memory. "That was something, wasn't it?" He eased his pant leg down and slid into a pair of loafers.

"I'll admit it was . . . unexpected."

"That was the whole point." He stood and finger-combed his hair behind his head, snapping on a rubber band to hold his ponytail in place. "How do you think it played?"

"Maybe you should tell me what you hoped to accomplish."

Bernard opened the exterior door, and a bright morning light strafed the room.

"I'm attempting what you might call a rebrand." He limped out to the parking lot and started hobbling toward a cluster of buildings in the distance.

Vicky set out after him, trying to keep him in frame as they walked. "This is what you meant by showing the world the real you?"

"Did you know," he said, "I used to be a well-respected academic?"

"I do," Vicky said. "I even read your dissertation on primate territorialism."

He stopped hobbling to look at her. "And?"

"It was good," she said. "At least the parts I could understand."

"Then you know." He set off walking again. "It's time for me to get back into real academics."

"Don't you think that ship sailed a long time ago?" Vicky asked.

"Maybe." He shrugged. "Then again, maybe not. It depends on how well this rebrand goes."

"And that's where I come in?" she said.

"It's not that I've lost the ability to bullshit," he said. "It's just that I no longer see the point in it."

"So you admit you're a fraud?"

"Of course," he said without breaking stride. "I'm a complete academic charlatan."

Vicky was stunned. She couldn't believe he'd admitted it so easily. Part of her wanted to shut the camera off, hop in her car, and drive home before he realized what he'd said. She could probably put together a decent short doc with the material she had right now. No point making this any harder than it had to be.

Bernard stopped walking and turned to look at her again. "Have you wondered why I agreed to work with you?"

Her voice caught in her throat. She'd never thought to ask herself this.

"I knew your film was a hit job on me the moment I read your first email."

"*Hit job* might be too strong a term," Vicky said. "My project is to find out the essence of who you are. And I think I've managed to do that."

"Hold that thought," Bernard said, then stepped into a small convenience store.

They'd walked into the middle of downtown Basic, which didn't look terribly different from the outskirts of Basic. Vicky—alone now—took in the dusty buildings and empty sidewalks. A tattered banner over the street read: *Basic Montana Celebrates Independence Day.*

This seemed like the kind of place with a story to tell, the kind of place Werner Herzog would plumb the depths of in order to reveal a profound meditation on the human condition.

Why can't I do that? Vicky thought to herself, then put the camera to her shoulder and started filming the building façades.

"It's a town like so many others," she narrated. "Streets lined with broken dreams. Crumbling under decades of disinvestment."

She fixed the camera on a square of cracked sidewalk with bone-dry weeds growing between the squares of concrete. Then she tilted upward until the frame settled on a gloomy stone building with a sign that read: SWAN ER H TEL.

"At first glance, you might say it looks like a place that time forgot." She paused, let a light breeze blow across the microphone. "Only that's not quite right. Because time never forgets. Time is relentless and undefeated."

She pulled the shot off the hotel and zoomed in tight on a light pole nearby, focusing on a chintzy American flag strapped to it.

"But if you look a little closer, you'll see something else here too." The flag fluttered and flapped itself flat against the light pole. "The only thing that's ever stood a chance against time: hope." She paused to let the word gather weight. "Under the patina of despair, there exists a belief—irrational as it may be—that life doesn't have to be this way. 'Things fall apart; the center cannot hold,' as the poem goes, but maybe . . . maybe instead of falling apart, things could be rebuilt."

Vicky pivoted to the horizon at the end of the street, and the mountains in the distance.

"As I stand here on Central Avenue, I find myself thinking about last night's convention. All those people in the audience waiting to hear someone tell them they're not crazy for believing in something irrational. Does Bigfoot somehow embody that indomitable piece of the American spirit? If an eight-foot primate has managed to survive undetected in our shrinking forests, is it so far-fetched to imagine that the economic engines of places like this town could one day turn over and hum again?"

A static charge sparked to life between Vicky's shoulder blades as she spoke. The words felt like an incantation, like the casting of a spell.

A bell clanged behind her. Dr. Bernard emerged from the store with a paper bag tucked under his arm and sat down on a bench. Vicky took a seat next to him and kept the camera rolling.

"One thing I can't figure out," she said. "If you really are trying to split with the Bigfoot community, why did you offer to go on that expedition with those guys you met last night?"

Bernard shook off his loafer and began peeling away the blood-encrusted sock. "This may come as a surprise to you, but Bigfoot people don't like being confronted with reality. If you've looked online this morning, you'll know my fans are already trying to explain away that speech."

He reached into the bag and withdrew a bottle of hydrogen peroxide. He lay his ankle across his knee and started pouring the antiseptic over the cut.

"I need to do one more Bigfoot expedition, but instead of playing my usual role of Bigfoot cheerleader, I'll go as a rational skeptic. We'll expose these guys here as loony tunes, or—even better—as frauds. Then maybe we can do our part to take down this whole delusional mindset."

"Did I hear you say *we*?"

"Yes," he said. "You've correctly identified the first-person plural."

The peroxide on his cut was turning foamy and pink.

"You want *me* to go on this expedition with you?"

"Of course," he said. "You're part of this . . . journey."

Vicky started to shake her head. "That's not what I signed up for," she said. "I don't have a lot of time to finish this. And I don't exactly have a budget to work with."

Bernard took a tube of superglue from his grocery bag and started lining up the loose flaps of skin on his ankle.

"If you think you have what you need, you can call it quits." He dabbed the superglue along the edges of his cut and pressed the skin together. "If a minor documentary exposing the hypocrisy of one deeply flawed individual was really your vision for this project, congratulations." He counted to ten under his breath, then prodded the glued skin a couple times to make sure it held. "But I have a feeling you want to make something more than that."

He pulled a pair of white cotton tube socks from his bag, bit through the plastic string that held them together.

"If we do this right, we'll both come out ahead." He removed the remaining loafer, slid the new socks over his feet, stepped back into his loafers, and stood up. "Me with my reputation restored; you with a biting satire exposing the dark corners of delusional thinking in American society."

Vicky didn't say anything for a several seconds. She pictured herself in the aisles of Jingletown Video, looking for the placard that best fit what this new film could possibly be. She hadn't considered Biting Satire before.

Just then, a plump woman in her mid-forties approached them on the sidewalk.

"You *are* that guy!" the woman said. "From that show!"

Bernard put on a rakish smile.

"I wasn't a hundred percent sure last night," she went on, "so I kept my mouth shut. Didn't want to make it seem like we're TMZ around here."

"It's always nice to meet a fan," Bernard said.

"Tammy Reynolds," she said, reaching out to shake his hand. "I'm the one who overserved you at St. Pete's last night."

Vicky slowly turned the camera toward Tammy, who wore heavy makeup, hair frosted blond at the tips.

Tammy pulled a cell phone from her pocket. "Is it okay if I get a selfie?"

As the two of them posed for the shot, it dawned on Vicky that Bernard was that rarest of species: a legitimately famous academic. Sure, your Cornel Wests and Noam Chomskys had higher Q Scores and vastly more substantive oeuvres. But drop them in the middle of Basic, Montana, and see if anyone even noticed. Dr. Marcus Bernard, on the other hand, was smack-dab in the middle of his target demographic, his socioeconomic wheelhouse.

"What brings you to our little corner of the world?" Tammy asked.

Bernard lowered his voice. "I'm not at liberty to disclose that information at the moment."

Tammy winked and leaned in closer. "If you're conducting an investigation, you picked the right place."

Vicky sensed an opening. "What makes you say that?" she asked.

Tammy tossed a side glance at the camera. "You hear things," she said. "The Native Americans have stories about these mountains. Places they'd never go into."

"That sounds . . . interesting," Vicky said.

"I don't care if you believe me or not." Tammy's voice turned cold. "It's more than just rumors."

"Do you have any specific examples?" Bernard asked. "Any *personal* experience?"

The color drained from her cheeks. She started to say something, but stopped.

"It's okay." Bernard rested a hand on her shoulder. "This is a safe space."

"My little sister," Tammy finally said. "Amber."

"Tell me about her." Bernard's voice softened into an empathetic register.

"In high school her and some friends were supposed to go to a Calobo concert in Bozeman, but instead went camping in the Elk-horns. Probably wanted to drink beer and screw is all. Normal teen stuff. Shouldn't've been a big deal, but . . ." Tammy paused, took in a sharp breath. "Something was out there."

"What was it?" Bernard leaned in closer. He put a finger to his chin. For a guy who claimed to not believe in this stuff, he was surprisingly good at faking it.

"No one's really sure." Tammy's face darkened. "Three of them went missing."

"Was your sister—"

"She made it out, thank God." Tammy shook her head. "Amber's story changed over the years, but the thing she described early on sounded a lot like it could be a Bigfoot."

"She's okay now?"

"Messed her up pretty good. Spent some time in the psych ward in Helena."

Vicky jumped in. "Do you think she'd talk to us if we—"

"She don't live here no more," Tammy said. "She's in Spokane. And she don't talk to no one about it. Put it behind her, best she could."

A car with a dangling muffler drove past. Once it got quiet again, Tammy leaned in. "If you decide to go into the woods around here, best be careful."

Vicky pushed in closer until she caught the tremor in Tammy's lip, the flutter of her eyelids. When the woman blinked, a tear welled up and raced down her cheek.

Vicky wasn't sure what to make of this story. It was secondhand, but not by much. And the basic facts were indisputable: four kids went out into these woods, and only one came back. Whatever happened to them out there, Tammy was obviously still shaken by it. Vicky began to consider the possibility that this film wasn't going to be a social commentary, or even a biting satire, but maybe something else entirely, something much darker.

June 20, 1932—Timber cruisers have established a forward outpost on behalf of Spring Creek Timber Company. Tree quality in this region appears high. Harvestable board feet of old growth timber runs in the millions, with vast majority being sawtimber and minimal amounts of pulpwood. Cruisers will begin work tomorrow, in advance of logging operations set to commence at summer's end.

*I find it desirable to keep an unofficial record of activities in this journal I discovered in the hollow of a ponderosa pine near camp.

June 21, 1932—1,000 acres platted. Estimated harvestable board feet: 70,000.

*Cruisers discovered abandoned mineshaft at base of nearby mountain. Shaft is flooded and appears to be unused for many years.

June 22, 1932—850 acres platted. Estimated harvestable board feet: 60,000.

*Terrain more challenging today.

June 23, 1932—900 acres platted. Estimated harvestable board feet: 65,000.

*Team reports seeing large human footprints in numerous locations. Most perplexing.

June 24, 1932—1,100 acres platted. Estimated harvestable board feet: 80,000.

June 25, 1932—350 acres platted. Estimated harvestable board feet: 25,000.

*Equipment locker broken into last night. Half of surveying equipment inoperable. Radioed base to send more. No response received.

June 26, 1932—450 acres platted. Estimated harvestable board feet: 40,000. Terrain extremely difficult today.

*Team members complain of poor sleep, disrupted by strange noises in forest. Others claim to find handmade objects placed outside tents. A state of unease has taken hold.

June 27, 1932—0 acres platted. Estimated harvestable board feet: 0.

*A timber cruiser, Cabot, turned up missing this morning. Drag marks indicate he was taken by force from his tent sometime in the night. A party has been raised to follow tracks and recover him.

June 28, 1932—0 acres platted. Estimated harvestable board feet: 0.

*I regret to report that Mr. Joseph Cabot was discovered several miles from camp. His body was suspended some ten feet off the ground, hung upon the branches of an ancient bristlecone pine. It was a ghoulish sight. While the incident has many hallmarks of a grizzly attack, there are those who remain unconvinced this was the creature responsible. His body was retrieved after some considerable effort. Once again tried to contact base via radio with no luck. Sending small team to hike out and reestablish connection.

June 29, 1932—72 acres platted. Estimated harvestable board feet: 3,000.

*Two cruisers have taken ill. Boils on the neck and armpits ooze and bleed. Muscles cramp violently. Fever, chills. Camp medic suspects improperly cooked meat. The rest of us have resumed work.

June 30, 1932—100 acres platted. Estimated harvestable board feet: 4,000.

*Six more cruisers show signs of boils. The first two cases have passed away. Camp medic now believes the contagion was brought into camp by Cabot's corpse. Have received no response from team sent to reestablish contact with base.

July 1, 1932—0 acres platted. Estimated harvestable board feet: 0.

*Illness continues to spread unchecked. The dead now number over a dozen. Camp medic is among the deceased.

July 2, 1932—0 acres platted. Estimated harvestable board feet: 0.

*Nearly entire camp suffers from boils, cramps, fever. No response from base. Only hope is for remaining able-bodied persons to hike out.

July 3, 1932—Four of us who remain alive are set to depart for base within minutes. Pray for us in this hour of need.

Chapter 8

Jute cracked three eggs into a skillet, and dropped a slice of bread in the toaster after inspecting it for mold. When his breakfast was ready, he doused everything with Tabasco sauce and brought it to the couch, where he wolfed it down under the stern gaze of his blobsquatch accent wall.

A Bigfoot cuckoo clock on the wall behind him knocked nine times. Pluto should be at the car wash by now. Normally Jute would be there to oversee the opening, but he was trying to establish a baseline of trust with his not always trustworthy protégé. After all, Jute knew how life-changing work at the car wash could be.

When his father finally disappeared for the last time, Jute was sixteen years old. He looked around at the world and all he felt was rage. Unloved and unwanted, just another useless thing slowly dying in this godforsaken place. Why not do everyone a favor and speed up the process? He spent the next year driving into Bozeman on weekends, looking to get into fights, itching for an excuse to hurt people. If he didn't wind up in jail or the hospital by the end of the night, he'd drive back to Basic with the speedometer pegged, tear-assing through Coyote Canyon, praying he'd miss a curve or a deer would leap into his path, causing a fiery wreck. There was always a part of him that was disappointed when he made it home safely.

Everything changed when Malachai Ricker offered Jute a part-time job at the local coin-operated car wash. The work mostly consisted of sitting for long stretches on a stool in the glassed-in booth next to the wash bays. But right away, Jute showed a natural proficiency with the machinery. What normally required three hours of downtime and possibly a service call to the distributorship in Spokane, Jute could often fix within an hour. And he loved the work, craved the regularity of it. The fact that he was wanted somewhere made him feel like he belonged in the world for the first time since the camping trip to Ramsey Lake.

Old Man Ricker, a widower with no children of his own, eventually asked Jute if he wanted to rent out the unused bedroom in his home on Second Avenue. Their conversations rarely consisted of more than a quick back-and-forth about which pieces of equipment were in need of maintenance, or how the following day's weather forecast might impact business. Yet they each provided a balm for the other. Jute even adopted the old man's signature look, a high and tight crew cut. By the time Jute graduated from high school, he was working at the car wash full-time, and the two of them were inseparable.

The day after Jute's twentieth birthday, Ricker had a massive stroke outside of Hoo Yin's. Jute heard the news while he was swabbing out one of the wash bays, and ran the three blocks across town to where the old man lay. He performed CPR until his arms shook.

The day of the funeral, Jute got a phone call from a lawyer in Bozeman. Apparently, Malachai Ricker had written and filed a will the year previous, and Julius Ramsey had been named in it. After the burial service in Sweetgrass Cemetery, Jute drove over to Bozeman, still wearing the suit he'd bought for the funeral, and sat down in the law office of James Anthony Messina, where he was told that Malachai Ricker had left Jute everything related to the business establishment known as Basic Car Wash, as well as the house where he'd been renting a room for the past two years, plus Ricker's white 1989 Chevrolet van. There were some loose ends to take care of, and documents to sign—lots of documents—but for all intents and purposes, everything was his.

Jute would be forever grateful to Malachai Ricker for what he'd done—giving him a home, a career, a stable base on which to build a life destined for something more.

Jute leaned over the mysterious map he'd discovered in his mailbox.

It had no lettering or legend, but there was a dotted line in faded brown ink that snaked up the page and ended in a small blob.

Vergil had not been pleased when Jute called him last night. He kept saying tomorrow, tomorrow, let's talk about it tomorrow, then hung up before Jute had a chance to explain what he'd found. The whole exchange had been very un-Vergil-like.

But something had been preoccupying his friend lately. His heart was walled off, and Jute couldn't break through to find out what was wrong. He hoped partnering with Dr. Bernard would snap Vergil out of it. Nothing like solving one of the world's greatest mysteries to lift a man's spirits. That was why Jute had gone ahead and called the number on Bernard's business card this morning. The sooner they could start this expedition, the sooner this next chapter of their lives could begin.

All her life, Vicky had been painfully aware of the fact that she was not the best at anything. Never the smartest, or the funniest, or even the prettiest. She wasn't the best musician, the best athlete, or the best daughter. (Her younger sister, Zoe, claimed all those superlatives.) Nothing ever came naturally to Vicky. Until she tried her hand at filmmaking.

The moment she first picked up a camera, everything changed. She saw angles, light, shadows differently. She intuitively knew how they could combine visually to make textures, express meaning. More than that, whenever she held a camera, she felt confident, powerful. Here, finally, was something she could do. Something she could maybe even be the best at.

She and Bernard spent a couple hours conducting man-on-the-street interviews while they waited to hear from either Jute or Vergil. Word had circulated around town that a bona fide celebrity was in their midst, and people were lining up to share their Bigfoot stories.

Bernard was a gifted camera presence. He always seemed to know what the next question should be, when to press harder and when to ease back. And even though Vicky was fairly certain he was doing it just to make these folks look silly, she found herself absorbed by their stories of high strangeness and could've listened to them all day. But when Jute Ramsey called to say he was ready to talk logistics for the expedition, she knew the real filmmaking was about to begin.

She and Bernard walked single file down Second Avenue. Vicky let the camera's gaze linger on decrepit trailer homes and sagging tar paper shacks, front yards adorned with old appliances, nonfunctioning vehicles, rusted satellite dishes.

"Here," Bernard said, pointing to a home so overgrown with weeds it looked abandoned. The only sign of occupancy was a beat-up old van parked in the yard with the words *Sasquatch One* stenciled on the side, along with a hand-painted American flag.

Bernard climbed the porch steps and knocked on the screen door. Meanwhile, Vicky waded through the waist-high weeds in the front yard to get a better angle on a wide shot, making a mental note to check herself for ticks later on.

"Hello, Mr. Ramsey, are you there?" Bernard peeked through a window and knocked again.

Vicky stepped on something buried in the weeds. Her ankle rolled, and a bolt of pain shot up through her shin.

"Dammit," she muttered, reaching down to find out what it was.

She found an envelope that looked like an electric bill, and a Bass Pro Shops catalog, but neither of those had been what she'd stepped on. She dug around some more, and that was when she saw it: an old book with a green leather cover. She flipped it open. The pages contained handwritten diary entries, the earliest ones going back over a hundred years.

Bernard knocked on the screen door again.

Vicky closed the book and bundled it with the rest of the mail. The moment she started up the porch steps, though, something gripped her—an irresistible urge telling her to keep the book for herself. It came on as a dull ache in her jaw that only went away when she stuffed the book into her backpack and zipped it closed. The rest of the mail she crammed into the mailbox just as Jute Ramsey threw open the front door. "Welcome to my humble abode," he said, "headquarters of the Basic Bigfoot Society."

The sheer volume of crap in his house was disorienting. A lot of it was normal stuff: magazines, books, mugs, plates, rumpled piles of clothes. But other things made no sense. A bowling ball in the foyer, a partially disassembled lawn mower engine on the dining room table, schematic blueprints on the kitchen counter, fishing tackle on the floor near the bathroom.

"You'll have to excuse the mess," Jute said.

Vicky swept the camera in a 360-degree shot, trying to take it all in. Then she came upon a wall entirely papered with blurry photographs.

"Any compelling evidence here?" Bernard nodded toward the wall, but kept his hands folded behind his back as if he were afraid to touch anything.

"Not yet," Jute said.

"Doesn't look like it's for lack of trying," Vicky murmured.

Bernard smiled. "So let's talk time lines?" he said. "When's the soonest you think we can get started on this expedition?"

"I don't know, Doctor." Jute scratched his chin. "It's a lot of work putting one of these together. Logistics. Supplies."

While they continued to talk, Vicky peered through the kitchen window. The toolshed out back had a sign posted over the door that read: *Bigfoot War Room Do Not Enter.*

She quietly stepped outside. When she poked her head into the shed, she saw that the walls were postered with black-and-white topographical maps and satellite images. Shelf after shelf of books and notebooks, all heavily dog-eared and bookmarked. The rest of the shed was overrun with stacks of ancient computers, hard drives, printers, scanners, CD burners, and cords—so many cords—laced throughout the room, crisscrossing the floor, dangling off tables, like a jungle overgrown with black vines.

Vicky stepped inside. Against the far wall she saw a whiteboard. On it was a series of bullet points with the following label:

THEORIES FOR LACK OF EVIDENCE

· Uses infrasound to disorient people
· Interdimensional travel
· Cloaking
· Mimicking abilities
· Extraterrestrial intervention

On the right side of the board, another list:

NEEDS FURTHER RESEARCH—

1. Encephalization quotient (Similar to robust australopithecine?)
2. Midtarsal flexion creases
3. Lorentzian traversable wormholes
4. Paranormal connection (Ghosts, orbs, UFOs)
5. Bigfoot language (Possibly use AI to decipher?)

In that moment, Vicky recalled a passage from one of Professor Moss's very first lectures: "The purpose of a documentary is not merely to provide a voyeuristic glimpse into people's lives. Its true purpose is to allow your audience to inhabit another person's soul. And when you accomplish this, it helps us understand the fundamental building blocks of what makes us human." She'd copied it word for word in her notebook, then marked it with a highlighter later on, even though she didn't fully understand what it meant at the time.

Vicky held the camera steady on the whiteboard for a moment, then zoomed in to make sure the writing was legible.

"I see you've found our command center," Jute said behind her.

She spun quickly. Bernard and Jute had come into the shed without her noticing. "Sorry," she said, "I was just looking."

"I'm glad you got the chance to see it for yourself," he said proudly. "This is where the magic happens."

"You sure do know a lot about this stuff," she said.

"That's kind of how my brain works," he said, smiling shyly. "When I'm interested in something, I have to find out everything there is to know about it."

"Listen." Bernard stepped into the camera frame. "Apparently, Mr. Ramsey can't make decisions about our expedition without a quorum present, so we're going on a field trip to find his partner."

Vicky stopped recording and walked out to the backyard. The shed, the scribblings on the whiteboard, that cluttered house—they were the by-products of some kind of madness. But she sensed something else at work here too: certainty. One hundred percent total belief. Vicky had never been that sure of anything in her entire life. And the overwhelming emotion she felt in that moment was jealousy.

Chapter 9

Vergil Barnes stood in his kitchen, listening to the crypt-like silence of the house. When the kettle on the stove finally started to whistle, he turned the burner off, poured water into his coffee mug, watched the steam rise.

Rye would be here soon. He already regretted what this announcement would do to her, the way it would tear her world apart again. For a while he'd thought about not telling either her or Jute at all. He'd carry on like normal for as long as he could, then when things got really bad, he'd get as far away as he could from the two people he loved most in the world so they wouldn't have to see him suffer. But he knew this instinct was a selfish one. His daughter had already had one parent snatched away without warning. She didn't need the other one to do the same.

Vergil spooned two heaps of instant coffee into his mug. He stirred and took a provisional sip. He glanced at the clock on the microwave: 9:04. He ought to go check on the library. Mrs. McGill was supposed to open this morning, but the deeper she got into her eighties the less reliable she was becoming. The Basic Public Library had always been Agnes Barnes's pet project. She—along with Claudia McGill—had devoted her life to its upkeep, believing it was her civic duty to shine a beacon of enlightenment into an otherwise anti-intellectual space. "Without a good library," his mother used to say, "the cretins take over." When she passed, it was clear Mrs. McGill would be unable to do all the work by herself, so Vergil had pitched in to keep the place running. That had been twenty years ago.

He took another sip of coffee and glanced at Flippy on the counter. He wished Rye had called before leaving campus. It would've given him a chance to chart her progress, worry at the appropriate times, as if the act of worrying itself might cast a spell that could protect her.

He stepped onto the front porch. The street was empty, so he went around to the backyard, where Hell Creek raged with spring runoff. This morning when he'd climbed out of bed, a discordant tremolo pulsed through his whole body. Ibuprofen helped quiet it down somewhat. But eventually, the doctors warned, he'd need to start taking something a lot stronger.

Vergil wasn't sure how long he'd been standing there, contemplating all he'd lost and had yet to lose, when he heard three sharp clicks behind him.

It was part of his and Rye's secret code, something only the two of them understood. The clicks had started as a way to get each other's attention on camping trips without alerting the entire forest to their presence. From there it evolved into a rudimentary code. Over time, this private language became a bubble—something that held them together and kept the outside world at bay. Three clicks was the first phrase they'd come up with: *I love you.*

Vergil turned to see Rye sitting on the porch steps, wearing jean shorts and a blue Bobcats hoodie, her long black hair parted in the middle, framing her face. His heart sagged with the knowledge of what he'd have to tell her in a few minutes' time. But for now, he put the tip of his tongue to the roof of his mouth and responded with four sharp clicks, the second phrase they'd invented: *I love you too.*

He crossed the backyard, conscious of not letting his daughter see how gingerly he was moving. When he got to the bottom step, he stopped. She looked thin, still pale from winter. Her legs were folded up beneath her like a newborn colt, the scar from her knee surgery a pink line splitting her kneecap down the middle.

They both smiled at each other uncertainly for a few seconds before

Rye finally asked a question she didn't know how to translate into clicks. "So what's this big announcement you need to make?"

Vergil thought he saw a trembling behind her eyes. He looked down at his feet. "Have you had any breakfast yet?"

Rye was piling her first load of laundry into the washer in the basement. Vergil turned the scrambled eggs over in the frying pan, waiting for her to come back upstairs.

From the moment he'd gotten the prognosis, he started keeping track of potential lasts. The last time he'd shovel the driveway, the last time he'd have to split firewood for the woodstove. He wondered if this would be the last time he'd stand in the kitchen cooking breakfast while his daughter did her laundry downstairs. It was an otherwise forgettable moment that now took on gargantuan weight and sorrow.

Footsteps on the basement steps. Vergil turned from the stove. To his surprise, Rye was holding a box of old paintbrushes.

"Tell me again why you quit painting." Her eyes were enormous, sincere—picture windows into her soul.

"That's a long story." Vergil spooned some eggs onto a plate and set it on the dining table.

"Have you ever thought about starting up again?"

"Maybe," he said, with neither enthusiasm nor commitment. "Someday."

"The lady who owns the coffee shop where I work always puts up paintings by local artists. If you want I could talk to her about displaying some of yours."

Her father gave her a sour look. "I don't think people are interested in what I have to paint."

"Mom always told me you were so good."

"Your mother saw more in my art than was actually there," he said. "She was blinded by love."

"I thought it might be something you'd enjoy getting back into." Rye set the brushes on the table next to her eggs.

"I'm afraid my painting days are behind me now," he said, trying for some reason to sound chipper. "Besides, I'm pretty busy with the library these days."

"Oh yeah?" Rye sat down and slid her plate closer. "How are things going?"

"People mostly use us for the free computers these days," Vergil said. "I guess nobody reads books anymore."

Rye nodded and looked off to the side.

"Mrs. McGill still puts me through my paces though," Vergil offered, trying to keep the conversation going. "Want to head over after breakfast and say hi? She'd love to see you. Always asks how you're doing."

"I'm good, I think." Rye picked up a fork and tried her eggs. "I don't have a lot of time for this trip."

Growing up, Rye spent every day after school at the library with Vergil. He would help her with homework or check out books while she read. Once she learned the Dewey decimal system, she'd file returned books. Every Thursday, Vergil picked a poem for her to memorize and recite by dinnertime. Then something happened in her midteens. Rye suddenly stopped coming to the library, preferring instead to stay at home or go out with friends. It was a natural part of growing up, Vergil told himself. He'd been lucky to get all those years with her. But there was no escaping the fact that overnight, the library had gone from being *their* space to just *his*.

Vergil took a seat on the bench facing hers. "How are things going with Jenny?" he asked.

Rye's cheeks went pink. "She's . . . okay."

"I didn't mean to pry."

"No, I'm glad you pried." She brought a forkful of eggs to her mouth. "It's just that we're probably breaking up."

"Oh," he said, "I'm sorry to hear that." He wanted to reach out and hug her, but it had been years since that had been a welcome response to tough news.

"It's fine," she said. "It's me, not her."

"Other fish, right?"

The thought occurred to Vergil that this might be the last girlfriend of hers he'd ever get to meet. An awkward silence spread across the table like a cup of spilled coffee.

He adjusted himself on the bench. He couldn't put this off forever. It was time.

"So," he said. "I suppose you're wondering why I asked you up here."

"Now that you mention it . . ." Rye set her fork across her plate and leaned on her elbow.

He drew in a deep breath, forced his hands to stop fidgeting.

Say it, Vergil. Say it and be done with it.

Before he could get the words out, a knock sounded at the front door, and they both jumped as if they'd heard a ghost.

Chapter 10

"A quorum now present, I hereby call to order an emergency meeting of the Basic Bigfoot Society." Jute typically gaveled his beer bottle on a tabletop to make the proceedings feel more official, but they were conducting today's meeting in Vergil's backyard, so he had neither bottle nor table at his disposal.

"Can someone please explain to me what's going on here?" Rye asked. "And who those people are?" She glanced up at the back porch, where Bernard and Vicky stood looking down on their conversation. They likely couldn't hear what was being said over the roaring of Hell Creek.

"We've got a rare opportunity to work with one of the best in the Bigfoot business," Jute said. "But we need to hold a formal vote before we can talk logistics."

"I thought you were supposed to be out scouting locations today," Vergil said.

"No need," Jute said, rocking back on his heels. "I already found this year's site."

"When did that happen?"

"If you would've heard me out when I called last night, you'd know." Jute unfolded a sheet of heavy paper decorated with graceful lines, hand-drawn in a pale brown ink. He held it flat across his palms. "Tell me what you see here."

Vergil leaned over it, tilting his head one way, then the other. "Is it supposed to be a drawing of something?"

Jute angled the paper so it caught the sunlight. "Look closer."

Vergil studied it again. One of the lines at the bottom of the page was a jagged lightning bolt, which reminded him of . . . what? A symbol? A logo? He reached out and rotated the page a few degrees. Two lines ran alongside each other, playfully crisscrossing up the page, ending at a figure-eight-shaped blob.

Vergil's stomach dropped.

"Is that . . ." he started to say.

A smile crept across Jute's face.

"Is that what?" Rye asked.

Vergil blinked three times, rubbed his eyes. How was this possible?

"I'm going to need someone to tell me what we're looking at." Rye was nearly shouting.

Her dad scratched his chin for a moment. "It's a map," he said.

"A map of what?" Rye asked. "Why are you guys being so weird all of a sudden?"

Vergil tapped the blob at the top of the page. "Judging by the stories your uncle Jute's told me, it's a place we've been trying to find for a very long time." He shook his head. "It's a map showing us how to get to Ramsey Lake."

Jute nodded.

"What's the big deal about Ramsey Lake?" Rye asked.

"Your uncle Jute saw Bigfoot there when he was a kid," Vergil said. "Actually, what he saw was a handprint that he *thinks* belonged to Bigfoot."

"I saw a lot more than that," Jute shot back, "and you know it."

Everything was happening so fast Vergil could barely keep up. His processors were overwhelmed with data to crunch, calculations to make, angles to consider.

"If we partner up with these people"—he jerked a thumb at the porch—"you realize you'll be sharing your family's lake with the world. Are you okay with that?"

"Think of the technology Dr. Bernard has access to," Jute said. "The years of experience he brings to the table."

Vergil twisted his mouth to the side and tilted his head. He wasn't sure how finding Ramsey Lake squared with the news he had to tell these two. Maybe it could wait until after the expedition. If the cancer wasn't too aggressive, he might make it through the trip without anyone noticing. Then, afterward, he could come clean. The more he thought about it, the more this new plan made sense.

"Don't tell me you're starting to waffle," Jute said.

"I'm not waffling," Vergil said. "I'm just making sure we cover all our bases."

"Think of the platform Bernard has," Jute said. "Our research will finally get the audience it deserves. Just in time for our greatest discovery—maybe of all time!"

"Hold on." Rye jumped in, calling a time-out with her hands. "How well do you know this guy?"

"He's only the most well-respected Bigfoot researcher in the world," Jute said. "You don't get an opportunity to work with someone of his caliber very often."

Rye lowered her hands, though it didn't look like her objections had been met.

"So are we ready to vote, or what?" Jute asked.

Vergil arched his eyebrows in response. He couldn't let his illness interfere with this partnership. If they really did find something on this expedition, Jute would be set for life, doing the thing he'd always wanted to do.

"Mr. Vice President," Jute intoned, "I move we take a vote on whether or not to accept this proposed collaboration with Dr. Bernard."

"Mr. President, I second the motion," Vergil said.

"All in favor of this collaboration, say aye."

Jute raised his hand. "Aye."

Vergil held his up. "Aye."

"The motion passes."

Jute started refolding the map.

"Don't I get a vote?" Rye asked.

Both men looked at each other. Nothing in the bylaws stated whether visitors were allowed to vote. Frankly, they'd never had anyone else attend one of their meetings before.

"Actually, I don't need to vote," she said. "But I want it noted for the record that you absolutely should *not* trust those people." She glanced up at the porch. "And I don't trust either of you not to."

Her words hung in the air for a moment, mingling with the spray coming off Hell Creek.

"That's why I'm going on this expedition too," she said. "Because I have a feeling you two are going to need someone to save you from yourselves."

Thurs Aug 13 1987

Two guys, two girls, two tents, a pony keg, and an ounce of weed! What could possibly go wrong?

Don't answer that!!! Ha-ha!

We're gonna be seniors in a week! We gotta live it up while we still can!!! Wendy and me told our parents we were going to a Calobo concert in Bozeman this weekend. Which they believed! Miraculously!! Travis and Dillon, who knows what their excuse was, as long as they don't go to jail their dad won't care. I don't know what Wendy and me see in those two, but it must be something.

Sidenote: Wendy and me were talking at lunch on Wednesday and we're both planning to do it on this trip!!!

Side-sidenote: I never kept a diary before. But I found this cool old book crammed under a rock out here and, I don't know, it seems like I ought to keep track of our adventure in it. Kinda reminds me of this chain letter my sister Tammy once got where she had to write letters to a bunch of people or all this bad stuff would happen. It's probably B.S. but I can't risk any bad vibes, not when I'm about to be a senior with my whole life in front of me!!!

We're officially in the middle of nowhere, by the way. Driving here, Dillon was like, Relax, I know where I'm going. Which I don't think he does, but whatever. It's a really pretty spot and I could totally cash in my V-card here.

One thing I did NOT plan on was how much the boys would race around on their stupid dirt bikes. Soon as we parked, all Travis and Dillon wanted to do was ride them nonstop!!! Those things are freaking loud and smelly and now I have a super big headache. I'm sure tonight Dillon'll try and get all romantic, but I'm not in the mood anymore. If that boy doesn't straighten up and fly right, he is not getting laid this weekend! Period!!!

Fri Aug 14 1987

Okay, last night was totally messed up. We got pretty buzzed sitting around the campfire, and I started to maybe forgive Dillon for some of his B.S. with the dirt bikes. We moved to the tent and things were getting hot and heavy, if you know what I mean, but then we heard something moving around outside the tent, so Dillon was like, Travis, quit being a perv, and Travis was all, F- you, I'm not doing anything.

So we started making out again but a second later something hits our tent. And we run out and what do we see but a bunch of, well, shit on our tent. Like actual dookie! From an animal or something!!! And Dillon is about to fight Travis because it's not very funny, but Travis comes out of his tent ready to fight too. It wasn't either of them who did it.

And it's like, who would do something like that? So Travis got his gun out and Dillon starts the campfire back up. Wendy looks at me and goes, Do you hear that? And at first I'm like, Hear what? But then I start to notice this whispering in the trees. And Wendy says, That sounds like my grandmother. Only her grandmother's been dead since she was a little girl, so I'm like, That's not your grandma, Wendy.

I have to admit I've never been so scared in my whole entire life.

Now that it's morning, Wendy and me want to leave, but the boys are being all macho, like, We're not getting chased out of here that easy. So now they're gassing up the dirt bikes to go find whoever was messing with us last night. This whole weekend is SCREWED!!!

Well, my hands are shaking so bad I can't hardly write. Things have got worse since this morning. The twins drove all over the place till they found a trail headed up the mountain. Keep in mind Wendy and me are riding on the backs of the bikes, winding back and forth up the side of a freaking mountain!!!

So we get to the top, and all the sudden we come up on this pretty little lake, but then, wait, there's this strange guy standing there. I just about fell off the bike. This guy was creep-y. His clothes were all ragged and gross, like the people you see who ride on the railroad tracks. I could tell Dillon was scared. But Travis gets in the guy's face like, Why were you messing with us last night, man?!?! But the stranger all calm-like goes, Magic protects this space, I'd advise you to leave at once. But that steams Travis up even more, so he goes, It's a free country, asshole!!! But the guy crosses his arms and is all, I told you magic protects this space, turn back now. I'm pretty sure Travis would've tried to kick that old guy's ass except Dillon convinced him to get back on his bike so we could get outta there.

When we finally got back to camp, we find these weird stick dolls sitting in front of our tents. Double-creep-y! I point out this must mean the old guy at the lake wasn't the one screwing with us last night, but Travis doesn't buy it. And even though we ate dinner and we're starting to chill out, Travis gets the stupidest idea ever. He jumps on his bike and says he's going to teach that old guy a lesson and we're all, That's the stupidest idea ever, but he roars off anyways. Just like that! In the dark! So STUPID!!! Dillon tried to go after him but I told him if he leaves Wendy and me alone out here he can forget about ever getting laid. Ever!!!

Now the three of us are waiting for Travis to come back. What else can we do? I'm signing off for tonight. Let's hope things are back to normal by morning.

Sat Aug 15 1987

Travis didn't come back last night. I say we should go get help because this is a real live situation, but Dillon says Travis might just be screwing around and it'd suck to ruin the weekend over a prank. And I'm all, Newsflash, the weekend's ALREADY RUINED!!!

Wendy's a mess. She keeps shouting Travis's name and crying. So I tell Dillon he needs to go find his brother, but I make him leave the truck keys with me because if he doesn't come back before dark we're out of here. It's been a long time since I prayed, but I'm about to start.

Praying didn't help. It was just getting dark when we hear a motorcycle coming our way, but then all the sudden there's this loud smashing sound and the motorcycle does this *weyeeew-weeyew* noise and stops. So Wendy and me take off and we see the dirt bike and there's Dillon bleeding like crazy. His neck was bent all funny and he couldn't move his arms or legs. And he's just screaming constantly, constantly, constantly. By the time we drag him back to camp it's too dark to drive out. So we build up a campfire and try to keep him warm.

We keep asking if he saw Travis but it's useless. When he's not screaming, he's half-comatose like he's not even there anymore. No matter what, we're getting outta here soon as there's enough light.

Sun Aug 16 1987

They're gone. Both of them. I woke up and Dillon and Wendy are 100% gone. I've shouted and shouted but nothing. I still have the truck keys, so I'm leaving now to try and get help. In case something happens to me, I'm leaving this journal here. If no one finds me, please know that I love you, mom, dad, and Tammy.

—Amber Reynolds

Chapter 11

As Jute guided Sasquatch One down a well-worn gravel road, he came to a sudden and stomach-churning realization: This supposedly secret map was taking them to a wilderness area he and Vergil had explored extensively over the years. The idea that the route to Ramsey Lake could begin anywhere around here was laughable.

The vote to join up with Dr. Bernard and Vicky had taken place two days ago. In a perfect world, Jute would have done some reconnaissance on this location yesterday. But he and Vergil had been so busy frantically gathering supplies for the expedition, they hadn't had time.

Jute wasn't sure why he'd been so confident in this map. If he'd thought about it for half a second, he would've seen it had all the hallmarks of a prank the Dodge brothers might orchestrate. Another chance for everyone to yuk it up at Jute's expense, reaffirm his role as the town joke.

He stole a nervous glance at Rye in the passenger seat. She alternated between studying the map spread out on her lap and taking the measure of their current surroundings. Jute swiveled his head farther to hazard a peek at Vergil in the back seat. Father and daughter wore identical expressions of concern. They could see where the map was taking them as well as Jute could.

The van came up on the distinctive hitch in the road Jute had used to orient himself. If this map was right, the trail should be somewhere up ahead on the left. Jute puttered along slowly with his window open, scanning the forest for a break in the foliage. Nothing appeared to be out of the ordinary. Everything looked the same as it did every other time he'd driven through here.

"How do you know this map is legit, Uncle Jute?"

"Look at how old that thing is." He tried to make himself sound confident. "Plus it's handmade. Why would anyone go through all that trouble to make such an authentic-looking fake map?"

Rye held it up by the corners as if it were a piece of dirty laundry. "Where did you find this thing?"

Jute turned the wheel sharply to avoid a small pothole and pretended not to hear the question. The legitimacy of the map wasn't the only thing nagging at him. Skimming the Bigfoot message boards last night, he came across a clip from a speech Dr. Bernard had given to the Montana Bigfoot Researchers Consortium. To say it was shocking would be an understatement. Like when Hulk Hogan—out of the blue—turned into Hollywood Hulk Hogan and started palling around with Kevin Nash and Scott Hall. Jute hated to admit it, but he was starting to wonder if Rye was right when she said they shouldn't trust these people.

Sasquatch One rolled slowly on. The sun had burned off the morning cloud cover. Dust kicked up from the gravel road, filtering in through the open windows. Grasshoppers leapt out of the way of the oncoming van and plinked off the windshield.

Just then, Jute noticed something on the left. A slight widening of the road, a thinning of the weeds. Probably nothing. But he stepped on the brakes anyway. Bernard's black Explorer skidded to a halt behind them.

"You two hang on." Jute shouldered open his door and stepped out onto the hardpan.

He put his hands on his knees and hunched down for a better angle. He squinted, tilted his head to the side.

He could swear he was looking at a soft spot in the brush, a narrow corridor where the trees appeared to be more slender, as if they hadn't been growing as long as the rest of the forest. Jute took a step back and saw the outline of an abandoned logging trail, so overgrown that if the map hadn't told him it was here, he never would have seen it.

"Well?" Vergil asked, once Jute had climbed back into the van.

"Might be onto something." Jute's throat was tight with excitement.

"Are you sure?" Rye asked. "Because it doesn't look like much."

Jute eased the van off the gravel road. Saplings grudgingly bent under the front bumper and whipped back up behind them. Branches scratched the side panels with cringe-inducing squeals. But once he'd gotten a couple dozen yards deep, the forest opened up.

The van labored on the uphills and lunged forward on the downhills. It spanned washouts and straddled ruts. All the while, Bernard's Explorer stuck close on their tail.

The logging road eventually petered out into a two-track, then a single-track, then it finally became nothing more than virgin forest. Jute had to feel his way along, looking for gaps between the trees to squeeze through. He occasionally stole glances at the map spread across Rye's lap, but everything at this point was guesswork. The forest out here was vast. All the map did was give them a slightly smaller piece of vastness to navigate.

Vergil could feel the cancer gathering strength. Originally the pain had centered on his lower back, but recently it had established outposts in various other parts of his body—his neck, his left shoulder, his right knee. At night when he lay in bed, he could feel these pain centers sounding different notes to each other through the taut wiring of his nerves. With each passing hour he sensed the cancer finding new parts of his body to invade, fresh bodily functions to disrupt. This morning he barely held down breakfast. And now his stomach was somersaulting.

"Dad, are you feeling okay?" Rye asked, turning to look at him.

"I'm great," he said. "Never better."

"This is why your old man always made me ride the rides with you at the county fair," Jute said. "Weak constitution."

"I'm not carsick," Vergil said, more angry than he ought to be.

The rear tires spun out in a muddy creek bed, then caught on a smooth rock face, and the van shot forward.

Vergil steadied himself against the seat back and stifled a groan. He wouldn't be able to hide what was happening much longer. He'd been rehearsing the speech he'd ultimately have to give, but couldn't figure out a way to deliver it that wouldn't destroy the two people he loved most in the world. Maybe there was no good way.

"I'm a little unclear," Jute said, "how your old man finally convinced his skeptic daughter to join us on one of our world-famous expeditions. Have we finally converted you into a Bigfoot believer?"

"You wish," Rye said.

"Then to what do we owe the honor?"

"I'm afraid my presence here is purely mercenary." Rye flashed him a puckish grin. "Now that you guys are about to go big-time, I figure you'll need an official media consultant."

"That's going to be a pretty big job," he said.

"Huge."

"Do you mind if I ask what your qualifications are?"

Rye leaned back and pretended to think about it. "I'd say my biggest strength is that I'm deeply familiar with you two goofballs."

"Okay, I'm listening," he said. "But how can we be sure you're not trying to cash in on our fame?"

"Aren't you paying attention, Uncle Jute? That's the *only* reason I'm here."

Sasquatch One barreled down a gully that was so steep they nearly scraped the winch mounted on the front bumper, but Jute tapped the brakes at the last minute and the van leveled out without incident.

"I think the real question," Rye said, "might be how you manage to get a van like this all the way into the backcountry."

"This old girl's gotten your dad and me through some tough spots." Jute patted the dash affectionately. "She's sturdy as a mountain goat."

"Sure-footed," Vergil said curtly.

"What's that?"

"The phrase is *sure-footed* as a mountain goat. Not *sturdy* as a mountain goat. Mountain goats aren't particularly sturdy. If you wanted to talk about the van's sturdiness, you'd compare it to a bison or a bull."

Jute sucked his teeth and looked off to the side.

Rye rolled her eyes. "Well, I, for one, think it's badass how you're able to take this thing so many places," she said.

Vergil knew he was being a jerk, but he couldn't help it. A constant ache reverberated through his body, an ever-rising din so loud it made his ears ring. It was worse when he had to sit still for long stretches, like now.

"Hey," Jute said, his tone letting everyone know he was trying to change the subject. "How's Jenny doing? Is she going to cry herself to sleep every night while you're gone?"

Rye let out a loud, uninhibited laugh. "I'm not sure," she said. "We actually broke up yesterday."

Jute idled the van while Bernard's Explorer bounced over a rough patch behind them. "Wait, so it's over?"

"But now"—Rye hesitated—"maybe we got back together this morning before I left campus?"

"Why do you say it like that?" Jute asked.

"How did I say it?"

"Your voice went up at the end, like you were asking a question."

"Oh crap," she said. "Did I really uptalk?"

"Is that what they call it?" Jute said. "I thought it was something they taught you to do in college so you sounded smart."

"It's actually the opposite, Uncle Jute. It's a vocal tic common among younger women. It implies a lack of security or power."

"I see," Jute said, nodding slowly. "Then what does your uptalk tell us about what's going on with you and Miss Jenny?"

"Probably not good things," Rye said. "Probably not good things at all."

"You know you always have your dad and me you can talk to," he said. "In case you need some advice."

"Relationship advice?" Rye said, smirking. "From you two?"

Jute toggled so easily between fun goofy uncle and serious father figure. Vergil had never quite known how to play the role of an actual father. That was probably why she'd stopped coming to the library right when she started having serious questions about herself and the world. She'd finally gotten tired of her dad not knowing how to be a dad.

"Hey, what's that!" Rye's arm shot over the dash, finger pointing out the windshield.

Jute slammed on the brakes. Everyone jolted forward then backward.

Stretched across the path were two logs propped against each other to form an upside-down V. Jute threw the van into park. Both men unfastened their seat belts. Before they stepped outside, Rye turned to them.

"Vicky's probably going to be filming you out there, so remember the rules we talked about. Number one: Don't look straight into the camera." Rye eyed them for a moment to make sure her advice sank in. "Number two: Say as little as possible so she doesn't have anything to use against you."

Both men nodded dutifully. Then they scrambled out of the van as if they'd been dismissed for recess.

Chapter 12

Vicky propped the camera over the dash, filming the back of Jute's van as it led them deeper into the forest. She knew this footage would turn out jumpy, but hoped the effect would work in service of the narrative—the jittery early moments of a voyage into the unknown.

She'd barely slept over the past forty-eight hours. After making arrangements with Jute and Vergil on Saturday, she'd raced back to Pocatello, where she spent Sunday borrowing (or purchasing) camping gear and packing up her film equipment. Then this morning Bernard picked her up at 3:30 for the drive back to Basic. Vicky hadn't even bothered to let anyone know where they were headed. She told herself it was because there'd been no time, but really it was because any sane person she knew would try to talk her out of going into the woods with four complete strangers.

And not just any woods.

Last night, Vicky had a chance to look at the green journal she'd found in the weeds in front of Jute's house. If the stories in it were even remotely true, it meant people had died out here, under bizarre (sometimes gruesome) circumstances. She sensed their caravan was right now heading toward the very same forest where it all took place. Was she about to accidentally make some kind of found-footage horror film? Of course not. What a silly question.

Vicky stopped recording. She popped the nearly full SD card out of the camera and slotted it into the plastic case where she kept everything she'd shot so far. Then she slid a fresh card into the camera, pressed record, and began to narrate:

"The Elkhorn Mountains are a chain of inactive volcanoes formed seventy-five million years ago when the Boulder Batholith—a mass of igneous rock stretching from present-day Butte to Helena—was forced to the surface by tectonic subduction, emerging from the earth's fiery center like an impacted molar."

This was all cribbed from the research she'd conducted earlier this morning during the drive back to Montana.

"Humans have lived in the Elkhorns for thousands of years," she went on. "The Crow, the Shoshone, the Confederated Salish and Kootenai, and the Blackfeet tribes have all called these slopes home at various points. White men came along too, much later, and etched their history onto these rocks."

The Explorer momentarily lost traction, then surged forward when the tires caught.

"Our vehicles labor deep into these mountains, laden with five souls and enough supplies to last us a week in the backcountry. It is Day One and we are still, essentially, strangers to each other. Even still, it's clear we each come seeking something different—knowledge, redemption, vindication, fortune, fame. Perhaps the member whose motives I'm least clear on is Dr. Marcus Bernard, who, up until three days ago, was a widely admired elder statesman of the Bigfoot community."

Bernard shot her a miffed look.

"He's what's known in the business as a legend tripper. Someone who parachutes in on other people's investigations to lend his expertise. What exactly that expertise is, I'm still a little unclear on."

"You know I can hear you," he said. "I'm right here."

Vicky ignored him and kept riffing:

"These mountains are majestic, yet treacherous. Their beauty is surpassed only by their ferocity. Some want to see the natural world as an indifferent force—unconcerned with our mundane lives, a neutral arbiter in the fates of man. But I don't see it that way." She paused, hoping this part didn't sound like bargain basement Werner Herzog. "Life is *not* random chaos; survival here is *more* than a spin of the roulette wheel. Nature is intentional, purposeful. It holds ancient secrets. And those secrets only last because Nature is ready to protect them."

"Laying it on a bit thick," Bernard grumbled. "Wouldn't you say?"

She looked up from the viewfinder. "I don't think it's over the top at all," she said. "In my opinion, it's one hundred percent accurate."

She set the camera on her lap and rotated it toward the driver's seat. "Why did you pick this moment to break up with the Bigfoot community?"

Bernard cut his eyes to Vicky, then back onto the van in front of them. "I have my reasons."

Vicky waited a moment, regrouped. "That day I came to your office," she said, "the day you agreed to let me film you . . . I noticed you'd been crying."

Bernard's face twitched—a tiny flicker on the surface. Vicky sensed she'd touched a nerve.

"You'd been looking at something on your computer," she said. "What was it?"

His nostrils flared. He tapped the steering wheel with the edge of his thumb. "I was reading an email," he said through gritted teeth.

"What did it say?"

Bernard shook his head and let out an exasperated sigh.

"You already know how persistent I am," she said. "Let's not draw this out any longer than we have to."

The Explorer shuddered over a choppy rock field for a few seconds.

"Fine," Bernard said. "Fine." He retrieved his phone from the center console. He clicked it open and held it toward her. Vicky pushed in tight with the camera.

The message had been sent five days ago from someone named Emmanuel Adebayo. Subject line: *We lost Benny.*

Vicky read the body of the email out loud:

My Dearest Marcus,

I regret to inform you that our beloved Benny has passed away. There was nothing I nor the staff could do; it was simply his time.

I know this loss is as great for you as it is for us. If there is a place better than this one, Benny is surely now at rest there.

> With brotherly love and affection,
> E. Adebayo

"I'm sorry for your loss," Vicky said, softening. "Was Benny someone you worked with?"

"In a way."

The car rocked from side to side. The gear stowed behind them shifted and groaned. Bernard leaned back against his headrest.

"I did my postdoc work in Virunga National Park," he said. "Adebayo was my partner. Our study focused on a particular troop of mountain gorillas who'd grown accustomed to our presence. We were able to glimpse their innermost lives—relationships, hierarchies, rituals . . ." Bernard lost focus for a moment, then quickly sharpened. "The research was very promising."

Vicky pulled the shot back to minimize the shakiness of the car.

"One morning we woke up to the sound of a child crying," he went on. "Twenty yards from camp we found an infant mountain gorilla clinging to his mother, who'd been shot by poachers sometime the day before." Bernard pursed his lips for a moment, swallowed hard. "I'll spare you the gruesome details of what poachers do with a gorilla once they've killed it."

Vicky looked down and saw that her hands were quaking.

"Anyway, her infant must have been off in the bush while the poachers attacked. He was scared when we found him, crying, but he took an instant liking to me. Seemed to calm down whenever I held him. Adebayo named him Bernard Junior because of that."

"Benny . . ." Vicky whispered.

"It was all our fault too. His mother most likely got killed because she'd been habituated to the presence of humans." Bernard's jaw muscle flexed. "So what were we going to do now? No way Benny could survive on his own. If we took him to a ranger station, they'd sell him to the same poachers who'd killed his mother, or else ship him off to a zoo."

The tachometer needle spiked as the tires spun out. Vicky squirmed in her seat. "What happened?"

"Adebayo decided right then and there he was going to start a great ape sanctuary. Walked away from a promising career in academia. Ballsiest thing I've ever seen." Bernard shook his head in admiration.

"What did *you* do?"

"I'm not nearly so ballsy," Bernard said. "I couldn't bring myself to give up this career I'd been working for my whole adult life. So instead I promised Adebayo I'd help fund the sanctuary." Bernard glanced at the camera for a second. "And I've honored that obligation."

"Let me see if I have this straight," Vicky said. "You found out Benny's gone, and you chose that moment to break up with Bigfoot World?" She let the time line sink in for a moment. "I don't see the connection."

Bernard hung his hand over the steering wheel and squinted as if he were trying to see a great distance ahead. "Have you ever wondered how I first got started in this racket?" he asked. "How a noted academic became the godfather of pseudoscience?"

"I've checked," Vicky said. "But I couldn't find that anywhere in my research."

"I was in my office one day. Producer for a show called *Monster Stalkers* calls me up. Must've found my dissertation online. Wants me to discuss how great ape territorialism correlates to patterns in alleged Bigfoot sightings. Five minutes on camera was all they'd need." Bernard chuckled for a moment. "Career suicide for any serious academic. I almost hung up the phone right then and there, but I must've just gotten out of an interminable department meeting, or maybe I'd had a grant rejected on some absurd technicality, or maybe it was a lousy student evaluation. One of those unavoidable professional annoyances that makes you reconsider all your life choices. So I stayed on the line to hear the guy out. And then he mentioned how much money they'd pay."

The van jostled over a series of fallen trees. The cases stored in back rattled against each other.

"I've given every nickel of my Bigfoot earnings to the sanctuary," Bernard said. "That was the least I could do."

"And now that Benny's gone ..."

"My moral ledger is as balanced as it's going to get," Bernard said. "Now it's time to atone for all the intellectual sins I've committed. See if the science gods can forgive me."

The Explorer lurched into a creek bed and darted up the other side.

"And part of that atonement is going scorched earth on Bigfoot World?" Vicky said.

Bernard nodded.

"Do you regret spending your career pretending to look for something you don't believe in?"

"Of course I have regrets," he said. "But at least I did it for a damn good reason."

The Explorer labored up an incline so steep it felt like the car might tip over backward.

"Isn't there a way to restore your reputation without humiliating the very people who helped fund your sanctuary all these years?"

"I don't look at it as humiliation." Bernard eyed her a moment. "What I'm doing is administering a strong tonic. It may cause some hurt feelings in the short term. But it's for the greater good."

"What's the greater good here?" Vicky said. "I don't see the harm in letting people have their stories."

"Where does the delusion stop, Vicky? When does belief in a fantasy become detrimental, dangerous even?"

"Who are the victims though?" she asked. "God knows, there's a lot worse ways to spend your time than walking through nature looking for Bigfoot."

The van in front of them lurched to a halt. Bernard crunched on the brakes. A moment later, the van doors popped open, and Jute and Vergil climbed out. Bernard threw the Explorer into park.

"Here we go," he said. "Lights, camera, action."

. . .

The sunlight was patchy, falling in golden pools surrounded by deep shadows. A thin buzz of insects droned over a gaping maw of silence underneath. Directly in front of the van, two stout logs leaned against each other at a sixty-degree angle, forming an upside-down V.

Vicky circled the structure in a slow tracking shot. "Don't some experts say tree structures like this are evidence of Bigfoot activity?" she asked.

Vergil bent down to inspect it. "It's odd," he said. "I'll give you that. Could be natural though."

"Natural my ass," Jute said.

Bernard had seen hundreds of supposed tree structures over the years. To his mind, they were the least compelling evidence Bigfooters tried to claim. Of course, skepticism didn't play well on the Bigfoot shows. So whenever he was presented with flimsy or nonexistent evidence, he'd respond with something noncommittal, yet vaguely encouraging. *What would Bigfoot do* sprang from just such a moment. Bernard had originally meant it as a sort of darkly ironic joke, but the question proved to be immensely popular among his growing fan base, eventually giving rise to a substantial revenue stream from merch sales.

"What do *you* think this is, Doctor?" Jute asked, nudging the structure with the toe of his boot.

Bernard hesitated. He had to be careful not to tip his hand in front of Jute and Vergil yet. They needed to think he was on their side for now.

"I'm stumped," he said, clefting his chin with his thumb and forefinger. "What do you guys think?"

Vergil and Jute exchanged glances, then looked blankly at the camera.

"My whole thing," Jute said, "is how did these logs fall so they're leaning *against* each other like that?"

"Except the wind knocks down trees all the time in the forest," Vergil jumped in. "Sometimes in ways we can't predict."

"I maintain Bigfoot use these structures as a primitive alarm system," Jute said. "If one of these gets moved, it lets them know something's been in their territory."

"*Or,*" Vergil jumped in, "it could just be a couple trees happened to randomly fall in the forest."

Vicky moved in closer to the structure. "There aren't any roots on the bottoms of these logs," she said. "I don't think they were growing here when they fell."

"Exactly!" Jute said as if he'd been vindicated.

A bird cawed loudly nearby. They all jumped and spun to look at a nearby lodgepole pine. Perched on one of the topmost branches was an enormous crow.

"Jesus, that thing is big," Vicky said.

The bird stared at the group, tilting its head as if it wanted to see them from multiple angles. Its eyes were bottomless, its tail feathers iridescent and sharp as knife blades.

"Let's get these out of the way and keep going," Vergil finally said.

"Wait," Vicky said. "Are you sure we want to trip the alarm?"

"That's *if* it's an alarm," Vergil said, giving one of the logs a stiff kick, causing the structure to creak and topple over. "Besides, I don't see any other way through here. Do you?"

Before climbing back into the Explorer, Bernard peered at the fallen logs for a moment. It *had* been strange, that structure. The chances of it being natural weren't high. But that didn't mean it was the work of a Bigfoot. Humans were far more likely culprits.

Chapter 13

Sasquatch One revved and sputtered as it crawled over a network of exposed tree roots. This was easily the most difficult terrain Jute had taken her into. The engine was running a little hotter than he'd like, and the tires were balder than they should be. But right now Jute was mostly worried about Vergil's lousy attitude. This expedition was supposed to lift his spirits, pull him out of the funk he'd been mired in lately. Instead he seemed to be getting worse.

"Would it kill you to agree with me for once?" Jute grumbled.

"What'd I do?" Vergil asked.

"You made me look like an idiot around some very influential people is what you did."

"We've never seen eye to eye on tree structures, Jute. You think they're all made by Bigfoot, and I don't happen to agree. I'm not going to change my opinion just because there's a famous researcher with us."

The van shook from side to side as it inched up a dry creek bed. Everyone jostled back and forth.

"You didn't have to openly disagree with me on camera," he said. "And you definitely didn't have to make it seem like you were enjoying it so much."

"I don't *enjoy* contradicting you." Vergil looked out the window for a moment. "Besides, maybe you *need* a reality check every once in a while."

"Give it a rest, you guys," Rye said.

"When did it become your job to give me reality checks?" Jute went on.

"See what happens next time you make an ass of yourself," Vergil said, "and I'm not around to smooth things over for you."

"What do you mean, *when you're not around*?" Jute asked.

The smell of juniper wafting through the windows was so strong it made Vergil's stomach curdle. On some level he knew why he'd said it. Like working up the courage to jump off a high-dive by inching yourself closer to the edge, at a certain point you had no choice but to take the plunge.

The van's AC hadn't worked in years, and the heat was stifling. A slick sweat beaded up on Vergil's face; droplets trickled down his back. "Can't I be in a bad mood for once?" he snapped.

"Maybe we can help," Rye said. "If you told us what's wrong."

"Yeah," Jute chimed in. "Tell us what the matter is."

Vergil let out a laugh. "I doubt very much you can help."

"See," Rye said, "this is what I hate about men. Everything has to be bottled up. Nobody talks about how they feel. That's toxic behavior, Dad, and I expect better from you."

Jute eased Sasquatch One down a steep incline, letting out the brakes inch by jerky inch. At that moment, Vergil felt something churn and burble inside him.

"Stop the car!" he shouted into the front seat.

"I'm not going to let you change the subject, Dad. Let's talk about this."

"Please," Vergil said. "Stop the car. I'm going to be sick."

Jute slammed on the brakes. Vergil clawed at the handle until the door slid open.

"What's going on up there now?" Bernard said, bringing the Explorer to a skidding halt inches before they rear-ended the van.

He and Vicky watched as Vergil stumbled out of the back seat.

"This doesn't look promising," Bernard said.

Vergil staggered a few feet into the woods, put his hands on his knees, and spewed what must have been the entire contents of his stomach into the forest.

"Oh god," Vicky said, hitting pause on the camera. She unrolled her window and stuck her head out. "Are you okay?"

Vergil waved her off without looking up.

"Let us know if you need anything," she called out.

Vergil remained there, hunched and heaving. After a few more minutes, he spit until his mouth was dry, and climbed back into the van.

Rye and Jute eyed him warily from the front seat.

"Thanks, guys," he said, mopping the sweat from his forehead with his shirtsleeve. "I'm better now."

"Are you sure?" Rye asked.

"Of *course* I'm sure." Try as he might, Vergil couldn't help sounding annoyed.

"What's wrong with you, Dad?"

"Jute already told you, I get carsick easily. That's all. Now let's get moving."

Jute eased his foot off the brake. The van continued its tortured journey into the forest.

Vergil leaned back in his seat. He felt better, relatively speaking, though he had a weird metallic taste in his mouth. The two up front wore expressions of mute concern. They weren't buying the carsick excuse, and the quiet was making him uneasy.

"How much farther do you think it is to base camp?" he asked.

"Should be close," Jute said. "If this actually is the right way."

The engine whined and strained, making the floorboards shake. Vergil took a swig from a bottle of Pepsi at his feet. The pop was warm and flat, but it helped kill the taste in his mouth.

"Ummm, Dad?"

"Yes, Rye."

"That throw-up . . . It looked kind of pinkish, like there might be blood in it."

"Did it?"

"That's, like, a really bad sign."

"I don't think anyone here is in a position to make a diagnosis."

"I'm being serious, Dad," she said. "I know what I'm talking about."

"Come to think of it, you *have* been moving awful slow lately." Jute was looking at him through the rearview mirror. "Is something else wrong, Verge?"

"I'm getting older," he said. "That's what happens when you reach a ripe old age like mine."

"You're not *that* old, Dad," Rye said.

"We're practically the same age," Jute added. "And you look thinner too."

"Seriously, Dad, what's wrong?"

It was hopeless. They'd caught a whiff of something amiss, and there'd be no shaking them off the scent. They'd hound him until they got what they were after. This wasn't where or when or how he'd expected to do this, but they'd given him no choice. He was trapped.

Vergil took in a deep breath and held it for a full three seconds. As he let it out, he was almost surprised to hear "I have cancer" come out with it.

Releasing those words—putting them out into the world—was an act of surrender, of submission, and he was surprised by how good it felt.

"It started in the pancreas," he went on, "but now it's pretty much everywhere. And it's terminal. Or whatever they call it when there's no cure."

A handful of loose change in the front seat cup holder jingled incessantly. It must've been doing it this whole time, but Vergil only noticed it now.

"I'm fine for the moment," he said. "Fine enough. But it's going to get worse, and you both have a right to know. I'm sorry if I've been a pain in the ass lately. I really am. But at least you understand why now."

.   .   .

Rye looked around the van, from her dad, to Jute, to the dashboard, to her own lap. She felt herself shrinking into the seat.

Her dad was still talking, saying more words. But she couldn't hear him anymore. Instead, all she heard was a gigantic ripping sound. Her life—this life she'd barely cobbled together after her mother died— was about to be torn apart again.

Rye's vision narrowed further until all she could see was the scar on her knee. She remembered the precise moment when it happened. It was the finals of the regional soccer tournament in Billings. She'd just lofted a gorgeous, arcing ball across the goalmouth, planted her foot to trail it into the box in case there were any table scraps, when she heard her knee pop, and she crumpled instantly to the ground. Her dad had been watching from the sidelines—he went to every game—and was the first to get to her on the field, even before the ref had a chance to stop play. Rye remembered her father picking her up—no easy feat for someone his size—and carrying her off the field. He'd laid her out in the back seat of the station wagon and driven like hell to the hospital across town.

To take her mind off the pain, he suggested they sing a song together. The only one they both could remember any of the words to was "You Are My Sunshine." But after the first verse, they had to make up their own lyrics. They were both so bad at it, Rye found herself laughing by the time they'd pulled into the ER.

> *I asked for mud pie*
> *Upon my birthday,*
> *But you forgot, dear*
> *And so did I.*
> *Now I'm so lost, dear*
> *My eyes are crossed, dear*
> *Couldn't see a pie in the sky.*

Those silly, stupid lyrics were all she could think about as Sasquatch One rolled onward into the forest, with everything, everything changed.

．　．　．

Jute was numb. His arms, legs, face, feet, hands—all of them useless, refusing to respond to even the most rudimentary of commands. Meanwhile, branches pummeled the sides of the van as it continued to putter along.

Through the mists of memory, Jute recalled the time when Vergil had moved back to Basic. They hadn't run into each other for the first couple weeks after his return. Then, one morning, Jute swung by the library to pick up a book on water hydraulics to help him figure out why the pump in Bay 3 kept crapping out.

The book had not been part of the library's normal collection, so they'd had to request it on interlibrary loan from Missoula. Vergil Barnes—his long-estranged childhood friend—sat behind the circulation desk. He was still new there, so it took him a few minutes to track down Jute's order in the mailroom.

"You know," Vergil said, removing the book from its packaging, "I heard they're thinking of cutting back mail service to once a week."

"Could you imagine?" Jute said.

Both men shook their heads and frowned.

Vergil stamped the book to check it out, then slid it across the desk. "Hey," he said, "are you still into that Bigfoot stuff?"

"Sure," Jute said, even though he wasn't. "A little."

"Remember that club we started when we were kids?" Vergil asked. "The Basic Bigfoot Society, right?"

"Oh, my gosh." Jute chuckled. "I think that's what we called it."

Jute tucked the book under his arm and turned to leave. He'd been doing fine in his life. Finer than he'd ever done before. He had a job, a thriving business, a house, a van. Everything a man could hope for. Except—Jute realized in that moment—he didn't have anyone to share these things with.

"You know," he said, turning back to the circulation desk, "it might be nice to start the club back up again."

"Let me know if you do," Vergil said. "That sounds like fun."

This moment, this pivot point in both their lives, was the only thing

Jute could cling to as Sasquatch One rumbled onward, crushing the ferns and brush in its path.

Vergil looked up at the ceiling of the van, scratched and scraped from all the equipment they'd hauled on all their expeditions over the years. The silence from the front seat was nearly unbearable, but he knew they would need some time to absorb this blow.

He wasn't proud of himself, detonating an emotional grenade out of the blue like that. But telling them both at the same time had been a fluky stroke of genius. Rather than having to go through it twice, separately, he'd only had to do it once.

"How long?" Jute finally asked. His face had shrunk in on itself, eyebrows drawn into the bridge of his nose.

"Six months maybe," Vergil said.

"What about treatment options?" Rye asked.

"Doctors said surgery and chemo might get me at most a couple more months. But I've already decided I'm not going to fight this."

"There's no way you get to make that decision on your own," Rye said. "How can we even be sure these doctors know what they're talking about?" She tried to unbuckle her seat belt, but she wound up pulling on the strap, making it lock and pin her to the seat. "I need to talk to them," she said. "Right now!" Her eyes were suddenly wide and wild. "Uncle Jute, stop this car!"

"Keep going," Vergil said. "We're not turning around."

"What are you talking about, Dad? This is insane!"

Vergil leaned forward, hoping his presence in the front seat airspace might prove reassuring. "I want to enjoy every minute of the time I have left," he said, "while I still can."

Jute let out a groan. Rye crossed her arms and shook her head.

"That means spending it with the two people I care about most in the world, doing something I love." He put a hand on each of their shoulders. "Can you give me that? One last Bigfoot expedition?" He gave them both a gentle squeeze. "Please?"

"So, what," Rye said, "we're supposed to just go along as if every-thing's fine?"

"Basically, yes."

"That's a big ask, Verge."

"I know."

Rye looked over helplessly at Jute, who still hadn't regained full control of his limbs.

"On one condition," Rye said, turning now to look at her father. "I get to talk to the doctors. I get to see the test results. I get to have a say in all the big decisions. If you can agree to that, I'll give you this expedition."

"Deal," Vergil said, then looked to Jute. "What about you?"

Jute's eyes were clouded with tears. His bottom lip quivered. But he managed to nod twice. And just like that, a promise had been secured. Vergil slumped with relief. Now he needed this expedition to start before either of them had a chance to renege.

At that precise moment, the forest went streaky. The tires on the van lost all traction, and it started skidding downhill sideways. Tree branches snapped. The steering wheel leapt uselessly in Jute's hands. Finally, the van crunched to a stop, and all three occupants rag-dolled against their seat belts.

Clouds of dust hung motionless outside the windows. The passengers blinked at each other, as if they'd just woken up from a long nap.

"Is everyone okay in there?" Vicky Xu's face appeared in the windshield. "It looks like you're all stuck pretty good."

"Yes," Rye said, her voice frail. "We're very, very stuck."

Sasquatch One was wedged at the bottom of a steep incline, left-side tires nearly buried in gravel.

Jute—back in control of his body now—put his boot on the rear bumper and gave it a slight bounce. Being confronted by a physical-world predicament like this allowed him to brush aside the cataclysmic news he'd just received. He felt his mind sharpening, whetting itself against the challenge at hand.

Vicky moved slowly around the pinned van, shooting it from multiple angles. "Think you can drive it out?" she asked.

"That'd only get us more stuck," Jute said. "Or else ruin the transmission."

Vicky panned onto Rye, who sat on a fallen log, her face pale and papery.

"Are you all right?" Vicky asked.

Rye shook her head tightly.

"I've got zero bars on my phone," Bernard said. "So what's the plan if you can't get that thing unstuck?"

Jute and Vergil exchanged glances, then opted to treat the question as if it had been rhetorical. They clambered up the hill to assess the situation from above. A light breeze carried the sweet smell of spring cottonwoods and fresh willow shrubs. A few tall pines nearby creaked as they swayed.

"Think your winch is up for the job?" Vergil asked.

"Pretty steep incline," Jute said. "Might be our only shot though."

He paced out the distance between Sasquatch One and some nearby trees at the top of the hill. Then he went back down and unhooked the winch mounted on the front bumper.

"Give me a hand?" he said to Vergil before considering whether his friend was physically capable of helping him, whether his body would allow it, and for how much longer.

Vergil—eager to demonstrate he *was* still capable—dragged the line to the top of the hill, where he looped it around a cluster of young spruce trees. He tugged on it once to see if it would hold, then he gave Jute a thumbs-up.

Back down at the vehicle, Jute turned the wheels to face the direction of the cable. He flipped on the winch and gritted his teeth. The low-geared motor made a loud grinding noise. The cable tightened and twanged. The van resisted at first, but slowly started to rise out of the depression. Rubble fell away from the tires.

Then a cracking sound tore through the forest, and the van lurched backward several feet. The trees they'd anchored the winch to had folded over. Jute lunged for the switch, but it was too late.

One more wrenching noise and Sasquatch One rolled back down to the bottom of the depression, dragging with it a clump of uprooted trees, like dead fish on a stringer.

Jute climbed up to the trees and rested a hand on their trunks. "I'm sorry, fellas. That was an accident." The view from the top of the hill was wide open now. As Jute stood there taking in this new vista, he felt a charge of recognition.

He'd seen this place before.

He stepped down into a clearing on the far side of the hill. The surrounding trees were bigger. Some of the rocks had shifted. But overall, the place hadn't changed much. He walked down to the bottom of the clearing until he was sure.

They'd found it.

The Ramsey Lake trailhead.

Over the years, Jute had sometimes wondered if he'd made the whole thing up. He'd come to doubt himself far more than he let on. But standing here now, where it happened, he knew it was real. All of it.

Chapter 14

The winch was still functioning, so getting the van unstuck was simply a matter of locating something sturdier to hook the cable up to. Which they found in the form of a boulder embedded in the hillside. Once the van had been retrieved, they parked both vehicles on top of the hill next to an earthen berm.

The forest here was a mixture of lodgepole and spruce, with a leafy underbrush that choked off visibility beyond a few feet in any direction. To the south, a steep-sided butte loomed over the clearing. Its crown was topped with spring snow sporting a heavy cornice, which overhung the ridgeline in outright defiance of gravity.

All five expeditioners stood in a semicircle between the cars.

"So what comes next?" Vicky asked from behind the camera.

Everyone glanced around the group, waiting for someone to take charge. In his capacity as president of the Basic Bigfoot Society, Jute was technically responsible for all expedition operations. But the glazed look on his face told the full story: He was in no shape to give orders at the moment. Fortunately, BBS bylaws allowed for the vice president to serve as acting president in the event that the president should become incapacitated.

"Welcome, everyone," Vergil said. "It's nice to see so many new faces here today. Let's start with a few ground rules. First off, protection. We're issuing everyone bear spray. This isn't grizzly country, but you never know when you might need it. Make sure you keep it on you at all times."

He handed everyone their own canister and demonstrated how the safety and trigger worked.

"Next is the itinerary," he said. "We'll establish a base camp here. Tomorrow morning we set out for Ramsey Lake. It's a two-day hike, so we'll travel light, bare essentials only." Vergil looked around the group. "As for sleeping arrangements, we've only got two tents so we can—"

"Three," Bernard said. "I brought my own."

"Fine, three tents," Vergil said. "Dr. Bernard will sleep by himself. The rest of us will split up boys and girls."

Vergil glanced around the group to make sure there were no objections so far.

"Now I get that we all want to start Bigfoot hunting right away," he went on, "but there are some basic camp chores we need to take care of first. Vicky and Rye, you two'll be in charge of scouting our water supply. Dr. Bernard, why don't you see about hanging our food bag?"

"Can't," he said. "I need to prep my equipment."

Vergil already didn't like this guy's attitude. "We're all expected to pull our own weight around here, Doctor."

"If you want me to furnish the tech," Bernard said, "it's going to require some setup."

Before Vergil could challenge him on this, Jute stepped between them. "You go ahead and set up your equipment, Doctor. Vergil and I will handle the camp chores."

"Cutting him a lot of slack, don't you think?" Vergil grumbled, once everyone had split up to pitch tents.

"The man's a living legend," Jute said, piecing together a set of poles. "We need to recognize where we are in the pecking order."

Vergil detected a note of anger in his friend's voice and realized he owed it to him to make sure things went smoothly on this trip. After all, this could be Jute's big break, the life-changing moment he'd always hoped for.

"You're right," Vergil said. "I can play nice."

Once the tents were pitched, Rye and Vicky each took a yellow bucket and disappeared over the lip of the hill in search of water. Bernard began unloading his equipment, which was stored in stoutly latched cases, the kind that usually held nuclear launch codes or Fabergé eggs in the movies. He stacked them on a foldout table in the center of the clearing. Meanwhile, Jute gawked at the gear they now had at their disposal.

"Come on," Vergil said, pulling a camp spade from the back of Sasquatch One. "Can't have a proper campsite without a proper *twah-lette*."

The two men walked into the woods until they found a natural depression with some billowy ferns nearby to provide privacy. Jute folded the spade open, stomped on the shoulder, and the blade sank into the soil.

"So..." he said, tossing a shovelful of dirt off to the side, "I know you don't want to talk about it, but can I at least ask you a few questions?"

"Of course, buddy."

"Are the doctors really sure there's nothing they can do? Like they *know* this?"

"Afraid so." Vergil looked down at the tops of his boots. "This kind I've got, they say it's the most aggressive kind."

"And how do you feel now?"

"Everything hurts," he said. "But that might not even be the cancer yet."

Jute stepped on the spade and it struck a rock with a metallic scrape, sending him careening off to the side. "But... you're going to be okay with all the hiking we're planning to do?"

"I'll be fine," Vergil said. "That's what ibuprofen's for."

Jute worked the rock loose and tossed it onto the dirt pile.

"Want me to dig a little?" Vergil offered.

Jute gave him a sidelong glance and continued to work on the hole.

As Vergil cleared brush and stacked it, he surveyed the forest his friend had dreamed of returning to for over thirty years. At first blush, it seemed like every other forest they'd camped in out here. Tall pines, thick underbrush, dry rocky soil, occasional granite outcroppings. But there was a density to the air here that Vergil couldn't explain, a heaviness. He felt it pressing against his skin, weighing him down.

"How does it feel," Vergil asked, "being back here after all this time?"

"Like I'm eleven years old again." Jute dug more dirt and tossed it onto the growing pile. "What do *you* think of it?" he asked.

Vergil inhaled the thick pine scent and looked around. "I'd say it definitely has Bigfoot potential."

When the hole was deep enough, Vergil dragged a thick log to the edge of it. "Perfect," he said, after he'd braced the log in place with rocks. "Now when it's time to recycle dinner, you sit down on this log like so, hang your ass out over the edge, and voilà. A *twah-lette* fit for a king."

Jute started laughing.

"What's so funny?" Vergil asked.

"Nothing. Except that's exactly what you say every time we dig one of these."

Vergil blushed. "Guess I'm getting predictable in my old age." Then, out of nowhere, he said, "God, I'm going to miss this."

Both men quickly looked at each other, as if one of them had broken a vow of silence. Jute's eyes started to tremble. Vergil set a hand on his friend's shoulder, and Jute leaned into it. They stood next to each other, the afternoon sun warm on their faces, silently commemorating what they both knew would be the last *twah-lette* the two of them would ever dig together.

Chapter 15

Rye and Vicky carried empty buckets down to the bottom of the clearing, toward the sound of running water.

Rye had promised her father she'd let him have this expedition. But that didn't preclude her from making plans for what she'd do the second it was over. As soon as she got someplace with a cell signal, she'd research the shit out of pancreatic cancer, find out everything there was to know about it. Then she'd mercilessly grill the doctors at St. Peter's to see if they had any clue what they were doing. Next she'd make inquiries, determine where the best oncology departments were, the most promising treatment options, clinical trials. Fuck it, she'd even check out Reiki and crystal therapy. If it was truly as bad as her father said, nothing would be off the table.

Handling all that would require pressing pause on her education again. Even worse, it would mean a soul-killing move back to Basic, just when she'd finally gotten a taste of the outside world. But that was how it would have to be. Rye had already lost her mother. If the Universe thought it could also take her father without a fight, then it didn't know Rye Barnes very well.

In the meantime, she'd have to pretend like everything was normal.

"Are you okay?" Vicky said. "You seem . . ."

"Not good?" Rye offered.

"Yes."

Rye nodded. "Let's just say I don't have much of a poker face."

"Is it anything you'd like to talk about?"

Rye glanced at the camera on Vicky's shoulder. "I'm not sure I can right now," she said. "But thanks."

Once they left the clearing, the forest took on a darker aspect. The shadows grew longer and colder. The sound of running water felt like it kept receding. The more they walked, the farther away it seemed to get.

"Are you originally from Idaho?" Rye asked. Idle conversation to take her mind off her dad. "That's where you're going to school, right?"

"Yeah, no, I'm from the Bay Area," Vicky said. "Oakland, actually."

"No way," Rye said. "I was supposed to go to school at San Francisco State."

"That's my alma mater!"

"Are you kidding?" Rye couldn't believe it. "What was it like?"

"It was . . . fine, I guess." Vicky shrugged. "Why were you going there?"

"You mean other than the fact that it's far from Basic, Montana?" Rye said. "They've got a decent physical therapy program," she said. "And their graduates get priority for the UCSF doc program."

"Why didn't you go?" Vicky asked.

Rye walked in silence for a few paces. "Unexpected family stuff," she said. "And no, I don't want to talk about that either."

"Understood," Vicky said. "I get family stuff."

The bunchgrass, still heavy with dew despite it being late afternoon, brushed against their legs and quickly soaked their boots.

"Can I ask why you decided to make a documentary about Bigfoot?" Rye said.

"The original idea was to do it about Dr. Bernard," Vicky clarified. "I saw him walking across campus one day. He had this entourage of students following him, and . . . I don't know, it hit me: Here's the most popular professor on campus, who's famous for this fringy idea, but it's also one that's like a guilty pleasure, you know?" She tucked a strand of hair behind her ear, even though it was too short to stay put for long.

"Then how did my dad and Uncle Jute get wrapped up in this?"

Vicky shot her a quick glance. "That was Dr. Bernard's decision," she said. "You'll have to ask him."

When they reached the bottom of the slope, they were confronted by a wall of vegetation—twelve feet high and impenetrably dense.

"Russian olive." Rye tore off a slender, silvery leaf. "Strange."

Vicky hoisted the camera to her shoulder and zoomed in. "Why's that strange?"

"Russian olive is an invasive species that usually follows human habitation," Rye explained. She stepped back to better gauge the size of the thicket. "You see it in cities all the time, but I've never heard of it growing up in these mountains. Technically, it shouldn't be here."

Vicky reached out to touch it.

"Careful!" Rye grabbed her by the wrist. "It's got huge thorns."

"Then how are we supposed to get to the water?"

"Unless you brought a machete," Rye said, "we'll have to see if there's a way around it."

Rye started edging along the thicket. Vicky followed behind her with the camera still rolling.

"So how often do you go Bigfoot hunting with your dad?"

"This is my first time," Rye said.

"Really? Why?"

Rye twirled her bucket a few times. "I find it childish," she said. "A waste of time."

"So you don't believe in Bigfoot."

Rye stopped walking and let out a belly laugh. "Not in the slightest."

"Does that put you at odds with your dad then?"

"All the time," Rye said. "But we have plenty of other things to be at odds about too."

Vicky's gaze slid off Rye's face to something over her shoulder. "Look." She pointed at a game trail cutting through the Russian olive, just wide enough to squeeze through if they turned their shoulders sideways.

Before Rye could react, Vicky headed into the gap, camera held out in front of her like a flashlight. The passageway narrowed as they went. At one point, Rye brushed against the shrub, and a thorn slashed her forearm. She almost yelped from the pain, but she bit her knuckle instead, not wanting to show weakness in front of Vicky or the camera.

When the thicket finally opened up, they were standing at the edge of a creek that sluiced through bottlenecks of downed timber and rock, thundering into calm holes where the water grew clear before swirling up at the next choke point.

"It's not supereasy to access," Rye said, "but we officially have ourselves a water supply." She knelt by the creek to rinse the scratch on her arm. "Let's fill these buckets and get back to camp."

Vicky didn't say anything. She lifted her camera, shot a slow 360, then started wandering downstream.

"Where do you think you're going?"

"I need to check something out," Vicky said without looking back.

"What we really need to do is stick together!" Rye called.

A few more steps.

"That's superimportant out here!"

The bunchgrass swished closed behind her like a curtain, and Vicky disappeared.

Rye waited, still crouched on the pebbly bank. A cold breeze pushed up the creek bed, swaying the stalks as if to taunt her. Goddammit, this was not what Rye signed up for. She kicked her bucket and took off after Vicky.

Rye had to march at least a hundred yards before she caught up with her companion. The slope had flattened out. The creek—slower here—split into multifingered trickles that seeped into a marshy pond. The ground was dotted with purple lupine. The air was filled with the medicinal scent of old cedars.

"It's a beaver pond," Rye said. "The dam should be farther downstream."

Vicky didn't say anything.

"Beavers are among the most ecologically important animals in North America."

Vicky turned the camera to Rye, as if this information might somehow change the focus of her documentary.

"They nearly got trapped to extinction," Rye went on. "Changed the entire ecosystem of the West."

"Trappers were here?" Vicky murmured.

"I wouldn't be surprised," Rye said. "It's fucking barbaric."

Vicky continued scanning the area as if she were looking for something specific.

"Listen," Rye said. "We need to fill these buckets farther back upstream, where the water's moving faster. Less risk of giardia."

But Vicky was off again, heading down through the willow reeds, past the beaver dam.

"This isn't funny!" Rye shouted. "It's a bad idea for us to get separated!"

Part of her wanted to let Vicky find her own way back, get a firsthand lesson in wilderness survival. She probably had no idea most people got lost within a mile of where they started hiking. And once you were alone out here, anything could happen. But Rye didn't need that hanging over her conscience, so she grudgingly gave chase.

Below the beaver dam, the creek picked up speed again. The air misted; the light got dim and flat. Vicky's tracks veered away from the water.

"Hold on one sec!" Rye shouted. "Wait for me!"

She followed the tracks up a rounded slope and found Vicky standing at the top. Her camera was fixed on a hulking object near her feet. Rusted metal, overgrown with weeds.

"What do we have here?" Rye bent down. She could make out gears, pipes, a fuel tank. "Looks like a machine of some kind," she said. "This is the engine here. Maybe an old piece of mining equipment or—"

"It's a motorcycle." Vicky's voice was cold with certainty. "A dirt bike."

"I highly doubt we'd find a motorcycle out in the middle of nowhere."

Rye brushed aside a creeping vine to reveal a pitted chrome Honda logo. She jumped back so quickly she nearly tripped over her own feet.

"How did you know that?" she demanded. "How did you know this was a motorcycle?"

Vicky tilted the camera onto Rye. She held it there a moment, unmoving. "It's a long story," she said.

Chapter 16

Once he'd strung up the food bag, Jute hustled back to check on the others, only to find himself overwhelmed by the pastoral beauty he beheld when he reached the edge of the clearing. Three tents formed a tight triangle around a crackling campfire. Rising over the tree line behind them, he saw the hollow-topped mountain where Ramsey Lake lay hidden. Vergil was busy organizing a camp kitchen, while Dr. Bernard—who'd donned his trademark fedora and safari vest—tinkered with various technological gizmos laid out on the foldout table. The scene seemed so perfect. Yet Jute was unable to savor the moment because his best friend and partner was seriously ill. What a cruel joke this all was.

He knew these kinds of self-pitying thoughts weren't helpful. The best course of action was to do exactly what Vergil wanted: focus on the expedition for as long as they were out here. After it was over, after they'd gotten back to Basic, then he could worry or cry or be as mad at the world as he wanted. Until then, not a word.

"Anyone need a hand with anything?" he asked, forcing himself to sound brighter than he felt.

"I'm about to start dinner," Vergil said without looking up. "Why don't you two place those trail cams."

Bernard scooped up a dozen Browning Recon Force Elite HP5s—each one of which was so expensive Jute had never even bothered to price them out—and slung them over his shoulder. The two men had only gone a couple dozen yards before the forest seemed to swallow them whole. Sounds from the clearing vanished, and it felt as if they were miles away from camp.

Jute tried to quiet his nerves at the thought of being alone with one of his personal idols. He wanted to impress Dr. Bernard. At the same time, he didn't want to seem like he was trying too hard. He thought about asking the doctor to clarify what he'd meant by that speech he gave in Helena. But it was impossible to tell what might upset these Hollywood types.

Ultimately, he decided to break the ice with a well-informed, mildly reverential question: "Should we set up a perimeter like you had your team do on *Monster Search*?"

"Looks like you've done your homework," Bernard said, nodding. "I think that's the right call."

Jute's throat tightened. His face broke into a stiff smile. "Thank you," he said, trying to play it cool, even though he was exuberant at the thought of receiving a compliment from a genuine legend in the Bigfoot game.

"How about placing one here," Bernard said when they reached a spot with a good vantage point. He lobbed a trail cam toward Jute, who managed to secure it with both hands, cradling it to his chest. He chose a stout lodgepole with a clear view of a nearby game trail and looped the strap around the trunk.

Bernard stepped up to the camera, opened a side panel, and pressed a few buttons. "Okay, now walk by," he said, "so I can make sure it's working."

Jute did his best loose-limbed Bigfoot stride past the camera. Then he glanced over his shoulder at Bernard. "I'm not sure if you noticed, but my gait is mimicking a midtarsal break."

"You don't say." Bernard didn't sound impressed.

"That's right," Jute went on. "I modeled my stride on your research on primate bipedalism."

Bernard stared blankly at Jute, who realized with a shudder that he'd overplayed his hand. Dr. Bernard had authored so many papers over the years, he'd probably forgotten about that one.

"After all," Jute went on, "it was you who first theorized that midfoot flexibility is one of the key anatomical differences in Bigfoot versus human bipedalism."

Bernard didn't say anything for several seconds. His eyes were so piercingly blue, they nearly induced vertigo. Maybe Jute had gotten his facts wrong. Maybe that wasn't Dr. Bernard's research at all.

"Should we keep going?" Bernard finally said, snapping the camera panel closed.

"One second." Jute pulled an apple from his daypack and speared it on a tree branch directly within the camera's line of sight. "Golden Delicious," he said by way of explanation.

Bernard frowned at the apple.

"On *Beast Hunters,* season three, episode eight, you baited all your trail cams with Golden Delicious apples," Jute said. "But then, on *Searching for Sasquatch,* season four, episode two, you didn't use any baits at all, so I wasn't sure which side of the bait debate you currently subscribe to."

Bernard hooked a thumb in a pocket of his safari vest and narrowed his gaze.

Jute shifted his weight nervously. This was not going well at all. "Maybe I'm not up-to-date on the latest research trends," he offered, hoping the admission might let the awkward moment pass. "I'd love to hear how your thinking has evolved."

But the doctor's face remained stony, his thoughts unfathomable.

Bernard was usually so good at reading people. That's what made him such a natural on camera. He instinctively knew how to measure the distance between what people *wanted* to hear and what they *needed* to hear, and how to come up with a line that managed to thread that needle, no matter how small or wide that gap was. But this Jute guy, for some reason, was proving difficult to pin down. Was he actually this naïve and sincere? Or did he know about the Helena speech and the controversy brewing on the message boards? Bernard hadn't been this unsure of himself in quite some time, and he found it deeply unnerving.

"Let's get the rest of these set up," he said.

They pushed their way through brush so dense it was hard to keep track of where they were in relation to base camp. Branches cracked and snapped. Pine needles scratched welted lines across their forearms. Bernard kept his GPS locator out, dropping pins at each camera location.

He'd been dealing with Jute's type his whole career—honest enough people who happened to be willfully, tragically misinformed. He didn't hate them. Hell, you could argue he was jealous of them. But if Bernard truly wanted to strike a blow for the forces of rational thought, a sacrifice needed to be made. This otherwise decent person standing before him would have to be turned into a poster child for a benighted populace more interested in superstition and pseudoscience than common sense.

Bernard wasn't entirely sure how he'd pull that off just yet. It was crucial he not come across sounding mean or hateful. Punching down would only hurt his cause. He needed to be cautious, roll with things for a while. Wait for the right moment to reveal itself. Then he'd pounce. Yes, there would be collateral damage, hurt feelings at the very least, but that was the price you paid to live in an enlightened world.

"I can't tell you what a huge honor it is to work with you, Doctor," Jute said as he strung up the next trail cam. "Really, really huge."

There was that tone again. Obsequious. But maybe *too* obsequious? Bernard eyed him closely and detected no undercurrent of subtext. Jute must not be aware of the Helena speech. And therefore couldn't possibly know the real reason Bernard was here. What *did* remain unclear was whether that ignorance would make what would eventually happen more painful, or less.

Just then, both men heard tromping in the forest. Footsteps coming their way. Trees shuddering. Rye and Vicky burst through the underbrush, nearly running into them.

"You got to check this out, Uncle Jute," Rye said, panting. "You're not going to believe what we found."

Chapter 17

Once the sun dipped behind a soaring peak to the west, the valley went black fast, like a set of jaws snapped shut overhead. They'd collected enough wood to last well into the night, and stoked up a good fire, which nudged the darkness back to the edges of the clearing.

Everyone sat on logs semicircled around the fire, except for Bernard, who'd brought a padded director's chair with his name stenciled on the backrest. Vicky had her camera out and swept it across the group.

"I always thought that story was an urban legend," Rye mused as she poked the fire with a stick she'd found in the brush. "Like something people said so we wouldn't throw keggers in the woods."

"I remember when it happened," Vergil said. "Jute, did you know those kids who went missing?"

Jute had a Coleman lantern resting between his ankles to supplement the uneven firelight. On his lap was the user's manual for a Klover MiK 26 parabolic microphone. His hands shook with excitement as he peered through his half-moon reading glasses, trying to make the diagrams align with the three-thousand-dollar piece of machinery on his lap. "What's that, Verge?"

"Amber Reynolds and those other kids. The twins and . . . one other girl, I think. Did you know them?"

"Barely," he said. "They were all a little older than me."

"Amber Reynolds," Vicky said. "She any relation to Tammy Reynolds?"

"Tammy's her younger sister," Vergil said. "How did you know?"

"We ran into her in town. She told us that story about her sister."

Vergil nodded and tried to wave the smoke out of his eyes.

"Did they ever determine what actually happened to those kids?" Vicky asked.

"I heard they were high on angel dust," Rye said. "And they went crazy and jumped off a cliff or something."

Vergil shook his head. "Amber was a good kid. She'd gotten accepted into Gonzaga. Those boys might not've been the best influence, but she had a good head on her shoulders."

"Did they ever find any of the—you know—remains?" Vicky asked.

"Not that I heard of."

"So what's the explanation?" She pushed the camera in tighter on Vergil. "What really happened?"

"No one knows for sure," he said. "Other than three kids never came out of the woods."

A log on the fire popped. Everyone jumped as a handful of embers floated up and scattered.

"Most likely explanation is they got attacked by a bear or a mountain lion," Vergil said.

"Tammy said her sister described something that could be a Bigfoot."

"That's what I heard too," Jute chimed in without looking up from the equipment.

"Oh please," Bernard said, leaning back in his chair. "I guarantee they weren't attacked by a Bigfoot."

"How can you be so sure?" Vicky asked.

Bernard hesitated. He glanced around the campfire. "Because," he said, "there's never been a single documented case of a Bigfoot attacking humans."

"Not documented maybe," Vergil said. "But what about all the people who disappear in the woods every year? It could be Bigfoot and we'd have no way of knowing."

"Counterpoint"—Rye jumped in—"it could be people go missing because they're not prepared, and the woods are pretty dangerous even without Bigfoot in them."

No one said anything for a few moments. A light breeze made the flames gutter and hiss.

"One thing I can't figure out though," Rye said, turning to look at Vicky, "is how you knew that hunk of metal was a dirt bike."

Vicky wasn't sure how to answer the question.

Ignoring the fact that she'd read about those kids in a journal she'd essentially stolen from one of the people in her documentary (an ethical lapse that could damage the credibility of her film and possibly warrant expulsion from the film program), the truth was, Vicky had no idea what to even think. The journal could be fake—written and planted by one of these people. Perhaps with the idea of creating confusion, priming the pump for a bigger hoax later on. But if it *wasn't* fake—if it was indeed genuine—then what was happening here defied all explanation. Either way, Vicky decided it was in her best interest to keep the journal a secret until she knew more.

"I used to date a guy who rode dirt bikes," she lied. "Guess some of it must've rubbed off."

"Must have." Rye flexed a stick against the ground, but kept a wary gaze fixed on Vicky. Those enormous brown eyes felt to Vicky like they were boring into her, digging for the truth.

Vicky turned the camera to Vergil. "So you've all been Bigfoot hunting for how long?" It was the first question she could think of to deflect Rye's scrutiny.

"Technically it started when we were kids," Vergil said. "But we've been serious about it a little over twenty years now."

"And in that time," she went on, "you must have developed some theories about what Bigfoot is."

Vergil hesitated. "I'm what the Bigfoot community refers to as an Aper."

"What's an Aper?"

"Apers believe Bigfoot must be an actual flesh-and-blood creature, something between an ape and a human. Most of us subscribe to the relict hominoid theory."

"Please explain," Vicky said, zooming in tighter.

"The relict hominoid theory"—Vergil looked around the circle as if he needed permission to keep going—"holds that a small group of one of our distant ancestors—maybe *Gigantopithecus* or *Australopithecus*—somehow survived and evolved in various forests around the world. I prefer this theory because it doesn't contradict any known laws of nature. And doesn't give Bigfoot supernatural abilities. It's just a normal animal that happens to be very good at hiding."

Vicky held the shot on Vergil a few extra beats. "I thought all our nearest ancestors supposedly died out like a hundred thousand years ago," she said.

"Supposedly," he said.

"Yet somehow an eight-foot-tall, manlike creature managed to remain undetected in the forests of North America all this time?" Vicky pressed.

Vergil glanced at Bernard, hoping he'd jump in with an explanation that would support the theory's plausibility. But Bernard stared at the fire, picking his teeth with a toothpick.

"It *hasn't* been undetected." This came from Jute.

Vicky spun the camera to find him. The parabolic microphone equipment was spread across his lap. He peered at the camera over the lenses of his readers.

"Ask any of the Native American tribes," he went on. "Ask anyone who's ever had a personal encounter with one. For those people it's been *very* detected."

"But that doesn't count as—"

"Sure, sure, I get it," he said, waving his hand. "That's not scientific proof. But can the skeptics explain away hundreds of eyewitness sightings every year? You can't tell me those people are *all* crazy. And if a single one of those reports is accurate, then it's time to rewrite the science books. *And* the history books."

Jute plugged a few more cords into an electronic box, then flipped a switch and the device gave off a pleasant hum.

"Parabolic is set up," he said. "How do you propose we investigate, Dr. Bernard?"

Bernard shifted his weight in the director's chair. He gave his tooth-pick one last suck and flicked it into the fire. "I haven't done much research in these parts," he said, "so I'm here to learn from you."

The fire crackled. A log slid off the pile and a burst of flames leapt up.

"We usually start with a wood-knocking session," Vergil said. "To see if we've got any company nearby."

When no one raised an objection, he climbed the slope to Sas-quatch One and dug around in back. He returned a moment later with a well-used Louisville Slugger. He stepped up to a thick lodgepole and took a few practice cuts.

"Hold on." Vicky swooped in close with the camera. "Could you explain what wood knocking is, please?"

Vergil rested the bat on his shoulder. "It's believed among research-ers that wood knocks—like loud knocking on wood—are one way Bigfoot communicate with each other." He held the bat handle under his nose until he caught a whiff of pine tar. "So what we want to do," he said, "is send out a signal that we're here. And if we get a response, we'll know we've got company."

He twisted his grip on the bat.

"I'm sorry," Vicky said, "but wouldn't it make more sense to sneak up on them?"

Vergil stared into the camera lens for several seconds.

"Forgive my naïveté," she went on, "but if Sasquatches are so elusive that they've managed to stay hidden for thousands of years, wouldn't announcing our presence simply let all the locals know it's time to move on?"

"Well . . ." Vergil said. "I mean . . ." He glanced over his shoulder to see if someone wanted to bail him out.

"None of us are sneaking up on anything out here," Rye finally said. "Even an imaginary creature like Bigfoot would see us coming a mile away."

Jute slid the parabolic headphones over his ears and was instantly immersed in a lush soundscape of scurries and rustles, squeaks and trills. It felt like he was plugged into Nature itself, his consciousness reaching outward until it was hard to tell where the forest ended and he began.

"Parabolic's hot," he said.

Vergil cleared his throat. "Wood knock experiment number one, night one of the Basic Bigfoot Society's summer expedition."

He faced the tree, dug his feet into the pine needles, and choked up on the bat. Then he let it rip.

The first crack rang out through the forest, hollow and hard. Two more followed in quick succession. An electric sting traveled up the hickory into Vergil's hands, so intense he had to lean his bat against the tree and shake them out. Everyone else waited, breathless, listening.

Jute waved the parabolic dish across the woods until he heard what might have been a knock—barely there—in his headphones. He stopped sweeping the dish, zeroed in on the direction.

He waited.

There it was again. A hollow pop. Distinctive this time.

"Did anyone else hear that?" he whispered.

"Hear what?" Rye asked.

"A response," he said. "Another wood knock coming back."

"Probably just an echo," Bernard said.

"I think I heard it too," Vicky said.

"Which direction was it?" Vergil asked.

"There." Jute jabbed his finger and only then realized he was pointing directly toward the part of the forest his father had called the Whispering Woods, the area he'd warned him about going into.

"Why don't you send a scout team to investigate?" Bernard said.

"Honestly," Jute said, "it was pretty far away. I don't know if it's worth scouting."

"I'll go." Rye raised her hand.

"Me too," Vicky chimed in.

Jute let out a shallow sigh. "Okay," he said. "Anyone else want to join us?"

"Hold on." Dr. Bernard went back to the foldout table and unlatched one of the cases. He pulled out a large piece of equipment, snapped a few struts into place, tightened some levers. When he turned around, he revealed a drone the size of a manhole cover, with eight rotors mounted on four stout arms. Below its nose was a camera angled like a turret. "A gift from a fan who used to run covert ops for the CIA."

Jute let out a low whistle. "What do you got mounted on that thing, Doctor?"

"Fifth-generation FLIR mobile thermal imager. Not yet available to the general public." Bernard flipped a switch and a tiny blue light turned on near its lens. "Once we're airborne, this baby'll pick up the heat signature of anything in the forest." He handed a tablet to Vergil. "We can direct the Scout Team wherever they need to go."

Bernard flipped several more switches until the drone let out a series of beeps. He nudged a controller. The rotors whirred to life. The machine rose straight up into the air.

As the drone steadied itself above them, the forest began to take shape on a tablet screen. Every branch, every leaf, had definition. They could see the heat signatures of ground squirrels and raccoons. Twenty yards into the forest, a large bird, probably an owl looking for its first meal of the night, was perched on a branch. When he angled the turret downward, it picked up the red images of all five of them standing in the clearing, the campfire hottest of all nearby.

"Look at that," Jute marveled. "You could see if Bigfoot had a hang-nail with that thing."

"Night vision goggles are over there on the table," Bernard said. "GoPros too."

Jute and Rye picked up a pair of PVS-14 night vision monoculars, each one of which was worth more than Sasquatch One. Vicky declined a set, saying she'd use her camera's IR mode to find her way.

They fastened the straps on the GoPro cameras and tightened them up. When they were done, it looked like they each had a small parrot perched on their shoulder.

"Here's your walkie-talkies," Vergil said, handing them out to the Scout Team. "If something's throwing off a heat signature, we'll guide you right to it."

"Everyone ready?" Vergil asked, once they were geared up.

They all waited for someone else to answer in the affirmative, but no one did. So the Scout Team slipped silently into the dark woods, ready or not.

Vicky fell into position behind Jute and Rye, trying to keep them both in frame as they ventured through the forest.

Yesterday, in anticipation of night hunts, she'd practiced walking in the dark using her camera's infrared viewfinder. Navigating this way turned out to be a lot easier to do in the familiar terrain of her apartment than out here in the field, where even the tiniest exposed root posed a perilous, ankle-twisting obstacle.

For a while there, Vicky had been thinking this film might turn into a buddy comedy, with Jute and Vergil doing a sort of *Odd Couple* bit. Now that Rye was squarely in the mix, it had the potential to turn into more of a family drama. It was hard to tell though. The nature of this film kept shifting, morphing into something different the moment she thought she had it pinned down.

Rye was getting out too far ahead. The camera wasn't picking her up with all this ground clutter. Vicky forced herself to speed up. She had to muscle her way through the brush, camera jostled by unseen branches and limbs.

The farther they got from base camp the darker it got. Vicky's view of the world shrank to the size of her two-by-three-inch viewfinder. Beyond it, she felt the cold immenseness of the forest rippling out in all directions.

Vergil and Bernard hovered over the tablet, their faces illuminated blue by the shifting pixels. The heat blobs of Jute and Rye fanned out ahead, while Vicky pulled up the rear. The triangle of red amoebas moved with eerie inevitability across the screen, leaving ghostly thermograms of heat on the forest floor.

"Base Camp"—Jute's voice crackled through the walkie-talkie—"do you see anything worth pursuing on the thermal?"

"Negative," Vergil said into the radio. "Proceed with caution, Scout Team."

"Let's increase altitude," Bernard said to Vergil, "and see what else is out there."

He nudged a stick on his controller, and somewhere above them a nearly inaudible whine lifted an octave higher. The three red splotches on the screen got smaller, and the greens and blues of the forest got vaster. Vergil moved in close to study the screen.

Then he saw it. Another hit on the thermal. A fourth red blob that materialized out of nowhere.

Vergil glanced at Bernard to confirm he wasn't imagining it. When he saw Bernard's mouth fall open, he knew this wasn't a false alarm.

"Scout Team, we have a target!" The excitement in Vergil's voice was evident, despite the hiss of the walkie-talkie.

"Copy, Base Camp," Jute responded. "Tell us which direction to head."

"Uh . . . it looks like it's behind you, Scout Team."

"Come again, Base Camp?" Jute snapped. "Did you say *behind* us?"

Vicky's heart was hammering in her chest as the exchange played out on her radio. "Base Camp, what does it look like?" she jumped in.

"Hard to say, Scout Team. Rough guess, it's about the size of you guys."

Vicky couldn't believe her luck. Something was out here with them. Something alive, and big enough to warrant this level of excitement.

"We read you, Base Camp," Jute said. "Circling back to investigate."

Vicky could sense it too. Something was here. Something different from all the other normal harmless forest stuff. She closed her eyes and took a deep breath.

Why can't I do that? she whispered to herself. *Why can't I do this?*

Then she turned around.

. . .

Vergil stared at the tablet as three blobs converged on a fourth, unidentified blob.

"That's it, Scout Team," he said into the radio. "Keep going. It should be coming into view any second."

But the responses on the walkie-talkies were growing increasingly fragmented.

"—where are the—"

"—not this way—"

"—need an idea what—"

It wasn't just the radios that were acting up either. The tablet screen started getting snowy, like an old-fashioned TV that needed its antenna adjusted. Even the lantern flickered, giving off a strobe effect in the clearing.

"You should see it by now, Scout Team!" Vergil shouted. "You're practically on top of it!"

Then, right before his eyes, the fourth blob vanished. It didn't move or run away. It simply faded out until it was the same blue-green color as the rest of the forest, as if it had never been there.

Vicky stared at the tiny box of light on her camera, trying to spot something hiding in the woods. The infrared's grayscale made everything a creepy inverse of real life. But all she saw were trees and brush and rocks.

She switched off the viewfinder, tried to let her eyes adjust to the dark. For the first time, she paid attention to what she was hearing. Crickets, a couple owl hoots, water running in the distance. But no rustling. No footsteps. Nothing that would indicate something big was sharing the forest with them.

"Base Camp," Jute said, "you need to tell us which direction to head."

Vicky could hear him on her walkie-talkie, but also over her right shoulder. It was comforting to have him close by.

"Come in, Base Camp," she said into the radio. "Do you read, Base Camp?"

Static.

Hiss.

Then from Base Camp: "It's gone."

"It's *what*?"

"Scout Team, the target has disappeared. Were you able to get visual confirmation?"

"Negative, Base Camp." Rye's voice came through loud and clear on the radio. "We didn't see jack shit out here."

Chapter 18

All five expeditioners scooched closer to the campfire, watching the dying flames like they were the last grains of sand running through an hourglass.

As far as Rye was concerned, their "research" tonight had been nothing more than a high-tech snipe hunt. That's not to say it wasn't interesting, fun even. Dodging in and out of the trees with those night vision goggles on made her feel like some kind of action movie superhero. She understood why people wanted to do this. But after a certain point, the novelty had to wear off, right? What would possibly keep a smart, educated person like her father coming back, year after year, never finding a shred of evidence? It seemed like such a waste of time. Rye would never understand it.

"What were you guys seeing on the thermal?" Vicky asked. "You sounded pretty excited."

"Decent-size heat signature," Vergil said.

"What do you think it was?"

"Sometimes rocks or tree stumps will hold in heat from the day." Bernard was disassembling his drone at the foldout table. "Once night falls, those tend to stand out."

"Some people theorize Bigfoot know how to cloak themselves," Jute said, "which would explain why the heat signature disappeared like that."

"Hold up, is it Big*feet* or Big*foots*?" Vicky said. "I can't believe I only thought to ask that now."

Jute chuckled. "Vergil and I use the same for singular and plural. One Bigfoot, several Bigfoot. Like *deer-deer* or *moose-moose*."

"Is that the standard usage?" she asked.

"Bigfoot people can't agree on what day of the week it is," Bernard said, returning to his chair by the fire. "This whole field is like the Wild West."

"Okay, fine." Vicky turned the camera back to Jute. "Now, about this cloaking."

"I'm not talking high-tech, sci-fi cloaking," Jute said. "More like maybe they can alter their heat signatures as a way to evade detection."

"That's ridiculous, Uncle Jute," Rye said. "If that were the case they'd be the only creature on the planet with that ability."

"Chameleons can change their color to match their surroundings. Mollusks can change the texture of their skin. Would this be so different?"

"Actually, yes," Rye said. "It would be quite different."

The group fell silent.

Rye felt bad for calling Jute out like that. But sometimes his nonsense was too much to sit still for. "You know I love you," she added as a peace offering. "I just happen to think you're nuts."

"That's okay," he said, "I happen to think you smell funny."

"Oooh, sick burn, Uncle Jute. Sick burn."

Vicky was having a hard time cloaking her disappointment over the night's events. She could have sworn she'd felt something out there, a presence hiding in the forest, just beyond her camera's reach. As it turned out, the one thing she hadn't been ready for was the one thing she'd seen: nothing.

She took a fresh SD card from her case and popped it into the camera. Then she panned around the campfire. "What happens if you guys never find Bigfoot?" she asked. "Like, not just on this trip, but ever."

"Nothing," Vergil said. "If we don't find Bigfoot, nothing happens."

Vicky pushed the shot back on him. "Okay, you got me," she said. "Then what happens if you *do* find Bigfoot?"

"Now, that's a much better question." He reached out and turned a log on the fire, momentarily causing a flame to cast shadows across his face. "Nothing," he said at last. "Nothing happens if we find Bigfoot."

"Is that supposed to be some kind of Zen riddle?" she asked.

Vergil shook his head. "Short of bringing back an actual specimen, no amount of evidence will convince the world Bigfoot exists. When you sign up for this business, you have to be okay with that."

"How is that possible?" Vicky was surprised by how loud her own voice was.

Vergil smiled. "Are you familiar with Albert Camus's essay on Sisyphus?"

"In passing," she said. "Which is to say I've heard of it."

"But you know about Sisyphus, yes?"

"The boulder guy," she said.

Vergil nodded. He leaned back and stretched his feet toward the fire. "So Sisyphus made the gods mad, and his punishment was to roll a boulder up a hill. The catch was, whenever he reached the top, the boulder would roll back down to the bottom. Every time. He had to start over again and again and again. But when Camus read that story, he didn't choose to see it as a punishment. Rolling that boulder up the hill, knowing full well what the outcome would be—he saw that as an act of defiance, of courage."

Vicky kept the camera fixed on Vergil's face, the campfire dancing in his eyes as he stared at it.

"And according to Camus, if you *really* wanted to make the gods mad, you should be *happy* in the punishment, find *joy* in it."

A log toppled over, exposing the raw, red embers underneath. Heat poured off it in waves.

"I remember you made me read that essay," Rye said. "I must've been like twelve."

Vergil looked over at his daughter. "Back when you still hung out with your old man in the library."

Rye snorted and tossed a stick into the flames. It quickly caught fire and turned into ash.

"That Sisyphus stuff is all fine and dandy," Jute said. "But I wouldn't mind staying at the top of the hill for a while. At least enjoy the view for a little bit." He looked over at Vicky. "Did you check the footage you shot? Maybe you caught something you didn't see the first time."

"Frame by frame," she said. "Three times."

Jute shrugged. "I don't need proof to tell me something's out here," he said. "I can feel it. And it's only a matter of time before we cross its path."

"Big day tomorrow," Vergil said, creakily standing up and patting his jeans. "Probably time to hit the hay."

He picked up a yellow bucket and swirled what was left at the bottom. "Looks like we'll need the last of this water to douse the fire," he said. "Any volunteers to get us a refill before bed?"

They all listened to the sound of the creek, distantly roaring on the other side of the Russian olive thicket. And they recalled the rusted-out motorcycle they'd found. Regardless of how it happened, three people had lost their lives out here. Which made the thought of filling the water buckets in the dark decidedly less appealing.

"On second thought," Vergil finally said, giving voice to what they all were thinking, "it can probably wait until morning."

The silence broke as everyone exhaled. They stood and stretched and yawned.

Vergil tipped the water bucket over the last of the flames. The embers sent off a chorus of hisses and pops as steam shot up into the night. The darkness, unchecked now, raced into the clearing and chased them all to their tents.

Chapter 19

Rye squirmed after she climbed into her sleeping bag, trying to find a comfortable spot on the hard, uneven ground. As the adrenaline from the forest jaunt wore off, and sleep began to fuzz the edges of her brain, her thoughts returned once again to her dad's illness, and the season of loss that loomed.

Rye used to think her tears were stored in a reservoir of sadness right behind her eyes. When she was growing up, she was afraid to wear swimming goggles in case something made her cry, and all that sadness would get trapped against her eyes. After her mother died, Rye was sure she'd cried that reservoir dry, emptied out every drop for good. What would she do now, she wondered, with a new season of loss on the way?

None of these thoughts were going to help her get any rest. She needed a distraction before her brain spun up and made it impossible to sleep. Rye turned onto her side, facing Vicky.

"Hey," she whispered.

Vicky didn't move, not even a flicker of her eyelids.

"Are you awake?"

It was no good. Her tentmate was either deeply asleep or deeply committed to ignoring her.

Rye rolled onto her back again and listened to Vicky's breathing—slow, steady, peaceful. She tried to sync their respiration. In, out, in, out—at the same time. After a moment, their chests were rising and falling in unison. Rye felt the tension in her brain unravel a little. Would their heartbeats fall in line too? Was that a thing that happened? She should probably know this after all the biology classes she'd taken.

As sleep began to overtake her, she opened her hearing up further. The forest sounds came to her in layers. At the bottom was the roar of the nearby creek, as constant as a white noise machine. Above that, trees creaked and clacked; pine needles whispered secrets to each other. On the surface, all the usual night creatures—owls, field mice, bats, raccoons—fluttered and scuttled and scurried as they went about their business. A lifetime of camping in the Elkhorns had accustomed Rye to this soundtrack, as familiar and comforting as a lullaby.

But then she heard something different. A short whoop that cut through the other layers. Coyotes were the most obvious source. They made all kinds of crazy noises, though she wasn't familiar with that one.

Rye held her breath, lifted her head off the ground.

There it was again. Louder this time.

The rest of the sound layers dampened, as if the forest had taken a deep breath and held it. Rye lay there motionless, ears straining to hear more.

And then she *did* hear more.

The moss-dampened timpani of a footfall. Heavy enough she could feel it vibrate the ground underneath her.

Rye's throat went tight. She tried to spot a silhouette against the tent wall, but it was too dark outside for shadows.

She told herself to chill out. This kind of thing happened all the time. She'd been in a tent when deer, elk, even moose walked through her camp. A black bear once too. As long as they'd strung up all their food—which they had—everything would be fine. Nothing to worry about whatsoever.

The footfalls outside grew more regular. The creature was moving between the tents, snuffling. Rye slowly craned her neck until she caught sight of the bear spray down by her feet. Getting it now would take too much time, make too much noise.

She'd been holding her breath for a while, and her chest was about to burst. She slowly let it out, trying not to make a sound.

The footsteps paused, then started moving toward her. They came right up to the other side of the tent wall and stopped. An animal heat radiated through the fabric.

Rye waited for what felt like hours.

Then a slight indentation formed on the tent wall, a quick poke that disappeared almost instantly, followed by a startled snort.

Rye's face tingled. Her ears itched. She gripped the edges of her sleeping bag so hard her knuckles hurt.

A moment later the indentation appeared again. This time it didn't go away. It grew wider, deeper.

It was one thing for an animal to be curious. This was something more, something intentional, provocative even.

The tent fabric started to make a ticking sound as it tightened. Rye tried to picture how she might get her arms out of her sleeping bag and lunge for the bear spray. She'd have to unzip the bag first, which would add so much extra time to the procedure. And if the zipper happened to get stuck—which this one did all the time—forget it; she'd be toast.

The tent pole started to bend as the indentation deepened. At some point the fabric would rip apart like string cheese. By then this thing would practically be on top of her—too late for Rye to do anything about it.

Her hands were sweating. Her face burned. She needed to take action. First, she'd try for the bear spray. If that didn't work, she'd have to fight this thing off with her bare hands. They said you were supposed to go for the eyes in these situations. That might at least buy her some time.

The indentation was pressing even harder. She couldn't wait any more. She'd give herself a three-count.

One.

Two.

Thr—

The indentation started to recede. The tent pole sprang back. One more huffing breath on the other side of the wall. Then the footsteps trailed off.

A moment later, another whoop rang out from somewhere deeper in the forest. After that, the normal nighttime soundtrack picked up where it left off.

Rye finally allowed herself to uncoil. She'd never had a sustained wildlife encounter like this before. Never this close, this personal.

It should've been impossible to sleep after that. But to her surprise, the opposite turned out to be true. Rye closed her eyes, her breathing fell back into rhythm with Vicky's, and she was out before she had a chance to ask herself what that thing had been.

Chapter 20

Vicky woke to the first rays of light bleeding into the tent. She'd managed to enjoy a deep, dreamless sleep, but now the screws in her mind began to tighten.

Time for a serious level-set on this film project. So far she'd seen some interesting things, hung out with a couple strange dreamers, and shot some beautiful scenery. Yet she didn't feel any closer to figuring out what kind of story she was trying to tell. Sometimes she pictured her film like it was a puzzle box. If she could only find the right hidden panel to slide, or secret button to push, the whole thing would open up and reveal itself to her.

Vicky pulled the green journal from her backpack and began leafing through it, looking for a clue that might jog an idea loose. The entries had an uncanny ability to suck her in, as if they were casting a spell. The second she started reading them, she felt herself slipping into these other stories, other adventures and calamities, until she hardly knew who or where she was anymore.

Rye woke to the sounds of her father priming the gas line on the stove. A moment later the dull hiss of the burner whispered through camp. Which meant he must've already filled up the water buckets. Rye was supposed to have done that this morning so he could conserve his energy for today's hike.

The least she could do now was get her ass out of bed to help him fix breakfast. But everything in the tent was covered with a layer of icy dew, and Rye hated climbing out of her warm sleeping bag in the mornings. She decided to give herself five more minutes' reprieve. Then she rolled over to check on her tentmate. To her surprise, Vicky was already awake, nose buried in an old green book.

"What are you reading?" Rye asked, her voice coming out louder than she'd intended.

Vicky slammed the book shut. "It's a . . . shot log," she said. "Helps me keep track of my footage. For when it's time to go back and edit."

"Don't stop reading on my account."

"It's fine," she said. "I was just finishing up." Vicky stowed the book in the rear pocket of her backpack and pulled out her camera. The red record light snapped on.

"Hey, no fair!" Rye pulled her sleeping bag over her face. "I just woke up."

"You look fine," Vicky said. "Top-notch bedhead."

Rye felt herself blushing.

Outside, birds were chirping. Vergil tapped a spoon on the coffee-pot as he added the grounds.

"I know you were passed out last night," Rye said, glancing around the tent to see where her clothes were, "but did you happen to hear anything weird?"

"Like what?" Vicky asked.

"Like . . . an animal or something."

"What kind of animal?"

"Not sure," Rye said. "Big though. As far as I could tell."

A tremor rippled across Vicky's face.

"Probably a deer wandering through camp," Rye said, brushing it off. "Happens all the time."

"But you definitely heard *something*?"

"It wasn't Bigfoot," Rye said, "if that's what you're worried about."

Vicky sat up and readjusted the camera on Rye. "Can I ask why you're so dismissive of this Bigfoot stuff?"

Rye let out a sharp laugh. "Really?"

"What?" Vicky said. "I'm being serious."

Out in the camp kitchen, Vergil opened a series of Tupperware containers. Each one gave off a satisfying pneumatic snap.

"I feel like it's my duty as a filmmaker to get everyone on record about this," Vicky said, her forehead furrowed. "Do you believe in Bigfoot?"

Even though she'd already been asked, Rye was momentarily taken aback by the directness of the question. It reminded her of the time her lab partner had looked up in the middle of cramming for a chemistry final and asked, point-blank, if Rye had accepted Jesus Christ as her Lord and Savior. Meanwhile, up until that moment, Rye had been mostly concerned with getting up the nerve to kiss the girl. Rye's response at the time had been to laugh so hard she dropped her textbook on the floor. And the two of them never studied together again.

"No," Rye said, meeting Vicky's eyes across the tent. "I do not believe in Bigfoot."

"You seem pretty sure of yourself."

"Don't get me wrong," Rye said. "Do I think the world would be a better place if things like Bigfoot or the Loch Ness Monster were running around in it? Sure. But I've seen pretty solid evidence that the world *isn't* a good place. At all. So in a way I'm glad they don't exist. Because they deserve a better world than this one."

Vicky glanced down at the camera. "Then why are you here?" she asked. "Why come on this Bigfoot expedition at all?"

"Honestly?" Rye fiddled with her sleeping bag zipper. "I want to make sure my dad and Uncle Jute get a fair shake from you."

Vicky nodded. "I can respect that," she said. "But I'm still trying to make a movie."

Rye unzipped her sleeping bag so she could start acclimating to the cold. "As long as we're asking questions this morning," she said, "can I ask what you're hoping to accomplish with this film of yours?"

Vicky started to say something, hesitated, then cleared her throat. "It's hard to know what a project is about until it's done."

"No, I mean, what are your *ambitions*? Like what do you hope happens once you're finished?"

"Oh," Vicky said. "No one's ever asked me that before." She squinted across the narrow space between them. "This project will be my graduate thesis. So assuming everything goes okay, I'll get my MFA at the end of the year."

"And then what?" Rye reached out and gathered a pile of clothes onto her lap. "What do you want to be when you grow up?"

Vicky hitched her head to the side. "I want to tell stories, I guess. Like real, interesting stories about real, interesting people. I know that sounds superbasic or clichéd or whatever, but that's it really."

Rye nodded, satisfied. "It sounds like you've got things figured out."

Both women searched each other with their eyes, as if each was just now seeing the other for the first time.

"San Francisco State's a good school," Vicky said. "I'm not sure if I gave that impression earlier. You should still go there if you can."

"Maybe," Rye said. "We'll see." She ripped open her sleeping bag, and the exposed skin on her legs goose bumped.

"Whoa." Vicky pointed at Rye's knee. "What happened there?"

Rye traced the jagged scar running down her kneecap. "Basically blew out my whole knee playing soccer."

"That looks awful."

"Gee, thanks."

"No . . . I mean it looks like it must've been painful."

"It was gnarly," Rye said. "Most knee surgery scars are pretty small these days. Little arthroscopic dots, basically. But mine was so bad they had to really get in there to fix it."

She pulled a pair of hiking pants out from the bundle of clothes. "Do you have any scars?" she asked.

"Not really," Vicky said. "No."

Rye wriggled into her hiking pants, zipped and buttoned them.

"Maybe that means I haven't taken enough risks in my life," Vicky mused.

"Well, you're here, in the middle of nowhere, with a bunch of weirdos, looking for Bigfoot." Rye pulled a clean T-shirt over her head. "I'd say that constitutes a pretty big risk." She loosely braided her hair and snapped a rubber band on the end of it. "I'm going to go help my dad," she said. "Breakfast'll be ready in a few."

Then she crawled through the tent flap and zipped it closed behind her.

A small campfire trickled smoke into the crisp morning air. Vergil was squatting in front of the camp stove, eyeing the pot of water he'd set on to boil. When he saw Rye, he stood and took a step toward her, but his knee buckled and he doubled over.

"Daddy!" She rushed to him.

"I'm fine."

"No, you're *not* fine," Rye said.

Vergil did a thing with his face where his mouth frowned but his eyes smiled.

Rye looked around the campsite. "Where's Dr. Bernard and Uncle Jute?"

"Sleeping still," he said. "Should be up soon."

The water on the stove reached a boil.

"How was . . ." He tilted his head toward her tent.

"Fine." She shrugged noncommittally.

"Water should be ready now." Vergil turned the heat down to a simmer. "Who wants oatmeal?" he intoned with an old-timey TV father voice.

Rye did a sarcastic halfway hand raise.

"Let me guess," he said. "Apple and cinnamon?"

She made an exaggerated frowny face.

This was a bit they'd honed over the course of countless camping trips, the whole thing as scripted as a Japanese tea ceremony.

"You don't want *plain* oatmeal, do you?"

She frowned even more deeply and drooped her shoulders. Even if Rye didn't feel like playing along, nostalgia alone compelled her.

"Oh . . . That's right," he said. "You're my maple-and-brown-sugar daughter."

She produced a sweet smile, and Vergil pulled a pouch from the

Tupperware container. It was a silly skit, but the ritual connected them to something larger. Camping had always been a refuge, the one place father and daughter could connect, even after she quit coming to the library, even when they were at each other's throats in every other facet of their lives. This was their first camping trip since Melody had died. And Rye now realized it might be their last.

She spooned some oatmeal into her mouth and tried to savor it. They both watched the morning sun creep red, then pink over the clearing, warming the dew, releasing thin wisps of steam from the forest floor.

"There's so much beauty in the world," Vergil said out of nowhere. "Isn't there?"

Rye looked up from the bowl. Her father was staring at her, his face taut with concern.

"You're crying." He tore a paper towel off the roll and folded it twice before handing it to her.

Rye blotted the tears from her cheeks. After her mother had died, she could have sworn she'd emptied that reservoir of sadness behind her eyes. Turned out she'd been wrong.

Chapter 21

After a quick breakfast, they pulled together all the gear they'd need for the Ramsey Lake excursion. Even though Jute made sure the heaviest stuff wound up in his own pack, Vergil's load still made his legs wobble. The illness was so apparent now. Gaunt face, eyes bulging. Jute couldn't believe he hadn't seen it before.

"You going to be okay carrying that?" he asked, trying not to henpeck.

"I'll manage fine," Vergil said. "You just worry about getting us to Ramsey Lake."

Once they were packed, the group gathered near the western edge of the clearing.

"Okay," Jute said. "I hope everyone's ready to do some hiking."

"Let's get the coordinates for where we're headed," Bernard said, pulling a GPS locator from his vest pocket.

"I don't have the exact coordinates," Jute admitted.

Bernard's brow furrowed.

"Last time I was there GPS hadn't been invented."

Bernard pushed up the brim of his fedora. "You're telling me we're going off-trail, into the backcountry, and you don't have coordinates?"

"We're headed toward that mountain over there," Jute said. "The shorter one with the hollow-looking top."

Everyone steered their gaze to where Jute was pointing.

"Our lake is near the summit."

"I'm sorry," Bernard said. "Then why does it look like you're about to have us head east?"

Jute thought about showing him the map tucked into the side pocket of his backpack. But a map with no markings, and no legend, whose provenance Jute couldn't explain, probably wouldn't do much to reassure him. "The direct route's too dangerous" was all he could come up with.

Bernard looked around to see if anyone else found this alarming.

"If you don't think you can handle it, Doctor"—Vergil jumped in— "by all means stay back here while the rest of us go find Bigfoot."

Jute was grateful for his friend's intervention. But Bernard had a point. The truth was, Jute remembered very little about the hike they were about to attempt. The only landmarks between here and the hollow-peaked mountain were the scree field and the egg-shaped meadow. From their location at the edge of the wide-open forest, with no trails or markers to guide them, the task of finding either of those waypoints—let alone Ramsey Lake—seemed more daunting than ever.

At 8:45 they filed out of base camp. Jute was in the lead, then Vicky, followed by Rye and Dr. Bernard. Vergil brought up the rear, claiming he'd taken that position to protect the group from wildlife, but Jute knew it was because his friend didn't want to slow the rest of them down.

The game trails were sporadic and meandering. When those disappeared, Jute tried to steer the group through sparser portions of the forest, all the while keeping a close eye on his compass, bearing due east. A bullet heading blindly toward its target.

It was hard watching Dr. Bernard belittle Jute like that, even though it was a pattern Vergil had seen play out often enough. Someone with a weak ego always felt the need to humiliate him. Never mind that Jute was big enough to physically dismantle most anyone who crossed his path.

Of course, Jute would never do anything like that. He had the kindest heart of any person Vergil had ever known. And the fact that people felt like they could tear him down was proof positive there was something fundamentally wrong with the world. Vergil worried what would happen to Jute when he was gone, when there was one less person to run interference on the forces of meanness.

Taking a group this size into this kind of terrain was always going to be a challenge. Bushwhacking through virgin forest took up lots of energy, demanded incredible patience. Frequently, when the branches and brambles got too thick, they had to backtrack to find an easier route. But the slower pace helped Vergil, who would not have been able to keep up otherwise. Even still, sometimes the others got far enough ahead that they disappeared for long stretches, until eventually Jute would call for a water break, which enabled Vergil to catch up.

Hiking alone, with only the sound of his own heartbeat, his own breathing to keep him company, Vergil found himself contemplating, in a very specific sense, how it would all end for him. Oddly enough, he found that he wasn't afraid of dying. It would be more accurate to say he was curious about it. To his mind, one of two things would likely happen. Either the lights would switch off and that would be it, or else there'd be the classic bright light, long tunnel to something or someplace else. He wasn't sure which theory he believed and wasn't looking forward to finding out which one was correct. But he at least found it interesting to consider.

Up ahead, Rye was snapping photos of tricky spots on the trail, like forks or sudden turns. Long ago Vergil had taught her to remember those spots—burn them into her brain—to help find her way back on a trail she was unfamiliar with. Using her phone was smarter though. Left a lot less to chance and the fickleness of memory.

Rye, of course, would insist on moving back to Basic when the illness took hold. She'd micromanage every aspect of his decline. Vergil would fight her on that, but he knew there'd be no stopping her. The only thing he could hope for was a quick battle, so his daughter didn't get stuck there, so she could get back to the life she was meant to lead.

His T-shirt was soaked. The backpack straps bit into his shoulders. He hadn't seen anyone ahead of him for several minutes. Maybe longer. He scanned the ground for tracks, a partial boot print or even some knocked-over brush to let him know he was still on the right path, but he saw no trace of the others.

Vergil spun right, left. The trees seemed to swirl around him. Normally he had an excellent sense of direction in the woods. But something about this forest kept disorienting him.

Panic started to climb up through his spine. He forced himself to stop, to be present and pay attention. That was when he heard a commotion ahead. Popping twigs. Footsteps. The junipers in front of him started to sway. Vergil put his hand on the bear spray canister hanging at his hip.

The brush parted to reveal Rye, looking worried. "There you are," she said. "We found a spot where we can rest."

The group had stopped in a small clearing littered with heavy stones. The ground was covered in tall grasses, the first shoots of which were starting to turn green.

A cold morning had given way to a warm afternoon. Vicky's skin was sticky, coated with a layer of grit and sweat. She took a long swig from her water bottle and shook what was left at the bottom. They'd crossed numerous streams where she could have refilled, but Jute had warned her that giardia was still a real concern, even this high up, so they'd have to either boil or purify anything they planned to drink.

Vergil distributed sandwiches and granola bars from his pack. Everyone scattered across the clearing and found a rock to perch on. Vicky set her camera on the ground to unwrap her sandwich. She wolfed down the first half in three bites. Then decided she'd better go slower with the second half to make it last longer.

She glanced around the clearing. Walled off by tall trees on all sides, it was darker here, with small patches of light streaming through. The place felt secluded, private even.

Vicky looked down and realized her attempt at eating the second half of her sandwich more slowly had been unsuccessful. At least she still had her granola bar, which she decided to save for later. To avoid thinking about the gnawing hunger in her stomach, she picked up the camera and began gathering more footage. She panned across the large stones strewn throughout the grassy open space. She lingered on each of the expeditioners for a moment. Everyone was focused on their food, unaware of the fact Vicky was filming them.

Maybe this project would turn out to be more of a nature documentary. A series of pretty outdoor shots spliced together, with an undertone of spirituality thrown in to give it a kind of paradise lost vibe. She wasn't sure what category that would have gotten shelved under at Jingletown Video. Probably something like Pretty but Pretentious.

Vicky strolled through the clearing and started to do more voice-over.

"The trail—if that's what you want to call what we're on—is almost nonexistent," she intoned. "Every step is contested, arduous. But this journey into the unknown feels ineluctable. We are willing pilgrims drawn by an unseen force, deeper into the heart of this primeval forest."

She let the camera refract on a shaft of afternoon light, causing a lens flare that would look either supercool or superdistracting later on.

"Something in me believes that Nature itself senses our presence," she went on. "I can hear it when the birds and squirrels fall silent on the trail as we approach. Then quickly resume their chatter as we plod past."

She paused to let the microphone pick up the ambient noises in the clearing.

"Even the trees seem to judge us, inconvenienced as they are by our presence."

Vicky went to the edge of the clearing and shot into the forest.

"Are these woods home to an eight-foot primate?" she wondered out loud. "Do they shelter a legend that's been living here since long before any of us arrived? Some believe; some don't. But none of us knows for certain. Maybe Bigfoot is a Rorschach test—less about what's out there, and more about what's inside each of us."

Vicky turned the camera in a slow circle. She stopped when she reached a patch of sun falling amid a grove of aspen. Stirrings of a caddis fly hatch floated aimlessly in the sunlight. Dozens at first, then hundreds. Each one illuminated, each one its own pinprick of light. Vicky moved in closer. They looked like spinning constellations, like a whole crazy galaxy. The way they fluttered in chaotic orbits, never once colliding with each other, felt miraculous somehow.

"Perhaps there's a better question we should be asking," she said after a few moments. "Does the forest really *need* an undiscovered, mythical creature roaming around in it? Isn't the world magical enough just the way it is?"

A breeze picked up and the caddis flies scattered. Vicky was about to stop recording and start working on that granola bar when she heard Rye shout:

"Hey, what the hell is this?"

Rye was kneeling next to one of the rocks in the clearing.

"This thing has writing on it." She leaned in and pried off a thick plait of moss. " 'Stephen Owens,' " she read. " 'Nineteen forty-seven.' "

Vicky pulled back the shot. From this angle, she could see the stones were laid out in rows, columns. Not a perfect grid, but clearly symmetrical.

Rye crawled over to another rock. " 'Clyde W——' " she said. "No date on this one."

"It's a graveyard," Vicky said.

" 'M. Vertreace, 1873,' " Rye called out from another rock.

"Technically that would make this a cemetery," Vergil said.

"What's the difference?" Vicky asked.

"A graveyard is attached to a church," he said. "A cemetery isn't."

Everyone looked around for a moment, as if they half expected to find a church looming in the trees nearby.

"Okay," Vicky said. "Then it's a cemetery."

"It could be from one of the old mining encampments," Bernard said. "Plenty of people died out here. And they had to do something with all the bodies."

Vicky felt a chill at the base of her neck when she thought of all the people in the green journal who didn't make it out of these woods. Could some of them be buried here? And if so, would that prove the green journal was genuine?

Rye tore a skin of dead vines off another gravestone. "Weird," she said, peering closer. "This one isn't in English."

"What does it say?" Jute asked.

"No, it's like . . ." She brushed it off, dug her fingers into the lettering to clean it out. "It's not in our *alphabet.*"

Vicky stood behind Rye and zoomed in on the characters, which looked like a cross between runes and hieroglyphics.

"Dr. Bernard, do you know what kind of writing this is?" she asked.

He came in close and squinted. "Can't say I'm familiar with it," he said. "Though languages were never my specialty."

"Do you remember seeing this place when you came here with your dad?" Vergil asked.

Jute shook his head, then turned in a slow circle, hands on hips. "You know," he said, "a surprising number of Bigfoot sightings take place in and around cemeteries."

"They do?" Vicky asked.

"I can think of at least thirty different reports I've read on the databases."

"Why is that?"

"Almost every Native American tribe believes Bigfoot is as much a spiritual creature as it is a physical one," he said. "So the theory is cemeteries, by their very nature, are places where you can have one foot in both worlds."

"*Or,*" Vergil said, "it could simply be they're attracted to cemeteries because deer come to them for the grass. And most experts believe deer make up a substantial portion of the Bigfoot diet."

"Spoken like a true Aper," Jute said.

Vicky turned the camera to Dr. Bernard to see if he wanted to weigh in on the two opposing theories. But he was staring at the gravestone with the strange markings. He looked lost, eyes jumpy, like he might be afraid.

"It's getting late," Jute said, glancing up at the sky. "Anyone want to make a motion we camp here tonight and conduct a more thorough investigation?"

"So moved," Vergil said, almost immediately.

Chapter 22

An emergency review of the bylaws conducted by the executive board determined that each member of the party was allowed to vote on major expedition decisions, even if they weren't actual BBS members. Furthermore, it was ruled that the motion to spend the night investigating the area around the cemetery did in fact constitute a major expedition decision.

In the end, the motion passed unanimously, and without debate.

A campfire was now going strong while the sky darkened around them. Out of respect for the dead, they'd pitched their tents on the western edge of the cemetery, as far from the graves as possible. Dinner was freeze-dried pouches of beef stroganoff or chicken and rice. Afterward everyone sat on logs staring at the fire, waiting for it to get dark enough to start investigating.

Spending the night here would mean a whole extra day before they reached Ramsey Lake. Jute wasn't thrilled about the delay, but the moment he saw that strange writing on the grave markers, he knew this area must be important somehow.

"I have to admit something," he said, staring into the flames. "I've seen writing like that before. A year after my dad disappeared, I found all these old books and maps he'd stashed in the attic. I didn't pay much attention to them at the time. But there were these papers filled with that writing."

"Are you sure it was the same?" Vergil asked. "That was a long time ago, buddy."

Jute nodded without taking his eyes off the fire.

"Did your dad know any foreign languages?" Vicky asked.

"He taught himself Latin when he was a kid," Jute said. "And he could get by in Spanish. But nothing like that."

"These old mining camps out west had immigrants from all over," Bernard said, working a toothpick between his teeth. "That writing is probably some script we're not familiar with. Russian or . . . I don't know . . . an Asian language maybe."

"It's possible your dad saw those gravestones when he came here as a kid," Vergil added. "And he was always a naturally curious guy, so maybe he copied down some of the writing in order to figure out where it was from."

Everyone nodded their agreement—even the ones who never knew Luther Ramsey III—because it was the only explanation that seemed to make sense.

A cold wind swept through the cemetery and blew against the back of Rye's neck. She'd situated herself so she was facing away from the gravestones because looking at them was a grim reminder of both her recent past and her possibly near future. And she was trying not to think about either right now.

"So whatever happened to your father?" Vicky asked.

Rye stifled a groan. She'd heard Uncle Jute tell his Ramsey Lake story dozens of times and knew this kind of question had a tendency to send him down a dark hole.

"There's not much to tell," Jute said. "We went camping at Ramsey Lake. He must've seen something, and it messed him up."

"What did he see?"

Jute shrugged. "I can't say. But when I woke up the next morning our gear was strung up in those trees, ten feet off the ground. And I only know one thing that could do that."

Rye was impressed at how well he was holding it together. Usually this story took a lot longer to tell, and he would at least have the sniffles by now.

"Once we got home," Jute went on, "he was a changed man. Never really fit in anymore. Drank a lot. Couldn't keep a job. A couple years later he went missing. They found his Jeep parked up near his favorite fishing hole on Hell Creek. Probably been there a couple weeks. People figured he'd been drunk-fishing and fell in. Others said it was maybe suicide. Who knows?"

"I never heard you tell that part before, Uncle Jute."

"What part?"

"The stuff about what happened to him afterwards," Rye said. "The fishing stuff. I didn't know about that."

"It was a long time ago," he said. "Before you were born."

Rye stood up and wrapped her arms around Jute, hugging him tight about the neck. He smelled like campfire and mosquito repellent, and tears welled up in her eyes.

"I think it's dark enough to start investigating now," Vergil suggested.

Rye sat back down and pulled on her hoodie. "Don't you think it's disrespectful to do this in a cemetery?" she said. "These are human beings."

"She's right," Jute said. "We shouldn't investigate inside the cemetery. We'll do a perimeter sweep of the forest surrounding it. Two groups, opposite directions, forming a pincer movement. We'll alternate vocalizations back and forth."

"What are vocalizations?" Vicky asked.

"It's where we imitate Bigfoot calls," he explained, "in the hopes of flushing one out."

"Does anyone really know what a Bigfoot call sounds like?"

"For sure," Jute said. "They've even got different types." He looked into the camera and shifted his weight unsteadily. "You've got your classic Ohio Howl. And of course the Michigan Night Moan."

"There's the Sierra Sounds," Vergil threw in. "And the Eastern Washington Warble."

"And then besides that, they're known to do whoops."

"Hold on," Vicky said. "Are those really *real*?"

"It's all speculation," Rye said, brushing off thoughts about the whoops she'd heard last night, and the thing pressing against their tent.

"No, these are actual recordings," Jute said.

"And don't forget about whistles," Vergil added. "They can definitely whistle."

"And some researchers believe Bigfoot can even imitate other animals, or people's voices," Jute said.

"So you're saying Bigfoot can sound like anything?" Vicky said.

"Sort of, yes," he said. "But different too, like always off just a little bit."

"And how do you know which sounds the Bigfoot around here will respond to?" Vicky asked.

Jute and Vergil looked at each other, both at a loss.

"I think," Rye jumped in, "she's asking how you know which dialect these Bigfoot speak."

Bernard let out a sharp laugh and tossed his toothpick into the fire. He'd been strangely aloof so far on this expedition, hesitant to participate or even speculate on anything Bigfoot related. If Rye didn't know any better, she'd say he was as big a skeptic as she was.

"That's not what I meant," Vicky said.

"I know what you meant." Jute's face grew serious. "That time I was a kid we heard something I call the Elkhorn Wail."

"The night your campsite got torn up?"

Jute nodded gravely.

"What does *that* sound like?"

"You'll hear it tonight," he said.

"How about we stop talking and get on with it," Bernard suggested as he started pulling the gear from his pack. "Rye, Vergil, and I will be in one group," he said. "Vicky, you can go with Jute, so you get a chance to witness this so-called Elkhorn Wail firsthand." He looked around. "Unless you think we need to take a vote on that too."

Everyone except Vicky donned night vision goggles and GoPros before heading to the southern edge of the clearing, where they ventured twenty yards deep into the forest. The foliage here was so thick they could no longer see the campfire.

"Each group will work the perimeter side by side," Jute said. "Stop every five minutes for a call and response."

The two groups parted, one moving clockwise, the other counter-clockwise around the cemetery. They pushed through the trees, stealthily climbing over rocks and roots, ducking under branches and boughs. What had been difficult during daylight was nearly impossible at night, even with the help of the night vision goggles.

Much like his daughter, Vergil found it morbid to search for Bigfoot near a cemetery. He'd only supported the motion because he wasn't going to last much longer on the trail today. It was more than pain he felt. It was physical exhaustion, his body brushing up against the limits of what it had left to give.

"Team One." Jute's voice crackled over the walkie-talkie. "Stand by for an Elkhorn Wail."

Vergil, Rye, and Bernard stopped walking. "Team Two, proceed with vocalization," Vergil replied.

The three of them stood stock-still, holding their breath so they could hear better.

Jute's howl started off quiet. Then it slowly built in intensity, until his voice cracked and broke nearly into a shout. It was the same call he always did on these expeditions, the closest he could come to approximating what he'd heard as a child with his father.

When it was done, and his voice had faded into the night, Vergil looked at the others. "Who wants to respond?"

Rye and Bernard both simultaneously pointed back at Vergil.

"Fine." He pressed the talk button on his radio. "Team Two, stand by for response."

"Awaiting vocalization, Team One."

Vergil stuffed the radio into his pocket. He cupped his hands to his mouth and drew in a deep breath. Before he could cut loose, he heard something in the distance. A sound that started low and mournful, but climbed and kept climbing until it was a clarion howl that shook the trees.

When it stopped, the forest went deathly still.

"Team Two," Vergil sputtered into the walkie-talkie, "was that you doing a second vocalization?"

"You mean that wasn't *you*?"

A chill lodged itself between Vergil's shoulder blades. With shaky fingers he pressed the talk button on his radio. "You guys," he said, "I don't think we're alone out here."

Once they'd set up camp, Vicky had gone around to each of the grave-stones, checking the names against anyone specifically mentioned in the green journal. Somehow she wasn't surprised when she found a match: Cabot 1932. He was the timber surveyor who'd been dragged from his tent in the night, whose body was later found suspended in the branches of a bristlecone pine tree.

Ever since then, Vicky had been trying to reason through what could be happening here. It was possible Jute and Vergil came to this spot beforehand, found all these strange things like that dirt bike and this graveyard and fabricated a bunch of wild tales, which they then wrote down in an old-looking journal. With a little sleight of hand, they could've easily made Vicky think she'd discovered the journal by accident in his front yard. Then they trotted out a couple confederates like Tammy and Rye to corroborate the stories, and it started to feel airtight.

But even if they *were* somehow pulling the strings here, it seemed like a lot of squeeze for very little juice.

Vicky and Jute stood facing each other. The camera's IR mode turned his skin a creepy bluish tint, his eyes black and lifeless.

One thing was certain: If the green journal *was* a fake, if it *was* part of an elaborate hoax, that would mean she was now alone in the woods with someone who was at best deranged, and at worst a sociopath. When she thought about it that way, it almost made her wish the jour-nal and all its grisly deaths were genuine. Though neither prospect gave her much solace.

Vicky filmed Jute doing his Elkhorn Wail (an impressive display of lung power, she had to admit), then scanned the trees to see if it generated a reaction.

"Awaiting your response, Team One," Jute called into his walkie-talkie.

They tilted their heads and waited. Then they heard it. Similar to Jute's but orders of magnitude more powerful. Vicky felt it in her chest, her skull. It went on for a solid fifteen seconds. Each time she thought it couldn't possibly get more powerful, it did.

And then it stopped, and everything went very quiet.

"Team Two"—Vergil's voice sounded panicked over the radio—"was that you doing a second vocalization?"

Vicky would never forget the mixture of surprise and fear that came over Jute's face when he heard those words. No one could fake that. He and Vicky stared at each other, the second howl still ringing in their ears. Then Jute pressed the talk button.

"You mean that wasn't *you*?"

The station went staticky.

"You guys . . ." Vergil's voice was thin and raspy. "I don't think we're alone out here." The radio crackled a little more. "Felt like it came from our twelve o'clock," he said.

"Both groups converge!" Jute shouted into the walkie-talkie. "Now!"

Everything broke loose. Jute charged into the forest, snapping branches and limbs as he went. Vicky tried to keep up, but it was impossible to see much of anything through her tiny viewfinder. Within a minute, she'd lost track of him. She kept stumbling, falling onto her hands and knees. Each time she forced herself to get up, to go on faster into the darkness.

As the sound of Jute bashing through the trees receded, Vicky became aware of another noise, coming from the woods behind her.

She slowed, then stopped. She made herself hold still.

Everything was quiet for a moment. Then she heard a stick break. Vicky brought the camera close and spun.

For one brief second, she saw it, standing between two scraggly pine trees. A figure, roughly the size and shape of a normal human. At first she thought it was Vergil or Bernard who'd somehow looped around behind her. But her blood ran cold when she saw two large antlers jutting up from the top of the figure's head.

It looked . . . wrong.

It looked . . . unnatural.

A high-pitched shriek seemed to scrape the inside of her skull, forcing her to drop the camera and muffle her ears with her palms.

Once she recovered enough to retrieve the camera, Vicky panned the forest, but the figure had disappeared. All she saw were trees and brush and more trees.

Then something latched onto her shoulder. She whirled around, ready to fight back, until she saw two familiar brown eyes.

"Hey!" Rye said. "Are you okay?"

Vicky had never been so happy to see someone in her entire life. She tried to say something but her mouth was too dry.

"Hey!" Rye said again. "You're okay. I'm right here. You're okay."

Vicky, still unable to speak, dropped her camera again, and threw her arms around Rye in relief.

Chapter 23

Everyone scooted closer to the campfire, trying to soak up what little heat it still threw off.

"It definitely wasn't us who did that second howl," Jute said.

"It wasn't us either," Vergil confirmed.

Despite how exhausted they were from a full day of bushwhacking, the adrenaline was coursing through the group's veins.

"That right there was a Class A vocalization, Dr. Bernard." Jute slapped his thigh. "How about that! Aren't you glad you teamed up with us?"

"There's no such thing as a Class A vocalization," Bernard snapped. "The only thing that gets a Class A ranking is a sighting. Any vocalization, no matter how good, is at most a Class B."

"Well, that was the best Class B you're ever going to hear."

Bernard eyed both men warily, trying to spot a crack in their story. He'd been with Vergil, so he knew the second howl hadn't come from him. Vicky confirmed Jute hadn't done it either. But Bernard was starting to question her sympathies. He'd have to keep an eye on her, make sure she was still going to produce the film they'd agreed to make.

"Have you ever heard a vocalization that good before, Doctor?" Jute asked.

Bernard considered how to answer. He needed to start being strategic in how he approached this. "I found it to be a prototypical Bigfoot call."

Vergil and Jute smiled, not realizing Bernard hadn't intended it as a compliment.

"What I mean is," he clarified, "it's the same howl I've heard a million Bigfoot hunters make over the years."

"Are you implying it wasn't genuine?" Vergil was indignant.

The fire crackled and smoked. "I'm saying I can't be sure."

"No human could make a sound like that," Jute said.

"What did *you* see out there, Vicky?" This came from Rye, who'd been eyeing her with concern across the campfire.

Ever since they'd gotten back to the clearing, Vicky had been glued to her camera's playback screen, reviewing the footage she'd shot in the woods. The clip she kept looking at started when she spun around. The forest blurred. Then, as the camera settled and the picture stopped whirling and the woods began to take discernible shape, she saw something else.

Vicky hit pause. She peered at the gray smudge on her screen.

Was that a figure standing between the trees? Maybe. But it was impossible to say for sure.

If she'd held the shot a tiny bit steadier for a tiny bit longer, it might've come into focus. But in that next instant Vicky dropped the camera, and the whole screen went haywire. A rookie mistake that left her with an image worthy of Jute's blobsquatch accent wall.

"I saw something," she said. "But I didn't get it on film."

"Oh, how inconvenient." Bernard's voice was thick with mockery.

"What happened?" Rye asked.

"I heard this other sound and got disoriented and I don't know . . . I guess I dropped the camera."

"Some experts theorize that Bigfoot are capable of producing infrasound," Jute offered.

"Uncle Jute . . ." Rye trailed off, shaking her head. "Do you even know what infrasound is?"

"It's superlow-frequency sound waves," he said. "Below the range humans can hear. It's how whales communicate across whole oceans. Lions use it to stun their prey."

"This is exactly why the scientific community looks at Bigfoot people like they're crazy," Bernard said. "How can we speculate on the abilities of a creature we've never seen in the flesh?"

"We do that all the time with dinosaurs," Jute said.

"That's not the same thing," Bernard said. "It's pointless to speculate on the sonic capabilities of a creature we haven't even proven to be real."

"Not to be rude or anything," Jute said. "But I first learned about infrasound from you—on season two, episode seven of *Alaska Bigfoot Files.*"

Bernard bit his lip and leveled a cold glare over the flames.

"But you saw *something*," Rye said, turning back to Vicky. "With your own eyes, right?"

"Well." Vicky set the camera down next to her boots. "I saw a figure. And it was standing on two legs."

"Was it a Bigfoot?" Jute asked, so keyed up he could barely get the words out.

"No." Vicky shook her head. "It was a little taller than me, maybe six foot, and slender."

"It could've been a juvenile Sasquatch?" Vergil offered.

Vicky frowned. "What I saw looked more like a man," she said. "Only . . ."

"Only what?"

"Only it had . . . antlers."

"*Antlers?*" Vergil said.

"I know, I know," Vicky said. "It weirds me out just to say it. But, yeah, like, it had antlers growing up out of its head."

Everyone was quiet for a moment. The fire popped. The flames dipped lower.

Vicky's eyes went unfocused as she stared past the flames, into the infinite blackness of the forest. Her father, raised on a steady diet of spaghetti westerns in his native Taiwan, had been determined to give his daughters a thorough appreciation for the vistas of their adopted country. So when Vicky was eleven years old, the family went on a road trip to Yosemite, Sequoia, and Death Valley National Parks. The showstopper, as far as her father had been concerned, was the Grand

Canyon, which was indeed breathtaking. But one last stop, a coda he'd tacked on to their itinerary at the last minute, took them nearly five hours north, where she encountered something she was just now recalling.

"Have you all ever heard of the pictographs in the Canyonlands National Park in Utah?" she asked.

"The Great Gallery?" Jute said, leaning forward.

"You've seen it?" she said.

"Only pictures," he said. "But I've read about it."

"I've never heard of it," Rye said.

Vicky drew in a shaky breath. "So the Great Gallery is this huge wall of rock with these paintings on it that are, like, thousands of years old."

"They say it was painted by a mysterious group of people we hardly know anything about," Jute said. "The Desert Archaic culture."

"How do *you* know about this, Uncle Jute?"

He shrugged sheepishly as if to say, How does anyone know anything?

"There were these figures on that painting," Vicky went on. "Slender, humanlike figures wearing robes. And some of them had antlers on their heads."

"There's a lot of speculation over who or what they represent," Jute said. "Most likely they were tribal shamans."

"Is that what you saw out here tonight?" Vergil asked.

Vicky nodded and looked at her hands, which were scraped up from her dash through the forest. "I know I probably sound crazy."

A crow cawed somewhere just outside the clearing.

"*Or*," Bernard said, "what you saw was simply a deer or an elk. Something that actually lives in these woods and actually has antlers."

"I know what I saw," Vicky hissed.

"Okay," Bernard said, "show us the proof then. Play back the footage."

"You guys don't believe me?" Vicky was pleading now.

"I do," Jute said, raising his hand like he was the only kid in the class who'd done his homework.

"I'm sure you saw something out of the ordinary," Vergil conceded. "I'm just not sure what it was."

She looked across the fire at Rye. For some reason Vicky needed her to believe what she was saying.

"I mean . . ." Rye leaned back on her log, buried her hands in the pockets of her hoodie. "I gotta say I'm with Dr. Bernard on this one," she said at last. "It seems pretty clear it had to've been an animal with antlers."

"What about that howl we heard?" Jute pointed out.

"Yeah, no." Rye shook her head. "Lots of animals make howls. It's kind of what they do. I'm sorry, guys, but I really honestly don't buy it."

Everyone was quiet after that. The flames dropped farther, then finally disappeared. With the last of the heat and light now gone, they all wordlessly stood and went to bed.

Chapter 24

Vicky spent the night with her ears pricked, muscles tensed and ready, in case the thing she'd seen in the forest decided to pay her a visit in camp.

Meanwhile, she kept thinking about that day with her family in the Canyonlands National Park. They'd been driving over twenty-five hours by that point. Vicky and her sister, Zoe, had long since stopped bickering over who got what territory in the back seat of the family minivan and were now allies in trying to convince their father to turn the car around and go home.

"One more stop," he kept saying as the car bounced down an old dirt road. "One more stop."

The parking lot was scorching, with only a few other cars baking under the noon sun. Her dad had made peanut butter and honey sandwiches in the motel room that morning, and they were smooshed beyond recognition by the time the family ate them on the rear bumper of the minivan.

Afterward, they clambered down a dusty trail until they found themselves in a low sandstone canyon. That was where they came upon the Great Gallery. Vicky froze when she saw those spindly figures painted on the rock wall. Her father recited factoids from the brochure he'd picked up at the ranger station, but Vicky wasn't paying attention. She felt a tickle at the base of her skull. She knew, instinctively, there was something magical about this place, something that set it apart from the rest of the world.

One figure in particular drew her in. It was smaller than the others, set back a little. The rock near its feet had chipped away, but its antlers arced gracefully over its head. The face (mostly featureless except for two hollow eyes) seemed to be watching Vicky. It felt like the figure was trying to convey a message she didn't know how to interpret. So all she could do was stand there, silently staring until the sun dipped behind the cliff wall, and the canyon slipped into shadow. Her dad eventually had to drag her back up to the car so they could check in to their motel.

What Vicky had seen last night looked like that painting come to life, as if it had stepped right off that rock face and into this forest. But that would be impossible, insane to even consider.

Maybe Rye was right. Maybe Vicky *had* seen a deer or an elk, and convinced herself it was something fantastical. Vicky knew how perceptual sets worked. You primed yourself to look for one thing, and it caused you to only see that one thing. That was how skeptics pooh-poohed most Bigfoot eyewitness encounters. Of *course* you thought that blurry shape in the woods was an eight-foot-tall primate, because that's what you were expecting to see.

Only Vicky *hadn't* expected to see an antlered man. Had she?

Once it was light enough to read, she fished the green journal from her backpack. Maybe it contained some reference to a figure with antlers that had incepted her subconscious.

One thing (among many) about this book that didn't make sense was how everyone writing in it started off so oblivious and naïve, as if they hadn't bothered to read what their predecessors had written in the previous pages. Yet they all wound up in similar predicaments, doomed to the same trials and fates. Maybe this journal was like the Bible, where the stories were written by different people at different times and only compiled after the fact. But who would bother to do that? And why?

Scanning the pages, Vicky saw plenty of passages mentioning a person called the Watcher, but he was only ever described as a normalish human being, never as a figure with antlers. And those would be pretty hard to miss.

"Funny how I haven't seen you write a single thing in that shot log of yours."

The sound of Rye's voice made Vicky jump.

"For all the footage you've been shooting, you sure don't seem to be keeping much track of it."

"Why don't you let me worry about how I make my film?" Vicky closed the journal and returned it to her pack.

"It was just a joke." Rye propped her head up on her elbow. "What's the matter with you this morning?"

Vicky unzipped her sleeping bag. The cold morning air stiffened the stubble on her shins like cactus needles. "I don't appreciate how you doubted what I saw last night."

"I didn't question whether you saw *something*." Rye sat up. "But it was dark, and everyone was shouting, so maybe in that chaos what you saw wasn't what you thought it was."

Outside the tent, the camp stove started to hiss. Vergil would be fixing breakfast soon.

"Besides," Rye said, "in case you haven't noticed, I doubt *all* of this stuff. That's kind of why I'm here."

"Oh, trust me, I've noticed." Vicky started pulling on her hiking pants. "And I think there's something more to it."

"More to what?"

The two women stared at each other a moment.

"I think your skepticism is a defense mechanism," Vicky said.

"Really," Rye said. "And what do you think I could possibly be defending myself from?"

"I'm not sure yet," Vicky said. "But I'll find out. Eventually." She arched her eyebrows to see if Rye had anything else she wanted to say. After a few seconds of tense silence, Vicky unzipped the tent flap and stepped outside.

Once she'd closed it back up, Rye finally responded from inside: "Oh yeah? Well, good luck with *that*!"

. . .

Everyone knew the drill by now. Cowboy coffee and a bowl of oatmeal, which was best eaten quickly, before it turned lumpy. Then it was time to pack up the gear and start moving.

Vergil was grateful to get back on the trail and leave the cemetery behind. All night long he'd felt a chilly wind whistling through his bones. He couldn't get warm, no matter how many layers he put on, or how deeply he burrowed into his sleeping bag, as if the ground itself were extracting the heat from his body.

Once he started moving his limbs, though, a warmth spread through his muscles and joints. He even managed to work up a good sweat. A stream was trickling softly somewhere on the left. He pushed through a thicket of mountain raspberry bushes. Vergil plucked one of the berries, even though it was still green. When it burst on his tongue the juice was brightly sour and made his lips pucker.

They were finally on the way to the spot where Jute had his childhood Bigfoot encounter. Last night's howl was by far the most conclusive evidence they'd ever collected. The kind of proof that could lead to interview requests, feature articles, invitations to speak at Bigfoot conferences. It was starting to look like this expedition really would be the game changer the Basic Bigfoot Society had been waiting for.

Up ahead, Vergil heard the others talking. Their elevated pitch and register told him something noteworthy was happening.

A little farther on, the trail began to rise.

A minute passed. The ground leveled out and the trees thinned.

Vergil found himself standing at the edge of a treeless expanse atop an isolated butte. The ground was covered in shards of iron-red granite. They'd made it to the scree field, the first landmark on the route to Ramsey Lake. And it was just like Jute had always described it.

Jute couldn't stop thinking about that howl last night. As he'd raced toward it, with his GoPro out and ready, he'd been certain he was about to come face-to-face with the thing he'd encountered all those years ago, a reckoning decades in the making. But then Vicky had let out that ear-piercing scream somewhere behind him, and he had to break off the chase.

She was clearly shaken up by whatever she'd seen. Jute wasn't sure what to make of her description. In all the stories his father had told him, he'd never once mentioned anything about a human figure with antlers. The notion that something other than a Bigfoot might be out here wasn't one Jute had ever entertained.

Rocks suddenly clinked beneath his feet. Without realizing it, he'd emerged from the forest onto a wide expanse of jagged stones. The others filed onto the bare hilltop, and looked around blearily at the sudden immensity of the sky. Mountains and valleys, gullies and ravines stretched out for miles in every direction. The whole wrinkled topography of the Elkhorns, covered in a shaggy coat of evergreen.

Vicky swept the camera, taking in the panorama. Then she lowered it and pushed in for a close-up of the bladelike stones they stood on. When she kicked at the ground with her toe, the rocks clinked like broken porcelain.

"What is this stuff?"

"It's called scree." Jute unclipped his canteen and took a slug of water. "Brittle rock that's been fractured and split over thousands of years of freezing and thawing."

A persistent wind blew across the bare hilltop, sounding a shrill whistle through the stone crevices at their feet.

"It looks like the surface of an alien planet," Vicky said.

The group decided to take a water break, hunkering down to escape the breeze while Jute scouted the route forward. He pulled out his map and studied it. If the small circle halfway up the dotted line was the scree field, then from here they needed to veer softly to the northeast.

Jute brought out his compass and held it flat on his palm. The needle ticked wildly back and forth like a Geiger counter. When he tapped the face, the needle spun counterclockwise, refusing to stop at a fixed point. It had been working fine a few minutes earlier.

No matter. They were close enough now, he could get them the rest of the way by dead reckoning.

Jute walked the perimeter of the scree field. At the far end, he found a game trail that matched what the map showed. He knelt down and stacked a stone cairn near this trail. When he returned to the group, everyone was stretched out, trying to get comfortable. This was their second full day of hiking, and they looked gassed. Faces lean and dirty, limbs limp and heavy.

"We pick up over there," Jute said, hoping the eagerness in his voice might rub off on the others. He knelt down and stacked another cairn where they'd entered the field. "A couple more hours should get us where we need to be."

They slowly redonned their packs and picked their way across the scree. On the far side of the field, they descended into a forest that was vastly different from the one they'd left.

It was warmer over here, more humid, filled with birch and broad-leaved licorice ferns. The canopy thickened. The shadows deepened. Off to the right, a grove of slender white aspen stood out amid the darkening greens of the forest.

Occasionally, Vicky pushed ahead so she could capture footage of the group coming toward her. Jute was impressed by her stamina. She'd matched him stride for stride all day long. Especially impressive, considering she'd been lugging that camera equipment, along with a full pack of camping gear.

Jute had forgotten how intense this leg of the hike had been. Fortunately, Vergil seemed to be holding up reasonably well. Even still, none of them could go on like this much longer. They'd need to stop soon.

"Should be coming up on the meadow any minute," he called out hopefully.

No one responded.

They had a half hour of usable daylight left. After that, navigating would get a lot more treacherous. Jute might have to suggest they stop short of the meadow, even though he'd prefer to sleep in a spot that gave them decent sight lines.

"Just a little farther." He tried his best to sound confident.

They passed through a quarter-mile stretch of boggy lowland. Mud caked on their boot soles, making their feet heavy as bricks.

He was trying to think of something else encouraging to say when they came upon an opening in the trees. There it was: the egg-shaped meadow. Tall grasses swayed and bent as if in greeting. And a quilt of yellow, purple, and blue wildflowers lent pops of color to the whole field. It was just the way Jute remembered it.

They'd done it. They'd reached the last of the Ramsey Lake landmarks. Just in time.

Chapter 25

"So how does this expedition compare with some of your previous ones?" Vicky asked, circling the campfire to take in their faces, one at a time. Everyone was present except Vergil, who was off washing the dinnerware at the edge of the meadow.

"This is already the most Bigfoot activity we've ever had," Jute said.

"Based on the strength of that howl we heard last night?"

Jute nodded emphatically.

"And you concur, Dr. Bernard?" She turned the camera to him.

"In my professional opinion, that was most likely a coyote," he said. "Maybe a bobcat."

"At least you're no longer saying we faked it," Jute said. "But coyotes and bobcats don't have the lung capacity to make a sound that powerful, Doctor."

"Could've been a mountain lion then." Rye jabbed a stick into the fire. "Or possibly a wolf."

It was quiet for a moment, except for the distant clinking of their camp plates as Vergil scrubbed them clean.

Vicky turned the camera back to Bernard. "Why don't you tell us about the most definitive Bigfoot encounter you've ever had."

"Yeah, Doctor," Jute chimed in. "What's the best Bigfoot story you've got from all your adventures?"

Bernard kicked his feet out toward the fire. "All my so-called encounters have been on TV. So you'd probably know them better than I would. Besides, they only ever amounted to vague noises, sketchy footprints. Nothing you might call real proof."

Vergil finished with the dishes and dumped the dirty water out in the woods. The crickets were starting to pick up their nightly song, like a symphony tuning itself before a performance.

"Okay, what about you?" Vicky said, pointing the camera at Jute. "Why don't you tell us about the time when you were most scared?"

Jute thought for a moment. "My scariest encounter was the time I heard my first Bigfoot howl," he said. "Back when I was eleven."

"Was it scary though?"

"Sure." He shifted his weight on the log. "Mostly because I didn't know what it was," he said. "The not-knowing is what scared me."

"What about when you heard it again last night?"

Jute rested both hands on his knees. "Last night was the opposite of scary. Because I know what it is now."

The campfire sparked and sputtered. Vergil stacked the dishes in the camp kitchen, and took a seat on the log next to Jute.

"Does anyone else have a spooky story?" Vicky asked, panning around the circle.

A plume of smoke blew toward Rye, and she had to wave it out of her eyes.

"What about you?" Vicky pinned the shot on her. "What's the most scared you've ever been in the woods?"

Rye cut a sidelong glance at the camera. "Why are you asking this again?"

Vicky shrugged. "Isn't that what campfires are for? Telling scary stories around?"

Rye set her stick across her lap and looked down at it. "I must've been ten or eleven when my Girl Scout troop went on a day hike to Lower Tizer Lake."

"Oh God, I remember that," Vergil said, drying his hands on his pants.

A crow cawed somewhere in the forest, followed by a series of owl hoots. Rye glanced toward them, then stared into the fire.

"Me and this other girl, Cynthia McKinney, we were picking wildflowers in a meadow during a water break. All of a sudden we looked up and everyone was gone. Like *gone*-gone. We panicked and tried to catch up, but we must've gotten on the wrong trail."

"I think that might've been scarier for me than you," Vergil said.

Rye looked up at him and shook her head. "We hiked and hiked but could *not* find the others. That's when we realized how lost we were, and finally did what we should've done from the beginning."

"Which is?" Vicky asked.

"Sit tight and wait for help to find us." Rye picked up her stick and rolled one of the logs until the exposed embers threw off rippling waves of heat. "We were lost maybe seven hours total. All you can do in that situation is listen and make noise. At first Cynthia and I talked about whatever. Then we sang songs. Then we did all the jump rope chants we could think of—the Cinderella one, and another one about a teddy bear, I think. But long about three, maybe four hours in, you run out of things to say. You get sick of hearing your own voice. And that's when doubt starts to creep in. I mean, who really knows if people realize you're lost? Or do they even have an idea where you are? Cynthia couldn't handle it. I had to talk her through it. Had to be brave and tell her everything was going to be fine, even if it didn't seem like it was." Rye sat back and huffed. "Anyway, waiting for help to find us in the woods, pretending not to be scared, *that* was the most scared I've ever been."

A pocket of sap inside one of the logs caught fire and sizzled. The crickets were in full swing across the meadow now.

"This is good," Vicky said. "Who else wants to go?"

Bernard crossed his arms.

"Come on, Doctor," Vicky pressed. "You must have something you can tell us about."

He looked off into the forest for a moment. Then, "I guess I do have one . . . *odd* story for you."

Vicky pushed in tight so she caught the firelight dancing in his blue eyes.

"This was back in the DRC," he said. "Early on in our research. We were still trying to find a good gorilla troop to base our study on—

one with a well-delineated family structure and territory that abutted another troop. Adebayo and I decided to split up. He'd take the north face of Mont Mambembe; I'd work the south slope. Imagine an environment where almost everything is looking at you like you're its next meal."

Jute let out a low whistle.

"I'd just settled into camp the first night on my own. Had dinner and decided to walk a short ways into the jungle to brush my teeth before bed." Bernard scratched his chin as the details came into focus. "So I finish up and head back to camp, ready to turn in for the night. But then all of a sudden, what do I see? Someone is sitting there next to my fire."

"What?" Rye nearly shouted.

"Oh hell no," Jute said.

"Yeah, seriously," Bernard said, clearly enjoying their enthusiasm. "A Mbuti elder, dressed in traditional hunting garb. Had a bow and arrow laying across his lap."

"What did you do?" Vicky asked.

"The Mbuti were friendly to us, knew we were only there to conduct research. But they rarely traveled alone in the forest, and never at night, so I knew something was off. My first instinct was to run. But where to? The nearest help was miles away. No, I had to see what this was all about. So I sat down at the fire across from him. My Efe was rough, at best, but I tried to say, 'Can I help you, friend?' And all he did was stare at the fire. Hardly looked up at me. After a minute he said, in English, 'Magic protects this space. You must not go any farther up the mountain.'

"I assured him I had no intention of climbing higher and was only planning to stay at the lower elevations. I remember him staring hard at me when I said this, stone-faced. It felt like he was looking deep inside me, and I got the sense that my life depended on whether or not he believed what I'd said. Then eventually he nodded and looked back at the fire."

An owl hooted and took flight somewhere in the trees. Everyone jumped.

"I didn't have a lot of provisions to spare," Bernard continued, "but I asked him if he was hungry and he nodded. So I went off to my tent to see if I could find him something to eat, and when I got back, he was gone. Just like that. Disappeared."

"Are you sure he was really there?"

"Maybe it was a ghost."

"Honestly, I'm not sure of anything," Bernard said. "Except here's the really weird part. When I met up with Adebayo a week later, I told him about it, and he said the very same thing happened to him. Same guy. Same night. Even gave the same warning. But on the opposite side of the mountain."

"No way," Jute said.

Bernard nodded slowly. "Out of all my expeditions, all the many nights I've spent in the field, that was the most scared I've ever been. Because the fact is, no matter where you are, the most dangerous, most scary thing you can encounter is another human being."

No one said anything else for quite some time. Vicky stopped recording and sat down on a log next to Rye. A pack of coyotes yipped somewhere in the distance. The darkness felt close and clingy.

"Okayyy," Bernard finally said. "What's the plan for tonight's investigation?"

Chapter 26

After several minutes of negotiation, Vergil and Jute decided that tonight's hunt would employ something they called the Potemkin Campsite Technique, which involved sending a team of Observers some distance outside camp to take up hidden locations along game trails and creek beds—corridors Bigfoot would likely use to travel. Then the smaller group, which had stayed back at camp, would make a racket, in the hope of drawing in a curious Bigfoot, who could then be spotted and documented by the Observers.

Bernard strapped on a pair of night vision goggles and powered them up. The forest instantly turned into a gray facsimile of daylight. A slinky pine marten scurried for cover through the grass. Bats charted herky-jerky flight patterns in the air above their heads. Bernard mounted the GoPro on his shoulder and pressed record.

There had been a time when he could tolerate these expeditions, maybe even enjoy them. Gearing up, venturing out into the darkest corners of the wilderness—he found it vastly preferable to the chalky lecture halls and lifeless faculty lounges of his day job. Set free in the backcountry, he could—early on at least—overlook the fact that his presence on these hunts was an endorsement of a pernicious belief system, a direct contribution to magical thinking. Eventually, he grew to despise the mindlessness of it all, the fanciful reading of "evidence," the pressure to say "Maybe that's something," instead of "Are you joking?"

And when Benny died, well, it was time to figure out an exit strategy. Now he had one last expedition to endure before he could put this chapter behind him. Once Vicky's film came out, Bernard would make sure it went viral, at least among the Bigfoot faithful. That should be enough to cement his split with them. Getting back into academia's good graces, however, would require more doing. The best way to do that would be a memoir, a grand apologia. In it, he'd prostrate himself before the altar of common sense and reason. He'd confess every sin and ask for absolution. He already had a title for it. *Goodnight Bigfoot: My Journey out of Darkness and into the Light.*

If all went to plan, he'd be welcomed back into the academic fold. Everyone loved a repentant apostate story. And they'd especially love his when they found out he'd done it all for Benny.

"Okay, Observers, let us know when you've taken up positions," Vergil said, switching on his walkie-talkie.

"Fine, fine," Bernard said, waving over his shoulder as he headed toward the edge of the meadow.

On the left, Jute was squirming through a dense stand of Douglas fir. Meanwhile, Rye was already huddled in some ferns off to the right. A whitetail leapt from behind a tall juniper bush nearby and darted off into the forest. Bernard spotted an enormous ponderosa pine, which he figured was as good a place as any to hole up until this charade was over.

He sat in a patch of dried pine needles, leaned back until the rough bark pressed hard against his skin. A cricket sawed away nearby. A daddy longlegs crept across his boots. He turned off his night vision goggles and closed his eyes.

"Observer Three?" a voice called over the walkie-talkie.

Nailing down phase one of his exit strategy was proving to be trickier than he'd expected. That howl they'd heard last night was tough to explain away. It was certainly possible Vergil and Jute were pulling off this hoax on their own. Or . . . there could be someone else out here helping them. Anything seemed possible at this point. Bernard needed to stay vigilant, keep his eyes open for the right moment. All he needed was one slipup, one tiny crack in the façade, and he'd pounce, showing the world how this Bigfoot business was nothing more than a myth.

"Observer Three, are you in position?"

It didn't help his cause that Vicky was compromised. She'd somehow developed sympathy for these people, possibly even crossed over to their side. Truth was, she probably lacked the killer instinct necessary to pull off genuine satire. So Bernard would have to set the trap and spring it himself. She could thank him later, once the truth was revealed.

"Observer Three?"

Bernard realized who Observer Three was.

"Yeah, I'm here," he said. "And yeah, I'm in position."

Rye burrowed herself into a stand of ferns. Through the trees she could make out a golden smudge from the campfire back in the clearing.

She switched off her night vision goggles, and the forest rushed at her.

"Observer Two is in position," she radioed.

"Roger, Observer Two," Vergil called. "Observer One, what is your location?"

"Observer One is in position," Jute said.

"Roger, Observer One. Observer Three?"

Rye grabbed a handful of leaves and piled them under her butt to make a cushion. No telling how long her dad and Uncle Jute would want to investigate tonight. She'd always pictured the two of them sitting around a campfire drinking cheap beer on these expeditions. Misguided as this enterprise may be, she at least had to give them credit for how seriously they took the whole thing.

"Observer Three, are you in position?"

The walkie-talkie crackled. Rye craned her neck, trying to remember which way Bernard had gone when they left camp. That story he told was a doozy. Pretty much her exact nightmare camping scenario. Kind of funny that the man didn't have a single Bigfoot story he wanted to share though. Wasn't that supposed to be his whole deal?

"Observer Three?"

Static. Hissing.

"Yeah, I'm here," Bernard finally growled over the radio. "And yeah, I'm in position."

"Very good," Vergil said. "Commencing Potemkin Campsite sequence."

A moment later, the campfire grew brighter through the trees. Pots and pans banged, followed by indistinguishable clanks.

Rye switched on the thermal and glassed the forest. A couple rocks and tree stumps glowed yellow. Everything else was blue and green. She pulled her hood over her head. She curled her knees up to her chest, wrapped her arms around her legs. She blinked and stifled a yawn. She turned the thermal off.

Two rocks clacked from the area of the meadow. Silverware tapped the side of a camping mug as if someone were demanding a woodland toast. The rest of the forest was silent.

Rye switched on the thermal again. The rocks and stumps appeared a little cooler than they had a few minutes ago. She picked up some red dots, probably jackrabbits, maybe muskrats, but nothing else.

She blinked, and this time kept her eyes closed. Just for a minute. Then she'd open them and check the thermal again. But for now she could use a little rest.

Now that the Observer Team was in place, Vergil rolled a fresh log onto the campfire, and a shower of sparks shot up, dancing in the air above them.

"Can I ask you something?" Vicky said.

Vergil shrugged as if he didn't have a choice.

"When I researched the Basic Bigfoot Society, I couldn't find a single thing about you guys online."

He chuckled. "Are you asking me why we're such nobodies?"

"I'd probably phrase it as 'Why do you have such a low profile?'"

"Maybe a high profile was never our goal," he suggested.

"Then why team up with someone like Marcus Bernard?"

Vergil scooped up a handful of silverware and dropped it piece by piece into a pan.

"We never had an opportunity like this before," he said. "And besides, it was time."

"Time for what?"

"To get serious about it. Maybe turn it into a real career."

"What do you do when you're not Bigfoot hunting?"

"I work at the town library." Vergil clapped twice and stomped on the ground.

They stared out into the forest, waiting to see any movement.

"Back when I was your age I fancied myself an artist," he said, "a painter."

"Interesting combination," Vicky said. "Painting and Bigfoot hunting seem so . . . incongruous somehow."

Vergil kicked one of the logs on the fire. The flames leapt higher, and another burst of sparks flared. He stared up at them until they cooled and vanished.

"Actually I think painting and Bigfoot hunting are very much alike," he said. "The only good reason to keep doing either one is if you love it. Once you start to worry about being a success, you're doing it for the wrong reason. That's when you're ruined. At least in my experience."

"Maybe that's why you've always had such a low profile," she offered, zooming in on his face.

"Quite possibly." He let out a long sigh. "I love being out here, chasing a mystery most people find foolish. I don't care if I never find Bigfoot. In some ways, I hope we don't. Because it would change this experience we're having right now." He pointed at the ground under his feet.

"Do you think Bigfoot hunting replaced painting for you?"

Vergil appeared to think about this for some time. "Could be."

He selected the biggest pot they had and moved to the edge of the meadow. He banged it with a spoon five times in quick succession. He and Vicky waited and scanned the woods.

Just then a noise came from back near the tents. They both spun, but saw nothing.

"You never answered my question earlier."

He looked at her blankly.

"What's something that most scares you?"

Vergil twisted his mouth to the side and looked down at his feet. "Not being able to take care of the people I love," he said.

The response hit Vicky square in the chest. She had to take a step back to keep the camera trained on him.

Vergil picked up two flat stones and clacked them together. They both paused and listened for several minutes. The forest was still and lifeless. Eventually, he pulled the walkie-talkie from his pocket. "Observers, what are you seeing out there?"

"Nothing, Base Camp," Jute came through. "There's nothing going on out here."

"Roger, Observers," Vergil said. "Let's call it a night."

One by one, the Observer Team dragged themselves out of the forest, back into camp.

Jute sat slumped on a log next to the campfire. "I can't believe how badly we struck out."

"I did everything I could on my end," Vergil said. "Honestly."

"I thought for sure we'd get something good tonight."

"Why do you think the Potemkin Campsite Technique was unsuccessful?" Vicky asked.

Jute tossed his hands up and let them fall heavily on his lap. "It should've worked."

"It feels like we're going the wrong direction, if you ask me," Bernard offered.

Jute sat up. "What are you suggesting, Doctor?"

Bernard glanced around and sniffed. "Seems pretty dead around here is all I'm saying."

"But we're so close to Ramsey Lake," Jute said.

"Maybe this lake of yours isn't the Bigfoot hot spot you thought it was."

Jute looked around at the others, hoping they'd be as upset to hear this as he was.

"I think," Bernard said, "we should consider heading back."

Jute's heart raced. Under BBS bylaws, Bernard didn't have the authority to summarily end an expedition. But he was allowed to call for a vote. And he might even get Rye to side with him. Then he'd only have to peel off one more vote to kill the rest of this trek.

"We need to give it more time." Jute's voice came out flighty with panic. "Ramsey Lake won't disappoint. I promise."

Vergil didn't look up from the fire. Vicky was busy filming the proceedings. Rye was whittling a stick.

"Who's with me?" Jute asked.

But no one else seemed to be paying much attention.

Rye was still sleepy from the nap she'd taken in the woods, so she was only half listening to the discussion. She took out her Swiss Army knife and began whittling a point on the end of her stick. She'd always enjoyed the feeling of a sharp blade slicing through green wood.

Bernard was making noise about turning around and heading back. As much as Rye would love returning to civilization, as much as she wanted to start tackling her father's medical condition ASAP, she could never vote to take this expedition from him.

"Who's with me?" Jute asked no one in particular.

That was when Rye noticed something. She blinked and rubbed her eyes to see if it might be a trick of the light.

"Uncle Jute," she said, "were you sitting on this log before we went out to investigate?"

"I think so," he said. "Why?"

"Did you write this?" Rye pointed at something scratched into the dirt at her feet:

MAGIC PROTECTS THIS SPACE
TURN BACK NOW

The letters were six inches tall and appeared to be freshly drawn, with soil furrowed along the edges.

"That was absolutely not me," Jute said.

"Then who did it?" Rye asked.

"Magic protects this space . . ." Vergil mused. "Just like your story, Dr. Bernard."

"It had to be someone from the Campsite Team," Bernard said.

Vergil and Vicky exchanged glances. "It wasn't either of us," she said.

"Maybe it was Dr. Bernard trying to scare us," Jute said, "since he's the one who wants to turn around so badly."

"Cheap theatrics aren't my style." Bernard chuckled. "Maybe it was Vicky's Antler Man."

He'd meant it as a joke, but others were now weighing the possibility.

"Seriously?" Rye said, incensed. "No one's going to admit to doing this?"

Everyone shifted their gazes around the campfire. They were all suspects.

Chapter 27

"All right, how about this," Bernard said, resting his hands on his knees. "Let's say you were doodling in the dirt absentmindedly, and didn't mean to cause a fuss. Just tell us so we can move on."

No one said anything.

"Oh come on," Rye said, tossing her stick into the fire. "This doesn't have to be a big deal. Come clean, for God's sake!"

The group continued to exchange suspicious glances in silence. Rye's stick flared up for a few seconds before turning to ash. The fire slowly dipped and dimmed until only embers were left. When it was clear no one was coming forward, they were forced to retire to the tents with the matter unresolved, the question hanging over them like a dark cloud.

Vergil barely managed to keep down the ibuprofens he'd taken after dinner, and they weren't doing much good anyway. So having his brain twisted up in knots over who wrote a somewhat cryptic message in the dirt at the very least provided a welcome distraction from the howling organ blasts of pain that wheezed through him.

He lay there in his sleeping bag, rolling from one side to the other whenever his position grew unbearable. He considered whether he himself could have left the message. Maybe he'd entered a fugue state and scrawled it in the dirt without remembering. But he'd never once been alone by the fire. So unless he and Vicky both blacked out and wrote it, the two of them were in the clear. That left Jute, Rye, and Bernard, but they all lacked the opportunity to pull it off.

There was, of course, another possibility . . .

Vergil shuddered when he thought about Bernard's story of a stranger wandering into his camp. He felt around to make sure the bear spray was close at hand. This stuff worked just as well on humans, should the need arise.

As soon as it was bright enough to fix breakfast, he unzipped his bag.

"How'd you sleep?" Jute asked as soon as he heard Vergil stirring.

"Barely," Vergil said. "You?"

Jute propped his head on his hand. "Same."

It got quiet for a moment.

"So I have to ask," Vergil said, "did you write it?"

Jute shook his head emphatically. "Of course not." He paused for a second. "Did you?"

"No," Vergil said. "And Vicky was with me the whole night, so that leaves Rye or Bernard. But I don't see how they could have done it."

Jute's brow furrowed. He ran a hand through his hair. "Was this a huge mistake?" he asked.

"Was *what* a mistake?"

"Bringing all these people here." He made a circling motion with his finger. "Maybe it should've been just you and me. Like old times."

Vergil surveyed his friend's wide face, the scars he'd accumulated in his bar fight days, the wrinkles that had started to deepen over the intervening years. "Would've been a lot fewer egos," he said.

"Simpler times . . ." Jute said, and looked at his knuckles.

"Let me go see about breakfast." Vergil eased himself out of the tent and stretched his torso from side to side—a move that made his lungs quiver. He remembered a conversation where the doctor told him that the more pain the body feels, the bigger the pain pathway becomes. It was a cycle that went only one direction—worse and worse and worse.

He was about to grab another handful of ibuprofens from the first aid kit when he noticed Vicky and Bernard standing on the far side of the clearing, engaged in conversation. Bernard was making a point, emphasizing it with a chopping motion. Vicky was looking off into the distance, half listening.

A more suspicious person might have wondered what secrets they were passing, what plans they could be hatching. But this was likely Vergil's last time out in this beautiful wilderness with his best friend and his daughter, and starting a feud wasn't something he wanted to do right now, so instead he raised a hand in friendly greeting.

"Good morning!" he called out to them. "Can I interest either of you in some oatmeal?"

The brightening of the tent fabric told Vicky the sun was about to break over the mountains. She rose to gather more footage around camp, even though the nature of this film was getting less clear the further they went.

Professor Moss, if he were here, would likely tell her to be patient. "The doc maker can *try* to craft a story," he'd said in the last lecture of his Intro to Doc Making class. "You can attempt to shape and sculpt it like marble. But I've found that that rarely works. The truest stories were written long before we ever thought to turn on the camera. And we probably won't recognize them until long after the film is in the can. Your task—the only way to do this—is to show up with your whole self, do the job with your whole heart, and hope for a little luck."

Vicky had been so moved by the lecture she stood and broke into applause when it was over, even though she was the only person in class who did.

Rye was still sleeping, so Vicky got dressed and opened the tent flap. When she crawled out into the dewy meadow grass, the knees of her hiking pants instantly soaked through. The mountains were close now, towering overhead. The hollowed-out peak they were headed toward was washed in a halo of clouds.

Vicky stepped into her hiking boots, brought the camera to her shoulder, and framed it on the letters, still legible in the sandy soil near the fire ring. "Magic protects this space, turn back now," she said, and held the shot steady for several seconds.

Vicky was desperate to make sense of what was happening here. The first time she'd encountered that statement was in the green journal, when it was spoken as a warning to Amber Reynolds and her friends. Yet Bernard, who couldn't *possibly* know anything about that incident, claimed to have received the same admonition decades ago on the other side of the planet. And now the five of them had apparently been given the same warning again last night. Vicky couldn't conceive of a logical explanation for this. Hell, she couldn't come up with an *illogical* one either.

"Is it possible someone knows we're out here?" she voice-overed. "And wants us to know we're being watched?"

She panned across the meadow until she settled the shot on a patch of purple lupine growing waist high.

"There's a phenomenon we've all experienced called scopaesthesia," she said. "The inescapable sense that you're being watched. People claim to feel it all the time. Yet psychologists have tried for decades to document it, with almost no success."

She crept toward the edge of the clearing. A nervous chipmunk froze in her path when she approached, then scampered off into the tall grass once she got too close for comfort.

"Just because we can't prove something, does that mean it doesn't exist? Absence of evidence doesn't equal evidence of absence, as Bigfoot researchers are so fond of pointing out."

Vicky reached the edge of the meadow. She turned the camera's gaze into the forest. The parallel lines of the lodgepoles created a disorienting lack of perspective.

"We've all felt it at one time or another, in a crowd, at a restaurant or bar. An unexpected pressure on the back of your neck, a chill along your spine. You turn, only to find that someone has been staring at you. Was it really that person's stare you felt? Or could it have been a reaction to external stimuli developed over eons of evolution, telling you—"

"Really going for it this morning, aren't you?"

Vicky whirled around. Bernard was standing behind her. He wasn't wearing his fedora. His ponytail was loose and scattered.

"I didn't . . ." she said. "I wasn't . . ."

"Relax," he said, stepping closer and lowering his voice. "I just wanted to see if it was you who pulled that stunt with the message last night."

Vicky shook her head. "It wasn't you?"

"No." Bernard glanced over his shoulder and smiled. "Which means it was one of them."

"How can you be so sure?"

He gave Vicky a querulous look as if to say, Who else could it be?

"I don't get the sense they're trying to pull one over on us," she added.

He nodded as if he weren't paying attention to her. "How do you think I'm doing?" he asked.

"Honestly?" she said. "You're coming across like a bit of an asshole."

Bernard sighed. "This isn't as easy as it looks, you know."

"I'm sure it's incredibly hard being you."

"But I think I've finally figured it out," he said, ignoring her.

"Figured what out?"

"This role I'm playing," he said. "Name one skeptical inquirer people love."

"I'm not sure I know any—"

"Sherlock Holmes." He beamed at the revelation. "People are nuts about that guy. That's who I need to be channeling."

"But why though?" she said. "What are we even trying to prove at this point?"

"I hate to tell you this," he said, "but your friends over there are taking advantage of your gullibility." Bernard leaned in closer. "They've started hoaxing," he whispered. "Couldn't even come up with an original line either. That message in the dirt is proof. All we need to do now is catch them red-handed."

Vicky stepped back to get some space, to clear her head.

"Listen," he said, "we've got them right where we want them. Stick with me and we'll both come out of this looking good."

"Good morning!" someone called from the other side of the clearing. "Can I interest either of you in some oatmeal?"

Vergil was standing outside his tent. Vicky had no idea how long he'd been watching, or if he'd heard any of their conversation.

Maybe scopaesthesia *was* a crock of shit.

Chapter 28

Jute knew the message was a warning. He also knew there was no way he could heed it. Not when he was this close to his goal, this close to finding the answers he'd been looking for. One way or another, he was going to Ramsey Lake today. He'd deal with the consequences later.

Once they'd broken camp, the group gathered at the north edge of the clearing. Jute stood before them, looking at the collection of vacant, sleep-deprived faces. What this moment called for was a pep talk, something to get the troops motivated for one last push.

"Okay, everyone," he said, making a huddle-up gesture with his hands. "We've got a mountain to climb this morning."

He turned and glanced at the hollow peak behind him. From this perspective, it looked like a giant golf ball had landed on top and left a divot before rolling off.

"It shouldn't take long, maybe half the morning. But it won't be easy. Lots of vertical feet, so if you start to feel light-headed or nauseous, let us know. That could be altitude sickness setting in."

Everyone shifted uneasily. Jute could already tell this wasn't motivating anyone. He was no leader. He didn't have it in him.

"The water over in that pot's been boiled," he went on. "So make sure you fill up your bottles and canteens. It's important to stay hydrated."

He gave one last lingering glance around the group to reinforce the point. When they'd gotten their water, and the pot had been stowed, Jute snapped the buckle of his waist belt and turned toward the mountain.

"All right then," he said. "Let's go."

The shadows from the mountain were deep here. The air grew colder. They had to hopscotch over streams of spring runoff. Jute pressed through spiderwebs glinting with dew, their threads catching on his face until he had to peel them off like a mask. His chest heaved; his scalp tingled with anticipation.

An hour later, they reached the base of the hollow-peaked mountain, and the trail began to climb. Gently at first, but the foothills soon gave way to the mountain proper, where it quickly grew steep. They rose above the canopy, and the forest spread out in a green expanse below. The oranges of the Indian paintbrushes turned pink and vivid as the route started to switchback into the higher elevations.

"Hey!" Vicky shouted. "Someone tell me what this is."

Jute backtracked to see what the matter was. Vicky was straddling the trail, camera pointed at the ground. "What kind of a footprint is this?" she asked.

The ground was dry hardpack, so the impression was indistinct, but it appeared to be an elongated footprint of some sort.

"Could be a Bigfoot track," Jute said.

"That looks like toes," Vergil added. "There. And there."

"Oh my God!" Vicky pushed in closer with the camera. "Are you telling me I just found an actual Bigfoot print?"

Bernard took off his fedora and wiped his brow with his shirtsleeve. "I'm afraid not," he said. "What we have here is a double-step, or an overlapping print." He tore off a feathery branch of sagebrush to point out the features. "Here you have the imprint of the forefoot." He circled an impression along the back half. "And here, you have the rear print, which in this case landed so it partially overlaps the front of the first print, thus creating what looks like one longish, *almost* humanlike print."

"What about those toeprints?" Vicky said.

"Look at this soil." Bernard scuffed the dirt with his boot, leaving a shallow mark. "There's no way you're getting a good impression here. Those so-called toeprints are simply the tips of the animal's hooves dragging out as it takes its next step."

Bernard slid his fedora back onto his head. "It's a classic misinterpretation made by Bigfooters who don't realize what it looks like when a quadruped moves at a trot." He gave them a patronizing smile. "Sorry to say, what we have here is the track of an adult moose."

Everyone stepped back and sipped their water, as if it might help wash down their disappointment. Then, without a word, they resumed the climb.

Jute's throat burned. His hamstrings felt tight and twitchy. He was starting to resent Dr. Bernard. Dismissing all this solid evidence out of hand was one thing. But doing it with such smug satisfaction was another. Constantly talking down to everyone, as if they were all a bunch of know-nothings. Jute forced himself to swallow his anger, let it fuel his legs as he pushed even harder up the mountain.

They were at the timberline now. The only trees that managed to grow here were scraggly and malnourished. Their route curled around to the eastern face of the peak, placing the morning sun on their backs. The footing was less secure. Jute's feet slid in gravel and snow every time he tried to push off. Still, he pressed on, somehow finding a way to go faster and faster.

The others were struggling. The party was dangerously strung out. Jute should've called a break fifteen minutes ago, should've gathered everyone up so they could make the final ascent together. But he was tired of waiting. Sick of everyone trying to hold him back. They didn't want this as much as he did. They couldn't know how important it was.

A shout from the rear finally stopped him in his tracks.

Bear!

Jute looked around. He'd been so absorbed in the ascent, he hadn't noticed that they'd hiked into a dense layer of clouds. Visibility was less than ten feet in any direction, and the only person in sight was Vicky. Voices filtered up from the clouds below.

"Who yelled 'Bear'?" he shouted as he peered into the strange, thick mist. Every time it seemed to clear, more clouds glided in.

No response.

This was Jute's fault. He'd ignored so many rules of basic out-doorsmanship, violated every notion of trail etiquette. What was he thinking?

"Talk to us!" Jute called again. "Whoever yelled 'Bear' let us know what you see!"

Nothing.

"Come on, people!" he tried again. "Communicate!"

"Whoa!" someone shouted.

"Hey!" someone else shouted.

Growling now.

Jute unholstered his bear spray.

"Don't run!" he shouted into the clouds. "Slowly back away!"

"What should *we* do?" Vicky had the camera trained on the mist behind them, but she was looking at Jute, terror etched across her face.

"We need to wait," he said, though honestly he wasn't sure what the right move was.

When he looked back down into the fog, he realized he couldn't hear the others anymore. It was as if they all had vanished.

Chapter 29

Jute set a brutal pace up the mountainside, showing zero concern for the others. A tricky climb like this should've been done in stages, with coordination and caution. Instead, he said nothing and kept going faster.

Rye was in decent shape—regularly attended spin classes, lifted weights at the school gym—but a half hour into the ascent, her lungs burned, and she had the sour taste of lactic acid in her throat.

Their route followed a twisty seam of black basalt up the northern face before zagging across to the eastern face. By the time they hit the hour mark, the trees had thinned and disappeared, replaced with sagebrush and scrub grass.

They ascended into a blanket of slushy snow atop an unstable base of glacial till, but nothing seemed to slow Jute down. The only person who managed to keep pace with him was Vicky, who stayed on his heels the whole way.

Rye tried to position herself midway between Dr. Bernard in front of her and her father behind. But Bernard was closer to the lead group, and Vergil kept falling farther back. The whole thing was an invitation to disaster.

Ninety minutes into the climb, a cold wet fog came out of nowhere and settled itself in. That was when the serious trouble began. Rye gave it a few minutes to see if it might clear up, but by then the mist was so thick Bernard was barely visible. To the rear, her dad was nowhere to be seen. Trail etiquette called for the lead hiker to pause and wait for everyone to catch up. But Jute was long gone by now.

Rye was about to turn back to find her dad, let go of the lead group entirely, when shit really went sideways.

It sounded like a huff and a snort. Guttural. Definitely not human.

Rye froze.

The only living thing in sight was a washed-out silhouette of Bernard up ahead of her. He stopped moving, spun left, right. Then a wraithlike cloud pushed between them, and he vanished along with everything else.

In that exact moment, someone yelled: "*Bear!*" But the fog was screwing with the acoustics so Rye couldn't tell who'd shouted it, or where it came from.

When the cloud passed, Bernard was working his way back down toward Rye. He kept glancing behind him, though the fog was still too thick for her to tell what he was looking at.

"What did you see up there?" she asked once he got within earshot.

Bernard snapped his head around as if he hadn't expected to run into her. His eyes were saucered, his pupils dilated. His lips moved without making a sound for a few seconds before he finally managed to get out: "What did *you* see?"

"Didn't you yell 'Bear'?" she asked.

"I thought that was you."

A small rockslide tumbled on the slope to their right. Bernard edged his way to the left.

"Don't get too far off-trail. A bear's nothing to freak out about." Even as she said it, a scalding panic was rising inside her.

Rye cupped her hands and shouted, "Hey, everybody, we need to communicate! Bernard and Rye are right here on the trail! Where are you? Let's sound off!"

She swiveled her neck to listen. It was silent for several seconds. Then she heard what sounded like her own voice saying: "What did *you* see?" The words seemed to come from so close by, they tickled her ear.

"Did you say something?" she asked.

Bernard shook his head.

The fog thickened. Layers of whites and grays overlapped, so Rye couldn't judge distance anymore. She'd never been caught in a fog this heavy before. She didn't know what the rules were, the smart things to do and—more important—the dumb things to avoid.

"We can't see you!" she called out. "But if you can hear me, come this way, toward the sound of my voice!"

Out of nowhere: A growl. Low and croaky.

Rye and Bernard shuffled a few steps back off the trail.

A voice shouted, "Hey!" coming from somewhere in the distance behind them.

"Dad?" she called out. "Is that you?"

A wind blew past her ears, billowing the hood on her sweatshirt. Rye swung her head around, looking for anyone else from their group.

That was when a figure materialized in the fog above them. At first she assumed it was Jute, finally coming to his senses to check on the others. Rye's neck muscles loosened, her stomach unknotted. She hadn't realized how scared she'd been.

"Not cool, Uncle Jute!" She put her hands on her hips. "You ought to pay more attention to the people you're hiking with. This is exactly how accidents happen."

But the figure didn't acknowledge her as it continued to approach.

Something wasn't right. Its proportions were off. The arms were too long. Its neck was too thick. And it was way, way too big, even for Uncle Jute.

Later on, Rye would try to gaslight herself, rationalize what she saw in order to explain away her own perceptions. But in that moment she knew, with absolute certainty, what she was looking at.

Bernard reached out to grab Rye. "What is that *thing*?"

His hand flailed until it brushed against her forearm and latched on.

"Take it easy," she whispered—to him, but also to herself.

The first and most important rule of the outdoors was to never run away from wildlife. That was one sure way to trigger a predator response. But what if this creature wasn't technically wildlife? They didn't make rules for things that shouldn't exist.

Rye unlatched the bear spray canister at her hip while she and Bernard stepped back a few more paces.

The figure took long strides down the uneven terrain, covering a huge distance with each step. Yet it moved so smoothly, with almost no head bob, as if it were riding an escalator.

Their footing got worse as they backpedaled into deeper snowdrifts with thick ice crusts on top. Their feet punched through, and they sank in up to their shins, setting off small avalanches below.

From very far away, someone shouted, "Don't run!" But it also might have been "Oh, run!"

Rye wanted to call out a response to the voice, let them know where they were, but any loud noise might provoke this thing coming toward them. Running was starting to feel like a viable option.

The figure was twenty feet away. Pure black against the white clouds. It was huge, at least a couple feet taller than Rye's five-ten. Even more striking was its width, its mass. Something this big, this heavy, shouldn't be physically possible.

As close as it was, though, she couldn't make out its features. Every time the fog started to dissipate, another cloud drifted in. Rye ran through a mental checklist of what it could be, something that made sense. A moose? An elk? A big black bear? Nothing squared with what she saw in front of her.

"What should we do?" she asked, hoping in all his TV appearances Bernard had developed some kind of expertise with encounters like this.

His eyes were jumpy. His mouth hung open. His face was slack and waxen. When he finally spoke, one word spilled out: "Run."

"No, we really shouldn't—"

But it was too late. He let go of her arm and took his own advice before she could talk him out of it. He bowleggedly picked his way over the snow and rocks, one hand holding his fedora on his head, zipper pulls on his safari vest clinking.

A moment later, the fog closed up behind him. And Rye was alone. Except for the thing above her, which continued to draw near.

She pulled the bear spray out of its holster, held it in front of her. She slipped off the safety catch.

The figure was in range.

Rye held her breath. She turned her head to the side. Then she mashed the trigger all the way down. The only thing that came out was a quick fizzling sound, like the last of the air being let out of a balloon.

"What the fuck!"

Rye shook the canister and squeezed the trigger again. Nothing at all happened this time.

How old was this bear spray?

She looked back up the slope, at the thing steadily approaching.

"Get out of here!" she yelled. "Shoo! Scat!"

Rye reared back and hurled the canister at the oncoming figure. It bounced off its shoulder with a harmless thwap. The creature didn't even flinch.

She was officially out of options. So she reluctantly gave in to the basest of all human instincts: flight.

The ground was loose, and her feet sank deep with each step. She wasn't running so much as taking giant leaps down the mountainside, hoping to avoid hidden snow moats, praying an ankle wouldn't roll, and that her knee held up.

Between bounds, Rye glanced over her shoulder. No sign of a chase. But she needed to put more distance between herself and that thing, so she continued her retreat.

She hadn't caught up with Bernard yet, which she found surprising since he hadn't gotten that much of a head start. Maybe they'd veered in different directions somehow.

Rye was just coming to the realization that she may have made a colossal mistake when she took one last leap down the mountain and her outstretched foot didn't touch solid ground. It kept traveling out into empty space, and she started somersaulting into nothingness. Then everything around her dimmed and went dark.

Chapter 30

What a fool Vicky had been, assuming a simple moose track was a Bigfoot print. Her imagination had gotten the best of her. More than likely, that meant her "sighting" of a man with antlers had been a figment of that same impaired judgment. And the "Magic Protects This Space" nonsense was either a bizarre coincidence or part of a hoax, as Bernard seemed to think. Vicky needed to get her head on straight if she hoped to make a thesis that wouldn't get her laughed out of film school.

Fortunately, she had this hike to focus on. She threw herself into it, relishing the pain, the physical sensation of her muscles straining to carry her body and her pack up the mountainside.

Jute's pace bordered on sadistic. The steeper the climb got, the more treacherous the route, the faster he seemed to go. Yet Vicky, eager to punish herself after the footprint debacle, matched him step for step, even as the others fell farther behind.

Then the fog hit. One minute they were trekking along with the morning sun bright on their backs and the next it was pea soup. Jute either didn't notice or didn't care, and Vicky was too busy keeping up to say anything. It wasn't until someone shouted "Bear" that he finally stopped and looked around. By then it was too thick to see much of anything, let alone a bear.

Vicky took a second to catch her breath, then pointed the camera into the curtain of fog below. It reminded her of the opening shots of *Aguirre, the Wrath of God*—ghostly images of the conquistadores dragging their rickety caravan down the Andes through layers of mist, to the doom lurking in the jungles below.

It was impossible to tell how this footage would turn out. Was the camera picking up the subtle complexities of the fog, the almost sentient way it moved around them? Could this footage convey the helplessness that took hold when you tried to peer through it? How its opacity seemed to smother your very soul?

"When was the last time you saw Dr. Bernard?" Jute asked.

Vicky moved the camera off the fog and onto him. "I was following you," she said. "No one told me to keep track of the people behind me."

He turned back down the trail and made a megaphone with his hands. "Hello!" he shouted. "Can anyone hear me?"

The silence from below was pervasive.

"If you *can* hear my voice, make a noise! We'll come find you!"

The fog wrapped itself around them like a heavy blanket.

"What should we do?" Vicky asked.

"This slope is exposed," he said. "If there's a bear nearby, it's not safe to stick around. We should head back down."

"I thought Rye said to stay in one place and wait for help when you're lost."

"We might be the only ones who aren't lost right now," he said. "Which by default would make us the help everyone else will be waiting for."

Before taking off, Jute turned and stared longingly up the mountain.

"How close are we to your lake?" Vicky asked.

"Mile, maybe less." Jute's eyes went glassy as he wrestled with the idea of abandoning the ascent. Finally, he pulled his gaze off the mountain and shook his head. "Best-case scenario, we run into the others on the way back and have enough time to try again this afternoon."

"Do you mind if I ask what the worst-case scenario is?" she said.

Jute opened his mouth to say something, then thought better of it. "Stick close," he finally answered. "And let's keep talking so the others'll hear us."

.   .   .

The footing was treacherous on the way down, the slope steep and uneven. Blisters on Vicky's feet screamed, and her toes mashed against the tips of her boots.

The lower they got, the more the fog thinned. Jute's head was on a swivel, searching for signs of the others, or the supposed bear. Vicky kept the camera loosely framed on his back. Not the greatest shot in the world, but it was the best she could do under the circumstances.

"What did you expect to find?" she asked. "Up at that lake?"

"I've only been there once." Jute's voice was thoughtful. "When I was a kid."

Vicky's foot slipped. She held her hand out to steady herself. "What happened that made you think it was a good place to look for Bigfoot?"

"A lot of . . . strange things. I remember the water didn't move like normal water. It acted"—his voice trailed off—"it acted like it was alive."

The fog was lifting. Visibility had increased to twenty feet in every direction. But the others were nowhere to be seen.

"Growing up, my dad told me stories about that lake," he went on. "How he'd gone there as a kid with his father. He said a special kind of fish lived in it. Called them wizard trout."

"Wizard trout?" Vicky said. "Is that even a real fish?"

"I'm not sure I believed that one." Jute let out a rueful laugh. "But my dad called it a thin place."

"I've heard of those before," Vicky said.

Jute glanced over his shoulder. "You have?"

"Sure," she said. "It's a Celtic term for places where the veil between the physical realm and the spirit realm is so thin it's permeable."

"I figured my dad might've made that up too."

"It wasn't just the Celts," she said. "Native Americans have lots of beliefs about sacred sites. My mother used to tell my sister and me an old Chinese legend about a girl named Li Chi, who was supposed to be sacrificed to a monster that lived on a mystical mountaintop. There's almost always some kind of monster guarding those places, keeping normal people out."

"What happened to her?" Jute asked.

"According to the story, she outwitted the monster and saved herself."

Jute stopped walking. "Did you believe it?" he asked. "That story your mother told you?"

Vicky sensed a lot was riding on how she answered this question.

"I believed those stories when I was a little girl," she said. "Now I guess you could say I believe *in* them."

Jute's face clouded. "What's the difference?"

"If you believe something, that means you believe it actually happened, like it's a historical fact," she said. "But if you believe *in* something, to me, that's like you don't believe it literally happened, but maybe it still has *meaning*, a lesson you can use in your everyday life."

"What was the lesson you were supposed to take from Li Chi?"

"Hmmm . . ." Vicky looked down and adjusted the aperture on the camera. "For me I guess the lesson was that little girls shouldn't listen to assholes who wanted to sacrifice them to monsters."

She couldn't tell if she was making the point she wanted to make.

"How about this," she said. "It's like the Noah's ark story. Do I believe God *actually* spoke to a man named Noah, and this Noah dude built a physical ark and loaded every single animal pair onto it in order to escape a divine flood as payback for humans behaving badly?" She paused for a moment. "Of course not. That's preposterous."

Jute's eyebrows knitted closer to the bridge of his nose.

"But then how do you account for all these different cultures around the world," she went on, "who never had any contact with each other, but somehow all have their own eerily similar flood myths?"

"Good question," he said. "How *do* you explain that?"

"Most scientific evidence indicates there really *was* a great flood," she said. "At the end of the last ice age, a huge meltwater pulse wiped out almost all civilization on the planet. The people who survived made up stories to explain what they'd lived through: Hence, Noah and his famous ark. The God-punishing-mankind stuff was just a convenient way to explain what we now know as climate change."

Jute unclipped his canteen and took a small swig. He offered some to Vicky but she declined. They started walking down the mountain again.

"So if those old stories are memories of actual events," he said, "why can't Bigfoot be like that too?"

"I suppose it could be," she said. "The Bigfoot myth might originate from our distant ancestors' memories of Neanderthal or *Gigantopithecus,* since early humans probably had to compete with them for resources."

"Relict hominoid theory," Jute said.

"In a way," she said. "Except they only survived into the present day as memories, hardwired into our brains."

When they finally emerged from the fog, Jute paused to survey the empty slope, making mental calculations—time, distance, the possible location of the others. Conclusion: If they hadn't run into them by now, the only place they could be was farther down the mountain.

"Let's keep going," he said.

They walked another few minutes, following the twisty seam of black basalt.

"The other day when Vergil was talking about the relict hominoid theory," Vicky said, "I noticed you didn't say anything."

Jute grunted agreement.

"Why is that?"

"Vergil's a committed Aper," he said. "And I respect that. But I'm more firmly in what's called the Woo camp."

"What's Woo?"

Jute smiled, apparently pleased that someone finally wanted to know his opinion on the matter. "People who buy into Woo believe Bigfoot to be more of a mystical creature."

"Mystical how?" she asked.

"I think Bigfoot is probably some kind of interdimensional being."

Vicky's eyes widened. This was the kind of stuff Bernard was hoping to get on film, something that would expose the kooky belief system underlying Bigfoot orthodoxy. She felt bad for pulling this out of Jute but told herself she wasn't forcing him to say anything.

"What does that even mean?" she asked.

Jute slid his thumbs under the straps of his backpack. "The way I see it, Bigfoot can exist on our plane, where we physically reside, when they choose to. But they can also teleport onto other planes."

"Teleport," she said. "I see. And what other planes are there for Bigfoot to teleport onto?"

Jute hesitated. "Like, other realms, I guess."

This was too easy. Almost unfair. All she had to do was ask the most obvious questions, turn his own words against him, and she'd twist him up like a pretzel.

"What other realms are there?" she asked. "Specifically?"

Jute didn't say anything for several seconds. "I'm not sure," he admitted.

"And what makes Bigfoot decide to be on *our* plane, versus all the other planes they could choose to be on?"

Jute waggled his jaw back and forth. "My personal theory is a Bigfoot comes to this plane when it needs to do something or send a message to someone."

"So it enters our plane in order to run errands?" Vicky deadpanned.

"Maybe it gathers strength from the other planes," Jute went on, "and that makes it more powerful when it's on ours."

The slope was flattening out now. The hiking was getting easier.

"Look, I didn't invent these theories," he said. "That's what most Native Americans believe. And they've been living on this land a lot longer than we have."

"Those are legends," Vicky said. "Myths."

"Didn't you just tell me legends are based on truth?"

"Yes, but never the *whole* truth," she said. "Not the *literal* truth."

A cold breeze rustled the sagebrush, waving its branches stiffly. Vicky was no longer comfortable with how this was going, the cruelty of it. She wondered if there was a more open-minded approach she could be taking.

"I have to be honest," she started, "when you talk like this, it sounds crazy. Like, I don't know . . . magical thinking."

"What's wrong with magical thinking?" Jute asked. "Magical thinking is how we've always explained things we can't understand. Until we *can* understand them. Then we call it science. People used to believe solar eclipses were God getting mad at us. Now we know better."

Jute walked a few paces in silence. "The problem is we think we know everything there is to know," he said. "That's hubris."

Vicky wanted to counter this point but wasn't sure how.

"Listen," he said, "I'm not saying there isn't a place for the scientific method when it comes to things like climate change, or communicable diseases."

"Then what *are* you saying?"

"Think about particle physics. String theory. Dark matter. Multiverses."

"What do you know about that stuff?"

"Not very much," he admitted. "But I *do* know all of them were considered punch lines within serious academic circles not so long ago. Only now we're starting to realize maybe those things are real."

They walked a little farther, and the slope began to lessen even more. They were getting close to the bottom of the mountain.

"Our biggest mistake as humans," Jute said, "is thinking we have everything figured out."

Vicky was trying her best to keep the camera steady. She didn't know how to process this conversation, or how it could possibly relate to her film. The longer she spoke with Jute like this, the more her certainties eroded, the more she found a world of possibilities opening up before her.

Chapter 31

Some kind of madness had gotten into Jute once they started up the mountain. His breakneck pace was reckless for a group this large. The party was splintering. And he'd neglected to pause even for a minute so they could reconnoiter. Vergil was planning to let him have it when he finally caught up. Assuming he ever could.

Then something went seriously wrong.

In the middle of the day, with an otherwise clear blue sky overhead, a thick fog rolled in. It had a strange, morphing quality to it. Vaporous tentacles coalesced and reached out to embrace Vergil before dissolving back into mist.

As he hiked farther into it, sounds became misshapen. Small rockslides tumbled to his right and left, even though no one should have been there. It got colder too. The sweat-soaked T-shirt underneath his backpack sent a chill down his spine.

That was when—out of nowhere—a voice he didn't recognize shouted:

"*Bear!*"

Vergil put his hand on his bear spray and peered into the fog, trying to make out a hunched, lumbering silhouette. This altitude should be too high for a bear this time of year. Even still, a bear didn't have to be a big deal. As long as everyone stayed calm, they could regroup and press on once it cleared off the trail.

He called out: "Who saw the bear?"

But his words hit the fog and fell flat.

"Someone let the rest of us know what's going on, please!"

It was quiet for a moment. Then a low growl came out of the mist. Vergil's head shot left, right. He unsnapped the bear spray holster.

Someone shouted, "Hey!" and it sounded like it was coming from right next to him.

"Who's there?"

Footsteps to his left.

Rocks tumbling to his right.

Up ahead, a figure emerged from the mist.

Vergil whipped out the bear spray and stiff-armed the canister in front of him. He took a step back to brace himself.

The figure coming toward him was running upright, taking long strides, feet crunching into the snow and gravel.

Vergil fumbled with the safety catch. His thumb found the trigger.

Right before he squeezed it, though, the mist parted to reveal Dr. Bernard charging his way.

"Christ, you scared me." Vergil reholstered the bear spray.

But Bernard didn't slow down. He kept sprinting headlong down the mountain, abject terror etched across his face.

"Hey, man!" he shouted. "Take it easy!"

Vergil stepped aside as Bernard blew past him without breaking stride.

What could have spooked him so badly? A glance back up the mountain provided no answers, only more rolling fog.

"Nothing's there!" he called out. "You can stop running!"

Bernard gave no indication he'd heard, only continued his mad dash down the slope. He was going to get himself killed if someone didn't stop him.

Vergil took one last look up the trail, hoping to see someone else from their group. But no one was there. Reluctantly, he began hobbling down the mountain, chasing after Bernard.

"It's okay, Doctor!" he shouted. "Stop running!"

Bernard was half visible at the edge of the fog.

"Hold up," Vergil called out. "It's me!"

Then Bernard vanished.

There one second. Gone the next.

"Dr. Bernard?"

Vergil reached the bottom edge of the cloud layer. The trail contin-ued another twenty yards before elbowing into a new switchback and dropping out of sight. No way Bernard could've made it all the way to that next turn so fast.

Vergil scanned the mountainside, hoping the doctor had come to his senses. Maybe he'd find him sitting on a rock, catching his breath, taking a swig from his water bottle. But Vergil was completely alone, surrounded by an empty slope of scraggly sagebrush.

On the ground he spotted two long skid marks that led off the trail, straight down the mountainside. He followed them. At first, the slope here was gently rounded, but it quickly grew steep and treacherous.

"Hello?" he called out. "Is anyone down there?"

"Help!"

He recognized the voice, though it wasn't the one he'd been expect-ing. He inched out onto the mountain face.

"Down here," the voice called.

Vergil forced himself farther out onto the slope until his daughter came into view. She was perched on a narrow ledge of gray andesite thirty feet below him. Beyond the ledge was a sheer drop into a vast couloir.

"Rye?" His voice oscillated between shock and relief. "How the hell did you get down there?"

"Bernard and I were running from that thing, and all of a sudden..." She looked around, as if she hadn't realized where she was until just this moment. "I don't know. I guess I lost my footing. Because here I am."

A wave of nausea washed over Vergil. A couple inches farther out and his daughter would have fallen hundreds of feet.

"Are you okay?"

"I scraped my arm pretty good," she said. "Hurts like a motherfucker."

"Nothing's broken, right?"

"I told you it hurts, Dad. I'm not a doctor."

She was scared—pacing like a trapped animal, head darting in all directions. This was when people made bad decisions. Vergil needed to act quickly.

"Have you tried finding a way back up?" he asked.

"It's too steep."

"What about over there?" He pointed to a spot that looked like a relatively easy route.

Rye edged over to it. She took one step with her right foot, then pulled back. She reassessed for a moment, then tried taking the first step with her left foot. She was able to get a little farther, but the fourth step produced a cascade of snow and gravel, and she quickly retreated to the safety of the ledge.

"It's no good," she said. "I can't do it."

The whole route was visible from Vergil's vantage point. If Rye could manage one more step, she'd reach a spot where it flattened out. From there, the rest of the climb would be a snap. But she couldn't see it from below, and she was too scared to do it blind.

Vergil glanced back up the mountain. None of the others had come into view, and there was no time to find them.

"I'll come down to you," he called out. "There's a way back up, but it's hard to see from your angle. We'll do it together."

Vergil faced the slope and leaned into it, digging the toes of his boots into the side of the mountain. The first step let loose a rivulet of till. This wasn't a good idea. But it was the least bad option he had right now.

Vergil backed his way down, kicking toeholds into the soft soil of the slope. He tested each one to make sure it held before putting his weight on it and setting to work on the next one. Focusing on the task at hand put the pain in his body on mute, and he felt, for the moment, at least, like his old self again.

He was a dozen feet above the ledge when he saw that the route was undercut from beneath, which explained why Rye hadn't been able to climb out on her own. No way she was getting off that ledge without a rope. Vergil would have to find the others now.

"Hey, where are you going?" Rye shouted when she saw him starting to climb back up. "Don't leave me down here!"

"We'll get you out as quick as we can," he said. "But I need to find some help."

When Vergil stepped into the next toehold, it crumbled under his weight. He flapped his arms to regain his balance, but his pack shifted, and the shoulder straps yanked at his chest. His center of gravity suddenly swung toward his unplanted foot.

He spotted a tuft of sagebrush near his hip and, in desperation, grabbed hold. As soon as he tried to steady himself, though, the roots pulled loose from the ground, and from there a fall became all but inevitable.

In a last-ditch effort to minimize the damage, he kicked his feet out and flattened himself against the slope, as if he were trying to hug the mountain. The maneuver prevented him from toppling backward, but he was unable to stop himself from sliding downhill. His face washboarded against the dirt and rocks until his feet hit solid ground, and his fall came to a juddering stop on the same ledge as his daughter.

Chapter 32

"When you really think about it," Jute said, glancing back at Vicky, "there's more evidence for the existence of Bigfoot than God."

They'd reached the bottom of the mountain without running into the others. Now they were retracing their steps to the egg-shaped meadow, where they hoped the rest of the group would be waiting.

"That seems like it might be a controversial opinion among the Bigfoot community," Vicky said.

"Why's that?"

"Aren't they all pretty . . . religiously inclined?"

"They are, yes," he said, "but there are other perspectives too."

"Such as?" Vicky was no longer interested in pursuing an angle or agenda with her questions. She was simply following whatever rabbit holes and tangents their conversation naturally took.

"A while back when I mentioned how the Native Americans all have stories about a Bigfoot-like creature, you said those were legends and myths."

"Aren't they?" Vicky said.

A breeze rustled through the canopy above them. Older trees swayed and groaned.

"That's not exactly how *they* view their stories," Jute said. "For them, those stories are based on real, lived experience. Thousands of years of careful observation of the natural world, trial and error. What we now call science, for them was just a way of life. In a way, you could say those stories operate more like textbooks."

The heavy boughs of an old Douglas fir stretched low across their path. They crouched and duckwalked underneath.

"So if they're saying there's this semicorporeal entity living out in the forests, don't you think it's the height of arrogance *not* to believe them?"

"You have a point there," Vicky admitted.

"Put it like this," Jute said. "The amount of knowledge of the natural world that we lost when the native tribes were decimated was a thousand times worse than what was lost when the great library of Alexandria burned to the ground."

He stopped walking and bent down to inspect a broken tree branch, trying to determine if it was snapped by the group this morning on the way to the mountain, or by someone heading back to the meadow later. Ultimately, he decided it was inconclusive.

He stood up and looked off into the forest for a few seconds. Then he hefted his backpack and tightened the shoulder straps. "Let's keep moving," he said.

"Your point's well taken," Vicky said, once they'd started up again. "But modern Bigfoot culture—the stuff we see on TV and podcasts—is almost entirely reliant on uncorroborated eyewitness accounts. Which I don't consider to be trustworthy."

"One single eyewitness account, taken by itself, *isn't* trustworthy," Jute said. "But when you add up all the sightings reported every year, that's when it starts to look like evidence, like quantitative data."

"Highly subjective and unreliable quantitative data," Vicky pointed out.

Jute cocked his ear to listen for the others. When he didn't hear them, he shook his head and kept going.

"Why in the world would anyone make up a Bigfoot sighting?" he asked. "Especially if they don't have any proof to support it."

"Isn't it obvious?" Vicky said. "They want to cash in."

"I know skeptics like to say that, but you realize it's a myth," he said. "Hardly anyone makes a cent off of claiming they saw a Bigfoot."

"Notoriety, then. Fame. You can't tell me those aren't motivating factors."

Jute swatted a mosquito off the back of his neck. "If you talk to most people who've had Bigfoot encounters—and I don't mean the nutjobs and the crackpots, but the normal, sane people going about their business, who swear they saw something in the woods—you'll find out that what they witnessed, more often than not, ruined their lives."

"How so?" she asked.

"They get labeled crazy. They lose their jobs. Family and friends stop talking to them. Their lives get completely upended."

Jute shouldered aside a springy pine branch and held it for Vicky as she passed.

"Is that what happened to you?" she asked.

Jute let the branch whip back into place.

"It's just a question," she said. "I didn't mean anything by it."

"No, you're not wrong," he said. "My life *is* a mess."

Somewhere in the distance a crow cawed several times. Jute looked around for it, but the bird was nowhere to be seen.

"One of the things that fascinates me about all of this," Vicky said, "is how something like Bigfoot can take over your whole life. It's like a religion, except instead of being a Catholic or a Jehovah's Witness, you become a Bigfoot believer."

Jute nodded slowly. "That camping trip was my road to Damascus moment," he said.

They both walked in silence for a few minutes. The crow cawed again, closer by this time.

When they finally got to the egg-shaped meadow, it was empty, other than the patches of flattened grass where their tents had been pitched. This was now, officially, an emergency. People were lost, lives were at stake, and Jute was out of ideas.

"Where do you think they could be?" Vicky asked.

He shook off his pack and sat down heavily on one of the tent patches. "I have no idea."

He leaned back, rested his head in the grass. The sky overhead was clear and cloudless. The sun was warm on his face. When he blinked, his eyelids shone red. Time was of the essence in situations like this; every second counted. But it was better to make a good decision slowly than a bad decision quickly.

Meanwhile, Vicky switched out her SD card and began gathering more footage of the empty meadow. Would she ever *not* be filming on this trip? The answer was no. Every facet of this fiasco would be recorded for posterity, and the world would get a front-row seat to the complete and utter failure that was Jute Ramsey.

"If they got here before us," she said, "and saw we weren't here, maybe they decided to try looking for us back at the scree field?"

Jute shrugged. He pulled up a blade of grass and chewed on the end of it.

"The scree field's elevated," Vicky went on, "so maybe they figured they could spot us a little better from up there."

No way Vergil would attempt to reach the scree field on his own. But if Rye and Bernard voted to head there, Vergil would've gone with them to keep the group together.

Jute felt a tiny flicker of hope as a new course of action took shape.

With the trail already broken, the scree field was probably a little over an hour's hike away. If he and Vicky got there and still didn't find the others, they could either double back here, or push on to base camp, where they might be able to call in Jefferson Valley Search and Rescue.

"You're right," Jute said. "Let's try the scree field."

He summoned whatever energy and enthusiasm he had left and rolled himself up from the ground. They poked around at the far edge of the meadow until they found the trail they'd taken yesterday. Then they set off for the scree field in search of their missing party.

Chapter 33

A stream of dirt and rocks sifted off the cliff above them. Vergil scooted to his left to avoid getting hit.

The ledge he and Rye stood on jutted out two feet from the cliff face, narrow enough to make Vergil's palms sweat when he glanced over the side at the jagged pickets of andesite below. Straight across from them, out over the mountain, a pair of red-tailed hawks silently circled on the updrafts, their wings stiff like boomerangs.

"I don't know how I wound up here." Rye closed her eyes and shuddered at a memory. "I saw that thing on the mountain and . . . I just ran."

"What did you see?"

"I'm not sure." She shook her head.

"I heard someone yell 'Bear,'" Vergil said. "Was that you?"

She opened her eyes and looked off vacantly into space. Her teeth were chattering. She was probably in shock.

"It doesn't matter," he said. "There's no time to worry about that now."

An invisible clock was ticking. Everyone in Montana, from an early age, learned the survival rule of threes: A person can survive three weeks without food, three days without water, three hours in extreme heat or cold, three minutes without oxygen. Based on what they had with them in their packs, lack of water was their most immediate concern, though as long as they were stuck on this ledge, any number of unforeseeable things could go wrong.

Vergil peered up the rock face. He cupped his hands to his mouth. "Can anyone hear me?"

The sound of his voice died on the hill, didn't even come back as an echo.

"Help us!" Rye shouted.

They both waited.

Once again, no response.

Vergil tried to calculate where the others might be right now. A lot would depend on where they'd been on the mountain when someone shouted "Bear." The most likely scenario had Jute coming to his senses and retracing his steps to find everyone. In that case, he would have no reason to look for them all the way over here.

Their best chance of survival hinged on getting themselves off this ledge. Vergil unbuckled his pack and leaned it against the slope. He sidestepped left to see if there was another way down. The cliff was pocked with a few scrubby pines that had taken root in the tiniest of cracks on the rock face.

He tried the right side of the ledge. The drop over here was so vertiginous he had to reach back and steady himself until the world stopped spinning.

"You know," Rye said, "I saw on this TV show one time, how these guys got off a balcony by tying their shoelaces together and climbing down."

"Shoelaces wouldn't support our weight," Vergil said, glancing over the edge again.

"Fine. What's your bright idea for getting us out of here?"

"I don't have one," he admitted. His face must have conveyed the gravity of their situation because Rye's eyes clouded and her teeth started chattering even harder.

Rye knew she was lucky to be stuck on this ledge and not a puddle of pancake batter on those rocks below. But their current scenario could wind up being just as bad. Her dad was trying to put on a brave face, even though the best acting job in the world couldn't hide what they both knew.

A cold wind caught her hoodie and nudged her toward the edge. She pressed her body flat against the rock wall to keep herself stabilized.

Her dad kept pacing back and forth, looking for a way down. At least she'd suggested that shoelace trick. What good ideas had he come up with?

"If you can hear me," she shouted, "come toward my voice!"

A wispy cloud drifted by, thin and cold. Rye was pretty sure that thing she'd seen in the fog had been a moose. It *must* have been. Looked at straight on, a cow moose could have an *almost* humanlike silhouette. And, being totally honest, she never got a great look at it. Add in the fact that she'd panicked when Bernard ditched her, and it made for a classic case of misidentification.

"I can't believe we're going to die Bigfooting," Rye said, surprised by her own candor. "Out of all the ways to go."

"It's not usually this dangerous," Vergil said. "If that makes a difference."

"Do you think they'll put that in our obituary, that we died looking for Bigfoot? God, I hope not. How humiliating."

"Let's not start writing our obituaries yet."

"I wonder if we can stipulate that it was a camping accident. Or a hiking mishap. Something respectable. Something sane people might actually die from." She felt around in her pockets. "Do you have a pen and paper in your pack? I want to leave a note for when they find our bodies."

"Knock it off, Rye!"

A sudden gust of wind slammed into the cliff face, making her ears roar. She ducked to steady herself. Her dad could be mad if he wanted, but she was only being realistic. They wouldn't last much longer up here.

.   .   .

Vergil tried to think of something to say that might make his daughter feel better. It was hard being positive when you didn't have a shred of positivity left to cling to.

"It's important to stay hydrated," he said, taking a water bottle from his pack. "Small sips. Make it last."

Rye stood up and took a single swallow before handing it back. She looked down and toed a pebble over the edge. A second later, Vergil heard a faint clack from below. He scooted to where his daughter stood. He nudged a rock over the side and heard a louder clack.

Vergil laid himself out flat, peering over the edge. An updraft pelted his face with grit, making his eyes water. Before his vision swam, he thought he saw an outcropping. No more than a foot wide.

"Give me your hand," he said.

They linked wrists and he swung his leg over the side.

"Do you have any idea what you're doing?" Rye asked.

"We'll know in a minute."

Vergil slowly eased his weight over the edge. Gravity tugged at his boot. He couldn't feel anything below. Maybe he'd only imagined the outcropping. If it *was* there, he'd have to swing both legs over the side to reach it.

What a terrifying sensation, putting your life into someone else's hands, particularly when that person was your baby daughter.

Vergil slid his other leg off the ledge and lowered his torso into the void. He felt his spine stretch out. Getting back up now would be difficult if that outcropping proved to be a mirage.

"Please be careful, Daddy."

In that moment, Vergil was struck by how much Rye looked like Melody. Little things, like the asymmetry of their eyebrows or the way their bottom lips curled out when they were concentrating hard.

"Listen," he said, looking directly into her eyes, "if something happens to me, you hunker down on this ledge and wait."

"Dad!"

"I'm serious, Rye. Bundle up and keep warm. Uncle Jute will be back soon enough with help. Okay?"

Rye tightened her grip. "Stop it, Dad!"

She wasn't a little girl anymore. She knew how to handle herself. That's what Vergil had been teaching her to do her whole life.

He inched himself lower. The rock ledge was pressing into his sternum now.

Still nothing.

His legs were almost fully extended. Rye's hand was sweaty. Her face was red from exertion, eyes squeezed shut with fear.

A half inch farther.

The tip of his boot grazed something.

A hair lower.

His foot scraped solid rock.

Vergil stretched his arm out and found the outcropping with his other foot. He bounced once to make sure it could hold their weight.

"You can let go now," he said. "I'm standing."

Rye opened her eyes. She released her grip.

"How did you know that was down there, Dad?"

"Lucky guess."

This new perch was narrower than the ledge they'd been on, but it snaked around the mountain, eventually reaching a more traversable face that led down into the couloir. Taking it meant they'd be giving up any pretense of getting back to the original trail. But they had no choice. Vergil needed to get his daughter and himself off this mountain.

"Hand me the packs," he said.

"Shouldn't we just leave them?" Rye asked.

Vergil shook his head. "We might need our gear later on."

Once they'd taken care of the packs, Vergil coached Rye down onto the new ledge.

"Where do you think this one leads?" she asked.

"It gets us out of here," he said. "That's all I care about right now."

Just then a prickling sensation pressed on the back of Vergil's neck. He turned.

A large black crow stood perched on the topmost branch of a dead spruce, silently eyeing them. Its head snapped from side to side in jerky tics. Vergil felt sure it was the same crow they'd seen yesterday. Was this a sign? A warning? He picked up a rock and tossed it toward the bird. He wasn't trying to hit it, just scare it off.

The crow watched the rock harmlessly pass by and tumble through the lower branches of the spruce. Then it looked at them again and cackled.

"Come on," Vergil said, turning his back on the bird. "Let's see what we've gotten ourselves into now."

Chapter 34

"Tell me about your niece," Vicky said as she untangled a vine that had snared her by the ankle.

"My niece?"

"Doesn't Rye call you Uncle Jute?"

"Oh right." Jute chuckled to himself. "She's not actually my niece, you know."

"I gathered that," Vicky said. "I just . . . wondered what her deal was."

"She's one of my all-time favorite humans," he said. "Smart. Funny. Thoughtful." He stepped over a fallen log covered in moss so green it looked like Astroturf. "I think it's been hard for her since she lost her mom."

"She lost her mom?"

"Couple years ago." Jute nodded grimly. "I'll let her tell you about it if she wants."

They came upon an oblong boulder, a glacial erratic with deep cracks running through it. Jute didn't remember this landmark from yesterday, so he pulled out his compass, took a reading, glanced at the map, scanned the forest. After all that, he chose a direction based mostly on instinct.

"Why did you ask me about her?" he said.

"I just . . ." Vicky hesitated. "It's good for me to know who the subjects of my film are."

"She's going to be part of your movie too?"

"Of course," Vicky said. "Everyone on this expedition will be."

"I guess I'm not really sure what your movie's supposed to be about."

"That makes two of us," she said.

Jute lifted up a low-hanging juniper branch. He picked one of the blue-gray berries and pinched it under his nose. Its ginny scent cleared his sinuses.

"I hope your movie doesn't entirely hinge on us finding Bigfoot," he said.

"It might be more accurate to say it's about the *idea* of Bigfoot," Vicky said.

"So kind of about the Bigfoot legend?" Jute offered.

"Maybe." Vicky squinted while she considered this. "There's a documentary called *Bells from the Deep*, about a lake in Siberia where the locals believe a hidden city lies submerged. And when the surface freezes over, they crawl out onto it and look down through the ice, because they think they'll hear the bells from the cathedral of this drowned city."

"Are we supposed to be like those villagers?" Jute asked. "Because that makes us sound pretty silly when you put it like that."

"It might seem like that at first," she said. "But that's not the point. For me, it's impressive. This giant faith in something unknowable and unprovable. I think there's something noble about that, heroic even."

They came upon a spot in the forest where there were no clear options for how to proceed. They stopped, and Jute glanced around.

"Then again, who knows?" she said. "At this point, I might be making a survival movie."

Jute grunted at this, then chose a route that skirted a dense stand of high-waisted lodgepoles.

"What do you think the others saw back there?" Vicky asked. "In the fog?"

"I heard someone yell 'Bear,'" he said.

"True, but neither of us actually saw anything." They walked in silence for a few seconds. "Is it possible someone yelled 'Bear' in order to cause confusion?"

"Why would anyone do that?" Jute asked.

Vicky waited a beat, to let the question linger and gather strength.

"I know you said no one profited from claiming they had a Bigfoot encounter," she said at last, "but I imagine plenty of people still try to hoax evidence. The temptation's too great."

"Do you really think we'd mess around on a climb like that?"

"Well—"

"Yelling 'Bear' when there's not one would be incredibly dangerous." He shook his head. "And highly irresponsible."

He did a swim move to get through a patch of shoulder-high ferns.

"So you're saying you haven't staged any of this?"

"If we were that good at hoaxing, we'd be world-famous Bigfoot researchers by now."

They hit a dense tangle of brush, where the leaves and branches pressed in so close they could barely see a foot ahead of them. Jute made a plow with his arms and sliced through.

A moment later his toe caught on a raised root and he felt himself tumbling headlong. The brush broke his momentum, and he wound up curled into a ball on a gravelly creek bottom. He shook his head to clear the leaves and sand from his hair.

"Are you okay?" Vicky asked from the bank above him.

Jute tried his limbs, flexed his joints. "I'm fine," he said. "Bruised ego is all."

She nodded her approval, but something caught her eye on the other side of the creek. Jute craned his neck to see a massive tree on the far bank. The fibers of its gray trunk were bent and twisted, the branches gnarled like arthritic arms. No other trees grew around it, as if they knew they had to give this one its proper space.

"That old beauty right there is a bristlecone pine," he said, dusting himself off. "You don't see many of these around here."

"Bristlecone . . ." Vicky murmured. She scrambled across the creek bed and rested a hand on its trunk. The swirling grain patterns looked like water, or wind, frozen in time.

"Amazing, right?" Jute said. "These trees are some of the oldest living things on the planet. Some have been known to reach almost five thousand years old." He shook his head. "Imagine all the things this tree has seen in its lifetime."

"Remarkable," Vicky said. But really she was thinking about the green journal—about Joseph Cabot, the man who'd been dragged from his tent, the man whose grave she found back at the abandoned cemetery. According to the journal, his body was discovered hung up in the branches of a bristlecone pine. That was a very specific detail she remembered. Was it possible this was that same tree?

She inspected the trunk as if she might find some forensic evidence, a clue telling her whether or not it was true. Then, out of nowhere, an irrepressible urge sprang up in Vicky. It came on so quickly she didn't have time to consider whether it was a good idea or not.

"I found something," she blurted. "In Basic. Right before we met up with you."

Jute shifted his weight from one foot to the other.

"I stumbled onto it," she said. "Like literally tripped over it."

Vicky took off her pack and unzipped the back pocket. She was relieved she'd finally decided to bring Jute in on the secret of the journal, to get his opinion on it and, yes, to gauge whether he had a hand in writing it or planting it.

"It's kind of a journal, I guess." She reached into the pocket, but nothing was there.

The blood drained from her face. Vicky shoved her hand all the way in, until she felt the bottom stitching.

Jute slipped his thumbs under his waist belt. "What kind of journal is it?" he asked.

"Give me a sec." Vicky set the camera down and opened the main compartment of her backpack. She started pulling everything out, tossing it onto the ground.

When her pack was empty, she squatted down to get a closer look. She picked up each item and moved it, one by one, as if the journal might be hiding underneath something. Then she checked every pocket of her pack again, turned it upside down and shook it.

"Are you okay?" Jute asked. "You look pale."

Vicky's hands were shaking. Her vision was tunneling.

"Maybe you left it back with the cars?" he offered.

Vicky shook her head. She'd looked at it yesterday in the tent. And she specifically remembered returning it to her pack when she was done.

"I'm sure it'll turn up," he said.

Losing the journal felt cataclysmic, like misplacing a piece of her own self. Vicky didn't want to get up, didn't want to repack her things, didn't want to start walking again. She only wanted to sit here on the trail until night came, until she froze to death. Hypothermia wasn't a bad way to go, supposedly.

"Okay, so . . ." Jute fumbled for the right words.

Vicky kept replaying their journey—the water breaks, the pauses, the moments she'd left her pack unattended—trying to figure out how she'd misplaced something so important.

"Yeah, so, we really need to get moving," he finally said.

But Vicky didn't respond. She couldn't.

Eventually Jute took the initiative and began gathering her things, sticking them haphazardly into her pack. When he finished, he held it up while she slipped her arms through the straps, centered it on her hips, cinched up the belt. A moment later, they set out again, in search of the scree field.

Chapter 35

Bernard's meltdown back there in the fog wound up bringing him down a completely different side of the mountain. It was anyone's guess where the others were by this point.

He stopped walking for a moment. He filtered out the sound of his breathing and his heartbeat so he could listen to what the forest was telling him.

Bernard heard the scritch-scratch of a grasshopper bowing its legs in the distance, a chipmunk scrabbling through ground clutter near his feet, a pair of magpies calling back and forth above him, and not much else.

He was disoriented, but he wasn't worried. Not yet. He could still recall Adebayo's advice: "All rivers lead to civilization, Marcus. You're never truly lost if you find running water." That one piece of advice had helped him survive some of the most inhospitable places on the planet.

He began hiking again, emerging from the shadow of the mountain.

Bernard still remembered how his senses had sharpened the first time they'd set out into Virunga National Park. The forests there felt ancient and untouched. The wind rustling through the leaves was a murmured prayer. Bernard would imagine himself merging with the landscape, becoming a tiny piece of a larger world. As dangerous as it could at times be, that was the only place he ever felt truly at home.

He paused again and listened. A pair of chipmunks bickered at each other across a fallen log. A woodpecker rattled its skull against a hollow trunk. No running water though.

Obviously Bernard had fallen victim to a coordinated hoax, a scheme so densely woven he hadn't yet been able to untangle it. That thing he'd seen on the mountain was clearly a man in a costume. A very good, very convincing costume, but a fake nonetheless. The real stroke of genius had been waiting until they'd hiked into that cloud layer for the big jump-scare. The fog created an air of helplessness, primed him to react out of fear, despite his better judgment. No one could blame Bernard for panicking the way he did. Still, he was grateful Vicky hadn't been there to film him hightailing it down the mountain, believing himself to be pursued by a Bigfoot. That image alone could have ruined him.

But did he really care about his reputation anymore? Was getting back into academia really what he wanted? When it came down to it, he'd never been happy in that world, insulated as it was from real life, from real experiences. Telling the story last night about that Mbuti elder at his campsite had freshened Bernard's memories of the time he'd spent in the forests of the DRC. If Bernard had been smart, if he had to do it all over again, he would have stayed there with Adebayo and Benny. He would have helped set up the sanctuary, not simply watched from afar, putting on a Bigfoot clown show in order to send money. A different life path, and probably a more fulfilling one.

But what good were regrets now? Some decisions couldn't be undone.

The ground suddenly went spongy under his boot, and he spilled onto his hands and knees. A swarm of mosquitoes descended. He waved wildly to swat them away before picking himself up off the forest floor.

Bernard scanned the vegetation for any semblance of the trail they'd blazed this morning. It was mostly old-growth timber back here, trees that had never heard the sound of a chain saw. But dotted among them, he already saw the familiar ominous brown patches of beetle kill. The warmer winters of climate change had enabled the mountain pine beetle to gain a foothold. Which meant the clock was ticking on this forest, just like all the others in these parts.

He pulled out his GPS locator. Something was wrong with it. The screen kept splitting into vertical bars, and it gave off an unhealthy electronic hiss. He slapped the device against his palm a few times, but the static only got louder. He switched it off and shoved the locator back into his vest pocket. The forest had grown strangely quiet. Buried somewhere in that silence, though, he heard a deep, resonant frequency, a sound so low it might not be a sound.

After a few seconds, he resumed walking. The ground started to rise. The trees thinned. Bernard caught a glimpse of clear sky through the canopy. He picked up his pace.

A few minutes later, the trees opened, and he stepped onto the scree field—empty, save for himself and tons of jagged rock. He must have overshot the egg-shaped meadow, but this was even better. Luck, it seemed (even the dumb variety), was on his side today. And he was another step closer to getting himself out of here.

Jute was starting to worry they'd missed the scree field. It had been two hours since they'd left the meadow. Occasionally they came across familiar-looking landmarks—a hollowed-out tree stump, a cluster of twisted lodgepoles—but they hadn't seen one in a while. So it was with some relief when he heard rocks clinking up ahead.

He stopped and cupped a hand to his ear.

"Did you hear that?" he whispered. "That must be the others."

Vicky nodded and double-checked to make sure her camera was rolling.

The trail began to rise. Eventually, they came upon an opening in the trees and found themselves standing on the edge of the scree field. At the far end, Dr. Bernard was stooped over, examining one of the rock cairns.

Truth be told, Jute would've much rather seen Vergil or Rye, preferably both. His only consolation was that if Bernard had managed to make it down from the mountain, there was a chance the others could have too.

Chapter 36

The outcropping below the ledge was a narrow quartz striation that snaked along the cliff face until it met up with a spine of blue granite, which Vergil and Rye were able to climb down on all fours like a ladder. From there, they traversed the mountainside eastward, looking for any chutes that could spit them out lower. Two hours after getting off the ledge, they reached the base of the mountain.

After a few minutes, Vergil found what looked like a well-worn trail cutting through the trees nearby. A quick compass check showed it was heading due south, more or less straight toward their original base camp, by his reckoning.

"Where do you think the others are right now?" Rye sat cross-legged on a rock, emptying dirt and pebbles from her boots.

"I'm sure they must've followed the trail we took on the way up," Vergil said. "Which means they're probably somewhere on the other side of this mountain."

"So what should we do?"

Vergil weighed their options. They could try circling back around, looking for the trail they'd taken this morning, which might in turn lead them to the others. Or they could try this new trail. Even as he considered it, though, he knew there was only one real choice.

"I think we should see where this trail here goes," he said.

"I was hoping you'd say that," Rye said.

She tugged her boots back on and double-knotted her laces. A couple minutes later, father and daughter set off from the base of the mountain, heading south into the forest.

The trail was crisscrossed by a series of raging spring creeks. Vergil and Rye crow-hopped over the smaller ones. But the larger ones required them to wade barefoot. Their feet got tenderized by the freezing glacier water, and they stubbed multiple toes against the algae-slick rocks. After each crossing, they had to let their feet throb and thaw before putting their boots back on and resuming their journey.

Vergil was warming up after one such fording when he noticed a flash of light. At first he assumed his eyes were playing a trick on him, so he went back to coaxing his dry sock over his wet foot.

Then he caught sight of it again.

Hanging from the branch of a good-size tree nearby was a string of monofilament fishing line. Tied to the string at six-inch intervals were tiny shards of mirror. Every time the slightest breeze came along, the mirror shards twisted, and polka dots of sunlight spun through the forest.

"What is that, Dad?"

Vergil plucked it like a harp string. "I've seen people use something like this to scare birds away from their crops."

Rye looked around. "Why would someone put one out here?"

The question hung in the air until Vergil decided he didn't like any of the answers that sprang to mind. "Better keep moving," he said.

They hadn't gone more than five minutes farther down the trail when he saw another flash in the forest—a second string of mirror shards, dangling from the bough of an old Douglas fir.

"Trail markers!" Rye pointed farther ahead. "See? There's the next one."

"If someone saw the need to mark this path," Vergil noted, "that means it must lead someplace."

Left unsaid was the fact that neither of them knew if it was leading someplace they wanted to go.

. . .

The mirror strings continued to appear anywhere between a hundred yards and a quarter mile apart along the path.

"Do you think the person who made them lives in these woods?" Rye asked as they climbed through a field of downed timber.

"When I was a kid I heard stories about mountain men living off the grid. I've even seen one or two come out from deep in the backcountry to barter for supplies."

This could explain what Rye had seen in the fog. That figure coming toward her on the mountain might have been nothing more than some old hermit out for a stroll. The moose theory still felt more plausible. But having a second explanation gave her some comfort.

Vergil stopped and pulled out his compass. He took a reading, then turned to get a bead on the hollow-topped mountain behind them. It seemed like a pointless gesture, since it wasn't like there were any other trails to choose from, but Rye didn't bother to point this out. When he was done, he slipped the compass into his pocket and they continued down the trail.

A couple hours of hiking brought them to an open, sandy spot where Vergil stopped to retrieve a flannel shirt from his pack. Rye leaned back to take a swig from her water bottle, but her eyes registered something and she froze.

Vergil followed her gaze to a dark hole bored into the side of the hill. A tunnel mouth, braced with heavy timbers. All around them the ground was littered with signs of mining activity: a rickety wooden sluice, pickaxes and shovels rusted almost beyond recognition, piles of spent tailings.

Growing up, he'd heard how the Elkhorns were riddled with abandoned mining claims that were never on any books. But this was the first time he'd stumbled across an actual encampment.

"It's like they dropped everything one day and disappeared," Rye said.

Vergil poked his head inside the tunnel mouth. A dripping sound came from somewhere deep inside the earth. Beneath it, the faint echo of churning water. "You know, some people say Bigfoot live in caves like these," he said.

"I'm more worried about any *actual* creatures that might be using it," Rye said.

Vergil stepped back to take a look. No tracks near the entrance. The brush was thick and undisturbed. Clearly unoccupied.

It was 6:30. They had their sleeping bags, but neither had a tent. Hunkering down in a tunnel like this would possibly be safer than sleeping out in the open. But if they stopped now, they'd be forfeiting valuable hours of daylight that could be taking them closer to safety, or the others.

"Let's keep going," Vergil said at last, hitching up his pack.

"Thank God," Rye said. "I thought you were going to say we had to sleep in there tonight."

"Then it's your lucky day," he said, as he turned down the trail, "because I almost did."

As the day slipped toward dusk, Vergil found himself thinking about who might come to help them should this trail end up going nowhere. Jute was an excellent outdoorsman, but what if he'd gotten lost too?

It would be at least four more days before someone back home realized the expedition was overdue. Most likely it would be Mrs. McGill at the library who'd sound the alarm. Though that scenario was entirely dependent on her remembering when Vergil said they'd be back.

He wondered how she was managing in his absence. He'd been nervous leaving her in charge of the library for so long. Gone were the days when she and Vergil's mother ruled that place with an iron shush. Now it was Vergil who handled most of the day-to-day duties. There was no succession plan either, so once his illness got too bad for him to work, that would likely mean the end of the Basic Public Library, an institution that had been in constant operation since the diphtheria epidemic of 1889. There had been a time when Vergil allowed himself to hope Rye might eventually step in and take it over. She certainly used to love spending her afternoons there. Until she didn't.

"One thing I never understood," Vergil said as they walked up a rolling incline, "why did you stop coming to the library?"

"What?"

"After school," he said. "That used to be our thing."

"Oh, Dad."

"I get that you were getting older and maybe it wasn't cool anymore," he said. "But it always felt like there was something more to it."

They walked in silence for several seconds.

"You don't want to know." Her voice was husky.

"Was it something I did?"

She reached out and snapped a dead twig off a tree. She rolled it between her fingers until the bark started to peel off.

"I used to love the library," she said. "Couldn't wait to get there after school. It always felt like home . . . even more than our actual home sometimes. I loved the way it smelled. I loved the feeling of being surrounded by so many books. I loved studying there, or sometimes just wandering around the stacks. And I loved spending time with you."

Vergil wanted to exclaim that he loved those things too—*so much*—so why did it have to stop? But he forced himself to listen.

"When I was fifteen," she went on, "I remember it was St. Patrick's Day because that was the only time I wore that ugly green sweater Mom gave me for Christmas. I was doing my homework and you were off somewhere, probably behind the circulation desk. I went to use the bathroom. And when I got back to the table, I found a yellow sticky note, stuck to my social studies notebook."

Rye went quiet for a moment. The only thing Vergil could hear was the sound of their feet treading on the trail.

"What did it say?"

"One word, written in all caps," Rye said. "DYKE."

Vergil felt his heart nearly stop beating in his chest. He spun around to face his daughter.

"The funny thing is, *I* didn't even know I was gay back then. So how could anyone else know that?"

"Why didn't you tell me?" Vergil asked. "I could have done something."

Rye shook her head. "That's exactly what I was afraid of," she said. "If I'd told someone, to me that would be the same as admitting it hurt me. And I didn't want to give them the satisfaction."

Vergil stared at his daughter's face, hands hanging uselessly at his sides.

"Afterwards," she went on, "I couldn't bring myself to step foot in there again. I just . . . couldn't."

"Did you tell your mother about this?"

"Good God, no."

Vergil wasn't sure why he felt relief knowing his wife never had to know how her daughter had been treated. It was the smallest of comforts.

"Anyway, I'm sure you probably thought I was just being obsessive about wanting to leave for college," she said. "But every time I'm back home I catch myself looking around at all the faces, wondering who did it, knowing it could've been any one of them."

Vergil was livid. The one place in Basic where he always felt like he belonged was the same place where his daughter was made to feel like an outcast. How had he missed this? Why hadn't he put the pieces together?

"I wish I would have known," he said. "If only so I could have supported you more."

"You've always supported me just fine, Dad." She grabbed her father's arm and tugged. "I didn't tell you that to make you feel bad. You asked, and I'm glad you know. Now let's get going."

And so they did the one thing they both knew how to do in that moment: keep walking.

The dark became viscous, like motor oil. They hadn't seen a trail marker in quite some time. The woods grew unnaturally quiet. Underneath the silence, something else. Murmurs. Whispers. Always when Vergil least expected. Always right after he'd convinced himself he must be imagining it.

"How are you feeling?" Vergil asked Rye, mostly to cut through the susurrations of the forest.

She walked for a few seconds without saying anything. "Kind of hungry," she said at last.

"Hold up then."

He propped his pack against a tree and dug around until he found two granola bars and two apples. They both sat down on the trail and tore open the wrappers. When the bars were done, they swigged water to wash the crumbs down.

Rye wadded up her granola wrapper and jammed it into her pants pocket. The apple gave a satisfying crunch when she bit into it. She chewed thoughtfully, staring at her outstretched boot tips.

"I wish I'd been a better daughter," she said, "to Mom."

"What are you talking about?" Vergil said. "You're a great daughter."

"I don't think I was really kind to her, as a human." Rye took another bite of her apple. "I remember when she used to get home from those late shifts at the hospital. I was always so glad she'd made it back. But I never once thought to tell her that."

"You were a kid, Rye, a teenager."

"Sometimes . . ." She paused as if she were trying make sure she found the right words. "Sometimes I wonder if Mom really knew me."

"Are you kidding?" Vergil said. "She knew you better than anyone."

Rye cast a steely gaze at her father. "Not really," she said. "Not the *real* me."

"You got cheated," Vergil said. "We all did."

They stared at each other for a long time.

Then she looked off to the side. "Do you think Mom would have approved of me?"

"Of *course* she would have," Vergil said. "She'd be so proud of you, of the person you are. I don't know a lot of things for sure in this world, but that's one thing I'm positive about."

Rye took the last bite of her apple and tossed the core into the woods. She stood up, brushed herself off. She was smiling. Vergil hadn't seen his daughter smile like that in a long time. He lifted his pack and tried to spear his arm through the strap but missed.

"Can you give me a hand with this?" he asked.

Rye reached for his pack, then froze.

"Wait." She shot a stiff finger into the air. "Did you hear that?"

Vergil set his pack down. A breeze pushed through the trees, causing the branches to hiss against each other. "What am I listening for?"

"You seriously can't hear anything?"

"I hear the wind," he said.

"It's coming from over there." Rye pulled out her flashlight and pointed it east, toward the blackest part of the woods. "It's . . . a voice."

"That's just the forest playing tricks," Vergil said. "Let's not get sidetracked."

"Oh my God, that voice!" Rye's eyes got big. Her mouth shrank into a tight circle. "It's *Mom*!"

Vergil tried to listen, tried to hear his wife speaking from beyond the grave. But there was nothing. What kind of madness was this?

"I honestly don't hear anything," he said.

Rye swept the trees with her flashlight, even though the beam didn't reach more than a few feet into the brush.

"I swear it's her," she said. "And she's saying she needs our help."

Vergil pulled out his flashlight and shone it in his daughter's face. Her pupils were dilated and jumpy. Her features looked hard and angular.

"Rye, honey, I'm telling you it's not real." He switched off his flashlight. "Now let's get these packs on and get going."

Rye didn't move. She was coiled up, ready to be set loose.

"Come on," he said. "The sooner we get going the sooner—"

But it was too late. She took off at a dead sprint, hurdling a fallen log, ducking through a gap in the trees. A second later, all he saw was her flashlight beam slicing into the woods, getting dimmer the deeper she went.

Vergil's legs were stiff. His knees creaked. But he quickly got up to speed, running full tilt, breaking branches, snapping saplings.

"Mom!" Rye shouted somewhere ahead of him. "Where are you?"

Everything was shaky. Everything was chaotic. Vergil caught sight of a low-hanging bough too late and it clipped him on the temple. His vision swam, but he forced himself to shake it off, to keep going.

Then Rye's flashlight beam went still. He veered toward it. When Vergil caught up with his daughter, she was standing in the middle of a small clearing. The arms of her sweatshirt were shredded; the skin beneath was lacerated and beading up red.

Rye didn't know what was happening. She only knew her mother needed her, and there was no way she could ignore it.

Rye! Help! Where are you!

Melody, of course, was dead. Rye had proofread the obituary. She'd attended her mother's funeral and helped scatter the ashes afterward. Yet somehow, inexplicably, her mother was calling to her right this very moment. Rye couldn't reconcile these two facts, couldn't explain how they could both be true.

Then there was another voice. It came to her muffled and muted, as if it were underwater:

Rye, honey, I'm telling you it's not real. Now let's get these packs on and get going.

Her father. He was here too. He had been all along.

But what if that really *was* her mother? What if there'd been some huge mix-up at the hospital, a mistake at the morgue? Rye would never be able to live with herself if she turned her back on her mother.

You're the only who can hear me, Rye. The only one who can help.

The voice didn't sound totally right. Hisses frayed the edges of the consonants, a strange tinniness narrowed the vowels. Was it possible Rye could be misremembering her mother's voice? That's what happened. You forgot people piece by piece. Trait by trait. Things like their favorite color first. The way they smelled. The way it felt to touch their skin. The visual image was the last to go. But Rye knew even that would slip away. It was inevitable. There was nothing she could do about it.

Help me, Rye! There's still time to save me.

That was all she needed to hear.

Rye bolted, her legs scissoring through the trees, carrying her into the darkness. Branches tore at her clothes. A twig caught her braid and pulled it loose at the bottom. But she kept running toward the voice.

When Rye finally found her mother, there'd be an explanation for what happened, a long chain of misunderstandings that could now be made right. Vergil was trying to stop her, but he'd see soon enough. Mom hadn't really died, and they could go back to the way things were before. Their family would be whole again.

Melody hadn't said anything in a few minutes, so Rye paused in a small clearing to listen, chest heaving, hands trembling.

A moment later, her father smashed his way into the clearing with her.

Vergil's lungs were on fire. His mouth tasted sour. He moved slowly toward his daughter, trying to make himself sound soothing. "Your mother's not here, okay?"

"You're wrong, Dad." Rye's body was still tense. "I can hear her and she needs our help."

"Whatever you're hearing, it's not Mom." Vergil reached his hand out. "I promise."

Rye cocked her head. Her nostrils flared. She was about to take off again. As soon as she heard that voice.

Vergil knew his body wouldn't let him run anymore. If she got away this time, there'd be no catching her. He lurched toward her, but Rye sidestepped him and took off again. In desperation, Vergil launched himself airborne in the direction of her receding flashlight beam.

For a moment he was flying, arms extended, body outstretched, cool air brushing his face. Then gravity took hold, his momentum slowed, and he began to drop. Right before he crashed, his fingertips grazed her boot heel, just enough to tangle her legs. She went tumbling headfirst to the forest floor, throwing up a spray of brown pine needles. Vergil seized hold of her ankle before she could gather herself.

"Let me go!" she screamed. "Mom needs me!"

She thrashed like an animal caught in a snare. But Vergil would not let go, not as long as he had an ounce of strength left in him.

Click-click-click, he said. *I love you.*

Rye tried to wrench her leg from his grasp.

Click-click-click, he tried again.

She snarled and spat.

Click-click-click.

Her struggle began to ease, her heart rate dropped. A few more seconds passed.

Click-click-click.

Finally, she responded: Click-click-click-click. *I love you too.*

Vergil let go of her ankle, and they both stood up.

A few feet beyond where they'd landed was a jagged ravine, an open wound in the forest floor. The drop was so deep their flashlight beams couldn't reach the bottom.

"My God." Rye's eyes were still blinking themselves clear. "What happened to me?"

"I think something was trying to lure you down there."

"Not Mom?" she asked.

"Definitely not your mother."

With almost no warning, Rye started to sob. Racking swells of anguish rose from somewhere deep within her and crashed against her chest.

"I miss her so fucking much," she finally managed to say.

"I do too," Vergil said.

Rye doubled over, hands on her knees. She drew in a long breath and stood up. "I can't lose both of you," she said. "I can't handle that, Dad. I can't."

Vergil nodded for a moment. "You're the strongest person I know," he said. "You get that from your mother."

Then Rye fell against her father's chest and cried into his flannel shirt until the reservoir of sadness behind her eyes once again ran dry.

Chapter 37

Jute was well versed in the rules for almost any outdoor survival scenario. When *this* happens, do *that*. When *X* occurs, avoid *Y*. But the rules never mentioned context. They never took into account all the contingencies and variables an actual emergency might entail, the messiness of real life. And this was indeed a mess.

Common sense said they should spend the night here at the scree field, maybe send one person back to the egg-shaped meadow so they had someone stationed at each of the two places Vergil and Rye were most likely to turn up. But Jute was secretly relieved when Vicky and Bernard voted in a bloc for all three of them to trek back to base camp tonight. A tiny piece of Jute held out hope that Vergil and Rye might make it back there on their own, and this nightmare scenario could end before it got any worse.

Within an hour, it was fully dark. A short while after that, the moon rose three-quarters full. It would have been a perfect night for Bigfoot hunting. Crisp air and low humidity meant wood knocks and vocalizations would carry a long distance. Jute would've been in favor of setting up a Honey Pot Trap. Vergil probably would have suggested they go with a classic Rope-a-Squatch scenario. These thoughts made Jute smile as he scrabbled through the brush. But they also laid bare a painful truth: He and Vergil would most likely never have a chance to do any of those things again.

Jute tried to dismiss these self-pitying ruminations, but once they took hold, he couldn't shake them off. His rib cage constricted and his lungs began to shudder. Sometimes he wondered if his sadness was bigger than other people's sadness—as if it were an emotion that took up physical space, and his enormous size gave it more room, more cubic inches to inhabit.

Around this time he began to notice sounds in the forest—off to the right—a gentle swish of branches, the occasional crunch of leaf litter.

Something was moving alongside them.

Jute didn't want to alarm Vicky and Bernard. So he quietly unclipped his bear spray holster and let his hand rest on the canister. He'd never had to deploy one of these in the field before. He wasn't even sure—now that he thought about it—if they had expiration dates.

He hoped he wouldn't have to find out.

Vicky didn't think anything could be worse than hiking on the mountain in the fog. But that was before she'd had to slog through this forest at night. Which was, it turned out, infinitely more scary.

She kept imagining things were touching her as she went along. Hands brushing against the back of her neck, fingers tapping her shoulders. Of course it was only branches, vines, cobwebs—the same stuff they'd been hiking through all day. But it was a lot harder to convince yourself of that when it was dark.

The chemistry of the group had been altered. Vicky had been enjoying her time with Jute, their free-flowing discussions on Bigfoot and myths and life. His quirky, monomaniacal intellect. With Bernard added to the mix, those conversations now felt silly, embarrassing even.

As the night deepened, she became aware of noises coming from the trees to their right. They weren't consistent. An occasional stick break, the gentle bass of a footpad landing on solid ground.

"Do you guys keep hearing something?" she finally asked.

All three of them stopped walking. One last swish sounded somewhere in the brush. Then the woods fell silent.

"Something's paralleling us," Jute whispered.

"*What's* paralleling us?" Vicky asked. "And what does *paralleling* mean?"

"It's a known Bigfoot behavior," Jute said. "Where they pace alongside people, staying just out of sight. It's their way of escorting intruders out of their territory."

Jute took out his flashlight and shone it into the trees. All three of them stared at the pale circle of light, breathless. A pine branch twitched, but nothing else happened.

"Before you assume it's a Bigfoot," Bernard chimed in, "you should know this is a common behavior among all territorial predators. Not unheard of for mountain lions, wolves, coyotes, even foxes."

Jute switched off his flashlight. Darkness instantly filled in the beam space. "The old Dr. Bernard would've at least entertained the possibility that we could be face-to-face with a Bigfoot right now," he said.

"You think so?"

"Season four, episode twelve of *Sasquatch Files*," Jute said. "Your team was investigating reports on the Olympic Peninsula when something just like this happened. In fact, I think it was you who said—"

"Stop it!" Bernard snapped. "Stop quoting my TV catalog back to me!"

The two men stared at each other for a moment, snarls frozen on their faces.

"Something happened to you," Jute finally said. "I don't know what, and I don't know why, but you used to see the world differently."

"Hey!" Vicky said. "Can we focus on the fact that a predator is stalking us?" She switched her camera to IR mode but couldn't see any farther.

"It's not an inherently aggressive behavior." Bernard waved his hand dismissively. "As long as we don't provoke it, there's nothing to fear."

Vicky cupped a hand to her mouth. "Is someone out there?" she called.

They waited, listened.

"Hellooooo," she tried again. "You have our attention. Is there something you want to tell us?"

A second later, they heard it: a two-note yoo-hoo whistle coming from just beyond their line of sight.

All three of them stumbled backward.

"Did something just whistle at us?" Vicky glanced at Bernard, hoping he had an explanation, but he only shook his head.

She stepped forward. "Whatever you are," she called out, "we don't want you around! We're tired, and we need to get back to camp! So just leave us alone. Please. Okay? Thank you."

Vicky did not see what happened next, but she heard it: a sizzle of displaced air as something sailed out of the trees and smacked her square on the forehead.

"Owww!" she said, rubbing a spot between her eyebrows. "What the actual fuck?"

When she looked down, a pine cone the size of her fist was resting next to her boot. It hadn't been there a second earlier.

Jute caught it in his peripheral vision. A gray streak sailing out of the forest, moving so fast he couldn't follow its trajectory. Then a crisp tap as the pine cone connected with Vicky's head and fell to the ground at her feet.

"You guys saw that, right?" Vicky asked.

"I think you made it mad," Jute whispered.

No one said anything for a few minutes. They continued staring into the trees, waiting for something else to happen.

"If that's a Bigfoot out there," Vicky said, "I mean . . . Isn't this the point where we should try to catch it on film?"

"Charging a wild animal is never a good idea," Bernard warned.

Jute agreed that it wasn't smart to race headlong into the forest when you didn't know what was out there. But this might be their last chance to get real, solid Bigfoot evidence.

"You're right," he said. "Let's do this."

"Really?" Vicky said. "I was kind of hoping you'd say we shouldn't."

Jute strapped a GoPro onto his shoulder and switched his phone to video.

"You realize this is insane," Bernard said.

"Ready?" Jute said.

Vicky wiped her palms on her pants and gripped the camera tight to her chest.

"On your marks . . ." Jute felt light-headed and giddy, like when the dentist gave him too much laughing gas.

"Get set . . ."

The air was thick and close around them.

"G—"

Before he could get the word out, an otherworldly roar came barreling out of the forest. A blast of sound so powerful it shook his bones and jostled his organs. It came at them in layers, as if multiple vocal cords were all sounding at once. By the time it finished, the trees were quaking.

"On second thought . . ." Vicky managed to say, her voice barely a squeak.

"Yeah," Jute said, sober now. "Maybe not such a good idea after all."

No one said anything for a few seconds.

"What do you think it is?" she asked.

Bernard shook his head, unwilling to hazard a guess. "I don't know," he finally said. "But we ought to get out of its territory."

Without discussing it further, they turned east again toward base camp.

The minute they resumed walking, the footsteps started up, twigs snapped, leaves jostled. Something was still paralleling them, and all they could do was pretend it wasn't there.

They'd hiked another couple hours when a point of light glimmered in the forest ahead of them.

"Is that eyeshine?" Vicky asked.

Jute paused and snapped on his flashlight. The beam revealed the western edge of their base camp. Ahead of them was the foldout table with Bernard's gear boxes stacked on top. Next to it, the kitchen supplies and fire ring. Beyond that, at the top of the clearing, the cars.

Once he'd had a chance to look around, though, Jute's heart sank. Vergil and Rye hadn't made it back.

"What should we do about the others?" Vicky asked.

"It's too dark to drive out now," he said. "We'll head out at first light and get help."

"What about in the meantime?"

"Getting a fire going might help. If they're anywhere in the vicinity, it'll guide them to us." Jute piled a couple handfuls of pine needles in the fire ring. "Plus it should scare off whatever was following us on the trail."

"I'll do a sweep with the thermal," Bernard said, "to see if that thing's gone." He began unlatching one of the cases on the foldout table.

Jute pulled a lighter from his pocket and flicked it. The kindling smoked and smoldered. He teepeed twigs and sticks until a healthy flame leapt up. Then he and Vicky peered into the wall of trees that surrounded them, at the twisting black kaleidoscope of the forest. Bernard began powering up the thermal imager.

"I'll go look for the others," Jute said, even though he was exhausted and didn't know how far he'd make it.

"I'm going with you," Vicky said.

Jute shook his head. "I need you to stay here and keep the fire going."

"Let Mr. PhD do that," she said.

"It's not a good idea to—"

"Got a hit!" Bernard was pointing the thermal into the forest. "Big heat signature," he said. "That thing must have circled the clearing to sneak up on us."

Jute and Vicky huddled behind Bernard. At the center of the tablet screen was a pulsing, red-and-yellow orb that lit up their faces. Occasionally an appendage would extend out from the blob, but it was impossible to tell if it was an arm or a leg or a tail.

"How far away is that?" Vicky asked.

"Thermal isn't good at reading distance," Bernard said.

"What should we do?"

"Better figure out something quick." Bernard's jaw was clamped tight. "Because it's coming this way."

Jute's pulse pounded in his head. This was it. The thing that left him that handprint all those years ago was back, and it was headed right toward them.

He stepped up to the edge of the clearing. He leaned his head out past the tree line. Even with the moon bright overhead, the canopy was too thick to let in enough light for him to see what was there. A stick snapped closer than Jute had expected, and his whole body flinched. He pulled the bear spray out of its holster.

More footfalls.

Very close now.

Jute peered into the trees. All he saw were morphing black shadows. He clutched the canister tight in his fist.

"It's splitting," Vicky said.

"*What?*" Jute gasped.

"Thermal's picking up two targets now," she said.

"Some predators are known to hunt in pairs," Bernard said.

That was all Jute needed to hear. He unlatched the safety on the bear spray and mashed the trigger all the way down. A hissing aerosol blast came out as he emptied the canister into the woods.

A moment later, a voice: "Hey, I think we made it back to base—"

Then he heard his best friend in the world break into a racking cough.

"Great," Rye gasped. "*Now* the fucking bear spray works!"

A second later she, too, started gasping as her throat swelled shut.

Before Jute could apologize or get them some water, a breeze kicked up, pushing the spray back into the clearing, and a light orange mist settled on them all.

Jute began to claw at his eyes. He collapsed to his knees. He turned to look at the others, but his eyelids had already swollen closed and the whole world had gone black.

Chapter 38

Sometime during the furthest depths of slumber, Jute's eyes shot open. He was seized by a dark panic—that he'd overslept, that it was late morning and everyone else was already awake. But when he stumbled out of the tent, he saw that it was still dark, and the others were fast asleep.

He looked at his wristwatch, but the crystal was fogged. He couldn't make out what it said, no matter how hard he peered at it.

"Am I dreaming?" The words felt thick and syrupy coming out of his mouth.

Jute snapped his fingers in front of his face, and the noise sent shimmering sound waves through the air.

Definitely dreaming, he decided.

He found this explanation comforting. His pulse slowed and his breathing stabilized.

Crickets chirruped in the grass nearby. An owl's ghostly hoot sounded twice. A light breeze made the branches sway and moan. Then, underneath the forest white noise, Jute picked up another sound—a voice so subtle and formless it could have been one of his own thoughts:

Go to the lake. Now.

As if on cue, the ragged patchwork of clouds overhead shifted to reveal a pearlescent moon, illuminating the forest north of the clearing. Another breeze swept past and Jute heard it again:

You've always wanted to see the lake. This is your last chance.

It was more insistent this time, like a dare. And it was right. He might never get this close again.

Before he could give the matter a second thought, Jute grabbed his canteen and set off into the forest.

He felt like he was on autopilot, following an ancient, invisible track in the earth. The vegetation seemed to open up a path before him, then knit back together once he'd passed.

In no time, he reached the hollow-peaked mountain, where he discovered a trail snaking clockwise around its base.

On the western slope, the trail met up with the spot where they'd made their ascent yesterday. Jute unclipped his canteen and greedily drank the last of his water. Then he began to climb.

The air thinned and cooled as the forest floor fell away. He came to the point where he and Vicky had been forced to turn back. Jute couldn't believe how quickly he'd gotten here, how easy it had been.

Before he knew it, he'd reached a wide saddle, and the slope flattened out. Above him the stars had never seemed so bright. They swirled in a pinwheel formation, and pulsed as if they were breathing.

The ground began to dip down into the crater at the top of the mountain. Then he heard water lapping against a rocky shore. A sound he'd imagined so many times that his heartbeat fell into sync with its gentle rhythms. A few more steps and the trees opened up.

Jute found himself standing on the shore of Ramsey Lake for the first time in thirty-five years. He was overcome with a strange elation, a euphoria building in his lungs. He knelt down and filled his canteen. Then he hoisted it and took giant gulps. The lake water's icy sting radiated outward into the tiniest capillaries, through every cell in his body.

Deep in the trees along the far shore, a slender curl of smoke rose into the sky. Jute knew this dream would not end until he faced whatever waited for him back in those woods.

He refilled the canteen and set out to circle the lake. But the forest was wildly overgrown with Russian olive. Try as he might, Jute couldn't find a way through, so he cut back to the shoreline, where he came upon a fragile-looking birchbark canoe, big enough to hold one person.

He slid the canoe out into the water, stepping in once it had cleared the sandy shallows. The boat wobbled and the gunwales creaked, but it quickly steadied itself. Jute found a hand-carved oar on the floor of the canoe and began paddling.

The water grew blacker the farther out he got. Every so often, before dipping the blade in for another stroke, he'd glance over the edge. He imagined formless shapes, degrees of darkness, shifting below him. And he remembered his great-grandfather's claim that they'd never found the bottom.

When he finally reached the far shore, Jute beached the canoe and reentered the forest, pushing his way through the trees until he came upon the structure. Logs leaned against each other at intentional angles. Gnarled roots grew from the ground and reached into mud walls, like fingers knitted in prayer.

Jute found a handle. He pulled, and a door swung open.

"You finally made it."

While it probably should have surprised him to hear the voice of a dead man, it turned out to be exactly who Jute had expected to find here tonight. He stepped over the threshold, and a dry heat warmed his face. Woodsmoke tickled his lungs.

When his eyes adjusted to the yellow light of a lantern that hung from the ceiling, he saw Luther Ramsey III reclining on a plastic camping chair, arms resting heavily on his lap. He wore a patchwork of animal skins roughly stitched together and draped over his shoulders. On his head was the growling visage of a wolf pelt, affixed with a rack of slender antlers. Behind him, the walls were festooned with dozens of stick figures, all shapes and sizes, woven from a variety of twigs and grasses.

"Take a seat." Luther nodded toward an empty chair.

Before him was a flat rock that served as a table, dotted with a handful of small animal bones. Next to them, Jute spotted the green journal his father had taken the last time they'd been here.

"I was hoping you'd arrive sooner." Luther's face, beneath his long hair and bushy beard, looked like it had barely aged.

"I've been trying to get back for a long time," Jute said.

"You felt the pull then?"

Jute had never considered the idea that something external might have been drawing him here. He'd always assumed it was something in him, his innate desire to find answers. "I guess so," he said.

Luther nodded with satisfaction. "We're bound to this place, you and me." He turned to his left and coughed. "Might say it's in our blood."

Behind him was a crude mud-and-stone fireplace, with a beat-up kettle perched on a grate over the flames. Luther retrieved the kettle and poured water into two tin camping mugs.

"Here," he said, offering a mug to Jute. "This'll help."

Jute eyed the leaves and stems floating in the hot water. "Help with what?"

"With what you're about to hear."

Luther drank from his own mug and waited for his son to do the same. Jute took a small sip and set the mug on the rock table.

"I suppose you want to know what happened on that camping trip," Luther said. "All those years ago."

"That might be a good place to start," Jute said.

Luther flicked the bones on the rock table, and a crow fluttered from a nest in the corner of the ceiling. Its wingbeats stirred the stale air in the hut, sending clouds of dust and smoke swirling. The crow eventually perched on one of Luther's antler points and glared at Jute skeptically.

"What happened was I learned the beautiful, horrible truth," his father said. "I learned the purpose of my existence. Accepting that burden changes a person." He smiled. "When it comes down to it, nobody wants to be a god."

"You think you're a god?"

"Under certain definitions." Luther shrugged as if he were trying to be modest. "We've gone by various names throughout history. Most recently, we've called ourselves the Watcher. It's an informal title, but it has its uses."

"Uses for what?"

"The Watcher is a servant." Luther laid his hands flat on the table and leaned forward. "Our job is to protect this lake."

"What do you protect it from?"

Luther appeared to think about the question for a moment. The crow shifted its weight from one foot to the other, cocked its head to the side.

"Most of the world's original sacred places are gone, Son. Bulldozed, paved over, fenced off. Their connection to the spiritual world permanently severed. So the short answer is, we're protecting it from humanity."

Jute was unimpressed. "I suppose that was more important than being a decent father."

"I didn't ask for this life." Luther's voice sounded wheezy and cracked, no longer the booming baritone Jute remembered from when he was growing up.

"Yet here you are," Jute said, looking around the shelter. "Training birds and weaving arts-and-crafts dolls."

Luther glanced at the stick figures on the walls. "Oh, I didn't make those." He chuckled. "The Beast did."

Jute's scalp tightened.

"You remember the Beast," Luther said. "It's what you and your friend have been searching for all these years. You'll get to know the Beast soon enough."

"What do you mean *get to know*?"

Luther turned and coughed a few more times.

"The Watcher and the Beast have the same job," he explained. "But utilize different skill sets. The Watcher is a trickster. The Beast, well, it's more of a blunt object."

"Why are you telling me all this?"

"You still don't see it?" Luther said.

Jute shook his head.

"The Watcher may live for a long time, but he isn't, ultimately, immortal."

"I thought you said you were a god."

"There's a lot that people don't understand about immortality." Luther leaned back in his chair, stroked his beard. "In the *Epic of Gilgamesh*, it was called the Plant of Heartbeat. But Ponce de León was closer to the mark when he went chasing after legends of the Fountain of Youth. Water *is* the key. Turns out he was looking in the wrong place though." Luther smirked as if he were enjoying a private joke. "The waters of Ramsey Lake have the power to heal a person, to extend life. That's why I still look like this." He leaned forward again so Jute could see him better in the lantern light. "But it's not permanent. Immortality is, alas, unattainable. Even for a god."

"I don't understand." Jute's eyes felt heavy. Floaters tumbled across his field of vision.

Luther picked up the green journal. "If you'd read this, you'd understand." He set it back down on the rock table. "Unfortunately it wound up in the wrong hands."

Jute leaned back in his chair. His vision felt fuzzy, warping at the edges. He rubbed his eyes, but it didn't help. Nothing seemed quite solid anymore, as if it all might melt away at the slightest touch.

"You've got a lot to learn." Luther slid the book toward Jute. "But there's still time."

"What do I have to learn?"

"Think of this as a job description for the Watcher."

"Why would I need to know about that?"

"Haven't I spelled it out for you?" Luther snapped. "I'm sick beyond the powers of the lake to heal me. Eventually, even gods have to die. And it's time for you to step up."

Jute's stomach let out a loud gurgle. He needed some fresh air before he got sick. He looked around, trying to locate the door he'd come in through.

"I worked my ass off to get things the way they're supposed to be around here," Luther said. "When you and I first came, this place was a disaster. I've done most of the hard work. All you'll need to do now is maintain it. And, eventually, find a successor. But that won't be for a long time."

"Me?" Jute couldn't believe what he was hearing. "Here?"

"It's not a bad life. You've still never tried fresh wizard trout."

"I don't want this life!" Jute said. "Find someone else."

Luther flicked the bones again. The crow lifted off its antler perch, flapped about the room twice, then landed on the table. Its glossy black eyes seemed to drill straight into Jute's soul.

"I could see how that might be your initial response," Luther said. "It's a lot to take in. If you need a few days to get your affairs in order, I'll understand."

A log in the fireplace popped. Luther stared hard across the table, apparently waiting for an answer, though Jute didn't remember being asked a question.

"My affairs *are* in order," he said. "I won't leave Vergil. He's family. And unlike you, I won't abandon my family."

Luther eyed the bones on the table, then glared coldly at Jute. "You're aware he's going to die soon, yes?"

"He needs me," Jute said. "Now more than ever."

"You always were a sentimental one," Luther said. "I'd forgotten about that."

Jute pushed his chair back from the table.

"I'm the only family you've got." Luther's voice took on an edge of menace. "And I need you now."

Jute stood so quickly his head bumped against the lantern. Shadows swung wildly. The crow spooked and took flight, scrabbling around the tiny hut, its wings flapping in Jute's face.

He stepped back and felt something loose against the wall behind him, one of the woven stick figures. He waved it like a flyswatter at the crow to drive it back, until it settled into its nest in the corner.

"This is all just a dream anyway." Jute rubbed his eyes again, hard. When he opened them, he was disappointed to find himself still in the shack with his father. He turned and put his shoulder to the door. Outside, he pushed blindly through the trees.

"This land demands a new servant!" Luther called out after him. "There isn't much time left!"

Finely needled branches clawed at Jute's face and arms, limbs and roots tripped him up—as if the forest itself were trying to prevent his escape. Eventually he made it back to the lakeshore. He launched the canoe and began paddling furiously toward the other side.

Something had disturbed the water. Choppy waves rode the surface and slapped the sides of the boat. Jute tried to stabilize the canoe. But the waves kept getting bigger.

Then one sloshed over the gunwale, and Jute felt the cold soak into his boots. He willed himself to wake up, to abandon this dream, shed its memory like an old skin. But he couldn't snap himself out of it.

A gust of wind roared across the water's surface. When it caught the canoe, the craft lurched to the side, dipped, and began scooping water.

That was all it took.

Jute was tossed into the lake. He kicked and paddled, but his boots, his clothes, his canteen, all weighed him down. He tried to shout for help, but water rushed into his throat.

Gravity took hold. Jute stopped fighting and began sinking into the lake's fathomless depths. He dropped for what seemed like hours, until he came to rest, lying on his back. And then he felt himself encased in something warm and downy.

His sleeping bag?

Must be.

The dream was finally over. Either that, or he was dead.

Chapter 39

Bernard was so close to connecting the dots.

He'd spent the night puzzling over what was shaping up to be a sprawling, multilayered Bigfoot hoax. But all he had right now were theories and suspicions, no proof, nothing that would definitively show how the deception worked.

And there wasn't much time left to figure it out. The expedition would probably end today. Once they packed up camp and left the scene of the crime, exposing these guys as frauds would become a lot harder, or at least less cinematic.

Outside the tent, a lone chickadee tweeted its two-note singsong. A moment later, someone started futzing around in the camp kitchen, probably Vergil getting breakfast ready.

What made exposing their scheme tricky was the shaggy nature of it all. Certain elements, like that paralleling sequence last night, had been so expertly orchestrated Bernard could barely comprehend how it was done. But the other non-Bigfoot things, like that rusted motorcycle they claimed belonged to those missing teenagers, or the note Rye found scratched in the dirt, were clearly intended as red herrings. Then there were the aspects of this operation, like the bear spray snafu, that played more like something the Three Stooges would cook up. Either way, the sheer number of phenomena demanding explanation made the whole thing a head-scratcher.

Thunder rumbled in the distance, eclipsing the sounds of Vergil fixing breakfast. A cool wind was picking up outside, pressing against the tent walls. Rain was coming. Bernard needed to stow his gear in the Explorer before it got ruined.

Maybe the problem was he hadn't been giving these guys enough credit. Maybe the bear spray incident was an intentional farce designed to throw Bernard off the scent. If they made themselves look like bumbling amateurs, no one would ever suspect they were clever enough to pull off all the other parts of the hoax.

Bernard heard someone else's tent zipper open and close. A moment later Vicky and Vergil started talking in hushed tones. This could not be good.

Untangling this scheme was hard enough without having to worry about Vicky being caught up in it. He'd better get out there and run some interference before she started colluding with them.

Vergil woke to the frosty chill of spring. Quite a difference from the scalding near suffocation he'd survived last night. They said bear spray was a nonlethal weapon, but it sure didn't feel that way when someone pumped a canister of it right in your face.

Vergil's throat had seized up, and his lungs convulsed. A cocktail of liquids streamed from his eyes, nose, and mouth. For a full minute, he'd been convinced he was about to die in the most absurd way imaginable—choked to death on his own snot after being mistaken for a Bigfoot.

A long peal of thunder rumbled in the distance. Storm on the way. Better get breakfast ready before things got sloppy. He climbed out of his sleeping bag and pulled on some clothes, careful not to wake Jute, who was still fully encased in his bag.

When Vergil got outside, every nerve in his body cried out at once. He'd pushed himself too hard yesterday, too far. The illness was taking advantage of his weakness to gain more ground. He limped to the fold-out table, shook a handful of ibuprofens from the bottle, and choked them down without water.

A breeze swirled through the clearing. The sky was overcast, clouds leaden and low. Wouldn't be long before the bad stuff hit.

Vergil primed the fuel line on the camp stove, opened the valve, and pressed ignition. The blue burner flame hissed to life. He set a pot of water on to boil. Might as well make a big breakfast today, finish off as many supplies as they could, since this was certainly the end of the expedition. If Jute didn't make the motion, Vergil would. Yesterday's repeated failures—not to mention multiple brushes with death—were all the signs anyone needed to know it was time to call this thing off.

Vergil felt bad about everything they hadn't accomplished. They hadn't made it to Ramsey Lake. Other than that one vocalization the first night, they hadn't gotten much closer to proving the existence of Bigfoot. Vergil even doubted Vicky had enough footage to make an interesting movie with. It was too bad, but sometimes you had to admit when you were snakebit. This expedition was at an end, and Vergil's Bigfooting days were officially over.

He tried to brace himself for what would come next. Sterile hospitals, invasive tests, hushed whispers among white-coated doctors, painful "procedures," poisonous therapies. All of them leading to the same inevitable conclusion.

He remembered a thing people used to say when he was a kid. "Today is the first day of the rest of your life." It was supposed to be inspirational, but from Vergil's perspective, it sounded more like a curse you'd wish upon your worst enemy.

Vicky was wide awake, still burrowed deep in her sleeping bag. In her mind, she was racing through Jingletown Video, looking frantically down the aisles, trying to figure out which shelf this film belonged on. There had to be some special category she'd missed, some obscure genre she hadn't spotted that would perfectly encapsulate what her project should be.

Outside, she heard the now-familiar sounds of Vergil getting breakfast ready. A moment later, the heavy bass of thunder boomed. Rain was on the way, which would likely hasten the end of this expedition, and further shorten the time she had left to figure this film out. Vicky quickly popped a new SD card into her camera and climbed outside to gather more footage while she still could.

When Vergil returned from Sasquatch One with bacon, eggs, and potatoes, Vicky was standing outside her tent, camera pointed up at the snow-encrusted cornice that overhung the butte just south of the clearing.

"Does that ice up there look . . . precarious?" she asked.

Vergil shook his head. "That'll melt slowly and feed the streams around here until midsummer." He strolled over to the foldout table and laid out the breakfast provisions. "How are you feeling this morning?" he asked.

Vicky turned the camera on him. "Fine," she said. "You?"

"Better now." He inhaled deeply. "Bear spray must be good for the sinuses."

He dropped a chunk of butter onto the skillet and swirled it around.

"We never got a chance to unpack everything that happened yesterday," Vicky said.

"I don't think anyone was in the mood to talk last night," he said. "I know I wasn't."

Vicky sat down on a log near the fire ring and pointed the camera up at Vergil. "Did anything happen to you yesterday?" she asked.

"Are you asking me if I saw Bigfoot?"

"That, or . . . anything else weird or inexplicable?"

Vergil thought about the voice Rye heard on the trail, the way it imitated Melody, luring her toward that gorge. That wasn't something he wanted to share with Vicky, let alone all the people who might watch her film. "Nothing I would call inexplicable," he said. "What about you?"

"I'm not sure." Vicky sighed. "All these things happened that, separately, have pretty good explanations. But taken together, it starts to feel like something . . . not normal is going on out here in these woods."

"Jute would call those things data."

"Right," she said, smiling. "He would."

"It's hard to know one way or the other." Vergil set the coffeepot on the burner. "It's possible something's going on." Beads of water on the pot steamed and vaporized. "Unfortunately, I don't think we'll be sticking around long enough to find out."

"That's what I figured." Vicky's voice was heavy with disappointment.

"At least we can have a good breakfast before we hit the road." He cracked some eggs into a bowl and started scrambling them. "Do you think you'll have enough footage to finish your film?"

"Maybe," she said. "I don't know."

Vicky glanced into the trees where a small black-and-white bird was preening itself.

"Are your parents proud of you?" Vergil asked.

Vicky's brow furrowed. "What?" she asked. "Why do you ask?"

"You're in an MFA program, right? Film school? That's pretty cool."

"My parents definitely do not share your enthusiasm," she said. "They're more worried I'll wind up a starving artist."

"I get it," he said. "When I told my mom I wanted to major in studio art, she said I should learn a useful trade, like mining."

They both laughed for a moment, even though neither of them found it that funny.

A squirrel chattered loudly in a tree overhead. Vergil emptied the bowl into the skillet and the eggs began to sizzle.

"Don't abandon your art," he said, eyes still fixed on their breakfast. "It's so hard to start up again once you've stopped. And one day you turn around and realize it's too late."

"It's never too late to get back into it," Vicky said.

"For me, it is," Vergil said, turning the eggs with a spatula.

Vicky sensed a quiet sadness in the way he said this, and she wondered what it meant. But before she could ask another question, the zipper on Bernard's tent started ticking open.

.   .   .

Bernard crawled outside to a sky socked in with dark clouds. Vicky and Vergil were over by the table. He was fixing breakfast while she interviewed him.

Bernard noticed something odd leaning against the side of his tent. An object woven from willow reeds. Human shaped, with an apple affixed to the top, forming an obscenely bulbous head. He bent down to pick it up. Strange and primordial, it looked like something the earth had digested in its large intestine, then coughed back up.

"What do you got there?" Vergil asked.

Bernard turned the figure over and noticed a white sticker on the underside of its apple head. It read: *Basic IGA.*

Of course. So sloppy.

Then an idea began to take shape. This was it. The key that would unlock the hoax, expose these people as frauds, and rehabilitate Bernard's image once and for all.

"Wake everyone up," he said in a clipped voice. "We need to have a conversation." Then he looked at Vicky. "Keep the camera rolling," he said. "You're not going to want to miss a second of this."

Chapter 40

Vergil put breakfast on hold while Vicky woke Rye and Jute. Bernard cleared some space on the foldout table, arranged a few items, and draped a blue tarp over it. He ran a comb through his hair, then refastened his ponytail and adjusted the brim of his fedora to make himself camera ready.

Within five minutes, everyone had assembled on logs around the fire ring. Bernard stood before them as if he were about to deliver a lecture.

"I must say this has been a most illuminating expedition," he started off. "Practically every turn has been full of sights and sounds and occurrences that beggar belief." He folded his hands behind his back and shifted his gaze from one person to the next. "Yet you'll soon see how each of these events has a thoroughly rational explanation. And the only thing out of the ordinary here is the length someone has gone to to perpetrate a deception."

He flashed a smug grin and strolled over to the table. Vicky hated how much he was enjoying himself. She wasn't looking forward to what would most likely be the public humiliation of Jute and Vergil. But she came here to make a documentary. No way she could turn the camera off now.

Bernard yanked the blue tarp off the foldout table with a flourish.

"I'd like to start by debunking one of the more perplexing moments we've encountered on this expedition: that paralleling sequence last night."

He pointed to a pile of debris on the table. "Let's say this tan pebble is Jute, the gray pebble is Vicky, and the pine cone is me." Bernard separated those items and moved them to the side. "Last night, around 7:45 P.M., the three of us were hiking from the scree field to base camp, when we discovered—quite to our dismay—something was tracking us. This thing was careful to stay just out of sight, and exhibited the ability to throw small objects."

"Yet somehow you refuse to accept it was a Bigfoot," Jute reminded him.

"That's correct," Bernard said. "Because Bigfoot doesn't exist."

Thunder clapped in the background, closer now than it had been a few minutes ago. The forest around the clearing was silent, as if it were holding its breath in anticipation of the coming storm.

"But do you know what *does* exist and also has the ability to throw small objects?" Bernard paused to give the question weight. "Human beings who are desperate to make a name for themselves in the Bigfoot World." He pointed at two other objects on the table. "Vergil and Rye Barnes."

"Wait, am I the stick, or am I that piece of moss?" Rye asked.

Bernard's face narrowed with annoyance. "It doesn't matter which one is you."

"Do we get to choose what we are?" Vicky chimed in. "Because I think I should be the pine cone."

"*I'm* the pine cone," Bernard said. "*You're* the gray pebble. Rye is this piece of moss. Now if you don't mind, I'd like to continue."

Thunder boomed again. Vicky felt the first raindrop splatter on her arm.

"What I'm suggesting is that the strange thing we encountered in the woods last night was in fact"—Bernard slid the moss and the stick next to the others—"a father and daughter team perpetrating a paralleling sequence on the rest of us."

"Except we were on the other side of the mountain," Vergil said. "We came back an entirely different way than you."

"So you say." Bernard frowned and tilted his head to the side. "Without a firm alibi, the fact remains it could have been either one, or the both of you."

"Hold up," Rye said. "You think *I'm* involved in this?"

"Why not?"

"Because I don't *believe* in any of it," she said. "I'm on *your* side. Haven't you been paying attention?"

"Oh, I have." Bernard's eyes flashed a deep blue. "And what I've seen is a dutiful daughter playing the role of a skeptic, thus conveniently making her a credible witness when it came time to verify any supposed Bigfoot evidence."

"That's circular reasoning," Rye said.

The rain was falling steadily now; cold drops thumped the tabletop. Vicky's camera was water resistant, but not waterproof. They'd need to wrap this up quickly before it got much worse.

"Besides, that still doesn't explain the thing you and I saw on the mountain," Rye said. "There's no way that could have been me or my dad, because I was with you and he was behind us."

"Great point," Bernard said, putting a finger to his chin. "How *do* we explain the person in the monkey suit?"

He arranged the tan pebble, the gray pebble, the pine cone, the moss, and the stick in a line on the table.

"While you and I were together, who does that leave as our possible, dare I say *likely*, suspect?"

Bernard cocked his head and pointed at the tan pebble at the front of the line.

"Me?" Jute said.

"Why not?" he said. "You're the right size for it. I figure you either had the costume in your pack or, more likely, you hid it on the mountain beforehand." He slid the tan pebble farther ahead of the other pieces. "Setting that rapid pace gave you enough time to change and circle back when we were least expecting it."

Jute shook his head feebly.

Bernard, sensing the advantage, put his finger in Jute's face. "Admit it," he said. "Own up to it, and we all can move on with our lives."

"That theory doesn't work," Vicky said. "I was with Jute the entire time on the mountain." She scooted the tan and gray pebbles so they were touching each other. "He was never once out of my sight. Which means there's no way he could've changed into a costume."

Bernard stared at her for several seconds, his eyes alive with anger. "Maybe you were in on it too," he said.

"Wait a minute," Rye said, "who in your mind *isn't* in on the conspiracy at this point?"

"It makes perfect sense when you think about it," Bernard went on. "You were desperate to find something that would make your film stand out. So you formed an alliance with the very people you came here to ridicule."

"I *never* came here to ridicule anyone," Vicky said. "That was *your* idea."

The rain's intensity picked up another notch. Drops detonated on the ground. Water was starting to puddle and trickle down the slope of the clearing.

"You and I were the only ones who saw that thing on the mountain," Rye said. "And we both know that wasn't a costume. That was . . . that was a monster."

Rye was surprised to hear herself say the word *monster* out loud. She'd spent the last twenty-four hours trying to convince herself what she'd seen up there had been something, anything else. Now that she'd given voice to it, though, there was no denying the truth anymore.

Bernard scoffed. "I think I know how to spot a man in a monkey suit."

"Laugh it off now," Rye said. "But that monkey suit was real enough to send you running like a scared little schoolboy up there."

Bernard started to say something, then stopped.

"Is this all you've got?" Vicky asked. "Because it's not very convincing, if you ask me."

The rain wasn't letting up. Heavy drops battered the tent roofs, creating a steady drumroll in the background. But something else deeper, more elemental, was going on—a vibration, a tremor. Vicky could have sworn she felt the ground shift ever so slightly beneath her feet.

"All it takes for the best planned conspiracy to fall apart is for one of the conspirators to get cold feet." Bernard waited a beat in case anyone appeared ready to crack. "Fine," he concluded. "Thus far, it seems you're all willing to toe the line."

"Or maybe there's no conspiracy at all," Vergil said.

"Hmm," Bernard mused, brow furrowing in thought. "If only we had some hard evidence to prove it one way or the other . . ." A smile slowly crept across his face. "For those of you who don't already know, I found something outside my tent this morning." He picked up the woven stick figure and held it out so everyone got a good look. "It's a curious object, no doubt. Not unlike a Congolese effigy doll or some kind of voodoo fetish. Though most people would recognize it as one of those creepy doodads from *The Blair Witch Project*." He hefted it once. "A strangely impressive piece," he said. "Hand woven, torn fibers, native materials. All except for this." He pointed to the oversize head on top. "I don't believe Golden Delicious apples are native to this region. Which perplexed me . . . until I spotted *this*."

He thrust the figure toward the camera and pointed at the produce tag for Basic IGA.

"How does that prove one of us had something to do with it?" Vergil asked.

"As you know," Bernard said, "these particular apples were set out as bait for the camera traps."

"The camera traps . . ." Jute gasped.

"That's right!" Bernard said. "One of our trail cams—triggered by motion—now contains irrefutable evidence of whoever, or whatever, repurposed this apple. Therefore, ladies and gentlemen, our hoaxer is about to be caught red-handed."

Jute could only watch the proceedings unfold in stunned silence.

That stick figure looked a lot like the one he'd used in his dream to fight off the crow in the hut. Except for the apple head—that hadn't been there. But the rest of it was the same. And now it was here on the foldout table, an object torn from his dream, manifested in the real world.

Jute wished the rain would get worse, bad enough so Bernard would have to postpone this dog and pony show. That would give Jute some time to sort out what happened.

Was last night real? Was his father actually alive, and living in a hut next to a magical lake he'd sworn to protect? Was Jute supposed to leave his life in Basic and join him? One of the videos on the trail cams might go a long way toward answering those questions.

Bernard opened a case and pulled out a tablet sealed in a protective rubber sleeve. He switched it on and tapped the screen several times.

Water was running down through the clearing in sheets now, carrying clumps of sticks and pine needles with it. Vicky felt the ground shake again. She looked around to see where the vibration was coming from.

"You see," Bernard continued, despite the rain pouring over the brim of his fedora, "if you interview enough Bigfoot eyewitnesses, as I have, one thing that's always struck me is how genuine most of these people sound, how deeply they appear to believe the stories they're telling. You look at Mr. Ramsey and Mr. Barnes here, and they seem so honest, so forthright." The tablet made a series of swooshing noises. "And now we can put that honesty to the test."

Bernard held his finger poised over the screen. "In the interest of fairness, if anyone wants to come clean, and spare yourself this indignity, now's your last chance."

The group shifted uneasily, but no one said anything.

"Very well," Bernard said. "Let's check the tape."

The first set of clips was from a camera placed at the eastern edge of the clearing. The footage showed a camp robber flying into the picture and eyeballing an apple. The next clip was more bird footage. And the next one, and the next one.

Bernard switched to a set of clips from a camera on the north-east corner of the perimeter. The first clip was a squirrel. The next several clips didn't appear to show much of anything. The apple was untouched in all of them.

Vicky used a finger to squeegee the water off her camera lens. She stepped back and panned around the huddled faces, which displayed a mixture of openmouthed curiosity and head-tilted disbelief. Until she got to Jute, who was cringing. Vicky pushed in close and held the shot.

Bernard scrolled to the pics from one of the other cameras. "Let's try this one."

The shot was a little farther from camp. It showed an apple resting on a craggy rock. A wide-eyed deer stepped into frame and nibbled at it until it finally took the whole thing in its mouth and wandered off.

"Okay, not that one." Bernard swiped to another set of clips.

This next camera angle had an open shot of a game trail with an apple speared on a tree branch. The camera had switched over to IR mode, so everything was gray and ghostly.

One clip showed a sparrow pecking at the apple. Another showed a long-quilled porcupine ambling by underneath it.

The last clip was time-stamped 5:13 A.M. Bernard pressed play. It took a second to buffer. Nothing seemed to be happening at first. But then a dark shadow appeared behind the tree.

"Hey!" Rye shouted. "What's that?"

A hand began reaching around the tree trunk, feeling for the apple.

"Here it is," Bernard said, holding a corner of the tarp over the tablet to shield it from the rain. "Almost there."

A figure started to emerge from behind the trunk.

"Here we are," Bernard said. "Moment of truth."

He paused the video. Everyone peered closer. It took them a moment to process what they were seeing.

"Uncle Jute," Rye said at last, "is that you?"

His face was partially obscured, but everything else—height, weight, haircut, clothes—was a match. Jute Ramsey was frozen on the screen, preserved in infrared grayscale for all to see.

As they looked closer, another detail stood out. Clearly visible in his other hand was the same willow stick figure that now rested on the foldout table in the middle of base camp.

Jute shrank under the weight of everyone's stares. "But . . . that was a dream," he stammered. "Wasn't it?"

"And now we know," Bernard said. "The sad, sad truth."

"That's *not* the truth," Jute said, backing up.

"With all due respect, this video says otherwise."

"I didn't fake anything. I swear." Jute had his hands out. "Give me a chance to explain."

"Start talking then," Bernard said. "We can't wait to hear how you'll get out of this."

Jute didn't know where to begin. So much of last night was shrouded in a gauzy haze. He remembered everything that happened, each tiny detail, up until he'd fallen into the lake. He had no idea how he'd gotten back here, or why he'd brought one of those stick figures with him.

"Well?" Bernard said. "We're waiting."

Jute opened his mouth, but before he could speak, something loud split the sky overhead. Not thunder and not rain. It was the sound of something big cracking wide open.

Chapter 41

All five expeditioners in the clearing watched helplessly as a geyser of water shot through a fissure in the crest of the butte above them. The overhanging cornice must have been acting as an ice dam, holding back months of spring runoff. Softened by the morning's rain, it finally burst, setting loose a cascade of melted glacier.

At first, all they heard was the rain clattering against their gear, but they soon heard a trickling in the forest. It was a small sound, like when Vergil overwatered a plant and it started to leak out the bottom of the pot. But the sound grew from a trickle, to a steady flow, to a whitewater roar. They began to hear limbs snapping, trees being torn apart and uprooted.

Then the forest at the top of the clearing came alive. Branches swayed, trees shuddered and bent. A moment later, a wall of water burst through the tree line.

While the wave barreled down on them, something else happened: Jute closed his eyes and drew in a deep breath. His lungs filled, and his whole body seemed to grow larger. He reached his arms out wide and shouted for the others to gather round. They were all so stunned, so unsure what to do, they complied without question. He folded everyone close until they were wrapped inside the shelter of his arms. He stepped forward so his feet were securely rooted to the earth, and just before the wave hit, he leaned his shoulder in to take the full force of the impact.

A second later, they were completely submerged. Everything went silent except for the swirling of water, the scurrying of bubbles past their ears. By all rights, they should have been shorn away like the rest of the debris in the clearing. But they weren't.

When the wave subsided, they were standing hip-deep in a raging river of slush and logs and rocks. The tents, the foldout table, all the gear were gone, washed down into the trees at the bottom of the clearing. But the water was still spraying like a fire hose from the top of the butte, and their purchase on the eroding soil was tenuous. They were not safe here.

Vergil spotted the cars thirty yards away at the top of the clearing. They were still dry, protected by a berm of earth. He tapped Jute on the shoulder and pointed. Jute nodded. With those two gestures, a plan had been made and agreed to.

"Everyone, grab hold!" Jute shouted.

All five of them linked arms and began working their way upstream in a line. Vergil was between Jute on his left and Bernard on his right. Rye and Vicky were on the other side of Jute, hooked onto his left arm. Cautiously, slowly, they all pushed toward the top of the clearing, and the safety of the cars beyond.

The water tore at their thighs and eddied behind them. Each step was a slow-motion, lumbering struggle to keep their footing in the relentless current.

They'd made it halfway to the tree line when a stone the size of a bowling ball tumbled toward them. Vergil couldn't get out of the way fast enough. It swept his legs and he plunged underwater.

His ears rang hollow. Everything felt far away and abstract. Time grew sludgy. Then, a tug at his elbows as Jute and Bernard hoisted him up out of the water. When Vergil exhaled, the air burst from his lungs like an explosion.

"Easy!" Bernard shouted. "We got you."

Vergil managed to reset his feet and start moving again.

Several minutes later, they were so close to the tree line Vergil could almost touch one of the dead lower branches of the nearest lodgepole, but the current was stronger here, more unpredictable. If the branch should snap off, they'd all be swept away.

Before Vergil could make up his mind what to do, Bernard got clipped by a tumbling log. He lost his footing and whipped loose. Vergil reached back and snared him by the wrist. He tried to reel him in but couldn't summon the strength.

Bernard flapped in the current at first, trying desperately to get his feet replanted until the water turned him over and pushed him under. Then he stopped struggling. Vergil grit his teeth and heaved—again and again—but the harder he pulled, the more his grip weakened.

Moments later, a stone spilled out from between the trees and caught Bernard on the shoulder. That was all it took to wrench him loose. Vergil tried to dive after him, but Jute wouldn't let go of his arm, so all he could do was watch.

Dr. Marcus Bernard slid out past the bottom of the clearing, caroming off stones, slaloming through the trees. He bumped along the edges of the Russian olive thicket until he was deposited into the still waters of the beaver pond below.

There, the slower current spun him in gentle circles as he drifted. Bernard was conscious enough to know he was about to die, from either drowning or hypothermia. It wouldn't be long now.

As his core cooled and his heart ticked slower and the last few seconds of consciousness fired across his synapses, Bernard found his mind reaching back to the day he and Adebayo first came upon an orphaned baby gorilla in the jungle of Virunga National Park.

It was evening, and the two men sat by their fire in camp. Adebayo had just decided to abandon his research, give up on academia, to start a sanctuary. Bernard knew he'd never follow those footsteps, knew he'd continue on his current path—a decision he would later come to regret, like so many other decisions that would eventually follow.

But the future didn't matter yet. The only thing that mattered was this moment, as Bernard looked down at his lap and saw Benny sitting there. The little creature was still dazed and uncertain, with his wrinkled face and heart-shaped nostrils. One tiny hand gripped Bernard's index finger; the other held on to his sleeve. This thing he had only ever studied from afar, through binoculars and field glasses, sat before him now—a living, breathing creature, a sacred, fragile life.

Bernard had to admit this was a pretty good memory to go out on. His facial muscles, barely functioning by this point, relaxed into a smile. He closed his eyes and waited for the end to come.

Only the end didn't come.

Splashing nearby. Footsteps.

Hands plucking him neatly from the water.

Bernard's eyelids fluttered open.

Two great brown eyes looked back at him, human but not human. A pronounced sagittal crest, heavy brow, shoulders wider than a Volkswagen, matted brown fur that the rain rolled off of in fat drops.

Even though he was too cold to speak, Bernard mouthed the words: *Benny, is that you?*

The Beast peered down at Bernard, as if it were trying to locate something buried deep inside him. Then, with a grunt that seemed to say, You'll be all right, it cradled Bernard to its chest and carried him off into the forest.

The people still fighting for their lives in the clearing inched their way upstream until they could safely enter the trees. From there, they used their hands to pull themselves up to the cars.

A few minutes later, they slid open the door to Sasquatch One and threw themselves inside.

Vergil lay on his back, staring at the ceiling. Raindrops sounded like buckshot bouncing off the rooftop. The four of them were exhausted, cold, alive. There was more that had to be done. They needed to mount a search for Bernard. They needed to get help. But first they needed to breathe, needed a minute to ponder the awful price they'd paid.

Chapter 42

Vergil and Jute immediately started scouring the forest for Bernard, while Rye and Vicky drove Sasquatch One out to get help.

They couldn't pick up a cell signal until they'd nearly reached the county road. Then they had to wait for Jefferson County Search and Rescue to mobilize so they could lead them back to base camp. By the time boots were on the ground, it was early afternoon.

EMTs determined Vicky had broken her collarbone and was dangerously hypothermic, so they medevaced her to Helena. Jute, Vergil, and Rye stuck around to answer the deputy sheriff's questions and direct the search crews but were eventually told to leave. So they salvaged what little gear they could from the trees below the clearing and headed home.

They were largely silent on the drive out, each ensconced in their own thoughts, trying to make sense of everything they'd seen and done.

The van reached the county road and Jute paused. "Anyone want some water?" he asked, holding up his canteen. He agitated it once so the water made a sloshing noise.

"No thanks," Vergil said.

"You haven't had anything to drink all day." Jute pushed the canteen up under his friend's nose. "You really ought to hydrate."

"Yeah, Dad," Rye chimed in from the back seat. "You're always telling me to drink more water."

"Fine."

Vergil grabbed the canteen and took a deep gulp. The coldness of the water caught him by surprise. An icy frisson traveled down his throat and spread through his whole body, even down to his fingertips, which began to tingle.

"That felt . . . strange," he said, smacking his lips. "What is this stuff?"

Jute shrugged. "Plain old camp water."

Before Vergil could say anything else, Jute eased the van onto the county road and set a course for Basic.

The storm that hammered their base camp had also passed through town. Everything seemed fresh and clean. Buildings that were normally gray with dust gave off a golden glow in the sun's dying rays.

Sasquatch One rolled straight down Central Avenue, left onto Rodeo Drive, past St. Francis, and left onto Batten Avenue, before coming to a stop in front of Vergil's house. Jute threw the gearshift into park and let his hands dangle over the steering wheel.

"You want some help with that?" Vergil nodded toward the mess of wet camping gear in back.

Jute shook his head. "Let me hang everything out to dry," he said. "We'll see if anything's worth keeping tomorrow."

Vergil climbed out of the van. He slid the back door open and helped Rye onto the sidewalk. Jute gave them a two-fingered wave before driving off.

They watched until the vehicle was gone before they started up the front walk. Vergil was surprised to note that the pain inside him had muted. A welcome, momentary reprieve.

"Are you hungry?" he asked as they climbed the porch steps.

"Starving."

"Don't think we have much to eat in the house," he said. "Only places open at this hour would be the Kit Kat or Hoo Yin's."

.   .   .

The bell hanging from the doorknob made a halfhearted clank when they stepped inside Hoo Yin's. Dallas Chow peeked his head out the kitchen window. Vergil and Rye took seats in a booth toward the back of the restaurant.

"What do you got there?" Vergil asked.

Rye held up a clear plastic box she'd been carrying in the pocket of her hoodie. "Vicky was storing her SD cards in this. I found it when we collected the gear." She set the case next to her place mat. "I'll send it off first thing tomorrow morning."

"You guys need menus?" Dallas was wearing a stained white apron over a T-shirt and jeans.

"Cashew chicken for me," Vergil said.

"Moo shu pork, please," Rye said.

Dallas jotted it down on his notepad. "That all?"

Vergil suddenly realized he was ravenous, hungry in a way he hadn't felt in a long time. "Let's throw in an order of pot stickers," he added. "And egg rolls."

"Crab rangoon maybe?" Rye said, getting into the spirit of it.

"And wonton soup for both of us," Vergil said. "Oh, and a pot of jasmine tea."

After he'd finished scratching out their order, Dallas tapped the notepad with his pen. He looked like he was about to say something, but instead nodded once and withdrew to the kitchen. Most likely some version of the incident had already begun to make the rounds of the local gossip circuit. No telling what relationship that version bore to the truth.

Rye was squinting at one of the Chinese zodiac animals on her place mat. "Do you think they'll find him?" she asked.

"They seem to think there's a chance," Vergil said.

The bell on the front door clanged. Dale and Christy Swinton scanned the restaurant as if they were trying to spot an empty seat, even though the place was deserted.

Rye looked up from her place mat. "Maybe I should have gone after him," she said.

Vergil shook his head. "Even if you'd caught him, that current would've taken you both down."

"Still," she said, holding out her empty hand. "I could've done more."

"There's a lot of good people looking for him right now."

"Looking for who?" It was Dale Swinton. He and his wife had wandered back to their booth.

"We heard about the incident," Christy said. She had stringy blond hair, lifeless from decades of home perms. "The one you all were involved with."

The Swintons had lived in Basic their whole lives. They used to work at Ten Pin Lanes before it shut down. Vergil didn't know what they did now, other than gamble over Yahtzee with the Loabs every night at St. Pete's.

"Sure were surprised when we heard about it," Dale said.

"Not *too* surprised though," Christy added. "I said to myself, if something like that's gonna happen to anyone, it's gotta be Vergil Barnes and Jute Ramsey."

The Swintons chortled. Rye cringed. Vergil smiled but said nothing.

"Word on the street," Dale said, leaning in, "is that nice doctor from those Bigfoot shows was with you all on the trip."

"And we wondered if he's maybe the one who went missing."

They were fishing for gossip they could leverage into free beer over at St. Pete's. "If you guys don't mind," Vergil said, "we're still trying to process what happened."

The curiosity on the Swintons' faces hardened into something meaner.

"Just how bad did you screw up out there, Verge?" Dale's eyes were heavy. The pockmarks on his cheeks glowed red.

Vergil sensed Rye taking in a deep breath to respond, so he gave her a preemptive nudge under the table. These were small people, not worthy of whatever emotion she was feeling toward them.

"Mother Nature had plans we didn't see coming," Vergil said.

"Order's up." Dallas Chow emerged from the kitchen balancing a tray full of food.

"Is it true the FBI is taking over the investigation?" Christy Swinton asked, desperate now for any scrap of news.

"I've heard reports of black helicopters spotted in the area," Dale added.

Dallas made a show of arranging the plates on the table, then he turned to the Swintons, blocking them from Vergil and Rye. "Are you ready to order?" he asked.

"We're not here to eat, Dallas," Christy said.

"We just wanted to offer support," Dale said.

"Okay then." Dallas crossed his arms over his chest. "It appears your support's been offered." He nodded toward the door. "Now why don't you let my customers eat?"

After a tense moment, the Swintons got the picture and left. Once the bell on the door clanked behind them, Dallas slipped back into the kitchen.

Vergil and Rye watched the steam rising from their plates for a few seconds. Then they dove in. Both of them ate with a greedy urgency, as if they hadn't had a decent meal in months. When they were done and their plates were clear, they sat back in their chairs, palms resting on bellies.

"So," Vergil said. "I suppose tomorrow you'll want to start in with the doctors?"

Rye nodded. "I already made you an appointment at St. Peter's, first thing in the morning."

"You did?"

She held up her phone. "The second I got a signal."

Vergil smiled and nodded. He listened to his body, tried to hear where the pain had migrated to, but it had gone strangely silent for the time being.

"Okay," he said, letting out a heavy breath. "Tomorrow it begins then."

"Tomorrow," Rye said, taking his hand. "You and me, Dad."

Chapter 43

Vicky drifted through a scrum of classmates and professors gathered in front of the Bengal Theater on campus. It was a chilly night and her collarbone ached, even though she no longer needed to wear a sling.

The university required every graduating MFA candidate to conduct a thesis defense. For film students, that meant screening their movie at a public venue, then answering questions from the crowd. Tonight was strictly a formality, since Vicky's committee had already approved her thesis, but she still felt jittery for some reason.

The fact that she'd gotten to this point was nothing short of miraculous. Six weeks ago Vicky had returned to Pocatello with a broken clavicle. She'd lost her film equipment in a flash flood. And worst of all, the principal subject of her thesis (not to mention a well-known faculty member and a prominent television personality) was missing somewhere in the Elkhorn Mountains. The AP ran an article on it, and for a while the news was inescapable.

Even if Vicky had wanted to make a movie at that point, all the footage she'd shot on the expedition had been washed away, along with her dreams of finishing film school. Her mother was already trying to line up an internship at a law firm in Oakland.

Then a package arrived in the mail. Inside it was Vicky's case of SD cards and a handwritten note:

I think these are yours. Whatever you do, tell the truth.

—Rye

The lobby lights blinked off and on four times. A few people put out cigarettes against the concrete planters on the sidewalk and tossed the butts into the street. Others were already shuffling inside.

When Vicky popped that first SD card into the reader and pulled up the raw footage on the monitor, something clicked. She was struck with a certainty so strong it bordered on truth: If she was patient, if she had faith, if she kept sliding the pieces around, eventually the story would come together.

The crowd migrated through the lobby toward the theater. Vicky had been hoping her mother or father or even her sister, Zoe, might surprise her by coming to town for this screening. But it didn't look like that was going to happen. Maybe her family would never be okay with her decisions. It was up to Vicky to be okay with that.

Her thesis adviser, Professor Moss, caught her eye from over by the concession stand and gave her a thumbs-up. When she'd emailed him a rough cut two weeks ago, his reply simply stated, "I believe there's something here to work with." Vicky, who at that point had barely slept over the last month, chose to interpret this as a compliment, though now she wasn't so sure.

Vicky took one last glance around the lobby. When she failed to spot a familiar face among the crowd, she ducked into the theater and sat in the front row, so she wouldn't have to watch the audience's reaction. If someone were to get up and walk out, she'd rather not know.

The lights dimmed. A spotlight turned on. Professor Moss stepped up to the lectern. He adjusted his spectacles and tapped the microphone to make sure it was on. The crowd hushed.

"Sometimes a film comes along that defies explanation, upends all notion of genre," he said. "Like an onion, each layer we peel off presents us with something new and unexpected."

Professor Moss paused and tipped a smile toward Vicky, who tried to bury herself in her seat cushion.

"At first blush, you might say this is a film that interrogates how our obsessions come to define us, a voyeuristic portrait of eccentricity bordering on affliction. But that would have been too easy, maybe even reductive. Look deeper and you'll see something else: a profound meditation on what it means to be human, what it means to be a family, and what it means to be a community."

This was easily the most effusive intro Moss had given for any of this year's screenings. Vicky could feel everyone in the theater staring at the back of her head.

"And when you examine this film at its deepest levels, you'll discover that it's whispering one of the divine secrets of life itself." Here Moss leaned in closer to the microphone and lowered his voice. "The difference between the mythic and the mundane, between the sublime and the silly, is all a matter of how we view the world around us. And the stories we tell each other can be shimmering threads that bind us together, as long as we open our hearts and let them."

Professor Moss stuffed his notes into his jacket pocket and looked up.

"That's why I'm honored to present Victoria Xu's graduate thesis in documentary filmmaking, *American Mythology*."

He took a seat to scattered clapping. The spotlight cut off. The projector turned on. And Vicky's story began to unspool on the screen.

The lobby lights had shut off a while ago. Even the pink neon piping above the marquee was dark. Everyone had gone home, but Vicky still lingered, like a ghost who didn't know how to cross over.

The screening had been a success by any possible measure. The applause lasted for a full five minutes after the movie had ended. The Q & A went fine. She got asked about the status of the search for Bernard, and why she thought they hadn't been able to locate his body yet. The last question, however, proved trickiest to answer, even though it was the most obvious one in the world: "Do you personally believe in Bigfoot?"

She came up with her response on the spot: "I don't know if I believe, but I think it's important to try."

Then it was over and the theater cleared out. Professor Moss shook her hand, said they should talk next week about submitting to film festivals.

Vicky could not have scripted a better conclusion to her career as a film student. And yet, she felt empty, like something important was missing. She pulled on her jacket and strolled past the concession stand. She pushed open the front door and stepped out into the night.

She was about to head back to her apartment, unsure what to do next, when she saw something lurking in the shadows by the planters. Vicky froze. A figure stepped into the glow of a nearby streetlight.

"Looks like you got my care package," Rye said.

Vicky cocked her hip to the side. "Looks like you got my invitation."

Rye tried to make her face look officious. "As chief media consultant to the Basic Bigfoot Society, I felt it was my duty to come down here and make sure you didn't screw this up."

"And?" Vicky said.

Rye drew a line on the sidewalk with the toe of her sneaker. "I noticed you took certain . . . liberties with the story."

"How so?"

"Well," Rye said, "you didn't include the part where my uncle Jute was caught maybe-probably hoaxing some of what happened to us out there."

Vicky nodded for a moment. "That didn't seem like it was a necessary or even very important part of the story I wanted to tell."

"I think you're right," Rye said. "It was an interesting choice though."

They drifted slightly closer to each other.

"So what happens next?" Vicky asked.

"Want to grab dinner before I head back to Bozeman?"

"You can't drive back *tonight*." Vicky was surprised to hear how alarmed her voice sounded. "It's already dark," she added.

"Let's eat first," Rye said. "We can figure the rest out later."

Then cautiously, slowly, they started off together, toward the city lights in the distance.

Chapter 44

Is there anything else to discuss?

A voice. Coming from far away.

Are-there-any-more-items-on-the-agenda?

There it was again. More insistent now.

"Earth to Jute! Come in, Jute!"

Jute blinked hard.

He heard notes in the distance, music, a Bon Jovi song.

Then the fog cleared, and the dark interior of St. Pete's Tavern came into focus. Vergil sat across from him, a half-empty beer bottle poised between tabletop and mouth.

"If you want, we can adjourn," Vergil said.

"Not so fast." Jute checked the agenda. "Two new media requests," he said. "One's an offer from Odyssey Productions, wanting to interview us for a series called *Bigfoot Files.*"

Jute heard a whistle over at the bar, Tammy Reynolds signaling to see if they needed another round. He shook his head. They were about done for the night.

"And the other?" Vergil asked.

Jute turned back to the table. "What's that?"

"You said we had *two* offers." Vergil polished off his beer and set it down with finality. "What's the other one?"

Jute looked at the agenda again. "Ah hell, who cares," he said. "Same answer as always, right?"

Vergil nodded. "Same as always."

Jute wrote DECLINE next to Items 5A and 5B.

"Anything else we need to cover?" Vergil asked.

"How's Rye doing?" Not technically an agenda item, but the meeting was almost over, so it could fall under the category of new business.

"Good, I think." Vergil spun his bottle on the tabletop. "Starting to get serious about PT programs now."

"Where's she thinking of applying?"

Vergil shrugged. "You can get the full list from her at Thanksgiving."

"She's coming?"

"Just got official confirmation this morning." Vergil smiled. "And Vicky too," he added.

"Full house," Jute said.

Someone rolled a Yahtzee over at the bar and a cheer went up. On the jukebox, Bon Jovi gave way to Travis Tritt.

Jute leaned back in his chair. "If there's no further business, I move we adjourn the November meeting of the Basic Bigfoot Society."

"Second."

"All in favor?"

Two hands went up.

"Opposed?"

Respectful pause.

"Meeting adjourned."

Vergil and Jute walked side by side down Central Avenue, past Basic IGA, past the bench where people had created a makeshift shrine for Dr. Bernard.

During the early days of the search, large swaths of the Bigfoot community showed up to assist, even though the sheriff's office specifically asked people not to. Having a bunch of yahoos running around in the woods only made their job harder. Even now, six months on, a steady trickle of people showed up asking questions. Most of them poked around for a few hours, had lunch at the Kit Kat or a beer at St. Pete's, then headed back to whatever larger city they'd come from.

The two men walked past First Federal Bank, the Kit Kat, the Silver

Museum. A light smell of pine smoke hinted at the coming winter. Jute had closed the car wash for the season earlier that week. They walked past Basic Public Library, Hoo Yin's, and Ten Pin Lanes. Then they turned right onto Rodeo Drive, up the hill, left onto Second Avenue where Jute's home—*their* home—came into view.

Neither Vergil nor Jute could remember who'd suggested it first, and Rye claimed it had been her idea, so the genesis was murky. But shortly after the expedition, Vergil put the family home up for sale. It sold within a week to someone from out of town hoping to turn it into an Airbnb.

Jute's place needed a lot of work. They cleared and seeded the front yard, bought planters with bright red and yellow flowers to line the walkway. The exterior got a fresh coat of sage-colored paint. But inside was where the real work took place. All the junk—and there'd been plenty of it—had to be removed. Even the wall of blobsquatches got dismantled. Then they gave it a deep cleaning, top to bottom, until it felt like a new home.

"What are you working on tonight?" Jute asked as they approached the front walk.

"Come see."

Jute followed him through the driveway. Out back, a motion sensor snapped on, and the backyard was flooded in light.

Vergil opened the door to the former Bigfoot War Room and flipped on the overheads. Gone were the computers and cords, the papers and books, the whiteboards and chalkboards, all the stray photographs. In their place was a rough-hewn wooden table cluttered with tubes of paint, dozens of brushes, half-filled mason jars. The walls were lined with finished and partially finished canvases.

Both men heard a thumping sound coming from the corner as an old Great Pyrenees slapped its tail against the floorboards. Yet another one of the many changes they'd had around here.

Three months ago, Vergil had read about a nine-year-old Great Pyrenees named Cargo at a rescue shelter in Cheyenne. The next day, Jute drove them there in Sasquatch One. Cargo's legs were arthritic. His eyes were frosted with cataracts. And both men fell immediately, hopelessly in love with him.

Cargo lifted his giant, jowly head when they came into the studio, then laid it back down once he saw who it was.

"Here's the latest." Vergil turned an easel to catch the light.

Jute stepped back and put a finger to his chin. The piece was heavily textured, with thick globs of paint rising from the surface. It took him a moment to see a mountainside, a craggy rock face striated with black fissures. It could almost be one of those squiggly paintings like they had in New York City.

"I like it," he said.

"Really?"

"I could definitely see this one hanging in a motel room somewhere." Jute smirked. "Maybe a Holiday Inn?"

"Gee thanks, buddy." Vergil dunked a paintbrush into a mason jar and flicked a spray of water at him. "Now, beat it," he said.

Jute crossed the driveway to the house. He went to the kitchen and opened the cabinet under the sink. He pushed aside bottles of cleaning supplies and retrieved an unlabeled milk jug half full of water. Jute looked out the window to make sure Vergil was still in his studio.

Then he tiptoed into his friend's bedroom. On the nightstand was a water glass, nearly empty. Jute filled the glass from the jug and returned it to the nightstand.

A *misdiagnosis*. That was how the doctors chose to rationalize an inexplicable recovery from stage 4 pancreatic cancer. Jute overheard two nurses outside the exam room using the word *miracle* in hushed tones. Neither of them was wrong. Science and religion simply used different words to describe the same phenomenon.

Jute, of course, had his own explanation: the water from Ramsey Lake did exactly what his father had said it would.

Since he only had a little left in his canteen after the expedition, and just to be on the safe side, Jute made a trip back to gather more of it.

He'd had to wait a month for the search crews to clear out, so he missed seeing his father again by about a week.

But Dr. Marcus Bernard—very much alive, very much not missing, very much embracing his role as the new Watcher—took Jute to the cemetery in the forest so he could pay his last respects to Luther Ramsey III. And in the few minutes he stood over the grave, marked by a headstone written in a strange language, Jute willed himself to find peace with the man who had been his father. Maybe it worked, maybe it didn't.

Jute left Vergil's bedroom and returned the jug to the cabinet under the kitchen sink. Then he went to the bathroom, where his swimsuit hung stiff on the hook behind the door. He changed into it and stepped onto the back porch. He shivered as he slid the cover off the hot tub and turned on the jets.

Vergil got an art studio from the proceeds from the house sale; Jute got a hot tub. That was the deal. The rest went to home improvements and Rye's grad school fund.

Jute enjoyed the burn on his skin as he eased himself into the water. Then he leaned back against one of the jets. In the studio across the yard, Vergil was darkening the clouds on his latest creation, spackling them with an ashy paste.

As Vergil stared at his painting, deciding what it needed next, he listened for any stray notes in his body—a habit he clung to even though he'd been pain-free for months. Tonight he heard nothing but the sound of his heart, still going strong despite the odds.

He was about to mix up a new color when Cargo started working himself out of bed. Vergil balanced his paintbrush across a mason jar and let the dog outside to do his business. Vergil stood in the doorway, looking over at the glow of the hot tub lights on the back porch and his friend's head bobbing above the water.

Both men regarded each other across the yard and raised a hand in wordless greeting. When Cargo finished, Vergil let him back into the studio and resumed his work.

. . .

Jute watched his friend squint and dab at the canvas, worsening the weather on his latest creation with every brushstroke.

The Basic Bigfoot Society never did find the proof they were looking for, and they probably never would. But that no longer bothered Jute. He'd come to see other things as more important. Like this moment right here, loosely shared with his oldest friend in the world. It felt like its own revelation, a mystery slowly unfolding before his eyes—so plain, so unassuming, if you blinked, you might miss it.

Acknowledgments

Okay well . . . With a book this long in the making, it's impossible to thank all the people who deserve thanking, with the commensurate levels of thankfulness. Regardless, these lines represent my own quixotic attempt to balance the gratitude ledgers.

First off, I must extend the deepest of thanks to my editor, Edward Kastenmeier, who had a vision for what this book could be and worked tirelessly to help me unlock it. A hearty thanks as well to the entire editorial team at Doubleday, especially Chris Howard-Woods, Brian Etling, Susan M. S. Brown, and Andrea Monagle, for their detailed work and unflagging enthusiasm. And to Marylin Eastwood for some timely lyrical assistance. Of course, a massive thank-you goes to agent extraordinaire Sarah Bedingfield, who saw the potential in this story right away and helped me chisel at the marble until it came to life. I wish every writer could have someone as thoughtful and passionate as she is in their corner.

You likely wouldn't be reading this book had it not been for the auspices of the BookEnds Fellowship. The biggest of thanks is reserved for Susan Scarf Merrell, who championed this book from the moment she first read it and was always ready with a paper bag when it seemed like I might start to hyperventilate. Meg Wolitzer, Karen Bender, JP Solheim, as well as all the members of Cohort Five, were integral in helping me make the big decisions that turned this from a behemoth of a book into something people might want to read. And of course, I must extend an enormous crying-emoji thanks to my BookEnds podmates: Kelly Anderson, Jena Salon, and Rachael Warecki. Their giant-hearted advice helped create the alchemy that turned these fictional characters into people who live and breathe and feel. I'm immensely grateful also to Tony Lipp and Adam Skilken, who have been there from the beginning and read it all. In addition, I must thank Jerry Brennan and Joseph Peterson, who read the first draft of this book way back when and convinced me it could be something.

My family, as always, deserves tremendous thanks for endlessly encouraging me to pursue this passion. Thank you, Brent Sr., Dorothea, Brent Jr., Taya, Jim, and Reed for riding out the highs and lows and never ever letting me give up. Special thanks are reserved for my sister-in-law, Millie Chou, who helped me get Vicky right. If that character rings true, it's due to the many conversations we had and questions she patiently answered. And of course, my wife, Natalie Vesga, the horizon upon whom the sun both sets and rises, who patiently puts up with my moods and indulges my enthusiasms; I couldn't have done this without you. Last, I started writing this manuscript in the early morning hours after daily walks with my beloved Great Pyrenees, Tanka. Those walks taught me how to find joy and peace in the daily discipline of writing. While Tanka is not here to see this book in its final form, his huge heart runs through every page of it.

Innumerable texts and films and podcasts were consumed as research for this book, but three stand out most of all: *Bigfoot: The Life and Times of a Legend* by Joshua Blu Buhs; *American Indian Myths and Legends,* edited by Richard Erdoes and Alfonso Ortiz; and the documentary *Not Your Typical Bigfoot Movie,* directed by Jay Delaney.

When I sat down to write this book, my goal was to tell a story about Bigfoot and friendship. In that vein, I would be remiss if I didn't thank all the wanderers and wonderers who strike out into the woods searching for something most people don't believe in. Even if you never find Bigfoot, I'm confident you'll discover something more important. And finally, I'd like to thank anyone who has ever been a friend of mine. I may not have always been the best friend in return, and we may not be as close as we once were, but—trust me—your impact on my life has been immeasurable.

A NOTE ABOUT THE AUTHOR

Born and raised in Montana, Giano Cromley is the author of two young adult novels and a collection of short stories. He is a recipient of an Artist Fellowship from the Illinois Arts Council and was a BookEnds fellow with Stony Brook University. He is an amateur woodworker, a certified wildlife tracker, and an English professor at Kennedy–King College, where he is chair of the Communications Department. He lives on the South Side of Chicago with his wife and two dogs.